Silent Interviews

Silent Interviews

on Language, Race, Sex, Science Fiction, and Some Comics

A COLLECTION OF WRITTEN INTERVIEWS

Samuel R. Delany

Wesleyan University Press

Published by University Press of New England • Hanover and London

Wesleyan University Press
Published by University Press of New England, Hanover, NH 03755

Printed in the United States of America 5 4 3 2
CIP data appear at the end of the book

Contents

Silent Interviews

Introduction: Reading and the Written Interview

> For a week you were wholly given up to the soft drift of the text that surrounded you as secretly, densely, and unceasingly as snowflakes. You entered it with limitless trust. The peacefulness of the book, that enticed you further and further! . . . [To the child] the hero's adventure can still be read in a swirl of letters like figures and messages in the drifting snowflakes . . . . He is unspeakably touched by the deeds, the words that are exchanged, and, when he gets up, is blanched over and over by the snow of his reading.—Walter Benjamin, *One-Way Street*

The alley was cradled wall to wall with white, which, out on the street, three days' traffic had beat down to gray batting. Curb and cobbles were edged with ice, and a January rain battered the frozen scabs into an aluminum crush. On a pristine stretch, strewn futilely again that morning, rock salt had melted black collars around central crystals suggesting the embroidered knoblets across last summer's chenille, till they too became slush.

What a wonderful day to stay indoors and read!

Drenched with light and immobile at well over ninety, the air was as thick as oiled excelsior. Where a child in seersucker had dropped her popsicle bit on the pavement, over three minutes by the watch on a chafed, damp wrist, the grape ice melted, spread for thirty seconds, till the wet patch began contracting, in inverse pseudopods, back toward the stick, to leave, finally, the faintest, driest stain—in the time it took to decide which of the doorways to duck into to block what hammered on the heated head, what, even with back to the sun, kept the eyelids low.

Surely it was time to go lounge with limeade and read!

But most of you who have come even this far into our text will know what it is to take pleasure from a book in a world too hot, or too cold, or too lonely, or too busy—too much with us, late and soon, one way or the other.

What is one to ask, then, of such readers—"What is it, perhaps, to read?"?

The romantic reads for relief from the old and release into the new. The classicist reads for instruction and delight. The poststructuralist reads for the delight falling out of rereading and the instruction accruing to misreading. Feminists and feminist sympathizers read alert to precisely the sort of gender skewing on which the nostalgia of our epigraph is grounded, ready to point out the split, gently here, powerfully there, in the classical world, in the unified subject, and the assumption of a transparent language on which any such self-satisfied vision of "man" (and the boy that fathers him, in our filiarchal society) must be grounded, always prepared for by (and constituted of) the shock that "you" are not "she" and (thus) "he" is not "you." (That split is not very far from the strange double marking that separates our two orders of interrogation—each signed with the question mark earlier.) The postmodern reads for the wild and wacky that insinuates itself in the crevices and crannies of every text—that is, for elements similar to those the deconstructionist reads for, so as to display, with long face and secret smile, the text's self-subversions and thus the impossibility of our ever mastering it.

Frank Lentricchia characterizes a radical as one who wants society to grow out of our education, while a conservative is someone who wants education to model itself on the society that exists—so that reading is (and what is education without it?) profoundly implicated in the very polarities of our politics.

The pleasure of the text, that exemplary reader Roland Barthes called the goal which, we like to hypostatize, all our readers, romantic, classic, feminist, conservative, and radical, share. Just to cite it, though, makes us suspect it is not at all single—but plural, rather, rich, and as articulately variegated as the number of readers around. Barthes marshaled the word *jouissance* to characterize it—"pleasure," yes, but derived from the French verb "to play." In the colloquial parlance of *boudoir* and back alley, "to cum."

What we need, Barthes suggested, before his death at the hand of an unseeing van driver at a *cinquième* intersection, is an "erotics" of reading—a wild and wacky idea if there ever was one—unless I seriously misread it. Barthes also said, "Those who fail to reread are obliged to read the same story everywhere," an *obiter dictum* I've been impressed with enough to repeat, I'm sure (a hundred, two hundred times?), far more, I'd guess, than Barthes ever did. That, from time to time, we have a choice between wandering through the sun and the slush and reading about wandering through the sun and the slush (and generally staying out of the sleet and the heat) is the freedom, I suspect, that redeems both experiences, the freedom that lets us get our insightful jollies from the one, the other, or both, that allows both—from time to time—to mean . . . when we can stand it.

"Symbolism." "Hidden meanings." "Themes." In my desultory experience as a teacher of reading, these seem to be what people who don't really read, or don't really like reading, are always afraid any reading worth the name is going to be about—at least when they come to class. Even if I tell them, as I always do (five or six times a term), "'Symbols,' 'hidden meanings,' and 'themes' don't really interest me—and, quite probably, refer to things that don't even exist," the papers at semester-end are usually awash with the terms, used often with great hostility and discomfort, so that the fear of them seems to trap the fearful in a self-fulfilling prophecy.

Now, it's very hard to talk about anything analytically without some specialized vocabulary. The one I favor for reading is nevertheless quite simple: "suggestion," "association," "convention," "allegory," "economy," and "conceit," along with the names for the various forms and genres encountered ("novel," "short story," "lyric," "longpoem," "science fiction," "essay," "pornography," "comic book," "narrative," "*récit,*" etc.), pretty much exhaust it for all save the most advanced purposes. (What I mean is that these are the terms that must be described and redescribed frequently because they cannot be defined.)

Metaphor? Metonymy? Apostrophe? Prosopoeia? I'll allow them in if someone else brings them up. But usually I can make do with "comparison" for the first. And the other three are pretty easily presented in simple language, with their associated problems pretty much covered by those suggestions, associations, and conventions—which is what I brought them in for in the first place.

Yet it is almost as if we *want* reading to be mysterious—to reveal, if we do it just right, symbols, mysteries, and signs. But I've been reading, as best I can, for on to forty-five years. And though many of the most important, intense, pleasurable, and wondrous experiences of my life have been granted me by reading, I am more and more convinced that the whole transcendental vocabulary is at best a set of historically interesting metaphors—and at worst a historically reprehensible shuck.

Today, my basic model for reading is one I've used with readers ranging from the remedial, struggling for any meaningful encounter at all with the text, to advanced graduates working tediously to tease out the meaning plays and slippages with which to construe the most delicate and arcane deconstructions.

To them both I say:

Consider the Instruction Manual.

How do we read it?

Even though it boldly declares, "Please Read ALL the Instructions Before You Begin Assembly," do we *ever* follow that particular exhortation? Doesn't that, rather, refer us to some idealized and ultimately nonextant and masterful reader who, finally, reflects none of us—whose only purpose is to intimidate all of us?

Does any one of us ever read a manual straight through?

What *do* we do when we read one?

We start. We stop. We look away. We look back. We backtrack. We skip ahead. We backtrack and skip ahead and stop and start again. We skim. We think about other things. We decide we'd better concentrate more on the text. We read with attention for a few moments. We read with less attention a moment on. We ignore this. We reread that—sometimes we reread that one section five, six, seven times. And what did it say up there? So we glance back. And read on. And almost always, as we read our manual, we tell ourselves we are reading with a purpose.

And when, as we've divined it, likely from previous expectations (and, possibly, from explanations offered by the manual itself), our purpose is accomplished, our reading, only a little after, stops—even if a tenth, or nine-tenths, of the manual demonstrably remains unread, an excess lingering among its pages, some unlooked at, but many others (at least we try, doubting as we say so, to tell ourselves) "read," to taunt us, to intimidate us, to lure us onward—or to be firmly ignored: We just don't have the interest. Or the time. . . .

And what about that excess? What about the instructions and passages pertaining to the hyperbolic functions, the Naperian logarithms, and the statistical and matrix capabilities that, while it's nice to know our little hand-held calculator can perform, you and I are never going to use and we know it?

The one thing we can say about it is that, by the time we've ended our reading, if only because our eyes have brushed across a section heading or snagged, while we were turning pages, on some bit of boldface type, we've already encountered *some* of it!

No matter how utilitarian we intended our trip through the text to be, if the music plays, if the picture—or the text—forms on the screen, if the engine turns over properly; if we feel as if we've made proper use of our manual at all, we've always (already) gotten caught in some of the excess. We've ended up reading a little more than we had to in terms of our purpose. In precisely the same way that, vis-à-vis some ideal of mastery, we never read it all or read what we read really carefully enough, at the same time we've always read a little *more* than we needed to, a little extra, as though our purpose in reading was itself attacked, changed, revised, and rendered, for a while, unstable by consulting the manual at all.

Well, I maintain *all* reading works this way—whether we're reading an epic poem, a magisterial philosophical treatise, a sweeping novel, or the instructions on the back of the box. And so, I maintain, do all readers, whether they be the beginning reader of three, four, or five, or the advanced student of Evelyn Wood, skimming along after an imaginary finger, overtaking it, hammering forward to avoid halting, missing this, regaining a ghost of what's missed from the context in that endless, headlong skim.

The only thing that characterizes the aesthetic text and makes it any different from the pamphlet under the Styrofoam around my new phone-answering machine is that, in the aesthetic text, the experience of the beautiful, the experience that intensifies that of excellence and beauty and insight (rather than the occurrence of simple explanation), at random and always differently for each of us each time we read (we cannot step into the same river twice; nor twice read the same text), functions through that excess, always—rather than through the task.

Because it is an excessive function (excessive to any readerly task), in matters of reading the aesthetic is difficult to discuss—and many readers, even very sophisticated ones, often would simply rather let it happen than try too hard to speak about it. We are talking, finally, about wonder—and isn't the initial response to wonder, properly, respectful silence?

Yes. Yet, turn two silent readers loose in the same room, and the moment they finish their books, invariably they start to talk. (I'm perfectly willing to admit that we are writing, here, about secondary, tertiary, or later responses . . . .) But I do think we can say something, if not about the wonder, then about the tasks that elicit our experiences of it.

Sometimes the task is simply to put together a story.

Sometimes the task is to create a coherent argument.

Sometimes—working with a poem, say, in a class—the task is to construct "a reading."

But whatever it is, the task is always a matter of expectation and/or explanation.

The task gives, then, the ideological dimension, which is to say our attempts to fulfill our readerly purposes are always both personal and political—which is to say in turn that with any and every readerly move we make, while there is always some element of freedom, there is also always an element of constraint. (When the task becomes wholly to construct an aesthetic, then the aesthetic becomes wholly ideological.)

The paradox it's hard to explain to the beginner is that, over any statistical range, it is they, even as this one labors toward a dimly misperceived originality or that one blunders into the hopelessly hokey, who are likely to be the most constrained; and it is the sophisticated readers who, over a statistical range, are likely to exercise the greatest readerly freedom.

True nonsense—that is, language in the lure of entropy rather than invention—leans overwhelmingly toward the conservative. And nonsense, let's face it, is often all beginning readers can find in too much of the text.

What assures our humility as instructors, however (and, at the same time, keeps us on our analytical toes), is that this is only a statistical lien. Any individual reader, beginner or advanced, may at any moment violate statistical expectations. We must be as careful readers of our students as we are of the solidly canonical—and, by extension, of everything in between. Even if blindness is inevitable, it is readerly vigilance that frees us.

I remember once encountering, at the University of Wisconsin, a young woman who had just finished an early volume of Proust over the same summer as had I. In talking, we discovered we had also both recently run into a passing point of Barthes'—that you never read Proust twice in the same way because each time you skim at different places.

"I didn't skim!" the young woman declared, over wine, white linen, and tangerines filled with Indian pudding drizzled with butter and rum. "I read every single word!"

"So did I!" I commiserated, toying with the Thanksgiving silver. "What does he mean, skim? How do you 'skim' Proust and get anything out of it at all?"

She nodded. Others of her guests chattered.

A few flakes flurried outside.

But the point is, it's the careful reader—the reader who "reads every single word"—who must be most attentive to her attention's wanderings. That's the reader who's always hauling herself or himself back to the text (and always at different times during different readings). Only the careful reader *knows* when she or he skims. Only through the vigilance needed to keep close to the text can the careful reader know just how distant (and idiosyncratic that distance is for each one) they are, text and reader, one from the other. Nor, I think, is it too much of a strain to read Barthes, given so many other things he said, as saying that.

But in today's climate of poststructuralism, psychoanalytic criticism, and new historicism, perhaps, like the climate itself, reading is just one of those things everyone talks of but never does anything about. Oh, we propose, and revise, and critique our various models. But which will weather, who can say?

Our struggle—and there is always, on some level, a struggle, be it the joyous struggle of the runner in love with jogging, the dancer who delights in leaping, the reader who relishes the sheer mental work of reading—to fulfill our task is always a tangle of glitches, inattentions, momentary snags, occasional snoozes, chance oversights, and habitual snarls—which set off and, finally, define the moments of clarity sometimes cited as the *Aha-Erlebnis* (the "Aha!-experience," when the manual actually lets us know how something works), which at once form the specificity of our encounter with the text and at the same time are all but repressed from our memory of it in precisely the way that, when listening to the stereo or shifting into cruise control, we forget our always faltering and fidgety initial manual perusals that impelled us into that moment of seeming mastery, when we once and finally, if only for a moment, give up our wills to be mastered.

That's what our manual model tells us.

And, once again, all reading works this way.

(In the same way we cannot read without repetitions, we cannot write without them either.)

Now this is a humble, very pedestrian model for reading. Its message is the simplest one: Whether you are just starting out or highly advanced, pay attention to what you're doing—even if that means paying attention to when your attention wanders. As a humble model will, it tends to reassure the beginner. And it keeps the sophisticated reader's feet conveniently grounded.

But notice, too, it's a disturbing model: With the same gesture that it reassures, it suggests to the beginning reader that there will never be any real, revelatory moment when some sweeping, all-encompassing, qualitative change in the reading experience occurs—that transcendental experience of understanding that, very possibly, the early reader deeply desires and that, alone, keeps him or her slogging on. And it tells the sophisticated reader: What you're doing isn't that hot after all. It's a very human, fragile, and faltering process—in some sense it rather knocks the feet out from under.

This model's tendency both to deflate excessive expectations for reading on the one hand and to undercut sophisticated readerly pretensions on the other may be why, in the face of it, all but the strongest readers seem to end up clinging to their symbols, hidden meanings, and themes—the unsophisticated reader as an excuse not to read in the first place, and the sophisticated one as a reward for having expended the effort.

Because my model simply does not speak of the wonder, people will read it (misread it?) as saying no wonder there's no wonder there to be found—at which I can only shrug; and perhaps offer a slight misreading (rereading?) of Wittgenstein's seventh proposition from the *Tractatus*: "That of which we *cannot* speak, we had best pass over in silence."

But even when the task we set ourselves is to construct the excellent, to recognize the beautiful, or to construe the insightful, it is the elements in the rich text that we are not paying attention to, that we don't precisely recall from the last time we read it, that sneak up and surprise us, that effect the task's accomplishment—if it occurs at all. Yes, we are working hard; but we are not in control.

Having said that what constitutes the aesthetic (note I did not say "the literary") is the inescapable excess to the (equally inescapable) task of reading in any text (even when the text is a painting or a sculpture; even when, as is so often the case in abstract work, the task is to locate the aesthetic in the text), I must note that much of the reading discussed in the pieces to come in this collection lies in realms generally considered excessive of the cultural mainstream—marginal to that canon for which we somehow feel we can easily assign the educational/historical tasks that are the post World-War-One academic constitution of literature.

The texts touched on here come out of literary theory and science fiction, comic books, and sexual rhetoric in the age of AIDS, as well as the discursive problems of texts that try to locate a theory adequate to them. The realities of race—if that is the proper term for what I take to be in all of its manifestations a system of political oppression grounded on a biological fantasy—also come up, now and again, as they must, in the discussion of any black man or women carried out extensively enough, in this or such a nation. (Anything "positive" in the system associated with "race" can be translated into terms of class—as class conflicts alone can explain the obfuscation, lies, and unspeakable cruelties that are the oppressive system itself.)

The three interviews in Part II—"The Kenneth James Interview," "The Susan Grossman Interview," and "The K. Leslie Steiner Interview"—are, I might introduce them here, introductory. By that I mean that they presume less familiarity with the topics discussed than do those in Part I. They also approach those topics at a rhetorical level that, for some, might make it easier to follow their instructionary thrusts.

They form, if you like, a beginners' manual for Part I. But I leave it to the reader to decide if she or he would rather read them before or after—if at all.

The seven pieces in Part I are, by contrast, professional interviews all.

(All began in association—even when they did not finish that way—with one journal or another.) The three in Part II all began as personal interviews—a small distinction but one that the reader may evaluate in the differences in focus, affect, and information.

And the Appendix—a conversation with Anthony Davis, composer of the opera *X: The Life and Times of Malcolm X*—gives the reader a chance to see what happens when the form turns tail and interviewee becomes interviewer.

Still, what is characteristic of most dealings with such texts on such topics in the past has been the assumption that they—as is assumed with actual manuals—are exhausted by their tasks: with science fiction and comic books, to tell a good story; in the case of literary theory or sexual rhetoric, to convey information. (Or, when the sexual rhetoric is presumed to be pornographic, to excite in such a way as to exhaust that excitement.) In the case of science fiction and comics, the aesthetic is assumed to be coextensive with the task—or not to exist. And most of us can respond to the even more astringent presupposition that the informative task of the sexual rhetoric of AIDS should, through the urgency that impels it, be such that it should have no aesthetic aspect at all; or that, certainly, here and now, to speak of an "appropriate aesthetic aspect" of such a rhetoric is in the nature of a scandal.

The contention here, however, is that the aesthetic remains an excess in all cases (even with real pamphlets on how to set up your word processor; or on how to have safe sex)—and that in any given manifestation the excess can still be profoundly, ideologically informative.

The genre in which we've situated our commentary on these marginal topics lies in an excessive and marginal space:

The written interview.

The marginality and necessity of this hemi-genre itself require some comment.

Without actually denoting voice, "Interview" still stresses mutual presence. If interviewer and interviewee are not within *sight* of one another, no inter-*view* takes place. Interview suggests an exchange of views—usually, today, between one who questions and one who answers—though this particular skewing away from the notion of intercourse between equals (one of whom might have questions and one of whom might have answers) toward a hierarchical interrogation comes through the appropriation of the seventeenth and eighteenth century's metaphorical/euphemistic use of "Interview" for a session of political torture, an appropriation controlling the twentieth century's postmedia development: an interlocutor who reports to a larger audience, and an interlocutee.

Perhaps because it is not self-presence but mutual presence positioned at the semantic core of the interview, a kind of cut remains between the participants—a fissure in which the truths there may be more malleable, less rigid, perhaps escaping the absolute and transcendental reading that still controls the ultimately logocentric concept of "dialogue."

But is that cut enough to allow writing to position itself within?

A telephone or radio interview substitutes sound for light—the voice carried at the same speed as light back and forth over whatever distances by means of an electromagnetic medium.

But what, then, of a written interview?

With its distinct connotation of absence, writing functions as an introductory minus sign, throwing the nominal term into reverse. A "written interview" is an inverse interview—an anti-interview—since it is the approach to truth vouchsafed by mutual presence which is struck by writing from the endeavor.

Yet, we can ask (as we asked what it was to read): What truth is the interviewer after? One interviews another person to find out what she or he truly thinks, what he or she truly feels. But I am a writer—which is another way of saying that my thoughts and feelings are intimately and intricately *formed* by writing.

Neither my "true thoughts" nor my "real feelings" would exist without writing. Writing has engendered them. Writing has developed them. Writing has stabilized them. Whatever specificity, range, or richness they possess, they have no basic existence apart from writing. The anxiety and forgetfulness playing through the face-to-face encounter confined to unrevised and unrevisable speech works (for me) against articulation, precision, sincerity—and ultimately against truth.

It might seem petty to some to discuss at this point the vagaries of transcription (so often compounded by the interviewer/transcriber's lack of familiarity with the topic under discussion) that plague traditional interviews, and their tendency to make oatmeal of the printed versions. If they were not so ubiquitous, we might skip over them and remain with more theoretical concerns. But for fifteen or more years now I've been interviewed between three and six times a year: Such vagaries are so prevalent that a theory of interview that does not take them into account is inadequate.

Here is simply a sampling to suggest the range to the category of transcription errors.

For more than ten years now, in my discussions of science fiction and its tense, marginal, critical relation to literature, I've had to make repeated and fine distinctions between "subject" and "object" as well as detailing their intricate overlap. But the ambiguity between philosophical usage ("subject-as-consciousness") and ordinary language usage ("subject-as-topic") often renders these distinctions difficult to follow in conversation, especially since, say, the "subject of a newspaper article" (in ordinary language) might easily be rendered (in philosophical jargon) "the newspaper article's object of consideration." My solution to this problem has been to employ three distinct terms very carefully: subject, object, and topic. And I always try to avoid the ordinary use of "subject" and use "topic" instead.

Sometimes I make mistakes. Far more frequently, however, even when I've been quite clear, the usage produces some rather odd or awkward sounding sentences. Transcribers in an attempt to smooth over such awkwardnesses have repeatedly rendered my statements meaningless by juggling the terms for euphony or for what they consider general flow. Thus, careful accounts of my critical notions are frequently bolixed by transcription.

Then there is simply the problem of the transcriber's ear. I recall one interview in which I spent a few paragraphs talking about the rhetorical relation, in fiction, between *récit,* dialogue, and action. But what got printed was a garbled passage on "racy dialogue in action."

In a recent interview that took place over the phone, I spoke of things about ourselves that we "are frequently the last ones to know"; later in the same interview, when talking about popular music, I mentioned "a standard C-major, A-minor, F, G-7th progression." Six weeks later, when the piece appeared in a Washington, D.C., literary supplement, I found myself reading about things that we "are free to be the last ones to know" and, a few paragraphs on, about "a standard teenager A-minor FG session"!

For a number of years now, when an interview is done, I've made a point of offering to go over the piece for precisely such mistakes. I stress to the interviewer that I will make no changes in the opinion passages of the article and that I will only clarify such verbal slips (mine as speaker or his as transcriber) or point out matters of fact. But while they all say thank you, less than a third take me up on the offer. And as recently as two months ago, when time went on and nothing arrived in the mails, I called the interviewer's editor to ask if I might take a glance at his finished piece, but was told, "Well, we don't like to let our interviewees see the articles before they come out. We don't want to impinge on the writers' freedom."

The young man who had done the actual interview (almost four hours of tapes, to be condensed into three pages of magazine text) had seen me for several follow-up sessions. At the end, we'd rather liked each other and had exchanged a couple of letters on topics completely unrelated to the interview per se. Since we had developed some sympatico, I trusted my feeling of mutual good will and contacted him, again stressing that I only wanted to clear up any ambiguities in the direct presentation of my own words within quotation marks.

Generously he invited me to come to the office and see the galleys which had just arrived. Still wrapped in my winter duds against the blustery January outside, while I was there in the old, wooden, ground floor rooms, I pointed out a couple of statements he'd made in the introductory section that, in terms of biographical facts, were just ambiguous, but left him to clear them up or leave them as he felt appropriate. Within quotation marks, I made two changes: In a discussion of representation and the human condition, I'd talked about certain events with the clumsy and awkward adjective "mirrorable." Transcription had turned at least one of my "mirrorable"s into a "manageable." So I put it back. At another point I straightened out the usual "subject"/"object" confusion.

When the article appeared, a couple of months later, though he'd adjusted the facts in the biographical passage, both quoted sections I'd corrected had simply been dropped from the piece. And I wondered if either the writer or his editor had felt that somehow the text at these points had been contaminated by my intervention and that surgery had been necessary to preserve its purity and health.

If such mistakes only appeared in, say, one out of three interviews, one might pass over them in silence. But I have never had an interview of more than nominal length that did not contain at least one—so that I begin to think such glitches are as constitutive of the listening process as similar glitches are constitutive of the reading process.

A first amendment fundamentalist, I believe wholly in writerly freedom, including the freedom of the interviewer—and am prepared to fight for it. Yet when that freedom is the freedom to hear "frequently" as "free to be," "C-major" as "teenager," "mirrorable" as "manageable," or "subject" as "object," the relation between freedom and truth slips perceptibly toward the problematic.

Yet for even these most fundamental sorts of mistakes to be corrected, the interview must become, at least in part, a written interview—with at least the correct versions of these words written into it by the interviewee.

The particular truth the traditional interview aspires to is a truth of mutual authority—and it loses access to this pinnacle primarily because mutual authority inescapably involves mutual intimidation.

The great American science fiction writer Theodore Sturgeon once wrote, "I write to make up for what I can't do in the living room."

But don't all traditional interviews presuppose a kind of ideal "living room" of the mind as their locus? And as Sturgeon's point suggests, there are simply times when we are less intimidated in the study alone than we are in the living room with others. If we turn to the interview for the verbal/social presentation an artist gives when cornered by someone arriving with the aura and authority of the media, fine: The transcriptive interview will do. But if we want to know what the writer thinks and feels, then a written interview may serve more forcefully, faithfully, and accurately.

A transcriptive interview is ideally part of the writer's life, not a part of her work. Several have pointed it out: While the work yields insights into the writer's motivations and attitudes on what was happening in her life, the life per se, apart from its historical aspect (that on a certain day so and so was working on such and such), tells us nothing about why the work achieved a certain aesthetic form—since the aesthetic enters into the text as an excess to the various tasks of writing as much as it is taken from the text via what is excessive to the tasks of reading. We should turn rather to the writer's work to find out what the transcriptive interview from life was probably a clumsy and ill-expressed version of. But reading it for insights into the writers' written pieces can be a doomed endeavor.

Writing is, of course, a construct. And one thing a writer constructs through her writing is a writerly persona. Indeed, writing is never more a construct than when the paper persona is an attempted self-portrait of the persona from the living room.

The written interview is, however, part of the writer's work. It's a kind of guided essay—certainly of a more careful guidance than the simple assignment of topic. As such, it preserves some of the mutuality of the interview, even if outside the "light"-and-"breath" locus of the western metaphorical structure in which metaphysical truth is deemed to dwell.

The written (or absent, or blind, or silent) interview will likely, for a while, if only because of its position marginal to this metaphysical/metaphoric structure, demarcate a modestly marginal genre—particularly fitting here, given these interviews' topics.

* * *

Two further marginal considerations remain to be introduced into the periphrastics of this introduction. One is the problem, the status, the politics of rhapsody. The other is my reason for resurrecting, in the title of what is, after all, my initial statement piece here, "The Semiology of Silence," the outmoded and currently unstylish term "semiology," rather than using the term preferred today, "semiotics"—which, certainly, the reader will note is the term generally used throughout the body of the same piece. Astute readers might even anticipate in this simple mention of this apparent contradiction a similar question of language that ultimately joins these considerations (of rhapsody and of style, the latter taking refuge in apparent unstylishness), one to the other: If I am someone who finally believes that race is an anabsolute term and refers to something that doesn't exist; if I feel similarly that all the socially meaningful effects of sexual difference are socially and politically—rather than biologically—contoured and that sexual difference is, therefore, another anabsolute, why not favor terms that already seem to acknowledge this, such as "class" and "gender"?

Almost all readers today know. The rules of Good Writing, of Forceful Language, tell us, use the Saxon term rather than the Latin. Use the short and common word rather than the polysyllabic, uncommon word—that is to say, the politics of rhapsody urges us to use the word most firmly anchored in its metaphysical, transcendental grounding. Does this mean that rhapsody—or, indeed, any other approach to "good writing" that you prefer—is innately conservative, fixedly metaphysical, inescapably transcendental?

I don't believe so.

I think, rather, what the "rules of good writing" are reminding us is that the metaphysical grounding we seek to cut loose from by our critical delirium is much more forceful than we give it credit for—and that it is precisely when we think we have cut loose from it that it is most strongly in place. Those rules remind us that it is not intellectual constructs that free us from metaphysics—other than as a fleeting, interim effect of a certain critique: a passing moment of vision. Rather, it is material changes alone that shift metaphysical grounds, and thus allow the newly critical intellectual constructs to emerge that will reveal where some of the older grounds once were. Those rules say: Do not forget the metaphysics you are always dealing with in your critique. They reiterate a position that has so often been associated with Derrida: "We are never outside of metaphysics." Thus they hold up the endless necessity for analytical vigilance.

The exhortation to the older Saxon term is a new version of an older rule: the exhortation to the Greek before the Latin. But why might one prefer the Greek "rhapsode" to the Latin "delirium"? Delirium speaks only of derangement, in deference to the enthusiasm and the ecstasy that still inheres in it. It is not as Gaiman's Prince of Dreams would sometimes have us believe: that Delirium was once Delight. Rather, Delirium was once madness—and is now Delight.

A rhaps-ode is a stitched-together song—traditionally from fragments of various narratives. (Though there's no etymological connection, how well it resonates with hip-hop's "rap"—which comes from the fifties and sixties drug term "rap," an apocopation of "rapid-fire.") Its fragmentary, incoherent, nondeveloped aspects all underlie what, by the Latin, becomes simply madness—or, at any rate, wildly improbable. (An interesting, rhapsodic characterization of theory.) The Greek holds us closer to the intertextuality of all song, all narrative; as well, it suggests the material underpinnings to what is later almost wholly a propositional attitude.

This is the spirit in which, at least in my opening title, I use "semiology" rather than "semiotics": because it suggests an area of study in which, by the very nature of such study, we will always be inclined to seek a system, a law, a "logos"—a logocentricity that, frankly, yes, contravenes the very enterprise I hope the term names. But let me remind you—

On his assumption of the Chair of Literary Semiology at the Collège de France in January 1977 in his Inaugural Lecture, Barthes described semiology as "the labor that collects the impurities of language, the wastes of linguistics, the immediate corruption of any message: nothing less than the desires, fears, expressions, intimidations, advances, blandishments, protests, excuses, aggressions, and melodies of which active language is made"—a description that certainly seems very different in tone, if not in substance, from the far more positivistic affect current semiotic studies—from animal semiotics to film semiotics—produce. It is also in the spirit, then, precisely through its contradiction with the letter, of this earlier description of a certain margin of language that I chose Barthes', rather than Kristeva's, term.

In short, we have a better chance referring to what we believe cannot exist—sex, race, and, yes, semiology (i.e., the systematic, logical, and exhaustive study of signs)—than we do referring to what we think does exist—gender, class, and semiotics—especially when, uncritically, we assume that such existence is possible without some metaphysical, transcendental ground . . . for in all three of these cases what grounds them is the very scientism that links them with the former three, denied terms, making the latter, positive three terms possible. Using such terms as sex, race, and semiology, then, in such an oppositional context, we already know we're in allegory, in fiction, in a condition where vigilance alone is proper. In matters written, a similar argument offers the justification for fantasy, science fiction, and magic realism.

I'd hoped that this insistently writerly hemi-genre, the written interview, might produce a more or less readerly text—readerly at least for those who enjoy reading criticism. (It is, in this day, left to our fiction[s] to be writerly.) I mean "readerly" in the sense that Barthes' essays, in the universe of theoretical discourse (where, in his *S/Z*, the readerly and the writerly—the lisible and the scriptible—were once so dramatically distinguished), are themselves readerly, pleasurable, at play in the fields of the familiar. (We pick up Derrida's *Of Grammatology* when we want to wrestle with the idea of play. We pick up Barthes' *Mythologies* when we want to play with the idea of wrestling.) The theoretical forays here work in the margins of a fictive enterprise, as rhapsodic speech lies in the margins of communication, as the fine points of reading lie in the margins of a mastery never ours. As theories, they represent the delirium of their objects, an excess, an aesthetic.

When rhapsody is an interplay between the excitement of a speaker and the involvement of a listener, as in some religious (or pedagogic) situations, rhapsody can, perhaps, be improvised.

But when rhapsody is written, if only because of the greater critical distance of the reader, it must be written carefully—often more carefully then more pedestrian instruction. And much of this theory—as does much theory—rhapsodizes. Rhapsody's status in contemporary critical discourse, now as (most importantly) Foucault's work assumes it, now as Lacan's work (in the radically edited transcriptions of his verbal "Écrits" and seminars) or Derrida's position themselves alongside it, is so determined. Its ecstatics/mechanics/politics function in the way they do because, even written, we read rhapsody above all as a vocal genre—and grant it a privilege that Derrida has (most importantly) examined vis-à-vis the suppression of just that privilege for writing. Rhapsody's problem—on the page—results from the tension between its status and its mechanic; nor would I be surprised to learn that a large part of the difficult collision between Anglo-American philosophy and the various modes of continental philosophy grows out of this same tension. Both sides are consistently too logical for it to be a matter of logic.

* * *

Language and theory, science fiction and comic books, sword-and-sorcery, the sociology of genres, AIDS, sex, and race: a more complete list of what you will find discussed ahead (here in our terminal margin) than the list that lies at the center of this essay. I am particularly grateful to the editors and interviewers who have taken on the role of guide among these topics. I have found the journeys they've led me along rewarding. I only hope my readers will find them so as well.

Marginality, lack of intimidation, accuracy—these are finally the reasons a writer might be tempted to favor the interview in written form.

For six of the pieces here ("The Semiology of Silence," "Refractions of Empire," "Science Fiction and Criticism," "Some *Real* Mothers . . . ,"

"The Susan Grossman Interview," and "Anthony Davis—A Conversation"), spoken texts were recorded, transcribed, and used as the base over which the writing was erected. For five others ("Toto, We're Back!," "Sword & Sorcery, S/M, and the Economics of Inadequation," "Sex, Race, and Science Fiction," "The Kenneth James Interview," and "The K. Leslie Steiner Interview"), the interviewers submitted questions to me in writing, and I wrote directly back—though in "Sword & Sorcery, S/M, and the Economics of Inadequation" those answers were discussed at several points during a many-layered composition process in person and in letter. Here I must mention that the written interview can be just as trying for the interviewer as the oral one can be for the interviewee. Takayuki Tatsumi of the English Department of the University of Tokyo ("Science Fiction and Criticism," "Some *Real* Mothers . . . ") twice produced, for example, careful and meticulous transcriptions of our lengthy oral tapes—and twice had to watch while, in version after version, I swallowed up and digested his work, to replace it with my second, third, and fourth thoughts on the matters he'd first raised. And *Camera Obscura*'s Constance Penley and Sharon Willis presented me with a dozen intricate and beautifully thought-out questions, of which, in thicker and thicker envelopes, I responded to fewer and fewer, till I reached the version here—which wrestles a mere three to a length of fifty pages: a text far too long for them to print in their very fine journal. I am particularly grateful to them for allowing me nevertheless to use the journal's name in its subtitle, since it was never actually published there. But to all my interviewers, I offer my sincerest gratitude for their acumen, patience, and generosity:

Sinda Gregory, Gary Groth, Susan Grossman, Johan Heye, Lloyd Hemingway, Kenneth James, Denny O'Neil, Larry McCaffery, Constance Penley, Robert Reid-Pharr, K. Leslie Steiner, Takayuki Tatsumi, and Sharon Willis—without whom, as it is so often said, this book could not have been written.

For help obtaining illustrations for "Refractions of *Empire*," my thanks go to Denny O'Neil, Darren Vincenzo, Len Schafer, Byron Preiss Visual Publications, Inc., and D.C. Comics; and, most warmly, to Ed Summer.

—Thank you.

Amherst, Massachusetts
February 1989/September 1990

Part I

1.

The Semiology of Silence: The *Science Fiction Studies* Interview

This text began as a recorded conversation in New York City in August 1983 with Sinda Gregory and Larry McCaffery (both of San Diego State University). I produced this written form over the next several weeks, which eventually appeared in Science Fiction Studies, *Volume 14 (1987). Another piece based on other parts of the same conversation is included in McCaffery's and Gregory's interview collection,* Alive and Writing: Interviews with American Authors of the 1980s *(Illinois University Press, 1987).*

Samuel R. Delany: I begin, a sentence lover. I'm forever delighted, then delighted all over, at the things sentences can trip and trick you into saying, into seeing. I'm astonished—just plain tickled!—at the sharp turns and tiny tremors they can whip your thoughts across. I'm entranced at their lollop and flow, their prickles and points. Poetry is made of words, Mallarmé told us a hundred years back. But I write prose.

And prose is made of sentences.

Oh, I've always been a bathroom dictionary browswer. Still—"In the beginning was the word . . . "? I suppose poets have to feel that way. But for me, the word's a degenerate sentence, a fragmentary utterance, something incomplete. Mollying along, lonesome Mrs. Masters asks, "Why aren't there any decent words?" Well, no word is decent by itself; and less than a dozen indecent—*shit, fuck,* and the like working the way they do because when they're blurted by counter women, construction workers, or traffic-bound drivers, they've got a clear capital at one end and an exclamation point at the other, so that the words alone (in the dictionary, say, or askew on the stall wall) are homonymous with the indecent expletive—which is a sentence. Declare "Sputum!" the way we do "Shit!" and we'll have it obscene in a season. It's highly reductive to take the toddler's tentative or passionate utterances, her one- and two-syllable grunts, his burble and blab, merely as practice *words;* they're questions, exclamations, protests, incantations, and demands. And tangible predicate or not, these are sentence forms. The late Russian critic M. M. Bakhtin (1895–1975) hit on the radical notion of considering the word not a locus of specified meaning but rather an arena in which all possible social values that might be expressed with and through it can engage in contest. But what calls up those differing values? What holds them stable long enough to get their dander up, if not the other words about, along with the punctuation that, here and there, surrounds and, there and here, sunders: in short, the different sentences the word occurs in? Without the sentence, the arena of the word has no walls, no demarcation. No contest takes place. Even historically, I suspect it's more accurate to think of the sentence as preceding the word. "Word"—or "logos"—is better considered a later, critical tool to analyze, understand, and master some of the rich and dazzling things that go on in statements, sentences, utterances, in the *énoncés* that cascade through life and make up so much of it.

The sentence is certainly the better model for the text. (The word is the model for the Bible, and that really *isn't* what most writers today want their texts to become.) The word is monolithic. You can't argue with it. At best it's got an etymology—which is to say it comes only from other words that most of us, speaking, don't have immediate access to. And an etymology is only a genealogy, not a real history of material pressures and complex influences. For that, you have to look to a history of rhetorical figures, of ideas (expressed by what . . . ?), of discourse.

The sentence is more flexible, sinuous, complex—one is always revising it—than the word. It's got style. Yet it holds real danger in its metaphorical compass. The wrong one condemns you to death.

Der Satz, the Germans say, philosophically: the sentence, or the proposition. We've got two terms for their one. They lead to very different areas of utterances about language, too. From the Greek Stoics on,[1] this split strongly suggested that meanings could come apart from words, from the sentences that evoked them. Philosophically speaking, a proposition was thought to be a particular kind of clear and delimitable meaning associated with a particular kind of rigorously simple sentence—or a combination of them in clear and lucid relations, indicated by truth tables and Venn diagrams; and any truly meaningful sentence could be broken down into them. Willard Van Orman Quine is among the more recent philosophers this side of the Herring Pond to suggest that view isn't right. Meanings just *aren't* hard-edged and delimitable. To use his word (in my sentence): They just can't be "individuated" as easily as that. Meanwhile, on the other side, Jacques Derrida is one of the new thinkers to make it disturbingly clear that the most fixed and irrefutable-seeming meaning is finally a more or less overdetermined play of undecidables.

"Words mean many things" is the old sentence that tried to illuminate some pivotal point in this complex situation. A comment about words, yes. But it takes a sentence to say it.

What interests me most about sentences is the codes by which we make them—and various combinations and embeddings and tortuosities of them (I was 19 when, in *Lectures in America,* I first read Gertrude Stein's bright and repeated observation: "The paragraph is the emotional unit of the English language." And you know what makes a paragraph)—make sense. An interest such as mine usually starts from the position: "Well, there are these things called words, sentences, paragraphs, texts. . . . And, by a more or less articulatable set of codes, we interpret them to mean certain things."

But as you articulate those codes more and more, you soon find, if you're honest with yourself, you're at a much more dangerous and uncertain place. You notice, for example, the convention of white spaces between groups of letters that separate out words is, itself, just a code. Knowing the simplest meaning of a word is a matter of knowing a code. Knowing printed letters—written characters—stand for language and are there to convey it is, itself, only a certain codic convention. "Word" (or, indeed, "sentence" or "paragraph") is only the codic term for the complex of codic conventions by which we recognize, respond to, understand, and act on whatever causes us to recognize, respond, understand, and act in such a way that, among those recognitions and responses and understandings, is the possible response: "word" (or, indeed, "sentence" or "paragraph").

But turn around now, and what we called "the real world" seems to be nothing *but* codes, codic systems and complexes, and the codic terms used to designate one part of one system, complex, or another. In the larger neural net, the colors we see and the sounds we hear are only codic markers for greater or lesser numbers of vibrations per second in electromagnetic fields or clouds of gas. Shapes among colors are markers coded to larger or smaller aggregates of atoms and molecules that reflect those vibrations. None of this can be perceived directly; and it's only by maneuvering and cross-comparing certain codic responses to certain others according to still other codes that we can theorize the universe's external existence in our own internal codic system—a system that, in practical terms, while it expands and develops on that theory at every turn, seems hardly set up to question it except under extremely speculative conditions.

The sentential, codic—or semiotic—view is dangerous because questions that, at least initially, seem inimical to the system *do* get asked. And inimical-seeming answers are arrived at. The comparatively stable objects posited by the limited codic system of the senses do not correlate well with the greater codic complexes that entail our memory of objects, our recognition of them, and our knowledge of their history and their related situations, which, finally, are what allow us to negotiate, maneuver, and control them. Sense-bound distinctions such as inside and outside become hugely questionable. Value-bound metaphors such as higher and lower stand revealed as arbitrary. And the physically inspired quality of identity becomes a highly rigid mentalistic ascription in a system that can clearly accommodate more flexibility.

"Solipsism" is what it's called—to call it with a sentence. And it feels very lonely.

The way out, however, is simply to remember that the code system isn't simple. It's terribly complex, recursive, self-critical, and self-revising; and redundancy, sometimes called overdetermination, is its hallmark at every perceivable point. The overdetermination of the codic system is the most forceful suggestion that the universe, from which the system is made and to which (we assume) it is a response, is itself overdetermined—which is to say: It operates by laws. (It is sentenced, if you will, to operate in certain ways and not in others.)

What does that overdetermination mean to the human codic system?

It means frequently you can knock out the most obvious appearance and still come up with pretty much the same understanding or one that feels even finer.

What *could* be more important than the spaces between for distinguishing individual words? YetyoucandropthewordspacesinalmostanyEnglish sentenceandstillreaditwellenough. Words seem to individuate more easily than meanings. The early Greeks used to write with all capital letters and no punctuation or spaces between words at all. There are a number of writing systems that have no way—or only a very impoverished way—of indicating vowel sounds. They still produce perfectly readable sentences. Nd y cn drp th vwls n Nglsh nd stll mk prtty gd gss t wht th txt sys. You can cut the bottom half of the print off an English sentence with no irretrievable loss of meaning.

That's all overdetermination.

What you can't do is drop the word spaces *and* the vowels *and* the bottom half of the print all at once. That over-determines chaos. Suddenly all meaningful pattern becomes massively underdetermined—far more so than the overdetermined current through all language that governs its flexibility and facilitates its deconstruction, though this chaos of the letter may well be the origin of that always inescapable current.

But the fact is, almost any codic convention we can talk of *in* language matters is likely to be overdetermined. Where there's communication, there's redundancy—starting with the one between what's in your mind and what's in mine, which allows words to call up similar meanings for both of us. Indeed, if there's a codic rule of thumb governing the vast complex of codes which makes up life in the world, it would seem to be: The more obvious, important, and indispensable a codic convention, the more redundant it is—including this one. That results from all the other little rules, often very hard to ferret out because the obvious hides them, that obliquely replicate parts of it, that manage to reinforce much of it, that give it its appearance—in short, that make it "obvious," "important," and "indispensable" in the first place.

Well, here I sit, in the middle of all these playful, sensuous sentences and codes, writing my SF, my sword-and-sorcery, more or less happily, more or less content. But I suspect there's little to say about writing, mine or anyone else's, that doesn't fall out of its sentences, or the codes which recognize and read them, the codes which the sentences are—and the sentences which are the only expressions, at least in verbal terms, we can have of the codes.

Larry McCaffery: Unlike Kurt Vonnegut, you have openly and proudly proclaimed your writing to be "science fiction." Indeed, in your critical writings, you have suggested that SF is a genre in its own right and not merely a subgenre of mainstream (or "mundane") fiction or of the romance or whatever. And you have resisted the notion that recent SF is "re-entering" the realms of serious fiction. Could you talk about these controversial notions, explain how you arrived at them, and why you feel they're important?

SRD: The easiest place to enter your question is at the idea of SF's "reentering" the realm of serious fiction. To be "re-entering" anything, SF has to have been there once before (presumably in the 17th, 18th, and 19th centuries' "feigned histories" and "utopias," from Kepler and Cyrano to More and Bellamy); then it has to have left (no doubt when SF stories began to appear in the adventure and pulp magazines of the early part of this century); and now, according to some people, it's coming back—while, according to me, it isn't.

Well, that whole model of the "history of SF" is, I think, ahistorical. More, Kepler, Cyrano, and even Bellamy would be absolutely at sea with the codic conventions by which we make sense of the sentences in a contemporary SF text. Indeed, they would be at sea with most modern and postmodern writing. It's just pedagogic snobbery (or insecurity), constructing these preposterous and historically insensitive genealogies, with Mary Shelley for our grandmother or Lucian of Samosata as our great-great grandfather. There's no reason to run SF too much back before 1926, when Hugo Gernsback coined the ugly and ponderous term, "scientifiction," which, in the letter columns written by the readers of his magazines, became over the next year or so "science fiction" and finally "SF." Ten years before or 30 years before is all right, I suppose, if you need an Ur-period. It depends on what aspect of it you're studying, of course. But 50 years is the absolute outside, and that's only to guess at the faintest rhetorical traces of the vaguest discursive practices. And in practical terms, most people who extend SF too much before 1910 are waffling.

Look. Currently our most historically sensitive literary critics are busily explaining to us that "literature" as we know it, read it, study it, and interpret it today hasn't existed more than 100 years. Yet somehow there is supposed to be a stable object, SF, that's endured since the 16th century (or 1818, when Mary Shelley published *Frankenstein,* an equally silly date)—though it only got named in 1929 . . . ?

That's preposterous.

Now, there've been serious writers of SF ever since SF developed its own publishing outlets among the paraliterary texts that trickled out on their own toward the end of the 19th century and that, thanks to technical developments in printing methods, became a flood by the end of World War I and today are an ocean. Some of those SF writers, like Stanley G. Weinbaum (1900–1935), were extraordinarily fine. Some of them, like Captain S. P. Meek (1894–1972), were unbelievably bad. And others, like Edward E. Smith (1890–1965), while bad, still had something going. But what they were all doing, both the bad ones and the good ones, was developing a new way of reading, a new way of making texts make sense—collectively producing a new set of codes. And they did it, in their good, bad, and indifferent ways, by writing new kinds of sentences, and embedding them in contexts in which those sentences were readable. And whether their intentions were serious or not, a new way of reading *is* serious business.

Between the beginning of the century and the decade after the Second World War—by the end of which we clearly have the set of codes we recognize today as SF—there are things of real historical interest to study in the developing interpretative codes and the texts that both exploited them and revised them in the pulp SF magazines and, later, in the SF book market, hardcover and paperback. But most academic critiques that equate 17th-, 18th-, and 19th-century didactic fables with 20th-century pulp texts just mystify history and suppress those historical developments, both in terms of what was seriously intended and what was simply interesting, however flip.

I've never *proclaimed* my work SF, proudly *or* humbly. I assume most of my published fiction is SF—and I assume most of my readers feel it is, too. But that's like a poet assuming she writes poems, or a playwright assuming he writes plays.

All I've ever "proclaimed" in my critical books, *The American Shore* (1978) or *Starboard Wine* (1984), is that, today, at this particular point in the intellectual history of various practices of writing, in the development of the greater complex of interpretative codes that we apply to the range of writing practices, "science fiction" is a useful designation and marks a useful distinction from literature. And I've even gone so far as to propose that when we bypass some of the most obvious appearances associated with the distinction and explore the ways in which the underlying codes and conventions overdetermine them, interesting things come to light.

In the vast play of codic conventions, there are *no* distinctions that are *always* useful for *all* situations and tasks. But there are many distinctions that are useful for many particular situations—so many, in fact, that their profligacy is itself a situation that makes it useful to call such distinctions "rules."

One place such distinctions are useful is when there's ambiguity on one side that can only be resolved by finding some overdetermined path to the other side where the ambiguity—if we're lucky—doesn't exist.

I've written a number of essays which have employed as examples strings of words that, if they appeared in an SF text, might be interpreted one way but that, if they appeared in a mundane text, might be interpreted another:

> Her world exploded
> He turned on his left side.

The point is not that the meaning of the sentences is ambiguous, however, but that the route to their possible mundane meanings and the route to their possible SF meanings are both clearly determined. And what's clearly determined is overdetermined. I've also written an essay on the way readers who have only acquired the literary codes of interpretation can go about misreading a typical SF phrase (just a fragment of a sentence): "The monopole magnet mining operations in the outer asteroid belt of Delta Cygni . . . ."[2]

Sentences such as "The door dilated" and "I rubbed depilatory soap over my face and rinsed it with the trickle from the fresh water tap" get special interpretative treatment when we encounter them in an SF text. And it's the nature of overdetermination that readers comfortable with SF will usually recognize these and many other such sentences and phrases as more than likely coming from SF texts, even if they have never actually encountered them in Niven or Heinlein or Pohl and Kornbluth.

The distinction between SF and literature is useful if we want to talk about what's happening to us at such moments of recognition, and how that differs from the recognition experience we have when we encounter such sentences as "A leaf stuck to Estreguil's pink cheek," "Gliding across Picadilly, the car turned down St James Street," "The Marquis went out at five o'clock," or "Ages ago, Alex, Allen, and Alva arrived at Antibes . . . ."[3]

LM: Until recently most critics have—fruitlessly, it seems to me—tried to define these differences in terms of subject matter: One text deals with outer space and the other deals with the world around us. But I gather that the basis of your view of these distinctions is different. You rely on an essentially semiological argument that the sentences in SF "mean" differently from sentences in ordinary fiction.

SRD: Again, it's overdetermination that causes the overwhelmingly important appearance of the subject matter differences. But that's simply to say with another sentence what I've said before: The most obvious distinctions and designations *are* the most overdetermined. And understanding doesn't really get under way until you can tease apart some of the ways in which the not so obvious conventions highlight, support, and even account for the obvious ones: what holds the system, as it were, stable. As far as the priority of subject matter itself, well: Poems often have different subject matter from mundane fiction. Dramas frequently have different subject matter from poems. And films frequently have different subject matter from dramas. But no sophisticated analysis of poetry, fiction, drama, or film would try to present an exhaustive analysis of each field, or its difference from the others, purely in terms of appropriate and inappropriate subject matter—purely in terms of traditional category themes. As Robert Graves noticed years ago, all poems tend to be about love, death, or the changing of the seasons. A clever observation, and it's insightful. But in the long run we still have to say that a poem *can* be about anything. Just as sword-and-sorcery stories tend to be about the changeover from a barter economy to a money economy, SF stories tend to be about the changeover from a money economy to a credit economy—also insightful. Still, SF stories (like sword-and-sorcery stories) can be about anything too. But the fact that some academic critics still seriously try to present an exhaustive discussion of SF in terms of traditional themes is just a sign of how unsophisticated much academic criticism of SF is.

The reader who can't respond properly to "The monopole magnet mining operations in the outer asteroid belt of Delta Cygni . . ."—the reader who doesn't know what monopole magnets are, who isn't sure if the mining is done *for* the magnets or *with* the magnets, who has no visualization of an asteroid belt, outer, inner, or otherwise, or who wonders how mine tunnels get from asteroid to asteroid—that reader is having the same kind of problem with the SF text that the contemporary reader of Elizabethan poetry is likely to have encountering, say, the opening clause of Shakespeare's "Sonnet 129":

> Th' expense of spirit in a waste of shame
> Is lust in action . . .

You have to know that "expense" here doesn't primarily mean cost: Its first meaning here is expenditure, or pouring out. You have to know that "spirit" here only secondarily means soul: Its primary meaning here is volatile liquid, such as alcohol. And "waste" doesn't have a primarily verbal thrust here: Its nominal meaning here is desert. "To act from lust is to pour out alcohol in a desert of shame . . ." was the immediate semantic perception for your ordinary Elizabethan—well before the level of interpretations began that set double (i.e., onanistic and commercial) meanings at play throughout this clause, the conclusion of its sentence, and the rest of the poem.

Before you can deconstruct a text, Robert Scholes writes somewhere, you have to be able to construe it. It's sobering to discover how many otherwise literate people have trouble with SF just at the construction level. And frequently these are the first people to condemn it as meaningless.

Since the complex of codes for SF (like that for Elizabethan poetry) *is* overdetermined and segues into and mixes inextricably with the codes for many other kinds of reading, one way to learn the SF complex is to read a lot of it—with a little critical help now and then. That's the way most 12-year-olds do it.

But these codic conventions operate at many levels. They not only affect what one is tempted to call the "what" of the information. They also affect the "way" the information is stored. And I see this storage pattern as fundamentally different for SF and literature—and that difference holds for all the subpractices of literature, too: poetry, realistic fiction, literary fantasy, philosophy . . . .

Sinda Gregory: You feel this distinction is true even if the literary text you're reading is a fantasy—say, something by Kafka?

SRD: All right. You have a text in front of you. For overdetermined reasons you know it's literature—it's in a large book called *The Norton Anthology,* and there are 17 books in *your* local library alone about the writer—this Kafka fellow. You read the first sentence: "One morning, waking from uneasy dreams, Gregor Samsa, still in bed, realized he'd transformed into a huge beetle." Because we know it's a literary text, certain questions associated with literature immediately come into play. The moment we recognize the situation as fantastic, yet still within the literary frame, we prepare certain questions: "What could this nonnormal situation be saying about the human personality? Is Samsa, perhaps, insane? If not, what in the range of *real* human experience is the *fantastic* situation a *metaphor* for?" And we pick out two areas in which we expect those answers to lie: One is that of a certain kind of psychosocial alienation associated with other literary characters, e.g., Conrad's Mr. Kurtz, Dostoevsky's Underground Man, and Sartre's Antoine Roquentin from *La Nausée,* although there are many others . . . . The other area we've already marked out to explore in the metaphoric light of the text is the area of artistic creativity itself. And you would be hard pressed to find a discussion of "The Metamorphosis" that, to the extent it sees the story as interpretable at all, does *not* present its interpretation as falling more or less under one or both of those rubrics. Even Kafka, in his diaries, talks about his writing as "a talent for portraying my dreamlike inner life"[4] (notice he specifically does *not* talk about it as portraying or critiquing his outer world), and we have very little choice but to take this inner life for anything but the inner life of the writer, or of alienated man and his psychological relations, no matter how objective the causes of that alienation may in fact be.

All right. There's a text in front of you. For overdetermined reasons you know it's SF—it's in a mass-market paperback anthology with the initials "SF" in the upper left-hand corner above the front-cover repeat of the ISBN number. And though you only vaguely recognize the writer's name, the blurb above the title tells you she won a Hugo award for best novella sometime in the early '70s. (Stories in SF anthologies often have introductory editorial paragraphs, as though they were all textbooks. But that's because SF has so little formal historiography.) You read the first sentence: "One morning, waking from uneasy dreams, Gregor Samsa, still in bed, realized he'd transformed into a huge beetle." The moment we recognize the situation as nonnormal (because it's SF, in most cases we don't even cognize it as fantastic), certain questions that are associated with SF come into play: "What in the *world* portrayed by the story is responsible for the transformation? Will Samsa turn out to be some neotenous life form that's just gone into another physical stage? Or has someone performed intricate biomechanical surgery during the night?" We want to know not only the agent of the transformation. Kenneth Burke's "dramatism" covers that very nicely, as it covers fantasy. But we also want to know the *condition of possibility* for the transformation. That condition may differ widely from SF story to SF story, even when the agent (a mad scientist, perhaps) and the transformation itself (the disappearance of an object, say) are the same; and I know of no literary or literarily based narrative theory which covers this specific SF aspect of the SF text. Most of our specific SF expectations will be organized around the question: What in the portrayed *world* of the story, by statement or by implication, must be *different from ours* in order for this sentence to be normally uttered? (That is, how does the condition of possibility in the world of the story differ from ours?) But whether the text satisfies or subverts these expectations, the reading experience is still controlled by them, just as the experience of reading the literary text is controlled by literary expectations. And because they are not the same expectations, the two experiences are different.

Needless to say, the conscientious SF writer tries to come up with a text that satisfies and subverts these expectations—exploits them, if you will—in rich, complex, and intriguing ways, satisfying in the long run whether satisfaction *or* subversion is the short-term effect at any local point. And, as I've also said, at the codic level, the two complexes of interpretative conventions (literature's and SF's) interpenetrate and overlap in many ways, many of which are linguistic, many extralinguistic. In fact, I'd go so far as to suggest that the overlap is probably *so* great that worrying about the purity of the genres on any level is even more futile than worrying about the purity of the races. Real understanding of the range and richness of codes, with their attendant recursions, revisions, and redundancies, makes absolute differentiation simply a nonproblem. Nevertheless, at certain heuristic points, when we're trying to clarify things at a certain historical level (which history, if it doesn't include the present, contours it at every point), distinctions among writing practices and between reading codes, like any others, can be useful *if* we keep a clear sense of how to dissolve them when *that* becomes necessary.

For the last hundred years, the interpretative conventions of all the literary reading codes have been organized, tyrannized even, by what, in philosophical jargon, you could call "the priority of the subject." Everything is taken to be about mind, about psychology. And, in literature, the odder or more fantastical or surreal it is, the *more* it's assumed to be about mind or psychology.

SF, developing in the statistically much wider field of paraliterature (comic books, pornography, film and television scripts, advertising copy, instructions on the back of the box, street signs, popular song lyrics, business letters, journalism—in short, the graphic flood from which most of the texts each of us encounters over any day come), has to some extent been able to escape this tyranny, at least a bit more than the straited stream of literary texts—in SF we used to call it "the mainstream," which is fine as long as you realize that paraliterary texts make an ocean.

Among paraliterary practices, popular song lyrics, which in historical terms are closest to poetry, have been able to escape the tyranny of the subject the least.

At the level where the distinction between it and paraliterature is meaningful, literature is a representation of, among other things, a complex codic system by which the codic system we call the "subject" (with which, in any given culture, literature must overlap) can be richly criticized. By virtue of the same distinction, SF is a representation of, among other things, a complex codic system by which the codic system we call the "object" (which, in those cultures that have SF, SF must ditto) can be richly criticized—unto its overlap with the subject.

At this point, of course, the poet gets righteously angry with me, for now I'm basically slogging about in a slough of jargon. I couldn't really blame any reader who'd just given up by now and gone home: There's overlap between poetry and prose too, and we must occasionally criticize prose by poetic standards—perhaps far more than we usually do.

This may be a good moment, then, to clarify a fundamental about fundamentals. When we look for a basic, should we assume that because it *is* a basic we're after, it will be simple, solid, monolithic, and a-tomic (that is, "un-cuttable")? Or should we assume that stability—the appearance of simplicity, solidity, unity—is a function of complexity, of organization (internal and external), of overdetermination? Shouldn't we perhaps assume anything that endures long enough to be noticed, anything that repeats often and clearly enough to be recognized—in short, any phenomenon that even flirts with the seeming of identity—must partake of the systematic, must exist as a balance of complexities, must persist through a combination and interchange of opened and closed subsystems, and thus must be potentially analyzable?

(Axioms are not objects. They're sentences.)

To choose the second is to choose the approach that privileges the sentence over the word, that models existence as a set of more or less stable complexities rather than as a set of atomic rigidities. That's really all the jargon grasps at.

And among the practices of writing today, "science fiction," "poetry," "pornography," "mundane fiction," "reportage," "drama," "comic books," "philosophy," *et alia,* all seem like fairly stable, fairly simple, fairly basic, fairly enduring and, above all, fairly recognizable categories.

Which is to say, each is complex.

SG: But you're saying that on the basis of reader expectation, mind-set makes SF a different genre from ordinary fiction.

SRD: That's not what I'm saying at all. Most readers' experience—specifically the experience of most readers familiar with a fair amount of SF—includes texts that feel indubitably science fictional as well as texts that feel indubitably literary. And, at this point, the texts that strike most competent readers as undecidable are experienced as few and anomalous. We talk about situations we agree on as ambiguous only to help develop an analytic vision of the world as we find it that feels logically and aesthetically satisfying. It's not simply to say that, just because it sounds sophisticated, things obviously black must be white, if only because what's obvious has to be wrong. One wants a theory that accounts for the obvious *and* the ambiguous. Not a theory which accounts only for the obvious but which the ambiguous contradicts.

"Mind-set" creates the SF text—or the literary text, for that matter? No.

You remember that phrase I was worrying over, a bit back? "The monopole magnet mining operations in the outer asteroid belt of Delta Cygni . . ." Well, that phrase, even without a predicate, states something; it's a statement about mines, as they exist in the world today. It says that the object, the location, the methodology, and the spatial organization of mines will *change.* And it says it far more strongly than, and well before, it says anything about, say, the inner chthonic profundities of any fictive character *in* those mines or about the psychology of the writer *writing* about them—which is where, immediately, the expectations of the literarily oriented critic are likely to lead her or him in constructing an interpretation.

Any faster-than-light spaceship drive met in the pages of any SF text written to date, be it mine or Isaac Asimov's or Joan Vinge's, basically poses a critique of the Einsteinian model of the universe, with its theoretical assertion of the speed of light as the upper limit on velocity: Those FTL drives are all saying, and saying it very conscientiously, that the Einsteinian model will be revised by new empirical and theoretical developments, just as the Einsteinian model was a revision of the older Newtonian model.

When Heinlein placed the clause "the door dilated" casually in one of the sentences of his 1942 novel, *Beyond This Horizon,* it was a way to portray clearly, forcefully, and with tremendous verbal economy that the world of his story contained a society in which the technology for constructing iris-aperture doorways was available.

But I don't think you can properly call the ability to read and understand any of these SF phrases, sentences, or conventions a matter of "mind-set" any more than you could call the ability to read French, Urdu, or Elizabethan English poetry a matter of "mind-set."

Another interesting point where a rhetorical convention has different meanings when it shows up in two different fields: The FTL drive which so delighted the audiences of *Star Wars* and *The Empire Strikes Back* simply doesn't carry the same critical thrust as the FTL drives that appear in written SF. As a number of SF writers noted when *Star Wars* first came out, perhaps the largest fantasy element in the film was the *sound* of the spaceships roaring across what was presumably hard vacuum. In a universe where sound can cross empty space, an FTL drive just can't support that kind of critical weight against the philosophy of real science.

Fifteen years ago, Australian SF critic John Foyster wrote: "The best science fiction does not contradict what's known to be known." When it does, at too great a degree, it becomes something else. Science fantasy, perhaps.

I'm the same person when I read an SF short story by Sturgeon or an SF novel by Bester and when I read a literary novel by Robert Musil or a literary short story by Guy Davenport—or when I listen to a David Bowie song or see a George Lucas film. Someone's *making* all these interpretations. Do differing "mind-sets" allow me to make them? Am I happy at one? Sad at the other? Serious and critical at one? Light-hearted and frivolous at the next? Yes, I interpret one differently from the other. And to whatever extent you agree with me, *you* recognize these different interpretations as valid. Do you, then, indulge several "mind-sets" at once to comprehend my several interpretations, if, say, two of them arrive in the same sentence? I think you'd have to work too hard to specify what you meant by mind-set in order to have it cover the needed situations; and when you had, you'd find you'd arrived at a meaning too far away from what most people designate when they use what is already, I'm sure you'll admit, a pretty informal term. So I'm just not sure how "mind-set" comes into it. I'll stick with expectations, conventions, and interpretative codes.

In terms of reader expectation, what makes SF different from literary fiction—naturalistic, fantastic, experimental, or surreal—is of the same order as what makes poetry different from naturalistic fiction. Let's start with the overlap, since it's the biggest part, despite the fact that it's the least interesting. A good prose writer is going to pay close attention to the sounds of the words in her prose; and a good poet *of course* pays attention to the sounds of the words in his poem. But that "of course" covers a multitude of expectational difference. Both John Gardner and William Gass are very phonically aware prose writers. Assonance and alliteration, not to mention phonic parallels and parallels disrupted, tumble from their sentences. But if Mona Van Duyn or James Merrill, Richard Howard or John Ashbery, Cynthia McDonald or Marie Ponsot wrote poems with the same blatant phonics, it would be ludicrous. A Judith Johnson or a Helen Adam succeeds with that open and above-board approach to sound only thanks to irony. I'm sure both Gass and Gardner suffered many well-intentioned suggestions: "Your prose is so poetic. Why don't you write poetry?" (Gardner, with *Jason and Medea,* tried). But precisely what makes them dazzling and stimulating prose writers would make them gross and clumsy poets, assuming they didn't curb it hugely. And that's all controlled by poetic vs. prosaic expectations. The fact that poetry is blatantly based on phonic expectations means, at this historical point, the phonics *must* be subtle.

Again, the vast overlap with literature aside, SF is a paraliterary practice of writing; its mimetic relation to the real world is of a different order from even literary fantasy. It grows out of a different tradition. It has a different history. Myself, I enjoy working with and within that tradition and struggling with and within that history.

SG: Of course, when your SF novel *Dhalgren* came out you had to deal with a lot of people claiming that you *weren't* writing SF, that you had gone outside the tradition.

SRD: Perhaps when a book sells seven or eight hundred thousand copies, the controversy contributes to the acceptance. You might even say the controversy *is* the acceptance—in which case the acceptance of *Dhalgren* was rather small. Most of the American reading public was quite oblivious to any controversy at all among the few thousand or, more likely, few hundred who, in that fanzine or this one, on one SF convention panel or another, expressed their conflicting opinions.

Myself, I never saw any *serious* controversy over whether or not *Dhalgren* was SF. When the idea was put forward at all, it was more in the line of name-calling. You know: "*That's* not science fiction! That's just self-indulgent drivel!" To me it seemed a much more modest argument—between the people who didn't like the book and the people who did. And my impression was that the contention centered mainly on discontinuities in the action and the lack of hard-edged explanation for the basic nonnormal situation . . . along with the type of people I chose to write about. This last is a point it's polite, today, to gloss over. But at least one academic (of highly liberal if not leftist tendencies, too) told me straight out: "I'm just not interested in the people you write about. I can't believe they're important in the greater scheme of things." What makes this significant is that the vast majority of fan letters the book received—many more, by a factor of ten, than any other of my books have ever gotten—were almost all in terms of ". . . this book is about my friends." "This book is about people I know." "This book is about the world I live in." "This book is about people nobody else writes of. . . ." These letters came from people in schools and people outside of schools. They came from SF fans and from non-SF fans. For these readers, the technical difficulties of the book, the eccentricity of structure, and the density of style went all but unmentioned. After all, if the book makes any social statement, it's that when society pulls the traditional supports out from under us, we all effectively become, not the proletariat, but the *lumpen* proletariat. It says that the complexity of "culture" functioning in a gang of delinquents led by some borderline mental case is no less and no more than that functioning at a middle-class dinner party. Well, there are millions of people in this country who have already experienced precisely this social condition, because for one reason or another their supports at one time or another were actually struck away. For them, *Dhalgren* confirms something they've experienced. It redeems those experiences for them. For them, the book reassures that what they saw was real and meaningful; and they like that. But there are many others who have not had these experiences. Often they are people who during their lives have been threatened by the possibility of their social supports all going, who fought very hard against it, and who have worked mightily to stabilize their lives in such a way that they will never have to endure these real social disasters. Needless to say, these readers do *not* like the book. For them, it trivializes real problems and presents as acceptable things (and I *don't* mean sex) they have specifically found unacceptable—and are to be avoided at all costs. But the arguments between those people who disliked the book intensely and those people who liked it exorbitantly helped it to become somewhat more widely known—and, presumably, to reach an even larger audience.

In the world of paperback sales, you know, 700,000 is actually a rather odd number.

The *average* paperback book still sells under 100,000 copies. To be a bona fide paperback bestseller, you have to get in sight of the solid 2,000,000 mark. So anything between, say, 250,000 and 1,500,000 is in a rather anomalous ballpark—especially if those sales are drawn out, as with *Dhalgren,* over ten years or more now. To appease the commercial anxiety that makes them want to name everything in case they need to sell it to somebody who hasn't seen it yet and doesn't want it, publishers have recently started calling such books "cult successes." So at Bantam I'm known as the author of a "cult" novel.

When you're passing an open door in a publishing company hallway, where people are talking in the offices, "cult" can sound close enough to "occult" so that, I gather, there's some small controversy within the company as to whether I write "cult" or "occult" books. But people who read me don't seem to have that problem. For them I'm still an SF writer. And my books are still SF.

SG: It's hard to me to think of a mainstream book as long and difficult and experimental as *Dhalgren* that has sold 700,000 copies. (I doubt if even *Gravity's Rainbow* has sold that many.) That seems to be another possible advantage to the SF field: An ambitious, serious writer who is interested in formal experimentation (even if this *is* part of the tradition) may have a greater chance to get his or her book out.

SRD: *Dhalgren* has outsold *Gravity's Rainbow*—by about 100,000 copies: we share a mass market publisher and statistics leak. But *Gravity's Rainbow* is a fantasy about a war most of its readers don't really remember, whereas *Dhalgren* is in fairly pointed dialogue with all the depressed and burned-out areas of America's great cities. To decide if *Gravity's Rainbow* is relevant, you have to spend time in a library—mostly with a lot of *Time/Life* books, which are pretty romanticized to begin with. To see what *Dhalgren* is about, you only have to walk along a mile of your own town's inner city. So *Dhalgren*'s a bit more threatening—and accordingly receives less formal attention.

Sadly, your description of a field of writing open to experimentation and ambition better fits SF when I began publishing in the early '60s than it does today. The period in the late '50s and early '60s known as the paperback revolution created a flood of books—and, with it, a relatively friendly climate for new writers. William Burroughs published his first novel, *Junky,* with Ace Books back in 1953. Those same economic forces probably account for why Vonnegut's books were, indeed, appearing as paperback original SF novels in the '50s and early '60s. Carl ("I'm with you in Rockland") Solomon, of *Howl* fame, worked at Ace as an "idea man." And when, in 1962, Ace became a publication possibility for me, I spent the odd minute smiling over the fact that names like Burroughs and Solomon seemed pretty good writerly company.

The economic crunch crunching through the last decade has left the publishing world far less accepting and more suspicious of the new and the vital than it was when the '60s dream of unlimited affluence and endless experimentation was about. Add to our economic hassles the current "block-buster" mentality that's infected the book business via the movies, as a hysterical response to that crunch, and you have a really nasty situation for any serious writer, in whatever field, trying to break in. And it strikes me as a very different situation from the particular style of endemic commercialism rampant in book publishing since it came under its present book distribution system just after World War II. (Most people are unaware that book distribution companies today are much bigger than book publishing companies. It's an open publisher's secret that the publishing companies work for the distributors, and not the other way around. But most readers can't name one distribution company.) Before, the court of sales was always there, at least as an ideal to talk about, no matter how difficult it was to get your work put before that court. Today, everybody in publishing is pretty well convinced that the court of sales itself has been hopelessly corrupted, by hype and other, nameless pressures, so that an editor who says, "I think there is an audience (however small or however large) that will enjoy this book," is no longer considered to be making a rational statement in business terms. The only statements considered rational in commercial publishing today are those which speak to the questions: "How can it be pushed? How can it be hyped? How can it be made bigger than it is?"—whereas *what* is being pushed is of secondary or even tertiary importance, save to the extent it's got a hot synopsizable angle. Today's publisher would much rather publish a book which, when described in three sentences, sounds catchy than a book which affects its readers so deeply and profoundly that, before speaking of it at all, the reader must pause. The desired book today is the one that prompts its readers to blurt, "Hey, it's about . . ." and go on with something snappy.

This not only ends up reducing everything to the lowest common denominator; it lowers the denominator itself, driving it constantly down. And in an already shaky capitalism when the quality of what you've got to sell is locked in a downward spiral, that doesn't leave you much to appeal to.

Of course, pulling together such a tenebrium of gloom-clouds is very easy from the Olympian perspective of 40-plus years—and always has been. It's not a bad idea to remember that 25 years ago the paperback revolution itself was seen by many, if not most, establishment critics

(Bernard DeVoto's name comes to mind) as the end of Literature with a capital L. Well, it's always surprising how writers—the people actually writing—have managed to articulate something over the range of the writing practices available; even invent new ones if they have to. And those articulations have their own character in each age. The writing practices that were most exciting and vital between 1890 and 1920—say, in the novels of James, Bennett, Conrad, the early Lawrence, and Proust—looked very different from the writing practices that were most vital between 1920 and 1950—say, those of Joyce, Barnes, Woolf, Faulkner, and Ellison. And the writing from 1950 to 1980 looks very different still. Are we going to go on to another change of style, concerns, and structure, in which the realities of contemporary publishing, from computer typesetting to distribution monopolies, play a large if ill-understood part?

Probably.

But I think it would also be a good idea for historically sensitive critics to take a look at how one practice of writing, science fiction, was positively helped by a situation which, at the time, was assumed in most cases to be a moral and aesthetic disaster. It might be instructive in terms of understanding what's to come.

SF benefitted hugely from those early years of the paperback revolution. Joanna Russ, Thomas M. Disch, Ursula K. Le Guin, Roger Zelazny, R. A. Lafferty—the number of markedly exciting SF writers whose careers were strongly shaped by that revolution makes your jaw drop. In 1951, there were only 15 volumes published which, by any stretch of the imagination, could be called SF novels, while last year SF made up approximately 16% of all new fiction published in the US. When, by the mid-'70s, crunch-crunch was undeniable, there still seemed to be some factors built into the geography of our particular SF precinct (or ghetto, if you like) that kept the damages at bay a *little* longer than in some other fields—primary among them, the vitality and commitment of SF's highly vocal and long-time organized readership, whose most energetic manifestation is the complex and fascinating phenomenon, fandom. But by now, the material hardships have made their inroads even into SF.

A few intriguing details of that history scatter through some of my essays of the last half dozen years.[5] Am I concerned about what's going to happen to this lively field over the next half dozen? Am I ever! But I'm also sure that, though it will be intimately connected with, it will also be markedly different from, what happens to literature.

LM: I heard an anecdote that very early in your career, you self-consciously resisted jumping on the treadmill of quick-writing-for-quick-money that exhausted writers like Philip K. Dick and others. What gave you the nerve to say to the SF publishing establishment, "Look, I'm going to take my time and write a good book—not in six weeks or six months, but in however long it takes me"?

SRD: Anecdotes often reduce the primary reasons for themselves right out of existence—especially when you tell them about yourself. And I think I once wrote about that situation—briefly and anecdotally—in an essay you may have come across. As an anecdote, it sounds very brave and moral; and I'm willing to take a *modest* bow. But the simple fact is: I'm constitutionally incapable of writing quickly. I'm highly dyslexic. That means, among other things, I must write slowly and revise endlessly, if only to get right what are so cavalierly called, by the lexic, the "basic mechanics." With all the time I spend looking for the dropped, misspelled, and transposed words that litter my early drafts, I might as well, while I'm at it, X the odd adjective, apocopate some terminal preposition, clarify a parallelism here, or strengthen an antithesis there. It goes, as they say, with the territory. Any text I write, I'm going to have to stay with a while—longer, anyway, than the lucky talents who whip out journeyman-like first drafts, which, once glanced at by the copy-editor for styling, can be sent on to the typesetter. It behooves me to think about what I'm doing a little more, if only to make sure it's complex enough to hold my interest during the extra time I have to live with it. (An apothegm in the SF community I've heard leveled at a number of our high-production moguls goes: "If he were a worse typist, he'd be a better writer"—meaning that such writers commit stylistic bloopers of the same blatancy as the mechanical ones automatically corrected by simply running the text once more around the platen. I've heard it said of both Harlan Ellison and Barry Malzberg—two dizzyingly talented writers, by the bye.) There've been a number of dyslexic writers, of course: Gustave Flaubert and William Butler Yeats are among the best known. Dyslexic writers tend to be slow and painstaking. The fascination of what's difficult, Yeats wrote, had dried him up and left him old. But for a writer who, like Yeats, didn't really learn to read until he was 16, more things are going to be difficult than most might expect. Such a writer has a push to substitute quality for quantity—which isn't *entirely* moral. A writer like Joyce, on the other hand, was as lexic as they come. And when he wanted to, he could write like a speed demon. Fully a third of *Ulysses* was written in galleys. That's over 250 of its 765 pages! Even in Paris in the '20s, you had galleys only for a couple of months, at the outside.

I could no more write 250 pages of fully realized fiction in two months—science or otherwise—than I could fly to the Moon flapping. And the more I'd thought about it and the more complicated a structure I'd planned it out to have, the longer it would take me actually to set down.

When I was 23, I wrote a long story in 11 days. The manuscript ran to 130 typescript pages—with wide margins: say, 75 pages of ordinary book type. But that was an endurance test I'd set myself, with mornings given over to first drafting, then, after a non-lunch, the rest of the day and a good bit of the night spent rewriting the previous day's work.

It's still moot whether I passed or not.

But that 11 days doesn't count the two weeks of notes on the early side to plan out a simple fabular structure that eschewed most of the complexities I'd previously (and have since) tried to work into fiction. (You could call it two weeks of testing the water before the plunge.) Nor does it take in yet another week on the far side for another retyping—in which much rewriting got done. As an anecdote, I'd like to say that the story—which was eventually published as a separate book, and has been called a novel—took 11 days. And certainly the hardest non-stop work *was* crammed into those 11. But I could as easily say that it took me 11 days plus two weeks at the beginning for notes, and a week of rewriting after. Composition times are almost as hard to individuate as propositional meanings.

SG: From early on, your books have explicitly dealt with some very controversial subject matter. Take, for example, your treatment of three-way or multiple sexual relationships, of gay and bisexual relationships (and all sorts of subgroups) in *Triton*, and your general call for the need to explore male and female sexual roles in all their guises. Do you think that working in the SF field has given you more freedom to explore these areas? I'm thinking of the controversy that surrounded, say, Mailer's *American Dream* or Roth's *Portnoy's Complaint*—books that are very mild in their sexual presentation compared with what you are dealing with in *Dhalgren* and *Triton*.

SRD: For a number of reasons, from my racial make-up to my sexuality to my chosen field of writing, SF—or even because, in this society, I've chosen to write at all—my life has always tended to have a large element of marginality to it, at least if you accept a certain range of experience that overlaps those of an ideal white, middle-class, heterosexual male as the definition of centrality. To write clearly, accurately, with knowledge of and respect for the marginal is to *be* controversial—especially if you're honest about the overlaps. Because that means it's harder to regard the marginal as "other." And at that point, the whole category system that has assigned values like central and marginal in the first place is threatened.

As to whether SF is more tolerant of what is usually called the marginal. . . . Well, it would be nice to think that because SF itself has traditionally been considered a kind of marginal writing, it recognizes the problems of life on the edges and welcomes them with insight and compassion. But that may just be a somewhat naïve anthropomorphism.

Basically the idea that a genre, or even an age or epoch, *gives* a freedom (or, indeed, imposes restraints) that any old writer, once he or she plops down in the middle of it, can turn around and exploit wonderfully (or be totally stymied by) is one I've heard before—and distrust.

It's not that I don't believe in history. Rather, I believe the historical process is more complicated than it's sometimes given credit for. The play of social forces lays down constraints (in sexual matters, say) that are internalized by individuals. Because society is not monolithic, these constraints are not necessarily the same for everyone; there may be class patterns, but even that's a reduction. There are going to be lots of variations, even individual to individual—which variations, if you squint at them from other angles, will make other kinds of patterns which aren't going to respect class boundaries at all.

The same play of social forces also lays down constraints for the various practices of writing—what, in practical terms, is generically acceptable, and what isn't.

But writers are not assigned their genres by God. Nor do they really choose them by conscious and considered acts of will. They move into them, even into literature, by a kind of ecological process. All through my adolescence I wrote novel after novel, pitched at the center of the literary tradition as I mistily saw it: you know, out of Hemingway by Faulkner and Joyce, with a good 19th-century underpinning. That was my adolescent reading history, at any rate. I sent them to publisher after publisher, but although they got me a couple of scholarships, and some of my shorter pieces even won me the odd amateur prize, they were all finally rejected.

Then I wrote an SF novel. Actually, it was rather borderline SF. (I had to go through four published SF novels before, in the fifth, I got brave enough to put in a spaceship!) And it was accepted, published, reviewed . . . !

Now there's a developmental aspect here that must be taken into account. I'm sure the SF novel I wrote at 19 was, indeed, a *little* better than the literary novels I wrote at 16, 17, and 18—though "literary" here is only a polemical distinction. None of them were good books.

Still, one does a lot of growing up, fast, in those years, and some of that goes onto the page. But even in my teens, what I was being *told* by literary editors, some of whom from time to time got rather excited about me, was that the final reason the novels weren't being published was that they were *too* literary—and weren't commercial. Even at 17 I knew some of this was an attempt to make a kid feel a little less crushed by rejection. Nevertheless, with all that taken into account, there's still a bottom-line situation here: Literary publishing wasn't very accepting—they didn't accept me through a *whole* lot of tries—while SF publishing was: They snapped me up on my first submission. And what they accepted was me, with all my socially-laid-down constraints, my limited talent, and my individual concerns, as manifested in what I wrote. And even during my first couple of years in the field, the genre tended to say to me: "You can do what you want."

Now that's not, "Anyone can do anything he or she wants." Rather, that's "The kind of things *you* seem to want to do are more or less within acceptable bounds."

If you look over my first four SF novels, all of which were written during my first three years in the SF field, as I've said you won't find spaceships. What you'll find is characters quoting poetry at each other. There's more than a passing interest in the female characters. Small sections are in play form. Other sections are in stream of consciousness. (The books that followed were, if anything, more technically conservative.) Bits of the story are told from multiple points of view. Once, in my sixth SF novel, written when I was 23, I was told that the printer simply couldn't handle one of the sections; it had to wait for computer typesetting and the most recent edition, in 1983, for the text to be printed as I wrote it back in 1965.

Now none of this is terribly profound as far as experimentation is concerned. The point is only that the SF publishing situation could accept it; my SF editor could say to me, "That's kind of interesting. I wonder what the readers will make of it." And for what it's worth, the books are still in print. And this is a very different situation from the one in which a literary editor in 1960 at Harcourt Brace, who liked an early novel of mine enough to recommend me for a scholarship to the Bread Loaf Writers' Conference, said to me about similar devices in the book I'd submitted: "Well, if we *do* publish it, those are the first things that will have to go in the editing." Then she looked at me, rather sadly, and said: "Chip, you tell a good story. But, right now, there's a housewife somewhere in Nebraska, and we can't publish a first novel here unless there's *something* in it that she can relate to. And the fact is, there's *nothing* in your book that she wants to know anything about at all. And that's probably why we *won't* publish it." And after two more readings and an editorial conference, they didn't.

The housewife in Nebraska has, of course, a male counterpart. In commercial terms, he's only about a third as important as she is. The basic model for the novel reader has traditionally been female since the time of Richardson. But his good opinion is considered far more prestigious. He's a high school English teacher in Montana who hikes for a hobby on weekends and has some military service behind him. He despises the housewife—though reputedly she wants to have an affair with him. Needless to say, there wasn't much in my adolescent "literary" novels for him either. But between them, that Nebraska housewife and that Montana English teacher tyrannized mid-century American fiction.

If you look at the first novels published by literary houses between 1950 and 1965, there's not one that doesn't have something in it for this ubiquitous non-couple.

Good-bye Columbus, The Floating Opera . . . ? Salinger, Heller, Pynchon? That doesn't mean that there weren't other things in their books as well. Some of those were not there for that obsessive pair, and some would quite offend them, were they noticed. The point is, however, that the things that *were* there for them come quite honestly from those writers. They were not there because Barth or Roth or Updike decided out of controlled, calculated, and manipulative intentions to put them there. These writers moved into the literary field in which they were most comfortable by the same ecological forces that moved me into mine. Writers are not born into the world the day they write their first salable work. There's a history of reading, a history of attempts made and attempts rejected that maneuvers a writer, however random it all seems at the time, into the position at which he or she is accepted; and that's also a position at which she or he *can* be accepted. That individual variation we started off with? The situation I sketched above is the overdetermined one by which generic demands are fitted to individual writerly talents. But that individual variation means the fit is *never* perfect; there's still going to be conflict.

I don't know about literary publishing today, but in SF I've always had the wheedling suspicion that when an editor says to a writer, "Your work is too far out for us to handle," there's usually a silent message that goes along with it: "And it's too clumsily written, ill-thought-out, and badly executed to be worth it, because it won't interest those readers with the higher stylistic standards that go along with broader topic interests." I felt this way back at 17 and 18 when my early "literary" novels were being rejected; I suppose I still feel it.

Now to assume that this is how the *entire* real and social world of art production—or, more accurately, art *re*production—works is, I suppose, finally a personal strategy to make rejection an occasion for initiating a personal attempt at improving what you do, a strategy for keeping rejection from being simply and hopelessly paralyzing. It's very hard to be any sort of artist without some belief to the effect that if the surface is crystalline *enough,* if the aesthetic logic is both vigorous and rigorous *enough,* someone somewhere will *have* to say "Yes" to it. On the other hand, we all know how frightening/baffling/boring the new can be to people who feel that they are guardians of a tradition, any tradition; so that to stand behind such a view too firmly as anything else *but* a personal strategy may be suicidally naïve.

Rejection and acceptance are both complex processes; and the complex truth is that writing must, itself, be complex enough to remain stable in the face of both. Current poststructuralist jargon would probably talk about this complex stability in terms something like: "The struggle between reification and deconstruction that any text worth the name initiates among its endless play of possible meanings. . . ." The older phrase—much less popular right through here—is: "The dialectical nature of art. . . ."

The last person to get any public mileage out of the image of the genre-stifled (or genre-unstifled) SF writer was Harlan Ellison, with his important *Dangerous Visions* anthologies that began in 1967. Exciting as they were, by the time two of them had appeared, they'd pretty much forced SF to grow up and realize that genre restrictions were a little more complex than sexually timid editors. (Or perhaps after *Dangerous Visions* any SF editor with a tendency toward sexual timidity was just embarrassed out of it.) Most of us have a conflict model for writer/publisher differences in which each is assumed to be after different goals and playing by different rules. But a better model is a game where both sides have internalized all the rules. Tensions arise between players, certainly—and high tensions. Sometimes even fist-fights. But they develop out of misread gestures, the bias that comes from a particular angle of observation, personality conflicts and personal goals as interpreted or misinterpreted within the game. And there are always teams you don't want to play on just because you love the game the way you do and that team's managers simply have a different notion of team goals. But an aesthetically significant conflict with a publisher with whom you are basically content is rather like a single player trying to get a team to run a new play when nobody quite understands how it will work or why it will be effective. The resistances—or, to call them by their right name, stupidities—you have to deal with are very much the collective sort; and if you have a truly new idea, you have to deal with that resistance in more or less the same way you would with a team. Any other approach dooms you to really frustrating failures.

LM: Your two most recent books, *Tales of Nevèrÿon* and *Neveryóna,* are obvious departures, in some ways, from your previous books. Instead of being set in some imagined future, both are set in some magical, distant past, just as civilization is being created. To begin with, do you consider these works to be SF at all?

SRD: They associate with SF via a subcategory of SF, "sword-and-sorcery"—SF's despised younger cousin. Certainly one thing that must have drawn me to SF in the first place was a propensity for working in despised genres. Sword-and-sorcery was invented, for all practical purposes, by an odd young man, Robert Ervin Howard (1906–1936), who spent most of his life in Cross Plains, Texas. He's remembered as a pleasant, personable, if somewhat shy, fellow. His surviving letters give an impression of a basically genial man, but with a good deal of almost belligerent rural modesty. Accounts of rare visits to him by others suggest a friendly and intelligent man, who, nevertheless, had more than his share of social paranoia. ("Do you have many enemies?" was one of the first questions he asked Edward Hoffman Price when Price drove down to visit him after Howard had become established in the pulps.) In 1925, Howard made his first sale, to *Weird Tales,* with a story he'd written at 15. By a program of physical exercise, he also managed to push his tall but frail body in the direction of his muscular, swashbuckling heroes, so that by his mid-20s he was quite an impressive hulk. From age 19 to 30 he wrote and sold reams of pulp adventure and western stories, about characters like Solomon Kane, Buckner J. Grimes, Bran Mak Born, King Kull, and—his most popular—Conan the Barbarian; and he wrote *lots* of poems. He was a sometime correspondent among a group of writers today known as "the Lovecraft Circle." One morning when he was 30, he went out to the car parked beside his home, got in, took up a gun, and put a bullet through his head.

His mother, lying sick in the house for some time, had recently gone into a terminal coma.

A doctor, Howard's father (also a doctor), a nurse, and the cook (who glimpsed the suicide through the kitchen window) were in the house when it happened. Howard lingered for eight hours without regaining consciousness. His mother died 31 hours later. Dr. Howard buried her and Robert together at nearby Brownwood, Texas.

What's intriguing about sword-and-sorcery is that it takes place in an aspecific, idealized past—rather than in Rome or Egypt or Babylonia or

Troy. This means whatever happens in this vision of the past that may have something to do with us today *doesn't* filter through any recognizable historical events—the Diaspora, say, or the Peloponnesian or Gallic Wars. So, once again—and this should sound familiar—it lets you look at the impact of certain cross-cultural concepts that nevertheless are often not given the same kind of spotlight in historical novels, concepts (like money, writing, weaving, or any early technological advances—the *techne* Pound got so obsessed with by the "Rock Drill" *Cantos*) that go so far in overdetermining the structure of the historical biggies: a war, a change of government, a large migration from country to city.

What makes S&S historically aspecific also makes it rather anachronistic. In most sword-and-sorcery, you find neolithic artifacts cheek-a-jowl with Greek and Roman elements, all in the shadow of late Medieval or High Gothic architecture. And because it's all supposed to be happening at an unknown time and place, *there* there be dragons!

SG: The *Nevèrÿon* stories all seem to deal with power—all kinds of power: sexual, economic, even racial power via the issue of slavery. Do you think this focus on power relationships seems especially interesting to you because you're black and especially sensitive to them?

SRD: Three of my grandparents were children of at least one parent born in slavery. And my father's father was born a slave in Georgia. Manumitted when she was eight, my great-grandmother Fitzgerald still told *my* grandmother stories about slavery times, as did my grandmother's grandparents, with whom my grandmother stayed in summer when she was a little girl in Virginia—stories which my grandmother, who was alive till only last year (she died when she was 102), told to me. In imaginary Nevèrÿon, slavery is an economic reality (fast fading into a historical memory) but also a persistent fantasy. The historic imaginative space, plus the paraliterary object priority S&S shares here and there with SF (which allows it to be read for what it is), lets me play with notions about how things-in-the-world, *including* the socially contoured organization of people's psyches, may be functioning in such correspondences. It's a ludic endeavor; but, however interesting or stimulating (or, indeed, crushingly trivial) people find the suggestions that grow out of it, it's still play.

But that's different from what I assume would be the corresponding literary endeavor: to sketch a psyche, a character, a mind caught up with such a fantasy (say, slavery), with the world shown only as the necessary frame to hold the canvas to shape. To me, right now, that just wouldn't be very interesting.

LM: What sort of overall plan have you been following in these books?

SRD: Only the traditional form SF has developed for its own brand of series stories. In the late '30s and all through the '40s, the overwhelming majority of American SF appeared in the pulp magazines. Many of these stories, by individual writers, would return to the same world or universe and pick up the time stream at different points. Sometimes there would be continuous characters. Sometimes not. Clifford Simak's *City* was such a series. Heinlein wrote a sequence of stories beginning in 1939 which were informally known after a few years as the "Future History" series, which also included novels. They were only collected in one volume, *The Past Through Tomorrow,* in 1967. Certainly the most famous SF series is the five short stories and four novellas by Isaac Asimov, known, since it was published in three volumes in the early '50s, as *The Foundation Trilogy,* to which, after 30 years, he added the full-length novel *Foundation's Edge* (1982).

The particular form I'm talking about is probably clearest in the "Foundation" tales, though you can trace it out in almost all the others. Put simply, the first story poses a problem and finally offers some solution. But in the next story, what was the solution of the first story is now the problem. In general, the solution for story N becomes the problem for story N + 1. This allows the writer to go back and critique his or her own ideas as they develop over time. Often, of course, the progression isn't all that linear. Sometimes a whole new problem will assert itself in the writer's concern—another kind of critique of past concerns. Sometimes you'll rethink things in stories more than one back. But the basic factor is the idea of a continuous, open-ended, self-critical dialogue with yourself.

The series is very flexible. Here's a short story. Next's a bulky novel. That can be followed by a novella, or another novel, or another short story. When publishers first began to collect SF series together in volume form, they did everything they could to try to make the resultant books look like novels. Because of that back-looking critical process, however, often a writer would have set a story further back in time from an earlier tale, instead of moving continually forward in strict chronological order. (One good form of criticism comes from asking the question: "What, historically, might have caused people to act in a particular way that, when I wrote the last story, I just assumed was unquestioned human nature?") When the stories appeared over months in magazines, this was no problem. But when the stories were collected, invariably they'd be put in chronological order, no matter how this obscured the self-critical development. In the first volume of the Foundation series, *Foundation,* the order of the stories "The Traders" and "The Merchant Princes" was reversed to accommodate internal chronology; and the first story in that book, "The Encyclopedists," was actually written after what's now the last novella in book three. They make much better dramatic and thematic sense if you start with "The Mayors" and read them in their compositional order.

I'm sure you can understand how, if a reader picks up the book version of one of these series, thinking it's an SF novel (and there's often no way to tell, since separate stories are frequently renamed "Chapters"), and begins it with the expectations ordinarily brought to a novel, the book's going to read strangely; and the self-critical development, especially if it's not blatantly obvious, might just slip by because the reader isn't looking for it.

The first volume of the Nevèrÿon series, *Tales of Nevèrÿon,* is five short and long stories that critique each other. The second volume, *Neveryóna,* is a full and rather fat novel that returns to a number of the notions in the stories and tries to rethink them. Right now I'm nearing the end of a novella that returns to one area in the novel that left me with some unsatisfied feelings.

In one sense, the SF series is something like a prose narrative version of that quintessentially American form, the open-ended serial composition longpoem—Pound's *Cantos,* Olson's *Maximus Poems,* Diane Wakowski's *Greed,* or Robert Duncan's *Passages.* You also find the same self-critical thrust at work there.

But that's a shock analogy.

You can only take it so far.

When you start a series, you may have some idea of things you might like to do in a later tale that will create some interesting reversal when you get to it, two, three, or four stories along. But that self-critical process usually means that by the time you reach the story in which, dramatically, you thought you might put one of these planned-out reversals, it ends up doing quite a different job from the one you envisioned for it when you first thought it up.

LM: You said once that you'd like readers to see in your works that "behind a deceptively cool, even disinterested, narrative exterior you can hear the resonances of the virulent anti-white critique that informs all aware black writing in America today." Early on, this critique seems to inform your work mainly in the way you say it does even in fascist works, like Heinlein's *Starship Trooper,* by your almost casual inclusion of black characters in positions of power and authority. But a bit later, in *Dhalgren,* for instance, and in the *Nevèrÿon* books, you seem to take up the issue of racism more directly.

SRD: What I actually wrote—and it's probably worth mentioning that I was writing to a white critic who was between drafts of an extended article on me, in the course of which he'd written me to ask why, as a black writer, my work wasn't, in effect, blacker—was: "If *you* wrote, 'Behind a deceptively cool, even disinterested, narrative exterior you can hear the resonances of the virulent anti-white critique that informs all aware black writing in America today,' I would think you were a downright perceptive reader" (italics, incidentally, added)—all of which he chose to quote in the final version of his article. I suppose this was my way of saying: "Hey, my experience as a black American runs all through my work. But why do you assume its traces will be such stereotypes?"

Some interesting facts about this particular critic: He's chairman of the combined English and Philosophy departments of his university; he's something of an expert in African literature and has collected, edited, transcribed, and published original African folk literature, about which he knows *far* more than I do; he's also co-editor of an extraordinarily perceptive anthology of Harlem Renaissance writers, about which I *do* know something; he and his wife have adopted a Korean daughter; and he's written a rather good biography of George Schuyler, an early black satirist, social critic, and father of the child prodigy pianist, Phillipa Schuyler, who was later killed in a freak helicopter accident in Viet Nam (where, as an adult, she'd gone to bring back Vietnamese children). In short, in terms of American culture, black or white, this critic's a *more* than interesting man.

But somehow black critics—and three or four, if not five or six, have written the odd article on me—just don't seem to be all that interested in how black a black writer's work is; or, when they are, they express that interest in—how shall I say?—a different tone of voice. The white, worried about some black's "blackness," always seem to be expressing the troubling anxiety that, indeed, you may not really *be* black, and that, therefore, somehow they've personally been fooled, taken in, or duped, either by your manipulative intentions or by some social accident—whereas the black critic is perfectly aware that you *are* black; I mean if you're born black in this country, you're going to know what it means to *be* black in this country; they're just kind of curious, therefore, to know what's going on with you. Now certainly there are things that can be going on with a black writer that a black critic who's had experience with them before may not approve of. He or she may even want to give that black writer down to the country for it, if not up-side the head. But so far, this is not the sort of critique I've received from black critics.

Still, to me, the tone in which the seemingly similar questions are put *feels* different, no matter if they're put to me or I hear them put to other black writers. But how subjective is this? How subjective is politics?

What I've said, with more than a little belligerence, to a number of whites who've chosen to question my blackness is (and you'd have to be black yourself to realize the astonishing number of whites who seem to have nothing else to do but worry about whether or not their black acquaintances are actually black *enough*): Look, I *am* black. Therefore what I do is part of the definition, the reality, the evidence of blackness. It's *your* job to interpret it. I mean, if you're interested in the behavior of redheads, and you look at three and think you see one pattern, then you look at a fourth and see something that, for some reason, strikes you as different, you don't then decide that this last person, despite the color of his hair, isn't really red-haired—not if you and yours have laid down for a hundred years the legal, social, and practical codes by which you decide what hair is red and what hair isn't, and have inflicted untold deprivations, genocide, and humiliations on those who've been so labeled by that code.

I was seven when, with quivering rage, my father told me—because of some racial incident at my New York private school—how, sometime in the 'teens or '20s, a cousin of his had been stopped with her husband by a gang of white men; she was perhaps eight months pregnant. Substantially darker than she, her husband was lynched, and she was dragged to a tree, hung up, her belly slit open, and, in my father's words, "her unborn baby was allowed to drop out on the ground"—because the men assumed she was a white woman and would not believe otherwise. My father was there when their bodies were brought back to the campus of the black southern college where his father and mother were vice-chancellor and dean of women. My father, I gather, was about the age I was when he told me; and while, pacing up and down our kitchen in a towering fit, he recounted all this, my mother—a black woman born in New York City—sat at the wide table, one hand holding tightly to the edge of the dark wood, and pleaded with him, "Sam! Sam, don't tell the boy things like that! Not now! Tell him later!"

What we've come face to face with here is, of course, the relation between writing and politics. And that's subsumed by the old philosophical problem of the relation between language and truth. It's got a venerable name: The problem of representation. And it's very close to some of the things we were discussing at the beginning.

You can never know for certain whether or not language is portraying reality rigorously, thanks to the problem of representation—really too ill-separated problems: the problem of verifiability and the problem of exhaustiveness. (This latter is sometimes called the problem of sufficiency.) Now I've just told you two anecdotes, one about an experience with a white critic, and one about an experience with my father I had as a child. Both are fraught with political significance, right? Well, here's a third, simpler than the others, that'll serve as an exemplar for both. . . .

There's a chair in the corner.

And that's the whole story. Assuming you are alone with only the language in which it's told, however, you have no way to determine its validity. Is it true, inspired by the real chair in the real corner of my real room? Or is it a polemical fiction? Perhaps it's just a downright lie. And assuming *I* believe there's a chair in the corner, could I possibly be mistaken? With such a simple account as that, real mistakes aren't too likely. But what possibility there is for mistake segues quickly into the second problem: exhaustiveness. Have I said enough about the situation to allow you, with only the verbal account, to verify it should you need or want to? Have I failed to mention that, though there is indeed a chair in the corner, it's one of these old bean-bag affairs from the '60s, gone so saggy that, today, half the people coming in here frown at it and ask, "What's that? Some kind of couch?" Is passion, tragedy, material or emotional catastrophe going on only a room away to my loved ones, acquaintances, or complete strangers that, even as I write, merits my (or indeed your) attention far more than fancies about dubiously extant chairs? Or, more eccentrically and polemically, have I just not bothered till now to mention that the chair is blue, lying on its side, about three inches from foot to upper back, and that in just two minutes I'm going to call my nine-year-old to come get it, take it in her room, and put it back with the rest of her doll furniture?

But now let's look at the more complex incidents we started with. Neither was simple. Both were important to me when they happened, and, for both polemical and personal reasons, I'm concerned with the accuracy of my account here. By this time, I've rescanned the accounts as written above a number of times already, and have—already—at a number of places, during the general editorial violence that such an "interview" as this gets subjected to, rephrased and reworded them here and there, with an eye to honesty and accuracy; and in places where time has blurred memory, I've been particularly careful with *perhaps*'s and *about*'s. The account *can't* be exhaustive. But *have* I told enough? Is my report sufficient? I didn't detail the racial incident at school that sparked my father's outburst. It was, indeed, minor, subtle, and complex—though it also could be seen as involving a great deal of money for the school, and was generally the sort of thing to make anyone with a tendency to be anxious over such things tear hair trying to figure out what hurt was done, what intentions were. (And, in 1949, what black parents with children in a predominately white private school *weren't* anxious over such things?) I couldn't clarify it much further in less than three pages—so I've chosen to omit it; or, rather, to represent it only with this sketch of its affect. *Was* I seven? I could have been six. I could have been eight. Did my father really see (or say he saw) the bodies, or did he only hear about them? It's unclear after more than 30 years. Did my mother's hand hold the table edge only a second or two? Or did it stay, locked there, for minutes? I don't remember.

Which of these elements is political? In what way are they political?

Talking to me about it years later, my mother told me that, through my father's tirade, I sobbed and cried out, "It isn't fair, Daddy! Oh, Daddy, it isn't fair!" I have only the vaguest memory of that part, which, by now, is hopelessly mixed up with my mother's telling me about it. I have an equally vague memory that my mother cried a little. But in general she was not a teary woman; she doesn't remember that. And my father has been dead 22 years.

In the case of the white critic, although I've now checked my own quotation (as it appeared in his article), I haven't checked his original letter which contained the questions to which my words responded—indeed, it's not at hand. How reductive am I being in my account of the exchange? Have memory and ideology introduced significant distortion? Anyone who comes across that actual article will notice immediately it's signed by *two* writers, who collaborated on it from the beginning. Since, at that stage, most of the queries came from the single writer, mentioning only one didn't seem too great a polemical streamlining—though conceivably the writers might not feel so if they read this. But not only did I not mention the co-writer (also white), I've also not mentioned that in the years since, though I've maintained a friendship with both men by letter, I've exchanged hundreds of pages of letters with the second writer of the article. . . .

Where does significant political detail stop? Or start?

This is the problem of exhaustiveness.

I said above that I made changes with an eye to honesty; but, in incidents so complex and emotional, can anyone maintain the clear line between changes for honesty and accuracy in reporting and changes made for effectiveness in recounting? Selection dominates any report of the real, and the line between relevance and irrelevance is as hard to fix as the line between meaning and meaning. Indeed, it *is* the line between meanings.

The kind of questions I've been asking of my own text above are, incidentally, just the sort that, along with the dramatic images they momentarily evoke in the writer's mind as she or he asks them, sends the writer back to do another story or novel in his or her SF or S&S series.

As the verifiability and exhaustiveness problems move into the political arena of accuracy, mistakes, distortions, lies, relevance, and suppression, the problem of representation becomes the linguistic bottom line at which Plato barred poets from his Republic and decided to make the heads of state philosophers—opening himself for ages to charges of self-interested bias. But like Heraclitus, Plato was already (as Karl Popper reminded us) a prince. And that same problem is what, so recently, has caused a number of critics to suggest that all fiction is really meta-fiction: Since language (and, by extension, fiction) *can't* be trusted to be rigorous about the world, maybe it all must be reinterpreted to be only about other language (and other fiction).

I said I thought that these problems were much like the ones we started with. That's because I think the way out of them is the same as the way out of the problem of the plethora of codic confusion: overdetermination. The key phrase in the discussion of the problem of representation is: "Assuming you are alone with only the language . . . ." That phrase itself assumes, somehow, that there *is* such a thing as language apart from the rest of the world—a language complete with meanings, grammar, syntax, logic, and thus the possibility of understanding—without a world to inform it, without a world in which it has been and will be developing, a world which is constantly changing it, and to which, changing or stable, it is always a response: a world that is, itself, constantly changing under language's operation. Similarly, it assumes that there is a world complete with its categories, its rules, and its patterns, apart from language.

It's not a matter of language's imposing its codes and categories on a simple, innocent, and ideally undifferentiated world, as some contemporary criticism tends to suggest. Rather, the reason that language is codic is because everything else in the world is too, as we saw at the outset; and language is in the world and of it. Language and world (or word and object) is another perfectly useful distinction, as much as any of the others we've glanced at; but, as with the others, the distinction is only useful *if* we acknowledge their hierarchical relation and do not demand they do the job of equal and parallel opposites where they clearly can not. The world absorbs language. Language does not encase the world—although the world displays language-like (that is, codic) properties at every turn; and these properties are no doubt what allow language, in a properly organized neural net, both to exist and to function. Because of that hierarchy, you can never be without the world and yet with language—"alone with only the language." Because language (and all that is language-like) *is* the social, you can only be alone without it.

By the time you get to wherever it is you are when the simplest or most complex story reaches you over whatever distance through time and space from whatever context was there for verification, you have already learned on your own enough about chairs, rooms, fathers, mothers, kitchen tables, the racial situation in America, interviews, critics, and writers to make a whole bevy of complex codic judgments, even if absolute veracity or sufficient exhaustiveness are not among them. These judgments range from your ability to reach a practical answer to the questions, "How important is it to me, right now, to verify this account? How important is it to me to have more exhaustive information?" to the strong feeling, "While x, y, and z have the ring of truth about them, there's no *way* you'll get me to believe p, q, and r—not unless a, b, and c were *very* different from the way the writer described them." And you may hold these opinions to the end of your life, forget them in an hour, or revise them three months hence in the light of further reading or experience. These opinions are all political judgments—interpretations, not perceptions—that we can make about the sentences in any text: poem, newspaper article, popular song lyric, letter, interview, pornographic pamphlet, 19th-century novel, Hollywood film, advertising copy, soap-opera dialogue, experimental fiction, comic book, Broadway drama, or contemporary SF story. Much of the process overlaps for all the different modes; and for each mode there will be distinctive codic processes entailed. Because of the differences, however, people who have been exposed to a great deal of, or have carefully studied, one or another of these language practices may have something interesting to say about the distinctive way in which these judgments usually occur, or are best carried out, in each.

Any text I present you with will be subjected to these judgments; and though the judging process will work slightly differently in each mode, there *is* enough codic overlap so that, whether it identifies itself as a scrupulously honest report or as a wholly invented fiction, no text I produce can escape them. Still, I'm the one who's got the responsibility to be honest (in whatever mode), because I think there's a correlation between what honestly happened (in the case of the report) or what I honestly thought might happen (in the case of the fiction) and my political judgments about it—which judgments, presumably, I'd hope you might recreate for yourself out of my account. At least I hope you might revise your own judgments in a direction sympathetic to mine.

But the fact I believe in that as possibility is, of course, also a philosophical and political judgment on my part.

In world terms, the text is an affluent luxury. Thanks to the problem of representation, no text can be considered, in any absolute sense, other than a more or less socially privileged lie (or, if you will, an ultimately undecidable play of biases, errors, and omissions)—and that's not only the texts traditionally thought of as fictive, either. The nature of the privilege, however, is social, recursive, self-supporting, self-critical, self-revising, memorial, codic, and complex . . . dialectical, if you will.

Or at any rate, it ought to be. Among the best readers, to a greater or lesser extent, it is. But it's the nature of the privilege that's in question, not the status of the text; for the text, finally, is almost wholly an experience—a process—rather than a thing.

As I said: Honesty is my problem (and a different problem in each mode), not yours; it's a factor of my motives. Interpretation—judging, if you prefer—is your problem (also different for different modes), not mine; it's a factor of your needs. Is there an overlap between your needs and my motives? As much as there's an overlap in the codes that let us recognize them, talk about them, agree *or* disagree.

But here might be a good place to begin a rather sweeping conclusion to all this . . . .

In high school, I had a friend who was a composer. For a time we were also part of a folk-singing quartet together. Somewhere during the autumn of 1961, when he was in his second year of college and I had dropped out, gotten married, and was writing my first SF novel, he completed an interesting musical composition that was to be performed at a concert of new music at Hunter College. It was complex, atonal, and at some of the rehearsals I helped out as a page-turner. At any point in the piece, the dozen-odd instruments would be playing all 12 notes of the scale—save one. Through the course of the composition, the missing note moved up and down through the cacophonous sonorities, so that the "melodic line," if you can call it that, was a silence that progressed, as a sort of absent melody, through it all. During rehearsals, while I sat by the metal music stand, waiting to turn over the page for the clarinetist, something became clear. When the piece, or more usually a stretch of it, was performed very, very well by all the players, with the dynamics and intonations truly under control and great attention fixed to its overall cohesion, then the travelling silence became clearly audible and its effect striking, disturbing, even moving. If, however, one or two of the players lost their concentration, or there was the least little dynamic wandering, or there was any noise at all in the rehearsal room, or indeed, if the attention of the listener strayed a moment, then the whole thing dissolved into acoustic mush.

I couldn't be at the concert, but some time later my friend told me that, no, he didn't feel it had gone very well. As far as he could tell, simply the change in the sonority of the auditorium that occurred when it was filled with people had been enough to muddy the subtle musical experience he'd contrived.

Possibly because I wasn't at the performance, I had an interested absence to think about, and my friend's piece became a kind of model for me of the situation of the serious writer—if not the artist in general. I thought about it a lot then, and I've thought about it a lot since.

It doesn't seem to matter whether the writer is a "hard-hitting journalist" or the farthest out constructor of experimental poems. All the writer's noise is finally an attempt to shape a silence in which something can go on.

Call it the silence of interpretation, if you will; but even that's too restrictive. The silence of response is probably better—if not just silence itself.

The writer tries to shape it carefully, conscientiously; but both forming and hearing it today can be equally hard.

The journalist may want a very different kind of thing to go on in that silence from what the experimental poet wants. One may well want the audience to use it as a lucid moment in which to make a decision for action, while the other may want the audience only to hear that it is there and to appreciate its opacities and malleabilities, its resistances to and acceptances of certain semiotic violences. The SF writer may want the audience to observe in it the play and fragile stability of the object world which its malleabilities and opacities alone can model.

The writer will mold it differently in terms of what she or he wants us to do with it, do in it, using a variety of codes. And the variety of codes that make that writing meaningful will differ here, will overlap there, depending on the writerly mode. Nevertheless, we can still, when it is useful, designate all writerly enterprises with the same terms: shaping the silence.

And we can *still* distinguish those enterprises.

And judge them.

That's more overdetermination.

NOTES

1. The Stoic philosophers have been generally presumed to be the earliest Western thinkers to have described the sign as consisting of a perceptible *signans* and an intelligible *signatum*—i.e., a signifier and a signified.

2. This fragment is based on a phrase from a science fiction story by Larry Niven, the exact title of which escapes me.

3. These four sentences come from, respectively, Guy Davenport's short story "Robot," in his collection *Tatlin!* (Charles Scribner's Sons, New York, 1974), Virginia Woolf's *Mrs. Dalloway* (Harcourt, Brace & World, New York, 1925), the French poet Paul Valéry, as an example of a sentence from a story he could not bear to write, and the opening sentence from Walter Abish's delightful *Alphabetical Africa* (New Directions, New York, 1976).

4. From the entry for August 6th, 1914, in *The Diaries of Franz Kafka,* 1910–1023, edited by Max Brod (London, Penguin Books, 1964).

5. Collected as *Starboard Wine* (Dragon Press, Pleasantville, NY, 1984).

2.

Toto, We're Back!

The *Cottonwood Review* Interview

This text began as a set of written questions from Lloyd Hemingway and Johan Heye (both then at the University of Kansas, at Lawrence) in October 1986. I responded in writing. About a third of that response was published in a special "contemporary black writers" issue of The Cottonwood Review *(38/39, Summer/Fall 1986), edited by Gerard Early.*

Samuel R. Delany: Let me begin with a theoretical precept that will probably color any answer I give, even to your simplest questions:

There are some today who would argue that there *is* no such thing as "experience"—lived experience, as it is sometimes called—save as it is reducible to language and desire. But it seems to me that the gesture abolishing at least *what happens* as an irreducible ontological order makes language and desire immediate, contiguous (in the sense that nothing mediates between them; that one is wholly flush with, wholly adequate to, the other), and has the same function as the metaphysical and mystificational gesture that makes language immediately and transparently adequate to the Real, or that makes experience the immediate cause and resolution of desire—and thus begins the myth of positivity that our precept here critiques:

Say rather (as another interim strategy): The mutual inadequations of language and desire constitute *what happens;* the mutual inadequations of desire and *what happens* constitute language; the mutual inadequations of *what happens* and language constitute desire. Then, to preserve ourselves from experiential or linguistic or sexual idealism (for what we are preparing is, after all, the theoretical aspect of a materialist practice), we must remember that the whole tripartite process is forever responding to a Real (I borrow the register from Lacan) that, if we "know" anything at all (and never forget that we may not!), we know is there (all else is belief), but that, other than as this tripartite process of discrepancy and inadequation encounters it, responds to it, shapes it when it can (forming genres, genders, semantic categories, and social classes) and is necessarily shaped by it (our constantly repeated realization of the inadequacy of all such categories, through the slightest shift in some response to the Real, apprehended through the same inadequations by which, a historical moment ago, the categories were formed), is inaccessible.

Desire . . .

Language . . .

What happens . . .

The point is that, because the inadequacy of any one to any other produces the field in which the third constitutes itself and registers, none of the three is a ground that can stabilize either of the other two. To negotiate their interrelations we must hold onto the fact that none is ultimately a privileged register or term. We only know any one of the three because of the gap between the other two. None operates as the ground against which events in the areas indicated by the other two are shadowed, highlighted, modeled in some way that is, itself, the privileged representation. Rather, each is a web, a net, a rhyzome—a revisable text, if you will—whose rhyzomatic aspects, whose gaps, whose flexibilities and rigidities, however temporary, are forever constituted by the coextensive failures, discrepancies, and gaps between the other areas we were precisely then *not* considering.

Lloyd Hemingway: Let *me* begin with a simple question. I'll be interested to see just how that precept contours your answer: When did you first discover science fiction, and what was that experience like?

SRD: Well! Your question suggests a moment of discontinuity before which—for the young and eager reader—there *was* no science fiction, but after which the genre, with its panoply of luminous and vivid worlds, lay there in all its potential to explore. This may be the point to remind ourselves that the rhetoric of revelation, the suggestion of a transcendent vision carried by even so innocent a phrase as "the discovery of science fiction," is basically part of the inflationary process by which genres survive, endure, propagate, and, in response to the material world, speciate.

But though it's sometimes fun to talk about them as if, indeed, that's the way they hit us, genres don't really come to us like that.

As curious and embattled children, busily absorbing the culture of childhood, first we hear a little bit about them. Then, perhaps, we see a book cover or an illustration—in the paraliterary genres, the visual is intimately involved with that inflationary rhetoric, through its commitment to the hyperreal, to the "slick," to the "professional" surface. Then we catch an older person reading something we already know to belong to that genre—in my case, in the case of science fiction, it was a very tall camp counselor named Roy, who, in pale framed glasses and blue baseball cap, read *Galaxy* each month, stretched out on his cot (Bunk Seven), sneakers crossed on the iron frame at the foot, while the rest of us took our afternoon naps.

But now, wishing at a stroke to encourage our reading and secure a moment's solitude, a harried adult declares how *exciting* we would find some genre juvenile (if we would only give it a try): Perhaps they're urging on us Jules Verne's *20,000 Leagues Under the Sea* (my father was a great proponent of that one), which, while it was not written as science fiction, has been, along with the most popular works by Stevenson, reduced to the status of "boys' book" (note that it is specifically *not* a "girls' book") and so can be foisted off on us as if it were, at least, auxiliary to the SF genre; and the inflation continues. But that's to get ahead of my story.

In the bunk with Roy, that summer, my bed was next to the bed of a camper named Eugene Gold, whose father was *Galaxy Science Fiction Magazine*'s editor. Mr. Gold used to send Gene cover proofs for the new issues, and I remember sitting with Gene on his cot and looking at the Ed Emshwiller cover illustrations for the first magazine publication of Pohl and Kornbluth's *Gladiators at Law,* and the black-bordered clutter of color for the first issue of a new fantasy magazine, *Beyond;* and, later, the *Galaxy* issue that commenced serial publication of Isaac Asimov's *Caves of Steel.*

Roy was quite impressed.

At the same summer camp, perhaps a year later, I stood on the wet matting along the pool's deep end, both of us beaded with water, talking to the swimming counselor, balding, beefy Barny—in black bathing briefs—who explained how disappointed he'd been in Bradbury's first novel, *Fahrenheit 451*. He'd been a fan of Bradbury's short stories for some years and had been looking forward to the book. But, when it had come out, he'd found it thin.

I'd just read two or three Bradbury stories that week, knowing nothing of Bradbury's special reputation within the SF field at the time—or that anyone besides me had ever read anything else he'd written. I just knew he wrote science fiction. But somehow the name had come up, and there beside the pool I'd been treated to this surprising burst of genre criticism—before, moments later, Barny and I were both back in the water.

But before you decide this particular summer camp was a hotbed of fifties science fiction readers, I have to say I could recount being on the end of any number of similar conversations during those same summers, with topics ranging from T. S. Eliot's *Cocktail Party* (standing on the junior camp swings with an older camper named Julius Novick—thin, blond, and bespectacled—who, as sunset turned to darkness, discoursed on "closet drama," Eliot's plays, and *Prometheus Unbound*) to the merits of Paddy Chayefsky's screenplay for *Marty*, a film we watched in the camp recreation hall, one blowy Thursday evening, a week or so after *The Grapes of Wrath* and *The Devil and Daniel Webster*, a week before *Citizen Kane* and *The Boy with Green Hair*.

Between these various summers' events (and I have no way to order which came in which year), I actually *read* my first science fiction story all the way through. (Several times before, I'd picked up one SF magazine or another, tried some tale by Sturgeon—a favorite of Roy's: I think it was "Granny Won't Knit"—or by Heinlein—already Gene's preferred writer: I believe it was "The Man Who Sold the Moon" in an old issue of *Astounding*, which belonged to an older camper—and had found them wholly dull and opaque. I'd abandoned both after a few pages—probably I was ten.) It was during a brief, autumn hospital stay. I was supposed to be observed for twenty-four hours, as I'd injured myself in some ridiculous school prank. In the patients' lounge were some oversized *Amazing*s. What I remember most clearly is the illustrations. I suspect they were Finlay's: Men in bulky spacesuits were entering some cave in which hung a lascivious cluster of all-but-nude, female vampires.

With bat wings.

In another picture some wizened little aliens with huge veined heads stood about examining a comatose Siegfried, encased in a great glass tube.

All I remember from the actual tale was that the secret weapon turned out to be light, whose speed had been dramatically slowed down—which meant that, correspondingly, its energy had gone way up. And by that time I'd read enough George Gamow books on popular science, relativity, and such to have an inkling of what the writer probably thought he meant—not much in the line of discovery and revelation.

The first science fiction *novel* I read all the way through was *The Red Planet Mars*, by John Kier Cross. The book I'd *wanted* to read, however, was Robert Heinlein's *Red Planet*, whose plot my elementary school friend Robert had detailed to me in intense and luminous particulars, as, in jackets and jeans, we'd wandered, shoulder to shoulder, down 89th Street half a block beyond Lexington Avenue to spend the afternoon in his penthouse apartment—watching Berr Tilstrom's *Kukla, Fran, and Ollie* on his mother's new television set (Robert's father, a large, white-haired, preoccupied man I'd met only two or three times, had died the year before—to me a mysterious and incomprehensible happening that I kept waiting to impinge, somehow, on our friendship. Only it didn't.) Robert's was the *first* television set I ever saw in anyone's house.

But it was Cross's book that, three whole exhausting weeks later, my mother returned with from the library, where she'd recently begun working as a clerk.

I was dubious. But she explained that it was *almost* the same title, was *probably* about the same thing—perhaps it even *was* the same book, and I was simply mistaken. And even I could see it was the same color (red) as the one Robert had been reading in school.

It *didn't,* however, have the same illustrations. But after two or three days, I gave it a try, reading it, even enjoying it—though I was still certain the other book, Robert's book, must be, somehow, better.

But by now Robert had been joined by another school friend, Johnny, in thrusting this book and that at me—more Heinlein and Clarke juveniles—some of which I read and some of which I balked at—while my friend and seventh grade confidante, Priscilla (who, a year later, was the first person I knew to have a *color* television), detailed the plot of *Titus Groan* to me over a two-and-a-half-hour phone call.

But the necessary feeling that greater excitement lay only a book away had already been clearly—and socially—established. It's a feeling—call it desire—that *must* be fixed to any genre if that genre is to be pursued; probably it must be fixed to any semantic category for that category to persist as a social reality. Like all desire it is formed on absence, the missed, the just-out-of-reach, the greater wonder and adventure waiting for us just over there that is what language, leaping ahead of experience, constantly creates via that gap. I did not know, then, that the same desire, the same absence, lay hidden within Robert's and Priscilla's and Johnny's reading, as it did within my own—that, indeed, should such an absence be absent, all feeling for genre, for identifiable category, would vanish with it; that this absence was what, more than anything else, generated our positive excitements and enthusiasms over the wonders and glories we shared with one another about the science fiction and fantasy we were actually reading, just as it drew us on, in the silent and most alienated hours of childish isolation, with an acidic pang, to find another book.

Here is the place to note that the same economy of silent desire and articulate inflation that controls the paraliterary genres—science fiction, comic books (Priscilla, inspired by her older brother, was the first person to enthuse to me over *Mad* comics; she loaned me my first copy, with the Kertzman *Raven* parody, which I spirited into the boy's john and, secreted in the stall with corduroys about my shins, read cover to cover), and, yes, pornography, controls just as surely the literary genres, poetry, fiction, and drama, as well as history and philosophy. Certainly it controls mathematics and the sciences. (I mention—and in our society to mention is to stress—pornography not for its salacious excitation but because, like seditious propaganda, it is always with us: Censure and prohibition are as effective speech acts as commercial hyperbole or even intelligent praise for establishing the experiential breech—the disappointment, if you will—necessarily constitutive of desire—desire which we are ethically bound to distinguish from want and hope.) How convenient it would be if desire lay, however silently and absently, in each of those signification practices at a locable, negotiable, circumscribable heart, crypt, or origin; and positive, inflationary, rhetorical articulation was equally placeable in a surrounding, supplementary, dismissible margin, leaving clear the uncontaminated "real experience" of the text, of the genre, of the meaning—perhaps in a kind of torus between, however that torus might be held to shape by the pressures within and without. Then all those discontinuities, discoveries, and transcendent visions would have their validation. And meaning and reference would be one (or, if not one, then immediate [or, if not immediate, then mediated by something we might call "the real-which-can-only-be-found, like a kernel or treasure, hidden-embedded-nested within its rhetorical layers-hyphens-quotation-marks-brackets-parentheses-punctuations"]). But it will always be hard to retain the fact that, in any discussion, such as and including this one, any representation of the real, any figuration of the thing in itself, whether given by the figures of "heart" or "kernel," or even "what happens," is, itself, only an extension of the rhetoric, the inflation, the mystification. Any escape from rhetoric is illusory, momentary, strategic—another transcendent vision, if you like, and finally, itself, rhetorical. Say, rather (as a momentary strategy), that desire is always in motion, working through any generic, any nameable, any categorical enterprise—just as is articulation, now in anticipation of desire, now lagging behind it, but never at one with it, so that at last the "experience" of any category—dogs, houses, science fiction—is finally the gap between them (language and desire), contoured by both at every point, constituted of the incongruency of their play.

I note here that Robert was somewhat the class oddball—Priscilla and Johnny only slightly less so. And my own history was certainly eccentric enough. A slim, black youngster named Carl, who lived a few houses away from me and who was two or three years older than I, was a friend of mine for a while: On a visit to his cramped, fourth-floor apartment, I found a volume of illustrated stories of the Knights of the Round Table in his living room bookshelf. It was a blue volume. The pictures were black and white and in the art nouveau style of the twenties. Carl told me he had read it and had enjoyed it. With his and his mother's permission, I borrowed it from him—and a few months later found myself forbidden to play with him any more because the rumor had gone around our Harlem neighborhood that Carl, the gentlest and most polite of thirteen-year-olds, had somehow become involved with drugs.

Before he was twenty, Carl was dead.

I never returned the book. And though every four or five months I took it out and looked at it, I did not read more than a chapter or two for several years. I mention all this to point out that even a fantasy as conservative as the Arthurian legends was somehow very early associated with the socially eccentric, the marginal, the outsider, the forbidden.

In June of 1956 I left the small classes and sunny classrooms with their movable chairs and tables at the private, progressive Dalton School for, a few weeks later, summer camp—again. In the tiny, middle-school library, two rungs up and one arm draped through, I'd hung on the library ladder for more than two hours, reading Sturgeon's *More Than Human*—dazzled, awed, moved far beyond what your or my rhetoric might suggest. At home, in my third-floor bedroom, sprawled over white appliqué rockets on the bedspread (and matching drapes—a notion of my mother's), I read Clarke's *Childhood's End,* and found it equally dazzling—*because* it dazzled in a wholy different way. And a year later in the attic of our summer house, stretched on the mattress on the floor, covered with its drab army blanket, where I slept, I read, once more, through the three issues of *Galaxy* containing the serialization of Bester's *The Stars My Destination,* and came downstairs to our country supper of chili and hot dogs a wholly different, and far more humble, human being, the transformation invisible to my parents and sister.

And that September, an avid reader of science fiction and fantasy (a process that had occurred over years, without any core, central, originary, discontinuous, and thematic moment I can reasonably hypostatize), I entered the large classes and cramped classrooms, with their desks nailed to the floor, of the public Bronx High School of Science, convinced I would go on to be a physicist and mathematician, but with such an excess of interests, in everything from music and ballet to literature and leftist politics, that I'm sure the wisest of my elders took my professions of professional interest with a silent smile, a grain of salt, and a considerable sense of wait-and-see.

The small point to all this anecdote, however, is that reading is still and always a murky business; and it always has a social (if not its political, which is simply the social articulated) side. While some of us—more and more rarely—will come upon an individual title, pick it up, and read it, knowing nothing in advance about book or writer, none of us *ever* reads a whole book in a *genre* we have heard nothing of before. And if, on occasion, we start such a book, we usually find it unreadable.

I've several times mentioned the process of generic inflation.

All genres, to repeat myself, survive, propagate, and reproduce themselves by taking some value and inflating it, then declaring that this is the value the reader may obtain by submitting to its text. The paraliterary genres—such as science fiction—survive through the inflation of pleasure or "entertainment value." The literary genres survive through the inflation of "aesthetic value." And there are always readers, seeking however sophisticated an ideological reading, who are ready to inflate the "political value" of a text. But to the extent that all three—"aesthetic value," "entertainment value," or "political value"—are posed as values *present in* the text, all three processes are inflationary and work fundamentally by the same means, as we humans seem not to care whether an a-, or even an anti-, social value of pleasure is inflated/created by language to establish the discrepancy with what happens that forms the irreducible and necessary locus of desire—or a socially condoned and eminently useful value of culture or pragmatic use effects the same experiential gap. (Proust dramatizes the process beautifully for literature in the "Combray" section of *A la Recherche du temps perdu.*)

"Aesthetic value."

"Entertainment value."

"Political value."

The reader who inflates "aesthetic value" in the text tends to privilege "language" as the grounding for desire and what happens.

The reader who inflates "entertainment value" in the text tends to privilege "desire" as the grounding for language and what happens.

The reader who inflates "political value" in the text tends to privilege "what happens" as the grounding for language and desire.

These privilegings, these groundings, are what produce so many of our false binaries, with their symptomatic hidden hierachies that we must again and again tease out and, if only momentarily, overturn in deconstructive delirium.

And at least one sign of the similarity of the process for all three cases is the ease with which each of us is one such reader on Tuesday and Thursday, another such on Monday and Wednesday, while we become still the third on Saturday night or Sunday morning.

But in neither the paraliterary ("entertainment") case nor the literary ("aesthetic") case, not to mention the extraliterary ("political") case of the reader who reads to change the world (or to learn how to install a new computer or a carburetor, say), will the value sought and socially prepared for ever correspond exactly to the experience of the text—for textual pleasure (better, perhaps, textual satisfaction?) is, in the paraliterary, certainly, as much as in the literary or in the extraliterary case, the result of a more or less masochistic submission *to* the text. (The ways that manuals must *always* be reread and reread, always submissively, always in part, and often incompletely, are at once a case in point, characteristic, and exemplary of the way reading actually occurs in *all* texts, literary and paraliterary as well.) This submission is composed as much of our shifting attentions and misreadings, backtrackings, rereadings, and sudden uncovering of associations, some conscious and some unconscious, some effervescent and joyous, some cool and cerebral, but all incomplete, all imprecise with a play always partly lost behind readerly blindness, as much as it is of those moments when, always with hindsight, we convince ourselves that we were, however briefly, at once satisfied and faithful.

In short, given my particular theoretical precepts, I am forced to respond to your question: One does not so much "discover" science fiction. Rather, we are always, however haltingly, mumblingly, or indirectly, *introduced* to it, socially, politically, materially—historical fragment (history *never* occurs in complete units) by historical fragment—an introduction never truly completed, even when we have gone on to become part of the historical mechanism by which others in turn are introduced; an introduction which, once we have recognized it to have been going on a while, we still stumble on into, hesitantly, humbly, now and again with moments of excitement to be sure, but by and large with eyes narrowed against the social glare of what we have already heard of it—the reading experience ("what happens" when we read) constituted by the discrepancy between articulation and desire, lagging behind or leaping ahead of expectations, less intense or more intense than anything we might have assumed . . . more intense at those moments when something clears enough to widen the eyes a while, before we return to our ploddings and reploddings with the squint of hazy comprehension that is what most reading, after all, is, even as we strive for a mastery over our chosen texts, a mastery which turns out, at best, to be a more or less benevolent enslavement.

Johan Heye: In your early years as a writer you were often mentioned as a representative of the New Wave in SF. Is this label at all meaningful today?

SRD: The real question is, of course, was it ever meaningful—and, if so, in what way?

At the time I was first being called "a representative of the New Wave" (that is, in the early 1970s, when I was very busy writing, but not publishing much), practically every writer who had emerged in the sixties was being lumbered with the same term.

This is a little sad, because there was a real, vigorous, and talented group of writers who were known as the New Wave at the end of the sixties—a group of interesting and energetic writers, whose output was very important for the development of science fiction. But they were a group with which, though I was friends with a number of them, I had almost nothing at all to do, at least in writerly terms.

These writers—Aldiss, Ballard, Brunner, Disch, Sladak, Zoline and a number of others—centered around Michael Moorcock's British SF magazine *New Worlds*, published largely out of the front room office of Moorcock's Ladbroke Grove flat in London. They started publishing with him around 1964 or 1965, became known at the New Wave in 1966, and continued to published with him through about 1970, when he stepped down as editor of *New Worlds*—though *New Worlds Quarterly* continued for some time under the editorship of Moorcock's then-wife, Hillary Bailly.

I always go to some length to dissociate myself from the New Wave when people make such statements, or ask such questions, as you just have. When I do, of course, my interlocutor usually smiles and quietly racks it up to the feisty, individualist writer's dislike of being associated with *any* group.

But, in my case, my insisting on the distinction is simply love and respect for the history of my genre, science fiction. To say that *I* was, somehow, a representative of the New Wave is tantamount to saying that science fiction *has* no history—that, today, we have no responsibility to keep the memory of aesthetic concerns, editorial directions, and publishing associations in some sort of reasonable and accurate order. It's to say that we can say anything about science fiction and it just doesn't matter. The vast majority of the distortion, by the bye, comes from lazy academics excited by the upsurge of critical interest in science fiction in the seventies—but who would not be caught dead *researching* the decade of their interest—though, Lord knows, there's enough to research!

JH: Do you feel that you as a writer belong to any group, trend, or movement?

SRD: Right now? No. During the mid-sixties, you could responsibly associate me with the *Dangerous Visions* writers—the writers who were, however briefly, organized around Harlan Ellison's multivolume *Dangerous Visions*[2] anthology project.

One thing that accounts for the "New Wave" mystification and obfuscation I've been discussing is a situation I've occasionally written about in my critical books on science fiction.

By the mid-sixties, the sea of science fiction production had grown large enough to support several productive islands. The most important of these islands was the historical New Wave, in England. Two other islands were both in the United States. One was organized around Damon Knight's continuing hardcover anthology series, *Orbit,*[3] which went through some twenty-one volumes. The other was the much broader if somewhat ill-formed island around *Dangerous Visions*—two immense volumes, which have several times been reprinted, broken up into smaller blocks. All three islands—*New Worlds* (focus of the historical New Wave), *Orbit,* and *Dangerous Visions*—had a different density, a different coherence, and a different organization; and all three represented different aesthetic and ideological priorities. As I said, my particular island was *Dangerous Visions.*

But even so, half a dozen groupings of SF writers including me that one might make would strike me as reasonable. Despite their homes on (or off) their various islands, during the sixties I always felt that Joanna Russ (an *Orbit* writer), Thomas Disch (who, along with the much younger James Sallis, was to publish almost equally in both *Orbit* and *New Worlds*), Roger Zelazny (who published a handful of wonderful, early stories in *New Worlds,* as well as in Cele Goldsmith's *Amazing,* where both Disch and LeGuin first appeared, but who, once he attained his peak popularity, with two successive Hugo awards for best SF novel of the year in 1966 and 1967, published his work almost exclusively in the American pulps—*Fantasy & Science Fiction* and *Galaxy*—which had more or less shepherded him to fame and also paid much more than *New Worlds*), and myself formed a kind of quartet. All four of us (Russ, Disch, Zelazny, and myself) are contemporaries among whom, in one way or the other, some kind of dialogue has constantly gone on since at least 1966. (I've always wondered why nobody ever thought to *give* the four of us a name!) It's a dialogue I see as still going on, by the bye.

So, you see, it's not the notion of "a group" or "a school" of writers I'm opposed to. It's only the historically demonstrable inaccuracy of locating me with the New Wave that I balk at. I would have very much *liked* to have been a member of the New Wave. But I wasn't.

LH: This question may be tantamount to asking, "Why do you write?" but what is there about science fiction that makes it an ideal medium for your aesthetic and imaginative faculties and your thematic concerns?

SRD: Here the presupposition I glimpse behind the question is the image of a writer, endowed with a kind of transcendental talent, complete, formed, and mastered, a writer with, as well, a set of "themes," "concerns," and "ideas," who stands outside of any and every genre, facing them all, surveying them for the one that best fits his wholly present set of intentions—till, in a moment of auctorial assumption, he or she declares, "*There*—!" at which point the writer assumes that genre like a new suit or a pair of contact lenses: Though there's some settling in, some learning how to be comfortable within it, basically writer and genre now cleave together in a perfect fit.

But just as no text can ever escape at least one (if not several) generic marks (there is no genreless text), there is no writerly talent that exists outside of at least one (if not several) genre(s).

And the fit, of course, is *never* perfect.

The cleavage—whether one takes the word to mean the joining of genre and writer or the split between them—is wholly problematic. The unsteady, progressive, and wholly social process by which the reader assumes the genre is, we must remember, the *same* process by which the writer assumes it. Remember, too, that, before all else, the writer is a reader of the text—perhaps the most violent reader in that she or he can always strike words away from the text and substitute others, but a reader nevertheless. And it is *reading* that forms the writer's themes, concerns, ideas—and talent.

It would be just as accurate to say that science fiction has given me my themes and ideas as it would be to say that I have brought certain themes and ideas to science fiction.

Nor can we forget that the genres exist in a certain tension with one another. These intergeneric tensions are always changing. We've seen a twenty-five-year period in which sex has been radically politicized, but in which, also, in the last fifteen years, a highly conservative socioeconomic field has grown up in the preserves traditionally thought of as the field for politics per se. These changes have altered the course of my own personal life. These changes *are* the tensions between genres, between types of discourse, the tensions that have contoured so many different practices of writing.

If your question *is* tantamount to asking, "Why do you write?" well, my answer is tantamount to explaining how, in my view, writing gets done at all. Writing is the articulating of responses to just such tensions between genres, between discourses, responses always under the mark of one discourse—one genre—or another (but *always* responding to tensions between that genre and one or several others), which, in their play of presences and absences, *are* texts.

LH: Some would find the overt concerns with language and contemporary literary theory in much of your work to be odd thematic material for science fiction and fantasy. Do you see yourself as breaking new ground in these genres by using them to express these concerns, or are you dealing with ideas that have been implicit in SF all along?

SRD: Your question invites me to boast, which is bad for the soul. I also find myself somewhat distrustful of your original/imminent distinction. Since the theory we speak of is a theory of language, of writing, presumably it should have some connection with the material practices of textuality. The simplest answer, however, is to say that science fiction has often spoken of itself as the literature of ideas. It dramatizes notions of critical theory in much the same way that it dramatizes notions from any hard or soft science. It approaches the notion of deconstruction in much the way it would approach the notion of navens or of ion transfers in the myelin sheath or of meson decay problems.

Critical theory as it has been recently practiced is very much a marginal activity—but it is a marginal activity that shatters the whole notion of a firm and fixed social center, as well as of a coherent and socially centered subject, into a series of political questions.

Now I've always seen literature's enterprise as marginal. And I see SF's enterprise as marginal to literature. And I see my current enterprise (the sword-and-sorcery series Return to Nevèrÿon I've been writing for the last decade) as marginal to SF. . . . But really I don't think our society *has* a center—nor, I suspect, did it ever. Centrality was, at best, a stabilizing illusion. At worst it was an oppressive and exploitative lie. All I think is or was is a system of intersecting margins; and the progression of margins neither stops nor starts with literature, with science fiction—nor with me.

This model of society as an all-but-endless intersecting system of marginal activities puts into question both the traditional Marxist division of infrastructure and superstructure as well as the Gramscian notion of cultural hegemony that attempts to revise it.

The margin of the margin. . . .

The phrase recalls Derrida's "the signifier of the signifier" as the model for all signification.

Analogously, I suspect, the margin of the margin may be a rich model for the place of all cultural productions, whether it be properly aesthetic productions (like operas or comics or poems or science fiction) or whether it be industrial productions: Just recently *Consumers' Union* published a list of the fifty products that have most changed the nature of our day-to-day lives in the last fifty years. It was a fascinating compilation, including air conditioners, disposable diapers, water-base housepaint, oral contraceptives, and microcircuit technology . . . none of these, taken individually, can be called "central." Yet, far more than any "central" idea or notion or thing, they and many like things are what organize contemporary material life to its present forms and values.

Science fiction has certainly had a long leaning toward a materialist explanation of history. I don't think there's anything particularly new in the Nevèrÿon series (or its overture, *Triton*) there. The rather fanciful discussions you get on social development, represented by, say, the switch from three-legged pots to four-legged pots, or from two-pronged yam sticks to three-pronged yam sticks, are pretty much in the same tradition that prompted Asimov's disquisition on the economy of metals that comprises the first three tales (in their order of composition and magazine publication—but not, alas, in their current bookbound order) of the Foundation series. There may be a bit more irony in my series than in Asimov's—my primitive materialists, while they have, indeed, laid hold of an idea, are really just congratulating themselves on the progress of their own technology, under the illusion that they have had a materialist insight. (Four-legged pots are *not* more efficient at standing up than three-legged pots; it simply means at some point you've invented the level.) But the two series are certainly in a dialogic—if not a dialectical—relation.

LH: Writers who are not white and writers working outside the realm of mainstream fiction often find themselves pigeonholed by the reading public, a process that gives you the unusual distinction of being doubly labeled—as a black writer and as a science fiction writer. In what ways do you think your work fulfills the unique expectations created by the combination of these two roles? Or are such attempts to categorize writers even relevant?

SRD: Your question leaves out—from what presumed politeness or well-intentioned disingenuousness, I would not dare to guess—that, as well, I am a gay writer, who writes about experiences that concern the gay community. My most recently published book, *Flight from Nevèrÿon* (1985), includes my 1984 novel about AIDS, "The Tale of Plagues and Carnivals."[4]

But the notion that *any* of these might be irrelevant categories—either of human experience or as a position from which to observe our society, comment on it, and to write—is only a kind of disarticulating embarrassment reveling in its own discomfort before any and every social difference that constitutes our society, a discomfort before the whole range of socially enforced distinctions—not to mention a discomfort before any attempt to protest or oppose that enforcement, at whatever level of complexity.

That the readerly expectations associated with any of these categories (black writing, gay writing, science fiction) are, if not unique, at least highly limited is not the problem of the writer but the problem of the reader.

The constant and insistent experience I have as a black man, as a gay man, as a science fiction writer in racist, sexist, homophobic America, with its carefully maintained tradition of high art and low, colors and contours every sentence I write. But it does not delimit and demarcate those sentences, either in their compass, meaning, or style. It does not reduce them in any way. And the expectations you mentioned in your question are, if *only* by their uniqueness (as I hope we can all recognize), reductive.

To remind anyone at this point that one of my protagonists is markedly brown, that another is an Oriental woman, or that still another is half American Indian, or that now and again one or another of my characters yearns for something other than standard missionary contact with the socially proper member of the socially prescribed sex, seems a tiresome and futile strategy whose only conceivable use would be to establish a preposterously disjunctive category: Not-Exclusively-Male-and-Caucasian-as-Well-as-Often-Polymorphously-Perverse Science Fiction, a category whose only conceivable function would be as some sort of satirical object—an object whose satiric thrust is entirely toward the genre-category we would have to stand it up against, that we would have to distinguish it from.

The speaking subject (or, indeed, the writing subject) must always speak (or write) from a real, material, and specific position. But this position is just that: a position from which to observe, from which to speak, to listen, to read, to write. It represents neither a perimeter around a given set of subject matters, around a certain predictable content, nor a signature that will always be discoverable in some inescapable rhetorical paraph appended either to the ideology or to the style.

(Remember, no matter how uncomfortable that fact makes us: Any position I—or you—cannot move from at will, be it my race, my sex, my aesthetic position, or my ideological allegiances or my economic status, is the mark of a political *im*-position.)

When writers write from the same position, sometimes we can recognize a shared horizon—if, indeed, these writers have all set their sights *on* the horizon. But when their observations are focused on the specificity of the material and mental life directly before the imaginative eye, while position determines all, it is in no way figured in all. And it is up to the reader, knowing what position was involved, to read its trajectories, its angle of incidence and reflection, with some sort of creative vigor. In many cases, such vigor may well be indistinguishable from ignoring the position in situations where it has become sedimented and clichéd to search for it, to appeal to it, to hypostatize it.

But the assumption that any vigorous reading can be carried out by an appeal to any set of unique expectations—and you have chosen the proper word for them—is the first step toward a critical tyranny.

JH: Which of your fictions have given you the greatest satisfaction?

SRD: Well, now . . . that's like asking a parent which is his or her favorite child. The book I enjoy most is, of course, the one I'm working on now. My 1975 novel *Dhalgren* is by far the most popular with general readers. 1968's *Nova* seems to be the favorite with hardcore SF fans. *Triton* (1976) seems to have generated the most intelligent criticism. And my last ten years' work on Return to Nevèrÿon seems to have been all but ignored—though it's certainly occupied the overwhelming majority of my own writerly energies for the decade.

LH: Your work has been very highly praised. Why haven't you ever written realistic—or mainstream—fiction?

SRD: I'm tempted simply to answer you with a tautology: "Because I write science fiction."

Yet there is an intriguing matrix of suggestions and implications that play through and support your question that we begin to be able to tease out when we ask, against it, why is this such a frequent question to the SF writer?

Those presuppositions actually come into focus, I think, when we begin to consider a like range of questions that, if I were any number of other writers, working in any number of other genres, you would likely never think of asking.

Does one ask the poet: "Why don't you write novels?"

Does one ask the playwright: "Why don't you write poems?"

If we look at the first one—"Why don't you write novels?" asked of the poet—clearly this is a question about money. Novels garner advances, frequently in the thousands of dollars. Poems, if the poet is very lucky and very famous, garner grants—maybe.

Yet, running against this is the notion that, one, money is vulgar—and, at the same time, poetry is the most sophisticated of all the arts. At the very least, then, the question says to the poet: Why don't you do something that will make you some money—a question that every poet who labors in our bourgeois society has had to deal with more times than most of us can imagine, and yet is still indicative of a stance most of us would like to dissociate ourselves from. If there is a secondary reading to the question confined purely to the aesthetic, it would be some form of: "Your skill is largely narrative, rather than lyric, placing you only on the foothills of Parnassus. Why don't you work in the less demanding fields of prose?" And while even Auden will state unequivocally that writing a novel takes more "work" than writing a sonnet, prose is still not traditionally thought to be as aesthetically demanding as poetry. Taken either socially then, or aesthetically, the question demeans. Yet even without the aesthetic reading, the vulgarity of commerce is enough to silence it in most aesthetically valorized situations.

To ask the playwright: "Why not write poems?" also has its bit of deprecation. Our first impression here is of a question about scale—about organization, about dramatic competency. Drama tends toward the gigantic, the spectacular, the epic. Ideas and images must be marshaled on the stage the way a general prepares for a war. We think of *Figaro's Marriage.* We think of *Hernani.* What else comes to mind when we think of drama? Trilogies of tragedies. Tetralogies of operas. Epic films—ten hours of *Greed,* five of *Napoleon,* seven of *Our Hitler.* O'Neil's *Strange Interlude,* Genet's *Les Paravants,* Shaw's *Man and Superman,* Strindberg's *Road to Damascus,* Sartre's *Freud* scenario . . . how many great dramatic works are nearly too long to be performed in full? Drama constantly strains toward a deployment of the unperformably huge: the Royal Shakespeare Company's *Nicholas Nickleby* (that one sees one act of in the afternoon and, after the most rushed dinner, an act of at night), or Robert Wilson's *The Civil WaRS* (that one sees another act of each season).

Poems, on the other hand, are small. Historically the epic, the narrative, the ode have all bowed before the lyric, which is, along with the epigram, their constitutive unit. The subject is the topic of the poem—all too often cut off from the sprawling social world. The poem, in its ideal form, is intimate, personal, singular, and brief.

The question insults therefore by suggesting, "You cannot deal with the scope and organization of drama. Why not try something less ambitious . . . like a poem." But it is finally the chasm between scalar concerns that stalls the question's expression. The very organizational differences between poems and dramas are so huge as to make their bridging an absurd concept. And those generically odd attempts to combine the two in something like a modern form—Hardy's *The Dy-*

nasts, Eliot's *Elder Statesman,* Barnes' *Antiphon*—seem the most quixotic of works, as if, indeed, there were some measure of the real world their authors were wholly incapable of taking.

Now at first the question to the science fiction writer, "Why not write mainstream?" seems one of competency of a more human—and less dramatic—order.

In the same way that the other two questions remain tacit because they insult, or because they suggest an impossible reconciliation, this question *achieves* expression because it appears to praise. Clearly this is not a question we would ask the *bad* science fiction writer—or of the SF writer we perceived at the moment as not up to snuff. While our question to the poet was one of money and our question to the playwright was one of scale, our question here is clearly a question of style. It says, most generously, to the science fiction writer: "You have an extraordinary control of the language, a critical sophistication, and an innovative approach to verbal effects: Why not use your gifts for something real, worthwhile, authentic?" It speaks from the contemporary impoverishment of literature. From within the literary precincts, the question gestures toward the paraliterary margin: Come, it says, and present your talents to us, where they are needed for the greater social good. There, where you now deploy them in your marginal activity, they are wasted, ignored, all but invisible.

Well, with that as my initial analysis, perhaps I can elaborate—can open up—my initial tautology: "Because I write science fiction. . . . "

It is precisely as a science fiction writer that I do not have to, or want to, deal with the impoverishment of literature. Indeed, I do not believe it exists. For now I admit it: Your initial question, to the extent that you speak "for the literary," has too much the air of General Motors asking the new graduate in engineering: "Come. Won't you join us? We *need* you. . . . "

Similarly, the abyss of scale is what, here, in science fiction I can express, interrogate, and attack directly. The genre presents me with a whole range of images, still very much alive, which I can use to bridge those unbridgeable abysses, the distance between here and the farthest star. Further, I can strive for a sentence by sentence lyricism even as I seek to organize a thousand pages of such sentences into dramatic vibrancy. And, here, no one even notes the gap. The vulgarity of capital is just not a force I could bear, silent and repressive, on the articulation of my work, which is, after all, very much a materialist exploration: I do not want such a force suppressing *any* question I might ask, any more than I want it contouring the manifest content of any answer I might offer.

JH: What is your assessment of the fantasy and science fiction scene in America today?

SRD: Currently science fiction is going through a very exciting period, with John Varley, Connie Willis, Nancy Kress, John Kessel, Paul Preuss, Joan Vinge, Terry Bisson, Jack Womack, Kim Stanley Robinson, Gregg Bear, Orson Scott Card. And, of course, there are the cyberpunk writers—William Gibson, Pat Cadigan, Tom Maddox, John Shirley, Bruce Sterling, Lewis Shiner, Rudy Rucker, Marc Laidlaw. . . . As an exciting node within an exciting sea, the cyberpunks represent a still more recent island—or rather an archipelago—of production. Unlike the individual islands of twenty years ago I've already mentioned, this archipelago has three editors and at *least* three publishing outlets associated with it. Also, the writers are far more dispersed geographically.

Ellen Datlow, at *Omni Magazine,* has been hugely supportive of the movement. So has David Hartwell, at the hardcover publishers Arbor House/William Morrow. And so has Gardner Dozois, at the old pulp-style SF magazine, *Isaac Asimov's SF.* (It was Dozois, of course, who first named the group.) And editor Terry Carr, who died most tragically of a long-time heart condition two weeks ago, published Gibson's Hugo and Nebula Award-winning novel *Neuromancer* in the recent revival of his prestigious Ace Special series, which brought Le Guin to fame sixteen years ago with *The Left Hand of Darkness.*

In a sense, this archipelago has been mapped out and given a much more coherent sense of itself than, certainly, the various writerly islands of the sixties—largely through the theoretical pressure of Bruce Sterling's critical writing in his Texas fanzine *Cheap Truth,* with much critical help from Shirley and Shiner. This is a very different field of organization, production, and writerly deployment from the situation of the *New Worlds* writers, the *Orbit* writers, or the *Dangerous Visions* writers. For the historical New Wave to have been of equal writerly force in 1967 as the cyberpunks were in 1987, it would have to have had the support not only of *New Worlds,* but of *Playboy* and *Doubleday Books* as well—which it simply didn't; though both *Playboy* and *Doubleday* were comparable outlets of SF at the time. But its differences are precisely what make it fascinating—although already I have seen the first lackadaisical attempts by those academics who have noticed the phenomenon at all to talk about it as if it were another "New Wave"—not the historical New Wave as I've elucidated it for you, but rather that unresearched and anhistorical myth of the "New Wave" (of which "I" am a "representative") that is seen as a free and unrestrained irruption of oppositional energies, without motive or locus, with neither ideological nor aesthetic specificities, yet somehow itself a Sign of the sixties and early seventies.

To the extent that the cyberpunks can be characterized at all, they seem to be very interested in the appurtanences of contemporary technology, that technology that combines computers, walkmen, and compact disks with artificial hearts, solar energy, designer drugs, and social control. Cyberpunk is the fiction of the microtechnologies that fall out of high-tech pockets to get swept up into life on the street. Their motto might be a line taken from Gibson (he uses one or another form of it in both his first two novels): "The street finds its own use for things."

They are very stylish writers.

They are also rather cynical.

And they are dazzled by data.

Myself, I find them intriguingly subversive.

Right now I'm teaching a course at Cornell University's Society for the Humanities in which I'm contrasting the world of (cyberpunk) William Gibson with the world of (non-cyberpunk) John Varley—all under the light that might be shed on it by Lacanian psychoanalysis.

Which is to say: The critical question is how *not* to psychologize their astonishing energies and effects out of existence—but rather to enlist psychoanalysis, in a strategy of mutual commentary, into preserving both writers' extraordinary object-critique of the world, as well as illuminating the equally astonishing range of ways each has come up with to impinge on, excite, and even shatter the subject.

The other aspect of the current science fiction scene that strikes me as formidable enough to make some notable changes in the shape of the field is the present erection of a critical apparatus—of which my own critical work may sadly but ultimately become a part—that seems to have no other objective than to drag science fiction away from its history and tradition and to haul it, protesting all the way, into the literary precincts—where, you may be sure, it will be assigned the most peripheral, noncanonical, and degraded tasks. One reason I find the particular vigor of the cyberpunks refreshing is because they seem savvy enough to recognize that particular critical program for what it is.

And because they have as canny a spokesperson as they do in Bruce Sterling—Chairman Bruce, as he is only *somewhat* jocularly known—I suspect they may be able to speak back to it in some meaningful way.

JH: How do you teach literature?

SRD: I don't. I teach science fiction. For me literature is not an innocent topic—a free and transparent space where good men and women have worked since the dawn of writing to purify the language of the tribe. For me literature is a set of historically sedimented ideological constraints and posited values that underwent a radical impoverishment and an astonishing concentration during the late-Edwardian institution of literature as an academic discipline, along lines sketched out years before by Matthew Arnold and Hypolyte Taine.

Certain academics from time to time cry out, "Let's keep science fiction in the gutter where it belongs," thinking, no doubt, that the ironic thrust of their words opens up the hearer to some vision that will honor and preserve the genre's vigor, autonomy, and integrity. They don't realize that one gutter services both the literary preserve and the paraliterary ghetto built on its margins. Condescension—no matter how ironic—is just not the answer. What is needed is a conscientious interpretive strategy grounded in historical sensitivity that can challenge the very form of the questions put to the genre and tease out their presuppositions so that they can then be judged adequate or inadequate to the object of study.

LH: How *would* you teach literature, then?

SRD: The same way I teach SF. With great energy, with great attention paid to the text, and at the same time an equally great attention paid to those historical presuppositions that allow us to make the text make sense—and I would explore the inherent limits on any notion of a mastery of the text, of a totalizing control of the play of meanings that constitute a text, in an attempt to tease out the ideological agendas behind all interpretations, radical, liberal, or conservative.

JH: What is the relation of science and fiction in SF?

SRD: The relation is intricate and intimate. It is intimate because, for better or worse, science provides the grounding of possibility that makes science fiction meaningful. It is intricate because it is only a grounding: What can be elaborated from that ground can, itself, be possible or impossible. Twenty-five years ago when the first information from the Mariner shots returned from Mars, then Venus, telling us once and for all the Percival Lowell view of rouged and canal-shot plains for Mars, or an ocean-covered world beneath roiling clouds of water vapor for Venus, was the impossibility that telescopes and common sense had already suggested it was—that, indeed, the clouds were masses of hydrocarbon vapor (hot oil) and that the scorched surface, above the boiling point of water, was an oil-scoured desert—SF writer Roger Zelazny, in response, wrote his wonderful and magical tale, "A Rose for Ecclesiastes,"[5] with its longevous Martian matriarchs living in their red desert, and "The Doors of His Face, the Lamps of His Mouth,"[6] with its monstrous sea beast, *Ichthyform Leviosaurus Levianthus,* which became two of the most popular SF stories of their decade.

Soon, possibly impelled by the astonishing success of the Zelazny stories, a whole anthology of "Mariner response" stories was published, called *Farewell, Fantastic Venus,*[7] and, soon after, writer John Varley produced his equally wonderful tales, "In the Bowl,"[8] set on a Venus whose landscape—a hot, lightless inferno, only visible in the infrared range of light—had first been described by the Mariner reports, as well as his Martian tale, "In the Hall of the Martian King"[9]—not so "scientific" as "In the Bowl," but not so romantic as "Rose."

Both Zelazny's and Varley's stories are very much science fiction.

Against them, one must look at films such as *Star Wars* and rehearse—yet again—the comment that swept through the science fiction community when the first of the filmic trilogy hit the nation's screens: "What makes *Star Wars* a *fantasy* more than anything else is the *sound* of the space ships presumably traveling across hard vacuum."

In a universe where all things are possible, eventually Lukas was interviewed by a number of science fictionally sophisticated people and questioned on this very point. His answer is illuminating. "Very early in the film project, this point was raised by a number of technicians on the crew. But it was finally decided that the ships would just be a lot more effective if you could hear them as well as see them. Besides, the majority of the audience would neither know nor care that a fundamental scientific reality was being violated."

This attitude is interesting to tease open in terms of the way, I suspect, most science fiction *writers* would have handled the same situation. First, if you feel that the ships are more effective with sound, you use your science to justify it: A bit of artfully dropped-in dialogue, in a subordinate clause here and there, explains that, Oh, that's not real sound. The ionic vibrations of the ships drives are translated into audible vibrations and broadcast over the speakers around us. Everybody feels better if they can aurally orient themselves. And we find it makes targeting and reflexes a lot faster. But really—out there, actually it's just silent.

Then, for the next few scenes, you play it just like *Star Wars* did—and there's no question. But what you now have set up the option for is a scene in which Han Solo, in his space suit, is out mending a patch on the hull of the Millennium Falcon, and suddenly a passing shadow makes him turn around—

An enemy ship is passing so close—while perfectly silent—that it fills up the screen. He sees one portal slip by, near enough to recognize the face of the officer at the window.

Solo barrels back through the airlock. Inside, as he pulls off his space helmet, the "sound" of the retreating space ship breaks in on him from the ship's speakers. . . .

Or something like that.

It becomes a devastatingly effective scene.

The point, however, is that the science fiction writer uses the "science" to expand the *aesthetic* options for his or her tale. What is basically non-science-fictional about Lukas' thinking is not simply the implied insult to his audience, but even more so the unquestioned assumption that the only thing "science" could be used for in such a situation is whether the ships make a sound *or* are silent—rather than having them be both.

In science fiction, what you use the science for is to *rationally justify* what would be, without it, precisely those violations of science. And that's how SF expands its aesthetic options over ordinary—or mundane—fiction.

And that far more subtle distinction in the intricate and intimate application of science is what leaves *Star Wars* and its sister films far closer to the axis that runs from realism on one end to fantasy on the other, than to science fiction.

It is when the grounding of possibility that science vouchsafes for us is left behind (both aesthetically and heuristically)—when the audience is assumed neither to know nor to care, and, what's more, when the creater assumes this is a situation to be exploited rather than to be rectified—that we leave science fiction at its best for fantasy at its worst. And certainly Lukas' attitude as expressed explains why cinematic SF is far closer to fantasy than is its written cousin.

Let me conclude by saying that there is much I admire in the *Star Wars* trilogy. But there is also much in it that is very shoddy.

JH: Have the 1980s and the Reagan era given you cause for new concerns that affect you as a writer or otherwise?

SRD: There is such a great discrepancy between what the Reagan administration says and what it does that it's almost impossible to judge it in the midst of this truly awful morass. There is one argument, of course, that the administration makes endless horrific statements while it contrives grandiosely behind our backs, letting the country coast downhill toward the pit of imperialism with all the momentum of a drugged pachyderm. (That, at any rate, is the most sanguine scenario I've heard.)

The stringently conservative era we seem to have entered is, I suspect, far more a factor of the country's economic condition than of anything Reagan has personally done. Being old enough to remember the politically turbulent fifties and sixties, I have to work hard to fight the traps memory lays out for me. As a writer I am actively interested in what is going on around me today. The problem is to heat one's desultory education to an active critical passion, and to keep its fragments from freezing into passive political nostalgia. The energy and cynicism I see in the new science fiction seems a very appropriate reaction to this conservative era. That's why I like to read it.

And to teach it.

NOTES

1. *Titus Groan* by Mervin Peake, initially published in 1947, currently available from the Overlook Press, Woodstock, N.Y., 1992.

2. *Dangerous Visions,* an anthology of science fiction stories edited by Harlan Ellison, Doubleday & Co., Garden City, N.Y., 1967.

3. *Orbit* was the name of a series of science fiction anthologies, edited by Damon Knight, Berkeley Putnam, New York. They ran from *Orbit 1* in 1966 to *Orbit 21* in 1980.

4. "The Tale of Plagues and Carnivals," first published by Bantam Books, New York, 1985, is a full-length novel currently included in *Flight from Nevèrÿon,* by Samuel R. Delany, Wesleyan University Press, Middletown, Conn., 1994.

5. "A Rose for Ecclesiastes" by Roger Zelazny, first appeared in *The Magazine of Fantasy and Science Fiction* in 1962.

6. "The Doors of His Face, the Lamps of His Mouth," by Roger Zelazny, first appeared in *The Magazine of Fantasy and Science Fiction* in 1965.

7. *Farewell Fantastic Venus,* edited by Brian Aldiss, Avon Books, New York, 1968.

8. "In the Bowl," in *The Persistence of Vision,* by John Varley, Dell Quasar Books, New York, 1978.

9. "In the Hall of the Martian Kings," in *The Persistence of Vision,* by John Varley, Dell Quasar Books, New York, 1978.

3.

Refractions of *Empire:* The *Comics Journal* Interview

In 1979, with artist Howard Chaykin, I published a 107-page comic book—or graphic novel—called Empire *(Berkeley Books, New York, 1979). Just before* Empire *appeared I was interviewed about it by comics writer Dennis O'Neil and, shortly after it appeared, by* Comics Journal *editor Gary Groth. I edited and reworked the transcripts of both interviews, which were published together in a 1980 issue of* The Comics Journal. *The version here has been rewritten substantially since.*

I

Dennis O'Neil: How would you compare *Empire* to your novels? Are there any essential differences in themes, characters, obsessions . . . ?

Samuel R. Delany: Well, obsessions are such that you don't get away from them. They'll probably be all too apparent. Still, I'm more aware of the differences between written and visual media. When you're working in a comics situation, the writer works for the artist, in much the same way a writer in a movie works for the director. That Howie and I like each other's work so much made things go very well: but I saw my job as essentially to inspire Howie to his highest moments—because he likes my stuff, he's more likely to be inspired. He's risen to the challenge wonderfully. I'm knocked out by what he's done.

DO'N: Which doesn't quite answer my question. How does *Empire* differ from your early work?

SRD: Again, essentially comics are a visual medium. Something I concentrated on here, in a way I wouldn't have in a written story, was the variations in landscape. In *Empire* the action moves very quickly from place to place. If you're writing a story, you want to stay more or less in one location till things resolve; only then do you move on to the next location. In *Empire*—in a comic—things work best if you shift from landscape to landscape pretty quickly: What starts against one background should resolve against another, to keep things moving.

DO'N: Let me be more specific. Almost all your novels to date—indeed, I can't think of any exceptions—are heavily influenced by mythology, reworkings of mythology in science fiction terms. Have you continued that particular mode?

SRD: I'm not aware of any myths that are directly followed in *Empire.* Indeed, I'm aware of a lot of mythical patterns that are broken. First of all, *Empire*'s main character is a woman. And she has a woman sidekick. There are very few presentations of active female friendships in contemporary western narratives, from top to bottom, whether it be in comics or in "serious" fiction.

DO'N: Mainstream?

SRD: Mundane fiction, as we call it. To try to deal with female friendships in any sense is to broach new, mythological territory. In *Empire* the point-of-view character is a young man—the character through whom most of the action is seen and (indeed) on whom the climax more or less hinges—a young man who gets involved with this very energetic pair of women. Since, I'd imagine, most of the audience for *Empire* is likely to be male, it provides a bridge for that male audience to get used to the idea of friendship between women. Also, because I'm male and the artist is male, it makes it easier for us to work with it. But at the same time I think it provides *something* for the women in the audience.

DO'N: You've used a woman protagonist before, in *Babel-17*. But there was a male sidekick in that.

SRD: Yes. A whole crew full of them. In fact, one problem I see, now that *Empire* is done, is that I don't think we did *enough* with the woman sidekick. There are times when the point-of-view character almost displaces her. If I had it do over. I'd spend *more* time working with the friendship. But I still think it's there—it's a step in the right direction. I'm happy with it.

DO'N: Why comic books?

SRD: I've always liked comic books—which is the understatement of the age. I don't believe the various media are replaceable. What you can do in comics you can't do in movies. What you can do on the stage you can't do in a novel. Once, in an introduction to a collection of some of your own work, I discussed some of the unique things comics can do. I talked about the way comics handle time. Unlike movies, comics are not bound to real time. In comics, you have far more flexibility in handling time than you do with the conventions of narrative film, because you're not held to a set performance duration. You can slip into slow motion and fast motion in comics without drawing attention to it, in a way you just can't in film—at least not without being very self-conscious. In a comic, you can have three panels in a row where the actions are half a second apart, followed by a fourth, the same size and on the same row, set a century later. Or you can skip decades between panels . . . and it just doesn't have the same egregious quality it would have in a movie. Peckinpah slows down the murder, and the body collapses through a space suddenly thickened to the consistency of clear Karo syrup. The intention is to model a psychological effect: the intensification of visual perception that occasionally occurs in the midst of physical violence. But the actual effect on the audience, what the slow motion violence conveys far more strongly, is that thickening of space and the intrusion of a particular aspect of filmic technology. And in the hands of a less skilled director than Peckinpah, the whole thing devolves into another of the pornographic caricatures that conventionalize filmic mayhem.

The same slowing down of a falling body—say, one just shot—over a series of comic panels, because of the cross sectional aspect, because of the lack of real motion, registers as a series of charts. The effect there is of a passage of analysis. The affect is intellectual, not sensual. The content of that analysis may, indeed, appear satirical when it's drawn from the pornography of violence. But the main point is that what superficially appears as two similar moves become profoundly different experiences, depending on which medium it's figured in.

An equal slowing down of the action in a comic and a film, in a time-bound and a non-time-bound medium, has very different results.

In movies there's what's often called the "Hitchcock rule." The camera's moving in, either in a single take or between cuts, signals the audience that the emotional charge of the scene is rising. If, however, you suddenly move the camera away from the action as you go from cut to cut, all the energy from the sequence releases. The camera's pulling away signals that the scene's emotional peak is past, that we're winding down, we're moving on. In comics, however, this rule doesn't apply. You can go back and forth, panel by panel, close-up to far-shot, building tremendous energy by their alternation, in a way that would just be incongruous (and unreadable) in conventional narrative film. The two—comics and film—really *are* different media. You can do things in comics and gain effects that just can't be duplicated in any other form. Howie's taken great advantage of this. He's given an aura to what Byron calls his "floating axis format," with three panels per page, now vertical, now horizontal, that's quite astonishing. We're working under a very restrictive template. But Howie has gotten the maximum flexibility out of it. The storytelling is unbelievably good—by storytelling, I don't mean my plot or anything like that. I mean the visual realization: Howie has learned all those Joe Kubert and Jack Kirby lessons *very* well.

DO'N: Were you aware of any specific comic book influences? Is there anything that's influenced this project that hasn't influenced your earlier work?

SRD: Again, this is something that Howie could answer much better than I could, simply because of the relationship between writer and artist in any comics endeavor. As I said, the writer is working *for* the artist—very much so. And that's very much the way I wrote *Empire.* Influences? Basically the comic book writers whom I admire very much—one of whom I have the pleasure to be sitting with and talking to right now.

DO'N: Aw, shucks.

SRD: I remember, half a dozen years ago, when you first told me maximum 35 words per panel—that's just on the most prosaic level. I believe you edited two of my comic scripts from barely passable to passable, which editing job I learned a great deal from. But that's the kind of thing that's gone into *Empire.* Some of the things that Len Wein has done I've liked very much. Kubert's storytelling: ways of presenting a story so that it will lend itself to certain kinds of visual analysis. Many of these Howie has taken and run with—and many of them he's thrown out and used approaches of his own. But he's the one who's done the real work. I'm infinitely more than pleased with the result.

DO'N: Did you use anything you learned in directing your movie, *The Orchid?*

SRD: Well, once I wrote an essay on what the differences were between oral and written storytelling. I had a lot of experience with oral storytelling when I was a kid. And most of what I know about written narrative has to do with the ways it differs from oral narrative—especially from exciting, convincing, *effective* oral narrative. I've had some limited experience directing movies. But the differences between film and comics are far more exciting than their similarities. People working in the comics field tend to talk about the cinematic aspects of their art. In fact, I think that's become so much the convention that if you want to talk about anything else, you can have a pretty hard time. But—again—I find the differences more interesting. Sure, I learned things from doing *The Orchid* film: but in terms of *Empire,* it's how the comic medium works *differently* from the movies that was most instructive.

DO'N: Do you have any idea of how readers perceive comics material? I'm groping for a theory of comics aesthetics. I would expect to hear something about the tension between the picture and the words; it's something I've thought about for years . . . and have come up with nothing.

SRD: I don't yet have that kind of theory. . . .

Let me put it this way:

My non-theory falls into two parts. First, there's what the Frankfurt School would call reception aesthetics, which has to do with the way people receive the comics. I think the basic thing to remember here is that people can take in a *lot;* and by people I mean eight-year-olds, seven-year-olds, five-year-olds like my daughter, and fifteen-year-olds and fifty-year-olds. We take in a lot more information than we put out. We take off the page a lot more than we can articulate back. Somebody may ask, "Okay. What did you just see?" and you stumble around for words to tell them. But that doesn't mean you didn't see a great deal. I think the information always goes in. Whether somebody can then give it out again is a whole different problem. But I think that's the main thing you have to remember: The six-year-old, the seven-year-old, the eight-year-old, not to mention the twenty-six-year-old and the thirty-eight-year-old, are taking in a hell of a lot more than they can articulate. Therefore, you have to *give* them a lot more than they may be able to talk about with any kind of articulated intelligence.

DO'N: Does the visual added to the verbal fulfill this need?

SRD: I suppose it does. But now we come to the second half of my non-theory: How you get all this to happen—how you get all this information into the thing to begin with. Which has to do with a more traditional notion of aesthetics. Yes, there's tension between the verbal and the visual. But I don't think *most* comic book fans pay that much attention to the words. I know I don't. [Laughter.] Yet for exactly that reason I believe the *writer* has to pay *more* attention to them, so that they will pack the highest power, because so many of them will be missed. That seems to be the comics writer's responsibility—or curse. Something that has already appeared in much the same format *Empire* will have is Richard Corben's *Den,* which is out now in a glossy, nine-by-twelve process color book. You really *don't* have to pay attention to the words in *Den.* The pictures more or less do the whole thing. After I'd looked through it eight or so times, I probably *had* read all the words in it. A couple of times over. But I *still* couldn't tell you the plot.

I think that's true for any number of comics.

Empire, for anybody who takes the time to read it, will have a plot; and the plot will begin here, go through its development, and come out there. But I think it's unfair to expect the audience to be all that interested in it. What the comics narrative has to do before it achieves coherence is push the action through one visually exciting situation after another, page by page, double-page spread by double-page spread, and panel by panel within that. I think that's the comics writer's *main* job. In a funny way, keeping the action coherent—which, yes, I've also tried to do—is secondary.

II

This interview is actually two in one. Prior to the appearance of Empire *(Berkeley Books, New York, 1979), Gary Groth asked veteran comics writer and editor Denny O'Neil to conduct an interview with his long-time friend (me). O'Neil interviewed me [above] in April 1978, before* Empire *was published. Groth felt I should have a chance to talk about the book after it was published as well, so in* The Comics Journal *he followed O'Neil's interview with his own, conducted some months later, after* Empire *appeared.*

Gary Groth: I understand Denny O'Neil got you interested in comics—at least interested in writing them.

Samuel R. Delany: Well, he was certainly the first person I met directly connected with the field. I think we were introduced at a Lunacon back in 1967. He was working for National at that time, having just left Marvel. I'd always liked comics. I grew up on E.C. and D.C. I missed the superhero renaissance. But once we hit the middle sixties and the explosion of D.C.'s "relevant comics," of which Denny and Neal Adams were both the cutting edge and the popular front, I got enthusiastic all over again—much more than I am now. I'm afraid I've sort of drifted away. If I remember, I pick up a copy of *Conan,* and even then, from time to time, a month will go by where I miss it. So there aren't very many comics today I follow regularly. But I was really interested in Neal Adams' work. Jim Aparo would knock me out. And of course I was a fan of the undergrounds—S. Clay Wilson, Strnad, Lee Mars, Corben, Trina, Spain, and Crumb. But, unfortunately, I really haven't been following comics the way I used to . . . so it makes them a *little* harder to comment on. [Laughter.] All my active experience as a comics fan is ten years out of date.

GG: Why have you lost interest in comics in the past few years?

SRD: I don't think it's anything in comics. I think it's something in me. When I acquired a daughter—she's now five—a lot of things just had to go out of my life; there wasn't time for them. Comics, unfortunately, were one of the things that fell by the wayside. Every once in a while I buy a couple of the specials—I bought the *Superman–Ali* thing, just to see what it would turn out to be: it spent so much time getting itself together, I wanted to see what it would finally look like.

GG: What did you think of it?

SRD: I thought the drawing was superb. I thought the story had its . . . rocky places. [Laughter.] I gather Denny and Neal had some problems coordinating the thing.

GG: I read that you had scripted *Wonder Woman.* I wasn't aware of that. How did that come about?

SRD: For two issues, I think. This was back when National was at the end of its "relevant" phase. They'd been trying to do the relevant bit with a number of standard titles: *Green Lantern* (with Green Arrow) was, of course, the great success. But now they were trying the same thing with *Wonder Woman.* Only it wasn't working. Mainly that was because the people they had writing it just didn't have much of a feel for the women's movement. Short of getting a woman writer for the series who did (Don't ask me why they didn't put some energy in *that* direction!), nobody could come up with anything. So at one point I said to Denny: "I think I have more of a sense of this thing. Why don't you let me do a couple?" So I *did.* A couple.

GG: This was while Denny was editing it?

SRD: Yes. From those two issues there was actually some very nice feedback. But then there was a big change. National decided to put Wonder Woman back into her American flag falsies and bring back the bullets and bracelets bit. For the previous ten years, basically she'd been wearing a gi and was a super karate expert. It was a lot more realistic and a lot more amenable to stories with some social bite.

But there was this nostalgia surge to take her back to her fifties incarnation. D.C. used a chance comment Gloria Steinem dropped while being shown through the National offices to throw out all of Wonder Woman's concerns for women's real, social problems. Instead of a believable woman, working with other women, fighting corrupt department store moguls and crusading for food cooperatives against supermarket monopolies—as she'd been doing in my scripts—she got back all her super powers . . . and went off to battle the Green Meanies from Mars who were Threatening the Earth's Very Survival. . . .

I wasn't interested in that. So I pulled out.

GG: When was it that you actually learned to write in the comics form?

SRD: Well, there're probably people who'll claim I never have. The first professional experience I got was with Denny, back when I was doing *Wonder Woman.* Writing for comics is very different from writing for any other medium.

GG: How difficult is changing from the novel to the comic form?

SRD: In a sense to call it a difficulty makes it the wrong kind of problem. It's not a difficulty. It's a matter or rethinking along a certain line. If you're used to saying what you want with words, then you can do it. But if you're the sort of writer who thinks of yourself as "expressing your inner feelings," then it's going to be difficult. Any kinds of restriction get in your way.

GG: How did *Empire* begin?

SRD: Howard Chaykin and I had always wanted to work together—since the late sixties, back when Howie, along with Bernie Wrightson, was a twenty-year-old boy wonder at D.C. . . . and I hadn't quite hit thirty. Back when I was doing *Wonder Woman,* we had one project together that never got going. In high school, Howie had been a friend of Byron Preiss, the producer and packager of *Empire.* Byron approached me about doing something with him and Howie. The whole thing came together very naturally. I'd met Byron a couple of times before—the comics world is fairly small and cheek-a-jowl with the SF world.

GG: I thought after reading *Empire*—

SRD: You know, I distrust people who "read" comics—in the same way I distrust people who go to "see" an opera. You don't go to see an opera. You go to *hear* an opera—no matter how lush or lovely the production. The visual, no matter how complex, is there to complement, comment on, and generally support that hearing. People who go to "see" an opera—and many do—simply start out with the wrong mind-set. Chances are they're not going to enjoy what they see all that much. You know: the soprano will be too fat and the tenor too old . . . it's a familiar story. Similarly, you don't "read" a comic book. You *look at* a comic book. ("Hey, you want to come over to my basement and look at some comics?" It's amazing how demotic language can find the problem knot and cut right through it.) While you're looking at a comic, sure, you read the words. As well, you learn to look at the panels in a certain order, to read the balloons and captions in a certain sequence—highest to lowest, left to right—just as you learn to hear an opera in a certain way, after you've gone to enough of them. You listen for the stretto at the end of Act I, whether it's in *Don Giovanni* or *West Side Story,* whether it's in Verdi or Gilbert and Sullivan. And if it's *not* there (as it often isn't in, say, Wagner), then the composer's telling you something about his particular view of music, theater, and the social world they relate to. You train yourself to listen for emotional progressions. But at the same time you train yourself *not* to listen for deep plot coherence—or you're likely to be just as disappointed as you'll be if you start looking for that kind of coherence in comic books. Words in opera have a similar position to words in comics. Librettos are notoriously mindless and so are comic book scripts. Yet simply in terms of musical demands—or visual demands—some are a lot better than others. Nobody understands *all* the words in an opera. The orchestra, the ensemble singing, the sheer volume the words must be produced at, not to mention the fact that in any given opera audience, half or more won't know the particular language the opera is sung in—all that fights the verbal side of opera. Yet great operas are unquestionably great art. Often the visual fights the verbal in comic books too—distracts you from it, or makes you skip over parts of it without really reading.

But even the words in a comic: You have to *look* at them first, before you read them. That's why comics sound effects are so important. That's why hand lettering can be so much more suggestive than print.

Myself, for *Empire,* I'd suggested printed captions, hand lettering for the dialogue balloons, as well as lots of artist-conceived and -executed sound effects from Howie—to get the full range to the possible *look* of the comics text.

But Byron couldn't see it. He had this notion of a "visual novel" in his mind—with the emphasis on novel. Finally he decided to do it all with set type. And no balloons. No sound effects, either.

The look of the comics page. . . .

The intense and commited silence with which one *looks at* a comic—or even the cursory silence with which one *looks through* a comic . . . that range of silences is terribly important. That silence is what allies comics with the novel, with painting, with sculpture, with philosophy, with pornography, and with historiography. That silence is what separates comics from theater, opera, television, concerts, and film. The noisy genres, entertaining as they are, as they fill up the space of looking with sound—words, music, the noise of crashing cars, the susurrus of breath that halts, suddenly, in anticipation of mayhem or violence—do so at the price of suppressing a certain inner dialogue, a certain internal critique, a space of concentration and criticism, which, I might add, our society desperately needs.

But if you start out to "read" a comic, you're starting out wrong. You won't really be able to get into what's going on. And I'm afraid that, because I'm a writer, and a writer who writes books that get real paperback covers put on them, not to mention occasionally reviewed in *The New York Times Book Review,* people are more apt to start *reading* a comic I write—rather than looking at it. But comics are to be looked at first—and reading is a subordinate process to that looking. And that's the medium itself, not me. I can't do anything about it. And I wouldn't want to. When I write a comic, I try to write it carefully, conscientiously, and as well as I possibly can *with* the priority of the visual in mind.

In movies, television, and comics, the operative factor is what some film theoreticians have taken to calling "the gaze." The gaze is a combination of the gaze of the viewer at the comic book page, or the television tube, or the film screen, modulated and directed by the looks the characters give to each other or to various objects. I look at character X who looks at situation Y in such a way that I now look at situation Y (*and* character X) in a way I wouldn't have before. The point, of course, is that the movie gaze, the TV gaze, and the comics gaze are all very different. What makes the comics gaze the privileged one in my estimation is that the gazer has the greatest control over the comic book gaze. The comics gaze is at once the most distanced and the least manipulated. In comics, the gazer can control the speed his or her gaze travels through the medium. The gazer can control how far away or close up to hold the page. The gazer can control whether to go back and regaze—and going back a panel or a page in a comic is very different from going back in a novel to reread a previous paragraph or to reskim an argument.

The gazer is a "coproducer" of the comic at a level of involvement and intensity, through the nature of the medium itself, that French critic Roland Barthes (as well as some experimental writers, such as Soller, Federman, or Kostelanetz) has been trying to make happen with words alone for some time—or words along with lines, used in highly comics-like ways.

It goes without saying: The vast majority of commerical comics don't take advantage of this aspect of the medium. (Though now and again individual commercial comics artists will produce stories that come far closer than most critic types are comfortable admitting.) But by the same token, the language in which a comics artist must take advantage of the medium—the medium's iconographics—is the language that has been, and is being, developed by commercial comics over the years, the Sunday and daily strips, the undergrounds.

Content changes sometimes *seem* revolutionary. Hey, let's show breasts and genitals! But the "eight-pagers" (or "eight-page Bibles" as they were once called) were doing that before I was born, and they're part of the comics' history and visual tradition too. Corben's and Wilson's lolloping lobs and ballooning bosoms have a lot more to do, in terms of draftsmanship, with the 1940s, black-and-white, pornographic carryings-on, drawn by anonymous teen-age boys, of Pop-Eye, Slugo, Little Lulu, Mickey, Minnie, and Fritzy Ritz than they do with the Praxitiles or Caravaggio cock, the Manet or Ingres breast. Nor could—nor should—it be otherwise. But formal changes—which change the nature of the gaze itself—happen much more slowly. The real genre geniuses are the comic artists who seize that gaze for themselves and do with it (always with the gazers' collaboration) what they will.

GG: Still, *Empire* lacked the description and background that fleshed out the characters in your novels. Is that a difficulty in comics—that you simply don't have the *number* of words necessary to building a character?

SRD: Certainly that's so if your basic assumption is that "depth" of character is inchoately a matter of words—which, in our culture, is pretty much the case. In ancient times, the word was made flesh. But since the seventeenth century there's been a general western tendency to recode the body, the soul, and everything in between in language. But "character" is a rather artificial concept. Which has "more" character? A written caricature by Dickens or a drawn caricature by Daumier? Which expresses the more "profound" character? Rembrandt's Aristotle, in his bourgeois library, contemplating the bust of Plato, or Shakespeare's Hamlet, by the graveside, soliloquizing on Yorick's skull? The implied conflation, in your question, between the pictorial and the graphic is, I think, a false and uncritical equivocation that muddles more than it clarifies.

The synopsis for *Empire,* by the time I finished it, was in the neighborhood of fifty-six pages. That's where the "character" descriptions were. They were pretty much in terms of things I wanted *shown*—literally pictured—about the characters. This was what I gave Howie. And my feeling is that everything in the synopsis and a good deal more are there in the drawings—paintings, I should say. *Empire*'s pages aren't outlines colored in, as most comic works are. Each page was worked up in color from the start—which, in terms of the all-important gaze (and doing it that way was Howie's own idea), is perhaps the *most* unusual and, at least for the traditional comics gazer, the most demanding thing about *Empire.*

The *look* of the comics page!

Howie was very much out to make you *see* things differently. The tiny splatters, the delicate lines zitzing across the broader strokes, the pallette-knife effects. The oil crayons laid in on top of highly painterly passages. This is all very *un*-comics-like stuff. It may take the audience a while to learn to look at it. There're a whole lot of simplicities that are givens of the comics medium—notions of movement, impact, and rebound in the world ("mechanics," the physicist would call them), concepts of inside and outside, in terms of outlined objects, ideas of figure and ground, subject and object—that Howie's panels simply start off, on first look, by declaring a loud and resounding "No!" to, then going on to depict a vastly more complex organization of visual space. Sure, often Howie's objects are outlined; but look at them a while . . . it's a rich, knotty, problematic line—not an uncritical and evanescent separation, which, to be seen properly at all, has, on some level or other, to be all but ignored; which is the way many inkers handle at least a goodly portion of their lines. Even as he layers his panels, again and again, in wonderful volumetric dimensionalities, Howie's planes still insist on the basic, true, two-dimensionality of the materials—paper and applied color—that is what he works with, so that, finally, there's a self-reflexivity to the work that makes Howie's a very modern eye.

It's all there. But you have to go with it.

And look at it. And look for it.

In comics, my own feeling is that what's in the visuals doesn't have to be done in the words. And if you spend a lot of time in the words repeating what's been done in the pictures, you're wasting word space.

Now for better or worse, a lot of comics writing does repeat—especially commercial comics writing—does repeat what's in the drawings. The comics audience tends to look for that. If they don't see it right away, they're unhappy . . . even if the stuff is all right out there, to be seen. I certainly thought the "character" should be in the drawing—which, in *Empire,* is where it is. Written words are pretty much restricted to what characters say (Howie could more than handle all the atmosphere problems) and a certain kind of analysis that can't be shown.

GG: I think you worked in what's been called Marvel style. I'd like to know what kind of interaction you had with Howie. For instance, the panel structure was such that the pages' images were all flush to the perimeters, so that the copy and the drawing fit perfectly. Did you write to fill the space allotted for your words, or did Howie draw to fit the space allotted for his drawings?

SRD: No, the drawings certainly weren't done around the dialogue and captions. Marvel style, yes. Only a couple of extra layers—Marvel style, but more so. I started by giving Howie a set of written landscape descriptions; also, a few written character sketches. We didn't begin with any story line. We only knew it was going to take place here, and here, and here. We worked up from that, in terms of what would be visually most exciting. We tried to arrange those landscapes in a progression that would be most dramatic—and satisfying.

The next step was to come up with a story line that would move the characters between these places in the required order. This was after Howie had done some character and landscape drawings, from my written sketches, to give me an idea of what it was all going to look like when realized. He also sketched out some things that he wanted to do. The visually sumptuous explosion in the dark, undersea mining city, which lets Qrelon get away from the guards, began as a purely visual notion of Howie's: As we drop down through the panels on the verso, things get darker and darker—then leap to the bright, upper panel of the recto, with the yellow-white explosion itself, and the figures, half behind the rocks, sketched in grisaille . . . and, again, as we drop down through the page, the light once more drops to darkness. . . .

At about this point, Byron came up with the notion of his "floating axis" format: That's a set of double-page spreads of three vertical panels on both pages, followed by a set of double-page spreads of horizontal panels—also three a page.

My first response to this, I confess, was, "Why . . . ?"

I can say now that I felt it was a mistake from the beginning. A page-high panel, only a third of a page wide, is a very awkward space to tell a story in. Basically it accommodates one Byzantine saint. It doesn't leave much room for landscape or action. Page after page of such panels, six to a spread, gets awfully dull. A double-page spread of six vertical panels is something you might want to use for a very specialized dramatic effect. But there're practically twenty-four such vertical spreads throughout *Empire.* Given the constraint, what Howie managed to work into them is astonishing: which is to say, after the third six or so, they lose all power to articulate and become the most empty sort of mannerism: and you can ignore them for the rest of the narrative. Similarly, the three-panel horizontal page, opened up over two pages, is simply and insistently dull. There're more or less twenty-one of *those.* Byron had used the vertical format for Starenko's *Chandler.* Everyone pretty much agreed it hadn't worked there, either. But, out of what notion I never quite understood, he wanted to try it again, hoping that minimal variation, coupled with the horizontal and the occasional splash, would release from it some kind of visual energy.

The one place where commercialism and aesthetics really fight each other in the comics is in panel structure. The sophisticated comics fan delights in inventive, energetic, ideosyncratic panel layouts. They give a story its visual energy. They involve the sophisticated fan in the narrative spacing.

But the commercial comics have discovered again and again that their primarily young audience, still learning the medium's iconographics, is just bewildered by that same visual variety. Again and again the comic book laid out at a simple four-panels-per-page outsells the more creatively laid out book. The result is that the artists are always trying to sneak in a slightly more interestingly organized page—and the editors are always telling them to cut it out.

The argument for Byron's "floating axis" format was that it was both simple *and* new. The argument against it was that the vertical pages, at least, fought against both active figure drawing and any sustained landscape effects.

It was also about this time Byron decided to omit dialogue balloons and thought balloons.

And sound effects.

Balloons! I looked at comics balloons and what did I see? . . . I saw that by taking the smooth line of a dialogue balloon and replacing it ı comics, different balloons indiate different types of language. Ionsters, supernatural beings, or ıe dead often speak in doubled balɔons, or in otherwise distorted figres. As well, balloons can indicate motion or tone of voice, a jagged alloon for an exclamation, a balɔon with icicles dripping from it for n icy statement or reply. Musical otes included in the balloon indiate song. Jagged edges indicate vords coming over some electronic nedium, radio or TV.

These panels Copyright © by D.C. Comics, 1993.

A smooth curve with a clear caret leading to the character indicates speech. A cloudlike curve with bubbles rather than a caret indicates unspoken thought. A broken line for the balloon boundary indicates a whisper.

with a cumuloform cycloid, around its pristine white, comics had managed to solve a problem Joyce could not overcome without distorting the entire surface of his fictive text: and, no matter how much we applaud his daring and his art, Joyce's solution *still* strikes contemporary readers, sixty years after *Ulysses*' publication, as a writerly move almost as eccentric as Sterne's in *Tristram Shandy*. Wrestling with the same problem in *Strange Interlude,* with all the mechanics of Broadway at his back, Eugene O'Neill still couldn't come up with anything more than a gimmick; whereas comics handle the whole problem of thought—literally—as naturally as speech. Is anything more sinister than the dashed outline of a whisper balloon, where, at regular intervals, the pure white reserved for articulated language bleeds into the vibrant, colored, silent surround, so that, for a moment, the whole structure of the medium seems about to break down under the pressure of the sedition? Take the doubled balloons, their outlined unsteadiness of a wholy different order from thought, a flat blob of yellow or green polluting the traditionally white space of articulation: The traditional form in which the monstrous speaks itself in comics indicates a separation from the pictorial at once total, thickened, twisted, moted, shaded, emphasized and such that the monster's hollow croak becomes the polar extreme of the hesitant human susurrus.

In the tradition of western art, the encounter of the living and the dead is the encounter of the recently executed thief, Aris Kint (aka Adriaan Adriaanszoon), and the doctors who gaze, none of them, at Kint's body but at the folio anatomy text propped beyond his wrinkled feet, while the anatomist Dr. Nicholas Tulp discourses rationally to them and to the unseen paying audience that fills the lecture theater. Rembrandt's *Anatomy Lesson* (1632—though we now know that two figures—Dr. Frans van Loenen, the uppermost figure, and Dr. Jacob Koolvelt, at the extreme left—paid, as the five first doctors had already done, to have themselves painted in some years later) encodes an entire seventeenth century's notion of the relation between life, death, discourse, text, vision, and the body.

In the comics, the living and the dead babble and stutter directly at one another, in mutual visual fascination, in endless verbal fragments, through the decay that shatters and splatters the space between them, torn between revenge and guilt, all rationality struck away. We can watch this process from the panels of Graham Ingels through the panels of Bernie Wrightson; it is their panels that will show you, by the same encoding, the *twentieth* century's view of life, death, discourse, text, vision, and the body—and the relation among them. But you *don't* ignore the balloons if you want to decode it! Asking the comics writer to give up balloons seemed far more extreme to me than asking the fiction writer to give up "she asked," "they whispered," "he thought," or "it rasped," if only because denying these to the comics writer is denying the writer's singular point of contact with the medium's visuality—which was denying access to its power.

Well, *Byron* looked at balloons and saw they made things look too comicky. . . . That's when I got the notion maybe it was time for me to pull out of it all.

It was sounding less and less interesting.

Byron was proposing all these things in terms of wanting to do "a visual novel." He really harbored an idea of starting a little—or maybe not so little—revolution in the panel arts. But the last thing in the *world* he wanted to do was a comic book. Comics, he was very quick to explain, was what he wanted to get *away* from. Well, as I said to him, I love the comics, and I love what comics can do. The idea of working with one of the great comic book artists of our time in order, I hoped, to produce a great comic book was why I'd gotten involved in the first place. But the particular restrictions Byron, as packager, was coming up with seemed geared to sabotage the whole enterprise. All the iconic rhetoric of the medium that made it flexible, incisive, and articulate he wanted to cut out, and for what pretty much struck me as vague, pretentious, and ill-thought-through reasons. A lot of it, I think, came from that innate inferiority complex so many people in the administrative side of the comics industry walk around with daily. Their ideal is to do comics that look like anything but comics. That was the basic reason, I suppose, Byron had begun with for bringing me in, as a hot-shot writer from another, more respectable medium, in hopes I'd somehow magically turn the lowly comics form into something wondrous and new—and, above all, respectable. Commercialism can be pretty deadening; but so can idealism—if it doesn't spring from an understanding of and sympathy with the workings of your medium. You make things new and exciting by going with all that—however idealistic you are. And Byron talked a pretty idealistic game.

Finally, however, *I* had a talk with Howie.

Howie more or less agreed with me that Byron's restrictions were misconceived. But he saw them, misconceived or not, as challenges. Like a lot of comics artists, he felt that balloons were basically big white blobs that got in front of the art. He'd always wanted to try something with an active story that avoided them. And the horizontal/vertical business? Well, he thought he could turn that into something positive. So, that morning as I left the studio Howie shared on Twenty-eighth Street with Walt Simonson, I told him: "I see myself as working for *you* in this whole

The Living, the Dead, and the Text, 1950.

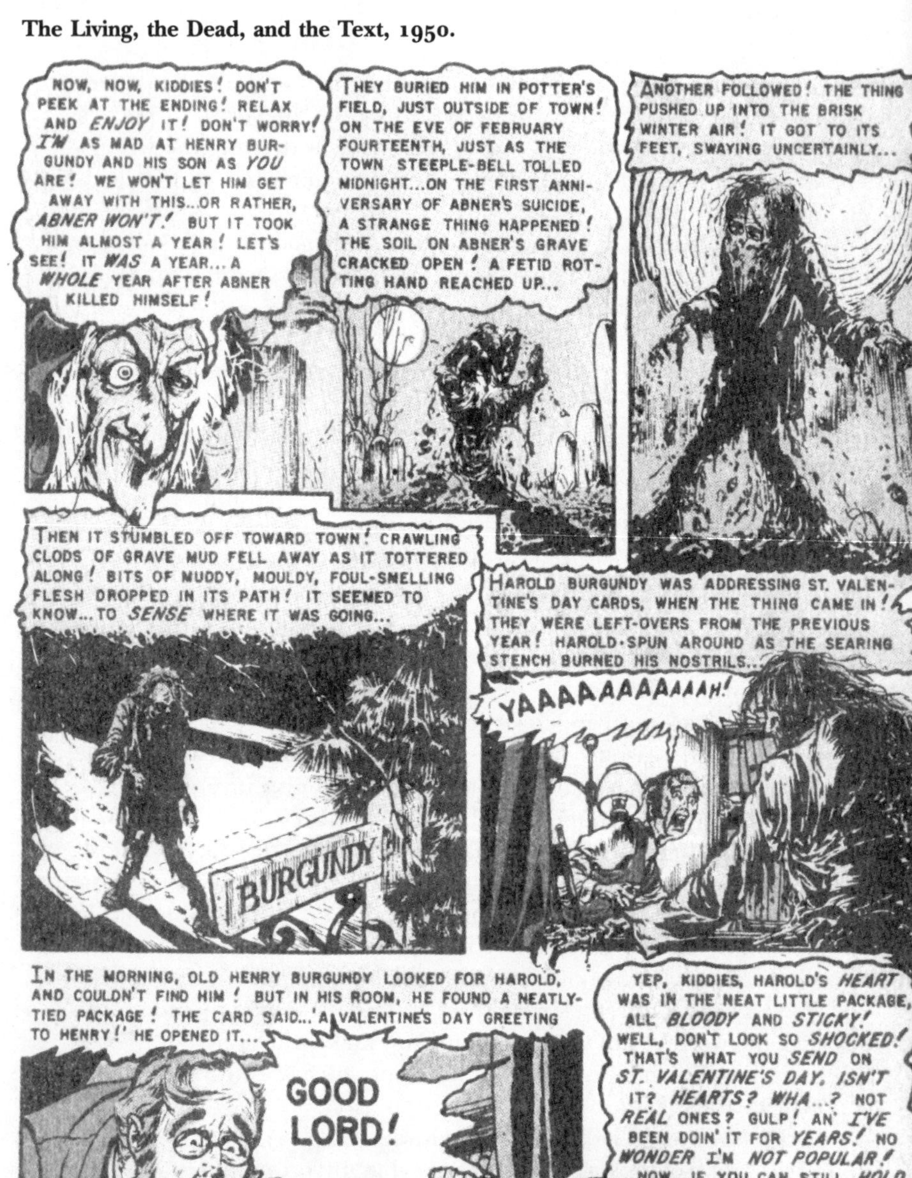

The last page of "Poetic Justice," a story drawn by Graham Ingels (1915–1991), first appeared in a 1950 issue of *The Crypt of Terror,* copyright © 1950 by William Gaines. Currently Copyright © by D.C. Comics.

The Living, the Dead, and the Text, 1632.

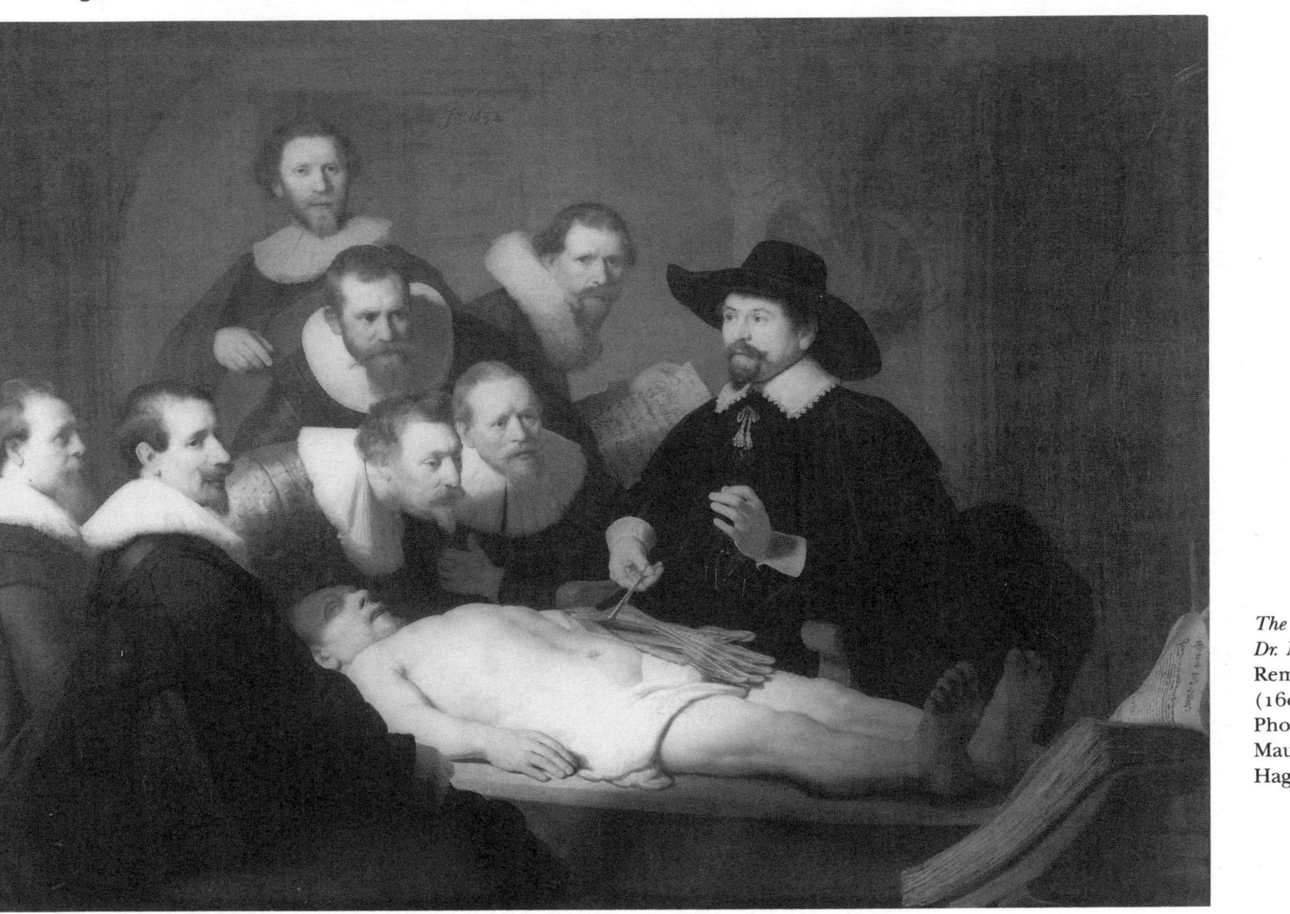

The Anatomy Lesson of Dr. Nicholas Tulp, by Rembrandt van Rijn (1609–1669). Photograph © Mauritshuis, The Hague, inv. nr. 146.

business. If you still think you can do something in the middle of all this, then I want to do it, too. And you seem to think you can. So we'll go on."

And I'm glad I did.

Howie is a very smart kid from Brooklyn. In the midst of a project, his energy, his visual invention, is endless. His work has a line for line, brush-stroke for brush-stroke authority that, personally, I associate with aging renaissance Italian and Flemish masters—which only sounds pretentious till you look at what he does. Artists aren't famous for being able to articulate either their own methods or, often, even what's going on around them. But Howie has a no-bullshit approach both to what he's doing and to the comics business in general. He can express himself pretty sharply. And since what he's doing has always been pretty exciting, it makes *him* very exciting to work with.

Howie was born red-green color-blind . . . a bit unusual for an artist. In fact, I kind of wonder if all that pink snow at the end of *Empire,* about the hue of Pepto Bismol, may not originate in that neurological red-green equivocation. But I doubt it. He's worked out all sorts of strategies for getting around it.

I'm dyslexic—not quite so unusual for a writer.

Still, it's a hurdle.

And it requires the same sort of strategic attack to go on producing with it. Also, we both started in our own fields particularly young and got a fair amount of attention relatively early. All that gave Howie and me a kind of *sympatico.*

He won't give in to a suggestion just because I make it. There's a cynical side to Howie (that, I think, masks a lot of larger, social idealism, where we're pretty much in agreement) that was a nice counterweight to my tendency to theoretical fancy-flights.

I think we were *all* for revolution.

But the kind of revolution in the medium Byron was hoping for—and we must give him that: he wanted to foment a revolution—almost always comes from *within* the field. And it rises from the visual area. Simply importing an outside writer—like me—won't make it happen. Back in the sixties when Neal Adams introduced tone-yellow into the comics coloring process, *that* was a visual revolution that changed the look of the color comics page. Once they've had it pointed out, eight-year-olds can look at comics and distinguish early flat-yellow comics from the later tone-yellow comics. You were talking about characterization, before. With tone yellow, a whole range of subdued, subjective, moody, interior colors could now depict all sorts of shadowy and subjective atmosphere effects (which is half of what you're really talking about when you talk about characterization in comics) right there on the panel's surface.[1]

The extraordinary sociological range to Neal's drawings was experienced by so many of us *as* just that—range—because, by smashing through the color barrier with what began as a purely technical move, he allowed his coloring (through what tone yellow freed up among the greys, tans, browns, and shadow tones in general) to establish an inner, subjective dimension that defines the imaginative distance between external social content and the inner subjective reality that range covers.

Sometimes you get a revolution by heaping more and more oppression on people—restrictions, if you're happier with the term. But it didn't happen in our case. The notion rampant in the administrative level of comics production that, somehow, you can effect a revolution in style, taste, and general seriousness if only you can get a good enough *story* is simply the industry's blindness to the fact that the action here is *all* visual. Don't get me wrong. There are some wonderful comic book writers. But a comic itself is wonderful because of what it *shows.* And because of what it shows *about* what is shown—and this second, aesthetic level is almost entirely a matter of exploiting the extant comics language. But a comic is never going to be *wonderful* because of (only) what it *says.*

Howie's Gideon Faust piece that came out a couple of months ago in *Heavy Metal* is probably more effective than any sequence in *Empire*—because, very pointedly, he did *not* have that ridiculous "floating axis" limitation to deal with. Free panel structure—and often *no* panel structure. That's certainly the way Howie works best.

GG: Not using balloons in *Empire* was Preiss's directive?

SRD: Yes

GG: Do you know *why* Preiss insisted upon that restrictive three-panel layout?

SRD: Well, besides wanting to repeat what Starenko had done in *Chandler,* I think there was *also* a bit of ass-backwards commercial thinking involved, which was really out of place in this project. All the commercial comic book companies believe the simpler the panel layout on the page, the easier time they'll have selling. The younger fans—eight to fourteen—really respond best to a simple four-panel layout. Only in our case, the three vertical panels didn't produce an effect of simplicity so much as an effect of affectation. Considered as a very real constraint, which both Howie and I felt was imposed from above, we did pretty well.

GG: What other contributions did Preiss make? Did he add his vision to the story?

SRD: Well, he rewrote a good number of my sentences.

GG: Are you kidding?

SRD: No. I take full responsibility for maybe *half* the sentences in the text. I don't understand the nature of a lot of the rewriting. Byron seems to have a phobia, amounting to psychotic terror, of parallel structure. Whenever I had a sentence in a nicely balanced form, he'd unweight one of the ends. [Laughter.] Also, the layout as to where type appears on the page was all Byron's. At a couple of places I managed to catch it when Byron put the wrong type on the wrong picture. And there were a couple more where everything had to be moved up one picture. I managed to catch some of those in time to fix. But there's still the odd panel where a dialogue caret drops to the wrong character. And of course we had the obligatory nudity problem in a couple places—nudity of the most ordinary and tasteful variety, I might add—that was finally covered up. Two pages ended up in the wrong order. This was pretty much all Byron's fault. I think the reason for this was, first, Byron had several projects going at the same time, and though he paid as much attention as possible to each one, some things just slipped up. Most of his attention, at least toward the end, was going into an illustrated album of Beach Boys lyrics. It's too bad.

GG: Let me ask you something specifically about the layout. On a panel where there was type over and under the panel, were you able to move the panel up and down to accomodate more or fewer words under and over it, as you saw fit?

SRD: No. We had a battle royal over the very first art page. Byron wanted the type on the second panel at the top. Now because of the iconic language of comics, a caption at the panel top means one thing and a caption at the panel bottom means something else. The way I'd written it, there was to be a caption at the top of the first panel, a caption at the bottom of the second panel (to pull the eye down through the first two panels, in order to exploit the meteor in the foreground that Howie painted overlapping the gutter between panels one and two), and a caption at the top *and* bottom of panel three—to make the eye rise and fall again through the third, largely red and black, and narratively most active of the panels.

Now a caption at the the top of a panel is supposed to do one job—set a mood, or provide a transition from the previous panel—while a caption at the bottom of a panel has to give you some further information about the picture right over it you've presumably just looked at. Those are two very different jobs.

Now if you put a mood caption—or a caption transitional with the panel before—at the *bottom* of a panel, it reads awkwardly; just as it does if you put a caption that gives you revelatory information about the panel at the top.

Well, anyway, what I had written as a revelatory, and thus clearly a bottom-panel, caption kept ending up at the *top* of the second panel! I'd say to Byron, "Would you please move that down there to the bottom of the page. It doesn't make any sense up there."

And besides: If you have three tall, thin panels, each right next to the others, and you have three captions all at the top, the eye just slides across them; you don't even *see* the caption at the bottom of the third—and more than likely you won't see the art in the first two panels, either. I tried to explain all this to Byron, but he couldn't quite see it. And all these concerns about how the text was supposed to modulate the gaze across the pictures sounded too comic-booky to him, and just not what he was interested in. Finally he gave in, but only, he said, because I wanted it that way. But by then, it was so late in the reproduction process—and I'd been saying this, literally, at every stage, and every stage he'd been ignoring me—you could no longer extend the middle panel's picture up to the margin of the other two pictures. The result to me looks very awkward.

GG: Did the original painting extend to the top?

SRDF: Yes. The top of the second panel was originally flush with the upper margin of the two panels either side of it.

GG: I was wondering why Howie didn't draw his panel the same height as the others.

SRD: The awkward white space above the second panel now is the place where the misplaced text had been set—before it got moved to the panel's bottom, where it belongs. But there're lots of little goofs like that all through . . . dropped words, the odd unnecessarily added word by Byron (Byron never *thinks* things. He only thinks *of* things—and he's damned well going to correct anyone else who does. There's a lovely little Byronic "of" in the first sentence of my introduction that certainly wasn't there when *I* wrote it), punctuation mistakes, type that, because it was sent back to be reset in a different font or point, nobody really got to proofread. . . .

GG: I assume you wrote the text from Howie's paintings—that you had the originals in front of you when you wrote the copy.

SRD: I had xeroxes of Howie's pencil sketches for the paintings. While I was writing, Howie was working on the paintings themselves.

GG: And I assume you indicated that certain captions went above and certain captions went below.

SRD: Yes. And I'd say about 60 percent of those directions were violated.

GG: That was Byron's job on the book?

SRD: Although he hired someone actually to paste up the mechanicals, yes, Byron laid out all the text again. What basically happened was this. When I wrote out the final text—working from xeroxes of Howie's pencil sketches (and, later, from tracings of the cartoons for the final paintings), as I said—I laid out small roughs of the pages, panel by panel, and typed the copy where it should go on each panel, top or bottom. I also wrote out the dialogue more or less in play form. Now Byron, when he read this over, *didn't* have the pencil sketches. He only had my roughs—just little boxes on the page, with some text at the top or bottom, but no pictures. And he had a copy of my fifty-six-page plot synopsis—which Howie was working from, on the pictures, over in his studio. By this time, of course, Byron had seen a handful of Howie's early finished pages. But I don't think he could have had more than a few of them—if any—in his possession when he went over my finished script to edit it. First he began to do little bits of rewriting on my text, most of it in an attempt to make the script coherent *without* reference to the visuals—with *only* the synopsis to go on.

For some sorts of commercial comics this is a reasonable way to edit a script—where, indeed, you don't care if the words repeat the pictures; where, from the editorial point of view, you want as much redundancy as possible, so that, between a weak script, weak visuals, and a young audience, what story there is will come through as strongly as possible. But this was *not* a weak story. And the visuals were anything *but* weak. And in a script where the writer has gone to infinite pains not to let such redundancies happen, it's just silly. I'm sure without the visuals, my script seemed extremely thin, if not incoherent. And I suspect a rather harried and busy Byron read it over and simply thought: Mmmm . . . this is obviously an inexperienced comics writer, who talks a good game but isn't delivering.

A lot of Byron's sentences tend to be in the present tense. I don't particularly like present tense narrative, and almost never write it. But in galleys a couple of my scenes had to be rewritten into present tense because Byron had stuck in so many present tense sentences that it involved fewer changes doing it that way than putting his additions back into the traditional narrative past.

Oh, yes. And on my original roughs-with-script, he crossed out all the characters' names for all the bits of dialogue—after all, he figured, the actual names weren't going to be set in the final version. The playform was only for his benefit—not anyone else's. Though he was right, crossing out the names was very silly. It may have saved the cost of setting a couple of hundred words. But it would have prevented endless confusion later if there'd been an easy way to identify which piece of text was spoken by which character. Next he sized the text to the panels, more or less following the vertical and horizontal pattern—which he could take from my roughs. Then he sent it to the foundry for typesetting.

What came back from the foundry was, of course, a series of pages with a lot of paragraphs of type on them, some sized for the narrow vertical panels, some sized for the horizontal panels. But there was no indication of what went at the top and what went to the bottom of the panels—or even what went with which panel. And of course the paragraphs of dialogue were not headed by any names. These pages were then sent to me for correction. By this time, I knew the visual/textual aspect of the project pretty well. I tried to put *some* of Byron's rewriting back the way it had first been; but you simply can't make major, substantive corrections at the galley stage. So I was very limited in what I could fix. *One* of Byron's particularly brainless additions, I remember, came in the scene in which the young hero, Wryn, is exploring the derelict spaceliner, *The Platinum Swan,* with the Nizerine Elyne, in their vaccuum suits. Looking over the galleys I read, at one point: "In his attempt to follow, a strut cracked the vacuum's silence." My God, I thought, a floating preposition (whose attempt? The strut's?), a piece of inaccurate wording (he meant, I assume, that the strut cracked), a cliché ("cracked the silence"), and a scientific impossibility (the silence cracked in a *vacuum?*)—all in one botched bag of words! (What *I'd* written was: "Suddenly, he lost his handhold . . . " because the previous panel had given a close-up Wryn following the Nizerine; this made a simple and wholly legible transition. But without the picture, my line simply struck Byron as not punchy enough. And the synopsis said something like: ". . . Through the viewplate of her space suit, the Nizerine stared at the bit of green glass. Behind her, a strut that Wryn was holding suddenly broke, and the boy began to topple through weightless space. . . ." Well, Byron probably figured the picture must show Wryn's hand slipping off some strut or girder. So that could probably be left out. But what Howie had actually *drawn* was much more imaginative: In the foreground, we have a close-up of the Nizerine, examining a fragment of the glass demon, the Meta-Max. Then, way in the background, a figure is involved in some ambiguous, awkward tumble that you can't read very clearly at all without the clarifying caption. My caption ignored the obvious foreground action and cleared what was going on in the background—which, a picture before, you'd just seen close up. *Looking* at it—the way you're supposed to do with comics—you see that whether Wryn slipped or a strut broke is unimportant. So I'd given that up. But without the progression of pictures, there was no way for Byron to tell that just from reading my text and/or my synopsis. At any rate, it had been a neat narrative word/picture tension—gone now.) Also, just at the level of awkward English, this one was too precious even to try to correct. I decided to leave it the way Byron had it, and if anyone ever asked me, I'd simply point out that it was one of Byron's (representative) contributions to the tale.

There were other problems, of course. The dialogue was supposed to be set within quotation marks (given the fact there were no balloons). Well, some of it had been, and some of it hadn't. And here and there quotation marks had been put around captions as if they were dialogue. Most of these we caught. But a few managed to slip by. When it came to laying in the text, a month or so later, when Howie was further along in the finished pages, Byron *didn't* go back to my roughs. He'd done too much rewriting for my original text to be easily recognizable from what was still readable on the roughs. By my estimate, over the general range of text, about 49% of the sentences had been reworded. And that's specifically *not* counting one whole *section* Byron rewrote from scratch—we'll get to that in a bit.

Then he sat down with the type (which now, you remember, had no indication as to which panel it went to, where on a panel it went, or which bit of dialogue went with which character) and the finished pages, and proceeded to go through it making notes for the paste-up artist on what text to drop in where. Some of it, miraculously, he got right. But a good deal of it he didn't. Some of the dialogue he assigned to the wrong characters. Since I'd gone to a lot of trouble *not* to have the text repeat the pictures, a number of captions ended up on the wrong panels entirely, since they didn't make direct references to the pictured actions.

I believe I saw one batch of finished pages with the acetate overlays, where I was able to make some corrections—but Byron had to pay the mechanical artist to implement those corrections, so that the changes that could be made were minimal, and only for gross sense. That, I recall, is the first time I told him to drop the type from the top of the second panel on the first art page to the bottom. The next thing I knew, I was handed a full set of color page proofs. Byron had been so rushed, he'd forgotten to specify numbers on the pages! (That's probably why two pages—the one beginning "Akbrum raged . . . " and the one beginning "On board the *Proteus* . . . "—ended up in reverse order in the finished book.) It's also at this stage I noticed again—and commented on—for the third time, that the dropping of the type, on that second panel, had still not been done.

Back when he'd made the decision not to use balloons, Byron had also decided not to use any boldface for text emphasis—a decision I wholly agreed with. But now, when the type came back, Byron thought that it all looked too thin. So, more or less at random, he had maybe eight or a dozen phrases reset in boldface type—or, sometimes, just italics. Among the three-hundred-odd panels, a dozen bits of boldface and/or italics just get lost. And when you come across one, it jumps out like a mistake—which, to my mind, is what it is.

But by now some of the goofs I'd already caught had embarrassed Byron. And at this point he was giving in to me on pretty much all the small points that, at this stage in the production, he reasonably could. So the second caption was—at last—moved to the bottom. But it was done by stripping the film, not by going back, correcting the acetate, and reshooting the page. That's why the picture couldn't be extended. They could lay something in over something already there. But they couldn't put back a section of the art that had already been dropped out.

That's why it looks so awkward now.

The other reason I suspect Byron was so capitulatory at this stage is that now he wanted to rewrite the climax sequence of the project. The way Howie and I had conceived the climax is rather complex. The action happens both in the Information Citadel called Ice and back in Loiptix's tent headquarters, where Loiptix is struggling with Qrelon, trying to get her to pull the lever that will destroy Ice and Wryn within it.

The way Howie had realized the ending was stunning; and it came as close as possible to making the horizontal/vertical structure of the rest of the book pay off.

Over a series of horizontal panels, Qrelon and her sidekick, Blaz, have been captured by Loiptix, among the dragon people who guard the Kunduke's information citadel, Ice. Qrelon and Blaz are brought to Loiptix's tent. On the screen in the tent's corner, they watch Wryn, whom Qrelon had sent to place the catastrophes, inherent in the glass demon called the Meta-Max, into the central information beam inside Ice. This will explode the citadel from the inside out: Wryn will be unharmed—but the citadel will cease to function. And the Kunduke will no longer have access to all the information of Empire—and thus no longer be able to rule and oppress.

In the tent, Loiptix grabs Qrelon's hand to force her to pull the lever that will cause Ice to collapse inward on top of Wryn and crush him and the Meta-Max he carries. That will leave the functioning of the citadel intact and impervious to defeat for the rest of eternity. The Kunduke's rule will be fixed forever.

It begins with the bottom horizontal panel of the last verso:

Oblivious to the struggle going on miles away, Wryn walks into Ice, carrying the glass demon. He's debating whether the destruction of the Information Citadel will, in the long run, be a good thing. After all, he *is* a student, dedicated to learning, to the preservation of information—not its destruction. As he remembers his classes at the university, he glances up to see that what he's thinking about—his class at the school—is pictured on Ice's walls. Whatever information he thinks of, Wryn realizes, Ice automatically pictures!

Turn over the page—

Verso: Instead of either horizontal or vertical panels, we have a full page splash, as Wryn wonders about the fate of his friend Burn, his parents, and his beloved teacher, Dr. Plong—all of whom, one way or the other, have been done in by the Kunduke villains, who control Ice . . . as he learns from the pictures that appear mistily on the citadel's walls. In each case, the Kunduke have broken their word. Burn and Dr. Plong are dead; and his parents have been told *he's* dead! Wryn is convinced: Ice must be destroyed—so that the Kunduke's power will end. He places the Meta-Max in the central information control beam; it starts to move toward the heart of the citadel. (When it reaches the heart, the citadel will explode outward, Wryn will be safe, and the citadel's power terminated.) As he does so, he wonders what's happened to Qrelon—

At the splash page's bottom, Howie shows Wryn as he places the Meta-Max in the sparkling, glittering beam; as he thinks of Qrelon's name, suddenly he looks back over his shoulder as (we don't see it, yet, but it's obvious from what's just happened) Qrelon's picture materializes behind him.

Next page: recto—

Three vertical panels.

Panel One: Wryn, astonished, looks at Qrelon's picture on the wall, as she struggles with Loiptix in the tent. He hears Loiptix raging, as he tries to force her hand to the lever, to destroy Wryn and the Meta-Max, before the demon reaches the heart of Ice. Wryn realizes his danger.

Panel Two: On the middle panel, the demon moves down the energy beam, coming closer and closer to the heart. . . .

Panel Three: We're in the tent. Loiptix tries to force Qrelon's hand closer. On the screen, behind the lever, we see an anxious Wryn press his hands against the glass (i.e., the walls of Ice), as if to break out, shouting for Qrelon to hold out just a *moment* longer. . . .

Turn the page:

A double-page spread, the explosion—or perhaps I should say the deconstruction—of Ice, happening off on the recto.

On the verso, three horizontal panels are dropped in, showing:

One: Qrelon manages to kick Loiptix down and break loose, while Wryn's face fills the screen.

Two: Blaz, also held in the tent, shouts, as Qrelon runs out the tent flap, "You're free!"

Three: Qrelon takes off on one of the corralled dragons, while Loiptix (who is all but insane in his anger at Qrelon, having forgotten about Ice—he can only think of catching her and destroying her), on another dragon, fires at her and misses.

Meanwhile, suggesting that all this is just about simultaneous with the explosion, the fragments of Ice scatter all over the two pages, behind the embedded panels. Qrelon is flying her dragon toward the explosion. Loiptix, on his, and firing after her, is in hot pursuit . . . through two more double-page spreads, in which—smash!—smash!—the rest of the plot elements resolve.

It was elegant, suspenseful, and done with beautiful economy. The collapse from the three verticals to, as you turned over the page, the three horizontals embedded in the double-page splash—the only embedded horizontals in the text—gave a tremendous sense of resolution and relief. Loiptix' face and body positions on those vertical panels gave you all of his enraged paranoia so that you didn't, for a moment, question why he didn't just reach up and pull the lever himself but chose instead to run after Qrelon (who, after all, has just kneed him in the groin). It was absolutely clear and flowed along with the energy of a river rapids. . . .

At this point, however, I found myself involved in a strange conversation with Byron.

"Once he gets into Ice, how does Wryn *find* the central energy beam, Chip?"

"What do you mean, how does he find it? He walks into this large citadel. And there is it, running right across the middle of the room. He sees it. That's how."

"No, no. There isn't any suspense in that, Chip. You have to have him try and find it, wondering where it is—he's got to look for it, among the levels of the citadel . . . and *finally* discover it."

"Byron," I said, "the suspense isn't in his looking for it. The suspense is whether he'll do the whole thing in *time.* Wryn's just finished a battle, which he thought he'd won. Now he just walks in, tired out, to do something that, by now, he thinks is simple, easy, and automatic. His mind's on other things; he's looking at the pictures on the wall. He's pondering the significance of what he's doing. Only at the last moment does he learn that a struggle is going on, miles away, that makes every second count."

"No, Chip. Believe me, it doesn't work the way you and Howie have it now. You have to balance the struggle in the tent with some sort of difficulty and drama in what Wryn's trying to do. He comes into the citadal. He knows he has to hurry. Where's the information beam? He can't find it. He thinks: Maybe the information beam generates heat. He feels heat coming from the left . . . climbs over some rocks. Is it this way? He climbs down among the rocks, slowly, making his way . . . there's a glow. Yes, that must be it! He comes out on a ledge. And there it is . . . !"

"Byron," I said, "the suspense is in the fact that Wryn *doesn't* know he has to hurry. Qrelon's struggle in the tent is balanced by Wryn's naiveté as he comes into Ice. He thinks he's come through all his struggles. The fighting's all behind him. He doesn't know that, a mile off, a fight's still going on that may destroy him in just seconds. (But *we* do . . . !) It's only his rising anger, as he learns from Ice how the Kunduke have killed his friend, his teacher, and deceived his parents that finally—when he thinks of Qrelon—reveals to him he, too, is *still* in danger . . . *that's* the suspense; and the climax. He realizes, in a moment, that all his speculation and wondering *may* just mean he's lost the battle—just when he thought it was finished and he'd won!"

"Believe me, Chip," Byron said, "that can all be in there, too. But you have to put some of my kind of suspense in it. Like I said, maybe if the beam sends out some heat. . . . Let me try it. You'll see."

I shrugged. "Okay." Since this was at the galley stage, anything that Bryon "tried" now would be in the finished book.

Even though I disagreed, I think I've given a fair account of what Byron wanted to do and why. But I don't think you could figure that out from what's there now. What Byron came up with for the sequence is just a botch. He hacked up Howie's art, had him draw three entirely new panels—none of which followed his own format that he'd imposed on us. From the horizontal where Wryn approaches Ice, with the demon in his backpack, on, Byron rewrote my text, cutting a lot of mine and adding what strikes me as mostly illogical nonsense, so that save a half a sentence here or some of a caption there, it's the one section in the story that really isn't mine at all. Or Howie's. I don't believe most readers can even follow what's going on across those pages. I don't feel it adds any suspense at all. It's just busy and incomprehensible. A piece has been cut out from the bottom full-page verso splash and moved up to the top of what would have been the second vertical panel on the facing recto. The second vertical panel, showing the demon moving toward the heart of Ice, has been moved over to vertical panel position three. Howie drew two new panels that now cover the bottom of the verso splash, making it a three-panel page, instead of a full page. And bits of the original recto's first and third panel have been cut down and placed in positions one and two where they don't fit, along with some other new art. The hacked down verticals are—visually—all but unreadable. Because they don't bear any compositional relation to the rest of the page (or to the rest of the book); the new panels don't advance the story. Nor do they retard it in any interesting way. It's very hard to locate what's going on where, back and forth between Ice and Loiptix's tent—which was lucidly clear in Howie's initial version. What little's left of my original intent just gets in the way of Byron's notion of "suspense." And Bryon's additions, instead of bringing out his own idea, are both verbally and visually without energy. Of the many tragic ironies of the thing, one of the saddest is that Byron, like most professional comics people, always urged me to remember to keep the words down: This is a visual medium. Well, these are by *far* the most text-heavy pages in the book; and three-quarters of that text is Byron's.

I don't know. In the middle of the climactic action, some comics writers, bored or trying for satiric effect, will follow what I call the de Bergerac ploy. Cyrano de Bergerac was the guy who, in Rostand's play, improvised a ballade which he recited to his opponent while they were having a sword fight. In the comics, the de Bergerac ploy is when a pair of superheroes—or superhero and supervillain—slug it out while exchanging what's supposed to be devastating repartee. But by and large, when the climax arrives and it's serious, you want to show it with a minimum of words and the strongest pictures possible. You want the viewer simply to look at it all happening.

That's just not the place to add "plot."

First art page of *Empire*.

It shot through lunar debris.

The world it sought was unimportant, half

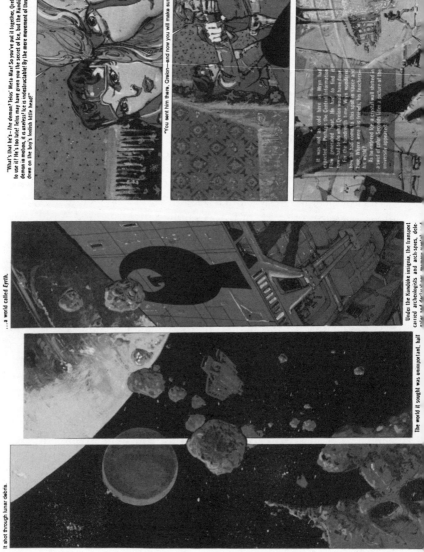

. . . a world called *Eyrth*.

Under the Kundüke insignia, the transport carried archeologists and arch-spies, dele-

Rewritten climax of *Empire* . . .

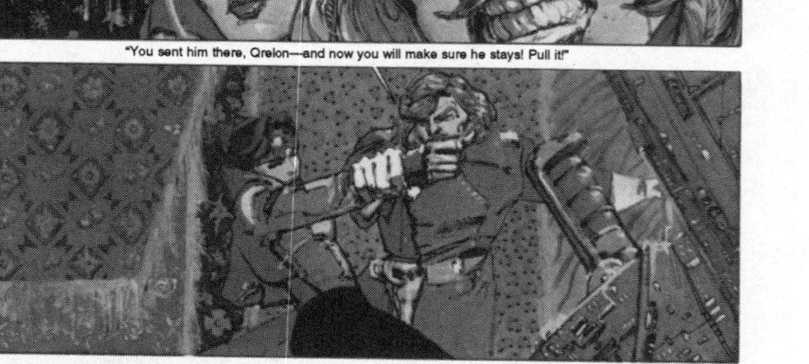

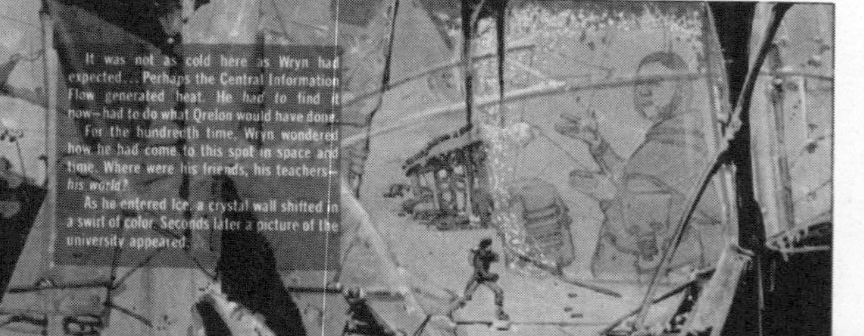

Artist: Howard V. Chaykin. Writer: Samuel R. Delany. *Empire* Copyright © 1978 Byron Preiss Visual Publications.

As the outlaw's name surfaced in his mind, a picture wrote itself in the crystalline sheets. Wryn suddenly knew his danger—her danger—as the raging figure of Loiplix appeared. Then he saw Qrelon's face, heard her scream, "The light, boy, the river of light!"

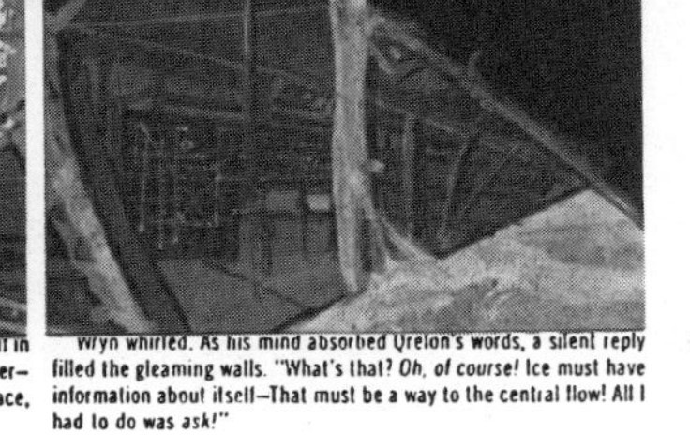

Wryn whirled. As his mind absorbed Qrelon's words, a silent reply filled the gleaming walls. "What's that? *Oh, of course!* Ice must have information about itself—That must be a way to the central flow! All I had to do was *ask!*"

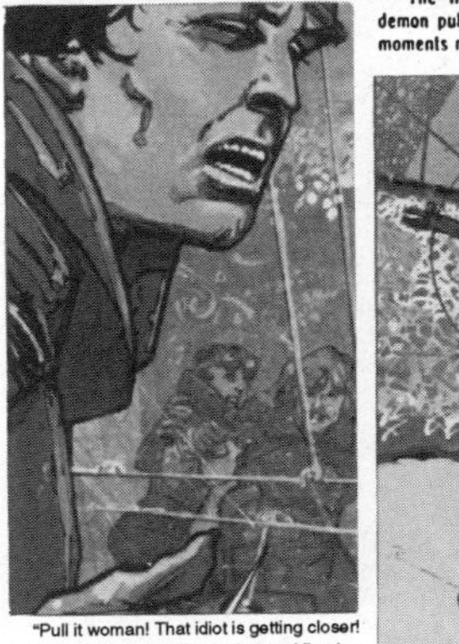

"Pull it woman! That idiot is getting closer! If the Meta-Max reaches the heart of fire, Ice will topple outward and the boy will live! Seize the lever and crush him and the Meta-Max . . . and the Kunduke triumphs! Pull it, I tell you!"

"The information flow! I can feel the demon pulling toward the heart! Just a few moments more—Qrelon?"

"No! Don't pull the lever! It's almost home! I saved you once, Qrelon! You said you wouldn't save me, but don't let him make you—! Don't!"

Loiplix forced the woman's hand closer and closer to the deadly lever.

Slowly, the demon, with its inscription of articulation and discontinuity, moved down the true shaft of light, swallowing it, engulfing it, empowered by a woman's anger at the wrongs of an age of ages . . .

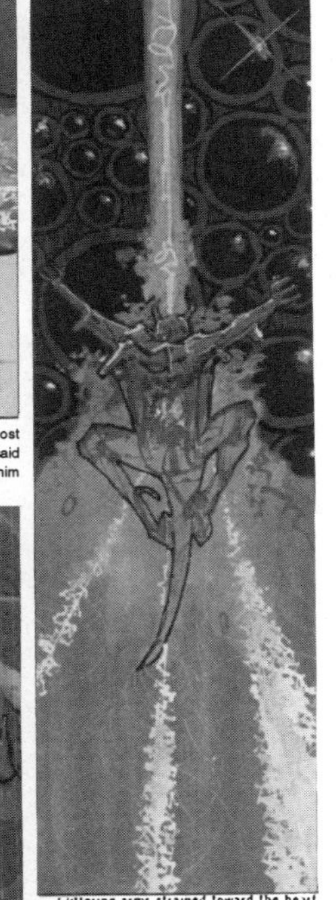

Glittering arms strained toward the heart, not like a thieving god after fire, but like a goddess welcoming the return of a light already her own. The light expanded before the demon, not like flaming swords guarding an inviolate garden, but like a sun's coronal flares, praising the worlds her womb has smelted.

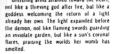

Artist: Howard V. Chaykin. Writer: Samuel R. Delany. *Empire* Copyright © 1978 Byron Preiss Visual Publications.

Continuation of rewritten *Empire* climax.

Artist: Howard V. Chaykin. Writer: Samuel R. Delany. *Empire* Copyright © 1978 Byron Preiss Visual Publi…

But what we have now, I'm afraid, is the *least* rewarding pages to *look* at—or to read—in the book.

And that's particularly sad because, before they were redone, they were two of the *most* rewarding—at least I thought so.

GG: Why would Preiss ask you to write a book and then rewrite so much of it? That seems counterproductive.

SRD: Well, I think he had his own sense of what would work and what wouldn't. I think these ideas grew out of a kind of misguided notion of what's commercial. The commercial tends to manifest itself as a number of rules of thumb—such as Byron's notion of a balance of difficulties. But rules of thumb are to be applied to places where you have a problem. You don't apply one at a place that works perfectly well only you don't quite understand how (because, say, it violates your rule); you don't employ it at a place where, according to your rule, there should *be* some little problem but that, after all, you just can't put your finger on.

You have to look at these things with your guts first, then use your response as a guide to when and where further thinking might do some good. But that requires time and sensitivity. And Byron was real short on the former—which probably got in the way of the latter.

Byron's a very sincere guy about what he wants to do, visually. He has very strong ideas about, say, the use of violence in comics. Myself, I quite unabashedly love the sex and violence in comic books. The only thing I find offensive is the way the sex and violence are politically skewed. You can show naked women's bodies but you *can't* show naked men's bodies. You can suggest rape but you *can't* show pleasant, satisfactory, recreational sex outside of marriage. And heaven forfend you depict methods of birth control. That's the kind of thing *I* find offensive. In art I'm all for sex and violence, in exactly the way I'm all for peace, love, and understanding. They're *all* part of life, and I want to see art deal with *all* of life—passionately, energetically, insightfully. It's only the political skewing of them that I hate. And right through here the unconscious political skewing I find substantially more hateful than the overtly propagandistic.

Now Bryon is different. He would really prefer that the comics simply not indulge in violence at all, save when it truly implements the plot. Of course I think plot is a wholly artificial construct, not that important at all in comics, and one of the least interesting sorts of progressions you can have through any narrative enterprise. That means the notion of violence (or sex) having to *implement* a plot is not one I find very congenial. There are too many other things you might want it to implement that are far more fascinating: any number of abstract progressions, say. That's probably also why I didn't get all that upset when Byron wanted to introduce what turns out to be some totally unnecessary and all but incomprehensible "plot" at the climax. It's just not that important—one way *or* the other. All I'm sad about is that, in doing it, he obliterated a handful of Howie's most powerful and pointed comics effects and pages to no purpose.

I think another part of it is, of course, a kind of power madness everyone I've ever met who's worked in the comics field is infected with to a greater or lesser extent. It's rather a paradox, but the farther down you go in the literary hierarchy, a hierarchy that runs from the *most* abstruse poetry at the top to the *most* bubble-headed comics at the bottom, the greater the power madness of the people who administer and edit. In the highest of high-falutin' literary magazines, when the editors receive work, they accept it or they reject it. But once they accept it, they're committed to every comma in it, every line break, every word. Should they find something in it they think might be a mistake, they bring it to the author's attention in the most polite and diffident manner, with the humblest query note. With comics on the other hand, which I maintain are just as difficult and complex as any other practice of art, everyone feels they can do them. Anyone can fix a dull stretch of plot. Anyone can jazz up a sagging story line. Well, telling effects in any art have to be set up, have to brought off. And Byron, because he started out with his own notions of plotting and storytelling, just couldn't see what we were setting up, what we were making happen.

With all this criticism, I've got to say I learned things from Byron, too. He was the first person to point out to me, just about comics writing, how powerful verbal descriptions of smells can be. Smell is the one sense it's hard, or often impossible, to call up visually. And that visual impossibility gives it, in the medium, a corresponding verbal strength.

In creative writing classes, you always have to remind your students to write through the senses—and the major sense you write through is, of course, the eyes. But a comics *writer* should *never* describe what anything looks like—at least not in the finished text, unless it's something off stage. The eye, for the ideal comics writer, should function only when writing the the artist's synopsis.

You know, it's very funny about overwriting in comics.

Any time I've done work in this medium, even back when I was with Denny, everyone would warn me: "Don't overwrite! Don't overwrite!" So I'd spend my time on the synopsis. And I was always very lucky with my artists: Dick Giradano, for example, back when we were doing *Wonder Woman,* with incredible clarity and economy, always gave me *everything* I wanted. And my synopses tended to be three times as long as anybody else's. That wasn't more action, either. It was a case of specifying more things panel by panel I wanted shown.

But as soon as I'd hand in my correspondingly thin script (because if it's all shown, you don't *have* to write it), Denny would say: "Where're the words?" and add two sentences here and three there. [Laughter.] The only thing any comics editor I've ever worked for has ever done to any of my texts, from Byron to Denny to Archie Goodwin, is *add* words to the text—and usually words that flat-out contradicted or obscured something perfectly clear from the pictures.

At first I thought it was just me, as a novice comics writer, who was getting this treatment. Then I saw it happening to other writers. There's a very ambivalent feeling in the field about which is privileged, the text or the pictures. Hitchcock at one point said he originally tried to conceive of every one of his films as a silent movie. Only after that did he add dialogue. Yet can you really imagine nine out of ten Hitchcock movies *without* their sound tracks?

GG: Hitchcock believes in something called "pure cinema."

SRD: Yeah. But I mean, there are so many places where the soundtrack —in fact, what's the famous one, with the knife?

GG: *Psycho*?

SRD: No, no, no. It's an early Hitchcock, where there's a woman at a table, and in her hand she's holding a butter knife. (*Blackmail,* that's its name!) She's talking to a man, about a murder that's been recently committed, and the man is watching her hand. As the man stares at her hand, Hitchcock blurs the sound at that point so that the only word you can hear from her clearly is "knife," over and over: ". . . knife . . . knife . . . knife. . . ."

Suddenly she drops the damn thing!

And you jump out of your seat! The whole sequence simply wouldn't exist without the sound track. People obviously feel two ways about words and pictures.

GG: It strikes me that this interview—how do I put this diplomatically? —has a very different feel to it from the one you did with Denny back in April. Yet, back then, *Empire* had just been completed. The production was just over with. Although the book hadn't actually appeared, you were just waiting for the copies to come from the printer. You were much closer to all these problems than you are now. Yet, in that interview, there's hardly a hint of any problem, though you were only weeks, or at most a few months away from them. They must have rankled even more back then.

SRD: You mean I'm being openly critical now of some of the things Byron did? Well, I suppose that was largely strategic. As you said, *Empire* wasn't actually out, yet, when I spoke to Denny. I assumed that first interview would appear about the time—or shortly after—the book reached the stores. I assumed most of the people who read it would not have actually read *Empire.* It didn't seem the time or the place to start carping about what I thought was wrong with it. Or why. Also, even if *I* really didn't think so, it was always possible that sales and/or reviews might prove Byron right. Each of those places, where it went either Byron's way, or my or Howie's way, was a kind of gamble.

At this point, *Empire*'s been out almost a year. It hasn't been particularly commercially successful. The sales peak has long since passed. But because of that, now I've got some reason to believe that if Howie had been allowed a looser and more flexible panel structure, that if, as writer, I'd been allowed to take advantage of balloons and captions in a more traditional comics format—that, indeed, if the production work had been more careful and the packaging more honest and less hyperbolic—we would have had a comics work at once more commercially successful and more critically appreciated.

But I'm also sure that Byron, at this very moment, is thinking that if *he'd* found a writer who had had more sympathy with his own vision of the visual novel—a form with a greater weight to a more novelistically formatted text—and an artist who was able to lower (I see it as lowering, of course; but I'm sure Byron would come up with a different metaphor—disciplining, perhaps) his narrative invention before such a text and who could treat the "floating axis" concept as a formal strength, rather than a hamstringing limitation, then *Byron* would have produced the more commercially and critically successful book. Oddly enough, had I been a *more* experienced comics writer, I might have welcomed much *more* eagerly the chance to work outside and against the usual conventions of the field. But to me, Byron's constraints just seemed to fly in the face of the medium.

There are certain composers—Chopin, Bach—who, no matter how difficult an individual piece of theirs may sound, always retain a supurb sense of keyboard logic. No matter the complexities of a particular piece, the performer will always tell you how essentially pianistic their keyboard work is. But there are other composers, such as the Russian composer Scriabin, whose piano pieces are basically "anti-pianistic." They employ intervals, arpegios, and fingerings that simply fight the traditional way the hand moves around the keyboard. Their work is very hard to learn. Even simple sounding pieces are often quite difficult to perform. It doesn't mean their compositions aren't moving, powerful, and extremely impressive. But I will say that I thought Byron's directives were, in much the way I was describing for the piano, "anti-comics." But that doesn't mean that, with another artist and writer, they wouldn't have resulted in something quite extraordinary.

Jack Katz's *First Kingdom,* with its lack of gutters, its crowding of text and image, the Goyaesque elongation of its figure drawing, strikes me as basically at odds with the comics medium the way Scriabin's piano work is at odds with the piano. Yet in spite of it, Katz's pages are full of wonder, strength, and intelligence.

Now you tell me which one of us—me or Byron—*you* think was right.

GG: [Laughter.] Let me ask you this instead. Do you personally adhere to thirty-five words per panel or somewhere thereabouts?

SRD: It's not a matter of following it as an absolute. But *after* thirty-five words, you should start asking yourself *why* there are more than thirty-five words per panel. If you come up with a good answer, fine. But it's a guideline, not a rule.

GG: Would you have written *Empire* as a novel? Or is it so visual that it could only work in a visual medium?

SRD: Given the kinds of revelations that occur in it, given the states people start out from and end up at—that is, given what *happens* in *Empire*—I suspect there's material enough for a twenty-five- to thirty-five-thousand-word novella. A *short* novel. I don't think the revelations offered at the end about Burn, Dr. Plong, and Wryn's parents would retain their power to move over too many more pages. But the very things that (I think) make it good comics material, such as the rapid moves from place to place, the emphasis on action, work *against* its being good short novel material. Short novels usually benefit by being more concentrated in their location. Also they need a psychological dimension it's silly even to try for in comics.[2] Unless you approached the location changes in *Empire*—novelistically, that is—as a writerly tour-de-force that works against the ordinary dictates of the form, I don't think it would come off too well as a written tale. On the other hand, it might be fun to try. Let me think. . . .

For better or worse, written narrative has fallen heir to all the classical unities, which somehow or other in its practice *must* be honored, if only in the breach—whereas those particular unities *really* don't apply to the visual forms. In the visual forms, they can be flagrantly ignored. Which is to say, the visual forms are stuck with other, visual conventions of organization, not narrative ones.

But Byron's whole idea of calling *Empire* a science fiction novel really bothered me.

GG: What would your classification be?

SRD: I think of it as a comic book. A very good comic book—or potentially a very good comic book.

GG: Do you think it's not science fiction, or not a novel?

SRD: I think it's science fiction. But it's certainly not a novel. And I think it's dishonest packaging to call it one. Anyone who looks through it doesn't get a sense that they're dealing with a novel. Saying "The Major New Science Fiction Novel by X, Y, or Z" on the cover just makes somebody who picks it up and looks at it take the whole thing a little less seriously.

GG: You didn't know the blurb about its being your major new novel was going on until the book came out?

SRD: Well, not till I saw the cover proofs. I said I didn't think it was a very good idea. But I was only the writer.

GG: You say that with some irony. Are you generally happy with the book?

SRD: Generally, yes. When all is said and done, for all the things that were done to it, done with it, I feel very much it's still—basically—Howie's and my story. Howie's and my characters, Howie's and my landscapes.

GG: How long did the book take, all told?

SRD: About two years. There was a six-month delay, when we changed from one publisher to another: In that six months, we didn't work on it at all. You could call it eighteen months of actual work.

GG: Are you interested in doing another graphic novel?

SRD: I'm interested in doing another comic book. But I'd like to do it with a lot more freedom. I wouldn't want to be constrained by this vertical-horizontal thing ever again. As I said, I thought that was a bad idea from the beginning. And I think, oddly enough, Byron, now that he's seen it, realizes it doesn't work. But he'd just produced the Starenko thing. . . .

GG: *Chandler?*

SRD: *Chandler,* which is done in this very rigid, wholly vertical style. But there the artist was also doing the writing; and it was a very different kind of story. The visuals concentrated almost entirely on a single character's progression. Sense of place was done almost wholly through atmosphere and indication.

You can't take the frames off one work, mash them up a bit, and impose them on another project. Such framing has to come from a consideration of the demands of the individual work. Given the fact, however, that such an imposition occurred, I think we did pretty well.

GG: Are there any other artists you'd like to work with?

SRD: If Neal Adams ever wanted to come back to the medium and do something, I'd like to work with him. There was a point where Neal was going to adapt a story of mine, "Driftglass."

GG: That might have taken a while.

SRD: Yeah. [Laughter.] Exactly. Of course I would like to work with Howie again. I enjoy what Howie does an awful lot. He's a very exciting person to work with. There's an awful lot of energy there.

GG: What did you think of *Chandler?*

SRD: I thought it was very ambitious. I liked very much what Starenko was trying to do. I think some of it worked—and some of it didn't.

GG: Do you like Chandler—Raymond Chandler?

SRD: Very much.

GG: Have you read *The Illustrated Harlan Ellison?*

SRD: There's some very nice stuff in that. Most of the 3-D thing I think works beautifully—though the separation in a couple of panels is *so* wide your eyes can't bring them together.

GG: What value do you think there is in transforming a short story in prose into the comics medium?

SRD: I think the value, really, is all to the illustrator. It gives the artist something to work with, something to take off from. The sources for many of Shakespeare's plays were other plays. But just as frequently the sources are texts in entirely different genres—Holinshed's *Chronicles* or Golding's translation of Ovid's *Metamorphoses*. "What's the value of transforming a section from a history into a play?" In Shakespeare's case, we hear that as a very odd question. I hope, eventually, we'll learn to hear *your* question as equally odd. If you've read the play, you certainly haven't read the history. And if you've looked at the comics version, you certainly haven't read the story. Both the play and the comics versions are new works. That's how they must be looked at. It's the same thing when novels become movies—when stories become panel art . . . does *anyone* use the term "panel art" any more?

GG: Well, we've come up with so many euphemisms, trying desperately to get away from the term "comic art."

SRD: I like "comics," myself. In this kind of situation I think, it's best to hold to the classical, conservative, demotic term and reinform it with meaning by the way you talk about it, by the way you do it—rather than try to come up with a neologism. Even if you come up with a good one, in six months the way you talk about it and the way you do it will have changed the meaning into exactly what the old term meant—if you haven't changed those, too. Searching out new terms is kind of wasted effort. You have to attack the problem of changing meanings by exerting effort at the places where meanings can be changed: at the critical level and at the creative level.

GG: *Empire* is one of the most ambitious comic projects, and it's obviously aimed at an older audience. Do you think comics will gain an older, more adult audience and, with that, the respect films and novels have?

SRD: I don't know if that's coming soon. As for the respect problem, the way to gain that is to act like someone who deserves that respect.

Eventually others fall into it. As far as comics go, I think that means specifically producing your art with energy, care, invention, and honesty; and it means talking among yourselves like people who take themselves seriously. And that means *talking* with great honesty, accuracy, and energy. Don't worry about pretentiousness. Concentrate on the honesty and accuracy, and the pretensions will take care of themselves.

And the other thing, of course, is simply not to waste too much time *caring* what other people think.

What I'm talking about, of course, *is* the level of creativity and the level of criticism.

You do interesting work.

People look in to learn more about it.

And they hear people talking about it intelligently.

As long as that's the case, you won't really have a respect problem.

The problem with comics—which is not much different from the problem with science fiction—is that there's a fairly long tradition of talking about it pretty stupidly, when all is said and done. But that's one of the good things about your own work in the *Comics Journal.*

Far more important than what they net in terms of respect, though, is that, when both levels are pursued with energy, insight, and invention, creativity and criticism feed one another. They strengthen one another. They help each other to grow. And that, I feel, is far more important than what some outside coterie that is neither part of the audience nor among the producers feels about you.

On the other hand, you don't get respect if you run around saying, "Hey! Respect me! I want it! I need it! I deserve it!" Whether you dress it up in fancy language, or demand it in full-out, four-letter belligerence, you'll still miss. The only thing you can do is assume your enterprise already *is* respectable and treat it as such.

Comics do something that can't be done in any other medium. If they weren't here, what they do would not get done. Enough pop apologists are already aware of that. People who already take comics seriously turn up in the oddest places. What you have to do is not be surprised, but be able to say, "Well, of course. . . . "

GG: Has *Empire* been reviewed by book critics in the media?

SRD: Algis Budrys reviewed it in *The Magazine of Fantasy and Science Fiction* a little while ago. A very nice review, too—quite a different review from the one you folks at the *Journal* gave it. By the bye, the Berkeley Books warehouse, where the copies of *Empire* are in storage, got flooded out in New Jersey, earlier this month, so anyone who has an *Empire* is on his or her way to owning a rare book. [Laughter.] A lot of copies just washed away.

GG: Is there anything you'd like to say to a comic book audience?

SRD: The only thing I'd like to say to a comics audience is: Take a look at *Empire*. Then go buy all of Howie Chaykin's other works; and look at them, too, lovingly and seriously.

NOTES

1. Endnote ten years later: Glance through any dozen pages of Frank Miller's *The Dark Knight Returns,* the most popular comic enterprise of 1986, and try to imagine it without colorist Lynn Varley's use of tone yellow. Simply, without it the book would not exist.

2. Another endnote ten years later: The Gibbons/Moore *Watchmen* series from D.C., which was certainly the most critically interesting work to come out of the comics field in the 1986/1987 year (Art Spiegelman's *Maus* aside), has opened up comics in a subjective direction inconceivable a decade ago. But, once again, this direction does not duplicate novelistic subjectivity. Largely it's achieved through illustrator Gibbons' brilliant handling of comics time, along with great formal and symetrical strength in the visual layout. This is the very opposite sort of layout from the one I was calling for in the interview above. But Moore and Gibbons, writer and illustrator together, make hay of my glib assertion of ten years back.

4.

Sword & Sorcery, S/M, and the Economics of Inadequation: The *Camera Obscura* Interview

This text began as a set of written questions posed to me by Camera Obscura *editors Constance Penley and Sharon Willis, in 1988. My written response became, finally, too long to include in the journal: it first appeared as an appendix to the English edition of my autobiography,* The Motion of Light in Water *(Grafton Books, London, 1989), under the title "The Column at the Market's Edge." I'm grateful to* Camera Obscura *and its astute editors for allowing me to use the journal name in the subtitle here.*

Libidinal Economy/The Marketplace

Return to Nevèrÿon (your series of tales and novels set in the imaginary land of prehistoric—or marginally historic—Nevèrÿon) foregrounds a transformation from a barter economy to a money economy, a transformation you've suggested is a common theme of the sword-and-sorcery subgenre. In these tales the marketplace becomes a central topos and a site of exchange between classes, sexes, and peoples (in the ethnic [or prenational] sense). In representing the marketplace as an intensely eroticized zone, these tales exhibit a certain reciprocal desire across class lines, and a particular fascination with the "lower classes," as well as with marginal or lumpen characters. How are these fascinations connected to the market? What does it mean to explicitly eroticize class relations, as well as economic exchange, in this way?

Samuel R. Delany: In Nevèrÿon, of course, everything happens under someone else's critical rubric, so I'll start by placing here, as a kind of motto or epigraph to our discussion, outside our text (yet, as you can see, already within it), the opening statement in a fascinating essay, "The Ring of Gyges," by Marc Shell, from his book *The Economy of Literature:*

> In *The Genealogy of Morals* Nietzsche argues that "the mind of early man was preoccupied to such an extent with price making . . . that in a certain sense that may be said to have constituted his thinking." A fundamental change in price making constitutes a fundamental change in thinking. The development of money was such a change.

In that essay, through a reading of Herodotus and Plato, Shell suggests that coins, tyranny, and philosophy all arose at approximately the same moment for intricately connected reasons, relating to power, visibility, and writing—a *type* of notion that readers who've sampled my Nevèrÿon tales will be familiar with. Considering Shell (whom I've only recently started reading—alas, he's neither a source nor an influence among the Nevèrÿon tales so far), considering as well your provocative and exciting question, with its numerous possible answers, its numerous satellite suggestions, I'm put in mind of walking into a new and wondrous market, a glorious intellectual mall, in which there are at once beautiful old objects to consider and shiny new ones to handle and examine, the range of them tainted only by the anxiety of exhaustion—will we have time to see and explore them? Will we be able to make a choice of what to commit ourselves to in hard cash or fluid currency? Will we even be able to hold onto the needs we entered with, now we are faced with such profusion? Before this array, under the sheer compulsion of impulse buying, how many expansions, exchanges, and omissions will distort, or even destroy, the order and specificity of the shopping list we brought in with us before we first took up our cart?

(Our motto tells us there is no real inside or outside to this market—or, rather, there are as many goods for sale without as within; and that whatever architectural separation we might fix on, if we only squint we will be able to make out the price tag, even if the ink in which the numbers have been printed is blurred. It is only another item on display.)

But let us, for a moment and once again (if we have not already done so), return to Nevèrÿon. You've read me as suggesting that sword-and-sorcery, such as Robert E. Howard's Conan stories, Joanna Russ's Alyx tales, and Fritz Leiber's Fafhrd and the Grey Mouser adventures, as well as my more humble Nevèrÿon series, foregrounds an economic transformation from a barter to a money economy. But the status of this observation is of the same order as Robert Graves' observation in *The White Goddess* that "all true poems are about love, death, or the changing of the seasons." It's true—but. . . . Along with theories such as René Girard's ideas of the collective violence at the origin of all religious rites, or various of Freud's notions about patient resistance, such ideas (as Hayden White once pointed out in a review of Girard's work in *Diacritics*) evade the scientific by avoiding falsifiability. It isn't just quibbling over semantics, then, when I say that sword-and-sorcery does not so much *foreground* that barter/money transformation as *background* it.

As it extends beyond any given S&S story to suggest the background of *all* possible sword-and-sorcery tales, this ground becomes the catalogue of all images from which any particular image in any particular S&S tale can come, the lexicon of all possible rhetorical figures from which any particular sword-and-sorcery rhetorical figure may be drawn, the mall from which all the ideas we may purchase (but at what price?) from this most despised sub-genre of paraliterary production, sword-and sorcery, are laid out, are compartmentalized, are organized for our inspection—in a stall positioned just east of the counter selling pornographic videos and sexual aids, and west of the one displaying marginally legal weapons, skull-and-cross-bone-, two-, three-, and four-finger rings, and black leather objects sporting metal studs and swastikas; and almost wholly out of sight of the wholegrains and insecticide-free vegetables, hand-thrown pottery, and handmade jewelry—though the stalls are all rented, remember, from the same array, and only the volumes of Celtic fantasy finally lie between.

Though markets are both mentioned in passing and described in detail throughout the Nevèrÿon tales, two (if I recall) hold the bulk of our attention. Both are in Nevèrÿon's newly capitalized capital city, Kolhari. One is the Old market, the "original" Kolhari market, that market in the oldest, poorest section of the city, the Spur. There's a suggestion that this is the market, the node, the occurrence around which Kolhari initially grew up, till finally the city itself outstripped it, leaving it a sort of economic memory and a site of barter/nostalgia, still—however—pristine as a concept, a site of magic, a font of art, a reliable map of the city, the nation, the world which it serves, however inefficient and shoddy its goods. In the margins of this market, specifically on the Bridge of Lost Desire leading to and from it, we find the "work space" of most of the city's prostitutes of both sexes, who cater to the range of sexual appetites that constitute the city's desiring engine. We learn that, at one point in history, there was even a prostitutes' guild, which, today in Nevèrÿon, no longer functions. (What *is* prostitution in a barter economy?) Its traces suggest, however, something almost utopian in this market.

The second market in Kolhari is the New Market—we might even call it the "meta-market". At any rate, the temptation to put quotation marks around it, or a *sous rature* line through it, is almost overwhelming. This is the market whose construction Madame Keyne, the wealthy merchant woman, is financing. This "New Market" grows up not as a natural and original response to the imminent and unauthored play of profit and loss, collectivity, and common good; it is not a market whose originary moment must be—however paradoxically—both just before (to inspire Kolhari to come into being) and just after (for the market to take its being from a nascent Kolhari) the founding of the city that it at once causes, grounds, and exists as a fundamental mirror of. The New Market grows, rather, from a conscious realization of, from an active pursuit after the principles of, profit and loss and exploitation of collective need. The New Market, for which a whole, impoverished neighborhood of Kolhari has had to be torn down, is constructed in Nevèrÿon because Madame Keyne and people like her have noticed ways in which the Old Market works—and are trying to abstract those principles, to improve on them, and to set them to work at greater intensity, over a greater range, at a manufactured site, in order to control loss, profit, capital in particular, and power in general.

As carefully as any psychoanalytically sophisticated modern advertising copywriter, Madame Keyne has observed the relation between sexual exchange and economic activity in the Old Market: she's quite willing to tear down the Bridge of Lost Desire and reconstruct it "stone by stone" next to the new—if that's what's required to make the New Market successful. But even without its reconstructed Bridge of Lost Desire (and she also notes, astutely, that the empress's public park just beside it seems already to have taken on the same, sexual functions as the Bridge, so that such a deconstruction/reconstruction may not be necessary in anything except—*Ahem* . . .!—theory), the New Market bears a relationship to the Old on the order of that which Pierre Menard's *Don Quixote* bears to Kathy Acker's. And when we have our major encounter with it, in *Neveryóna,* the New Market turns out to be very much a market of the mind. (The only time we enter it as a completed reality is during the AIDS novel, *The Tale of Plagues and Carnivals*—which I can only suggest is *not* a writerly accident.) The New Market around which so much of Madame Keyne's desires are organized is all possibility and potential.

Now let us consider:

The Old Market is an innocent market. It can absorb and produce endless analysis. Indeed, it is constituted in the sixth tale and first novel of the series (*Neveryóna,* in which, during Chapter 3, we take our major trip through it), by almost nothing *but* that analysis!

The New Market, on the other hand, is always in excess of (or inadequate to) the theory around which it has been built. Its very construction marks a site and a surround of political pain and inequity at the very moment Madame Keyne uses it as the stage and the occasion for her explanation of capital—a conceptual locus and occasion which the Old Market simply could not provide.

The two markets are thus profoundly different places. And I would suggest that the sexual exchanges that occur in and around them, as those exchanges form the "parergon" of the economic work that goes on in these markets proper, will have as different a meaning and affect as the meaning and affect of the barter and money exchanges that give way, one to another, in the proper sites of the markets themselves.

(In Robert E. Howard's letters to Price, Smith, and the other writers of the Lovecraft Circle, writing itself is often discussed in terms of "the writing market." Let us consider:)

The catalogue, the lexicon, the conceptual background, like the New Market, is primarily a catalogue, lexicon, or background of the mind. Any given sword-and-sorcery text will always be in excess of, or inadequate to, it. The assumption of adequacy between background and text (between *langue* and *parole*) is the metaphysical move that shuts out sword-and-sorcery's specific textuality, its textual specificity.

Somehow, without sexuality, without textuality, the market, like the sword-and-sorcery subgenre itself, is incomplete.

The New Market, the background, the lexicon, the catalogue, the site of theory (always inadequate *to* its object, as opposed to the analysis *of* an object) is posited on the real and unquestioned existence of that originary, nostalgic, and metaphysically adequate Old Market—that market somehow founded and grounded before the transformation from barter to money begins, to which, by beginning, by ushering in its confusions, its exploitative grandeur, and its fall from any adequate analysis of markets (Walter Benjamin suggests that sales in the Old Market are based on knowledge of the goods, while sales in the New Market are based on questions of taste), the New Market is the response and effect.

When, as a child, I first read *The Hour of the Dragon* and the other of Howard's Conan stories, certainly the market scenes fascinated me most. (In Russ' marvelous Ourdh, the Street of Conspicuous Display of *course* leads to the market . . .) Here, in our mall, recall that other.

Thieves went slipping through it. People dashed up to other people in it, whispered mysterious or menacing messages, then dashed off again to be absorbed in the crowd. How many quarrels there erupted into vicious, bloody sword fights? Rumors had lives there as complex as the lives of human beings. There the high met the low, to discuss quickly and quietly their secret off-stage (i.e., obscene) relations. The market gave you a vision, not of the average citizen, but of the range of specific economic individuals, beggar and student, housewife and horse-dealer, farmer and potter, acrobat and army man, barmaid and baron, the vendor hustling belt buckles and the farmgirl on her day off looking for entertainment, from which that average is drawn (and "the average" is the theoretical principle-of-inadequation-to-the-actual by which the New Market manages).

For years, it seemed, the classic S&S tale went like this:

Scene i: In some secret chamber, high in a palace tower, deep in a temple cellar, in some cave, magician's crypt, or beggar's culvert, a politician and a sorcerer plot.

Scene ii: As Conan or Jeril or Fafhrd or Sonya enters the marketplace, they notice some public effect of that plotting: a guard menaces a beggar or a thief; with a wave of her cloak, a sorceress halts what would otherwise have been an ordinary sale; a nobleman with his guards and henchmen flagrantly violates the rules and customs of exchange ("No—*I'll* take that, thank you very much! And if you protest, I'll have you killed"), which either directly discommodes our protagonist or clearly oppresses the people.

Scenes iii, iv, v, and vi . . . here we have a kind of narrative free play, in which natural and supernatural aids (in the better organized tales, minor characters we have met in the market scene itself—the young barmaid, the runaway boy from the provinces, the slumming princess, the friendly guard—may give the protagonist a hand) mix with plot turns and plot developments, in which the social evils are matched with magical, metaphysical ones, and the hero strives to avert the one by comprehending the other.

And always, somewhere among these scenes . . .

In the market, once again, hero pursues villain, knocking down counters, overturning stalls, strewing tools, vegetables, baskets, smashing pottery, wreaking havoc, disrupting, violating, over-turning the market. Often in this scene, the ire of the merchants before such mayhem is halted when a minor character shouts accusingly about the villain (when someone else tries to hinder the fight's progress): "But don't you realize that *he's* the one who . . ." and the information, the revelation, the knowledge saturates the entire disruption of the public space of capital with moral right.

It could not have escaped your notice: in our wandering, we've paused right beside Cinemas One, Two, Three, and Four . . . where, if we wanted to right now, we could purchase tickets to any number of espionage films or exotic adventures . . . the filmic apparatus itself through which our market is so regularly displayed suggests that this mayhem is never accomplished without some minimal gesture toward technology, usually that of weaponry: Conan crouches at its center brandishing mace, mallet, or broadsword; Bond gambols about its edges with a gun, the barrel swollen by its silencer; and, in *Romancing the Stone,* Mike Douglas and Kathleen Turner manage their obligatory act of mercantile devastation using a grounded Leer jet!

And why, in those particular films in which our antagonists snatch their weapons, their battering objects, their hammers to be hurled, their knives to slash, their pots to throw, from the smashing, crashing stalls around them, is the effect both comic yet scarifying, as well as, somehow, both more intimately (i.e., psychologically) and allegorically (i.e., politically) right?

Isn't the "obligatory car chase" of the more contemporaneous slant of film merely the same scene replayed with props from the immense used car lot just to our right, written out in linear form to accommodate the axis of speed (its fundamentally cinematic order first delineated by René Clair in the runaway funeral procession of *Entr'acte* [1929?]) with its escalating scale of violence represented by smashed vehicle after smashed vehicle? (The automobile: major American sales object and symbol for both sexual and economic [i.e., *oikos,* the home, vid. domestic] success.) On the screen each car is reduced, at the point of impact, to a symbol of the quintessentially inessential consumption (visual, conspicuous) of the movie, the video tape, the paperback book it actually *is*—exactly what, on a smaller scale, each overturned potato and tomato basket, each shattered egg, each broken pot becomes at the point of spillage, smash-up, smithereens.

Each violence erases itself, or more accurately sublates itself into art, the moment it occurs. (How else could Ballard use precisely these crashes, divorced from their traditional narrative context, as *the* symbol of art?) Only in animation is this process rendered legible, vocal, self critical and thus free to signify outside the range we have here demarcated.

Political, economic, and commercial forces, all three, strive to drag this scene to both the temporal and conceptual center of the film. Those forces that are so lightly called aesthetic work mightily to position it at the story's "climax." Between the two, then, it circulates endlessly through all those positions that ellipse about these twin epicenters.

And in film after film, tale after tale, the violence erupts in a market whose unruffled order returns with each new story, invisibly and inevitably restored along with the famously and fabulously incorruptible leading lady's hairdo, an order that is always replaced—off camera and effortlessly—a moment beyond the sequence's final cut, a background order that foregrounds the violence playing across it in such a way as to suggest that, finally, the most popular item for sale *in* the market is the endlessly iterated image of its own devastation (an image wholly allied to the iterated ability of such devastation mystically, magically, and invisibly to heal itself, of the market's potential to absorb any and every violence to it). In the usual art/life reversal of values, it suggests that an imminent, unbounded, and originary field of violence is the grounding on which the market is actually built, over which, now and then, an instrumental order is, for that illusory moment at the beginning of such tales, such scenes, temporarily set in place, but only to initiate, operationalize, and empower its own devastation.

Then, in the penultimate scene—always somewhat anticlimactic to me—the antagonists have their final and fatal encounter, this time alone on some lightning lashed crag, in some rustling graveyard, or on a stormy spit thrust into the loud and moaning sea, in some sunken cleft, housing deep underground its dank, silent, glittering hoard, guarded by a demon or a corpse straddling the border between local life and eternal legend, where magical (read: metaphysical) values have replaced, or been revealed to lie beneath, those market values we just saw overturned. In the course of Kull's or Valeria's ultimate triumph, usually we glimpse some appalling depth or horror or monstrosity that suggests a realm of evil and secrets "man was not meant to know." Perhaps disingenuously, I take this as a conventional figuration of the inadequacy, not of humanity to metaphysics but of metaphysics to humanity—as well as the usual inverse through which the situation is traditionally mystified. At any rate, because of this encounter, our protagonist leaves the scene of triumph a little less surely than he or she might, pensive, contaminated by the encounter with metaphysics—but, presumably, to return to the market (restored, whole, harmonious), to everyday life, to the beggar girl or the merchant's son or the prostitute or the runaway boy or the barmaid or the slumming prince or princess, for whom the encounter itself will become another wondershot tale, another glittering, terrifying, and seductive object which, back in the market again, can enter the circuit of exchange as knowledge, as power, as tradition, where, precisely at the stall we began at, it ultimately stands for sale.

What I have recounted is, of course, the archetypal sword-and-sorcery tale that places my entire series—and, perhaps, every sword-and-sorcery story actually written—in the margins of this already marginal genre. For what we have described is an object of the background, of the lexicon, of analysis, only to be found in the Old Market, whereas what is actually to be read in Michael Moorcock and Karl E. Wagner, in C. L. Moore and Fritz Leiber, not to mention in Delany, is our always theoretically inadequate expressions of it, our endless battle with it, that always devalued material we are always purchasing (for inflated prices) in the New.

But let's turn from this central market activity that we have here valorized (and remember that term is itself from economics, and—unlike validate—means increasing the price of one object by lowering the price of others) to the parergon that connects it to (and separates it from) the rest of the city: desire.

It's been my pet notion for years (and you will find me offering it up for examination in various guises throughout the Nevèrÿon series) that the reason cities grow is that people in the provinces universally believe sex is more available there. Tribes leave an exhausted hunting ground for better hunting grounds because of food and the talk of good food. Individuals leave tribes for cities because of sex and the talk of sex—in a tribal context where, because of food, sex must be fairly carefully controlled. Each decade we discover cities are five hundred to a thousand years older than we previously thought. I wouldn't be surprised to find cities among the oldest of human institutions, rather than among the youngest. (It is only the *history* of cities that is new.) Çatal Hüyük is no longer the Enoch of archeology.

The economic underpinnings that stabilize cities at the infrastructural level are just that—the stabilizing factors in what is at base a structure of desire. (Language stabilizes thoughts, feelings, and behaviors in the individual and the group; cities stabilize culture, civilization, and forms of desire in groups and individuals—an amalgam that should also be called civilization or perhaps politics, but for which we really have no easy and accessible term.) I make this suggestion as only a diehard, card-carrying materialist can.

Sodom and Babel are our two archetypal cities, both destroyed by God (read: a mystified market collapse), both more than likely mirror images, if not intimate explanations, one for the other.

But now let me counter your specific, terminal question ("What does it mean to explicitly eroticize class relations?") with what, in a less rich array of notions, should have perhaps been my specific, initial offer:

Is anything ever eroticized *other* than class relations—or the signs of class relations, which, simply because they are not quite the same thing, allow for the necessary *shift* in class relations themselves despite the fixes of desire? (I choose not to read you as saying that eroticizing them *implicitly* is somehow better than eroticizing them explicitly . . .? Our Markets, both old and new, are places of display.) The racist term "fetishism" has a pejorative ring to it, thanks to its (racist) use in both Marxism and psychoanalysis. But I seriously ask you to consider the following.

Look at the Size Queen who is primarily interested in finding the biggest ones available: certainly this pursuit of genital or mammary proportions takes place wholly within a mythology of ethnic expectation: Slavs, Africans, Celts . . . French, Italians, Spanish—which, in any national landscape, is immediately reinscribed within and around specific class parameters. Consider, as another sort of limit case, the well-brought-up middle-class heterosexual white woman, who declares: "There isn't any physical type at all that I'm particularly sexually attracted to. All I'm really interested in in a man is personality and intelligence. . . ." Certainly to the extent this is an honest self-evaluation, we recognize this as code for: The people I find erotically acceptable are generally those in or near my own social class. (Only people in *other* ethnic/class groups *have* physical "characteristics" to be eroticized. Those in our own group are simply "normal.") Even bestiality or, say, wristwatch fetishism (worn low on the wrist, the watch is erotic; worn high on the wrist, anti-erotic) have their class decodings. Since all human signs have their class associated aspects, anything we find erotic *must* be an eroticizing of 'class relations'. Class relations are what the human universe—and by extension, the erotic universe—is made up of. The adolescent boy who masturbates to the image of the movie star pin-up or the Bunny of the Month, the adolescent girl who gets all dreamy over this season's Brat Pack sex symbol or MTV rock idol: both are eroticizing class relationships as much as any of the rest of us. The question should be, rather, why is the eroticizing of certain class relationships egregious and always made explicit in an accusatory tone, while the eroticizing of certain others is always mystified and allowed to remain implicit by calling that process anything other than what it is?

Like so many other questions, we begin to tease out the answer when we start to ask: Who *benefits* by the eroticization of certain class relationships? Who *suffers* by the eroticization of certain class relationships?

Let me hazard twin rules of thumb:

First rule: The harder a set of eroticized class relations is to name, the harder it is to name that set as specifically erotic, the harder it is to accuse that set of any taint of pathology (and the rhetoric of the erotic exists primarily to articulate minor or major socially constituted pathologies), then the more the eroticization of that particular set of class relationships benefits patriarchal *status quo* phallocentric society.

Second rule (and inversely): The easier it is to name, survey, and pathologize the eroticization of any particular set of class relations, then the more *dangerous* that set of relations—and their eroticization—is to patriarchal *status quo* phallocentric society.

What makes certain such relationships dangerous is that they represent lines of communication, fields of interest, and exchanges of power. Fundamentally, the working of these patterns is simple.

She or he who desires, listens. She or he who is desired, speaks. (At the stalls of desire it's always a seller's market.)

I might go so far as to say that to speak is to constitute oneself as a desired subject. To listen is to constitute oneself as a desiring subject. The archetypal domestic American complaint, "You don't really love me: you never listen to a word I say," is almost always justified. Why is the single greatest American phobia that of having to speak in front of a group? Because it requires not only bravery but a whole range of mental judo to act and feel as though one is loved by that group, which is what speaking effectively before a group demands. To anticipate our discussion here just a bit, at the same time as I would be the first to warn against posing any simple and uncritical relation or correlation between the two topics, I'd nevertheless hazard that the reason there are far more people who enjoy sitting in a theater than there are people who enjoy standing on a stage is the reason there are far more masochists than there are sadists. (The desire to love is masochism. The desire to be loved is sadism.) This is why the pedagogic relation always has its erotic side: people speak and listen, and the amount of speaking and listening is seldom equal. The Greeks understood it: the one who speaks (or is desired) has the one who listens (or who desires) under a certain power. For a middle-class man or woman to desire the lower or the marginal classes means that, whatever he or she makes of it, a middle-class man or woman spends a lot of time *listening* to what the lower or marginal classes have to say. It means that they are under that class's influence. This is, of course, dangerous to the *status quo.*

The argument that grows up against this situation is an old one—but finally disingenuous. It is the argument of the New Market. Just because you desire them, that doesn't stop your class from exploiting their class. It doesn't stop you, on a class level, from contributing to their oppression. You can't be friends with—or certainly not love—someone you buy something from. (It was the upper middle class who preserved a separate entrance for tradesmen.) Especially if what you buy is love or friendship. In this case, love/desire is hypostatized as the originary, metaphysical absolute to which any material exchange is always inadequate. (Your desire simply allegorizes, extends, and continues the class exploitation.) This inadequacy contaminates all relationships, pathologizes them, and renders them somehow unauthentic. But this is simple mystification laid over the fact that such relations are, over any statistical range, subversive—and they are dangerous particularly for the established, more powerful class.

What we're left considering after such a demystification is the question, where does sex actually lie in the range of marketable commodities? Does it provide a frame for the market in the sense of a frame for a house? Does it pervade the market, supporting it, holding it erect, giving it strength and structure, solidity, form, and endurance? Or does it frame the market as the frame of a picture, acting as a supplement mediating between the greater architecture of the city and this central site of exchange? Does it at once connect and set off what is inside from what is outside? Does an examination of the frame tell us more about the world outside the frame than the play of color and convention within it?

(The ambiguity marks, of course, Derrida's parergon.)

I'll begin to withdraw from between the aisles of this infinitely fascinating and wonderfully attractive—at least to me—set of speculations, suggestions, and interrogations by making only a few more points.

In the imaginary land of Nevèrÿon as, over the course of a decade or more I've envisioned it, I have tried—and failed—to write it, with its changes, its exchanges, its self-criticisms, its developments, its surprises, its constantly turning out to be in excess of, or inadequate to, any theory I could come up with for it, I have tried to show desire working in both directions, across all sorts of class lines. The only one I've consciously attempted to downplay is the one on which patriarchy grounds itself and through which it heals, over an historical period, all its wounds: that is the desire of women for men a microclass above their own. This is, of course, the one "sexualization of class relationships" perceived as somehow not really sexual at all. Its implicitness is its exploitability. This is the mode of desire by which most of the major, easy, and hardly ever redressable exploitations of women by men occur. The men are desired and talk. The women desire and listen. The women are under the men's influence. We know how the power relations run. In the Nevèrÿon tales, rather than subject it to analysis *or* theory, I chose simply not to support it with representation. Such desire is real; it is certainly no more evil than any other mapping of desire. But I try not to write about it—in the same way that a generation of liberal American writers simply decided that the rape of white women by black men was too politically exploitable a subject to reify at a particular historical moment. There are too many other desiring modes to explore, a major subversive battery of desires. But (your question) why do some of these others seem to get so much emphasis? Finally the answer must be in that strangely inseparable set of reasons that marks the indisseverable boundary between how I write and how you read.

The "fascination" with the lower classes, with lumpen characters, you find in the Nevèrÿon tales is probably more visible in the later stories.

Without downplaying the sexual component that hovers over your use of the word fascination, I suspect you'll find more such characters presented sympathetically, even seductively, in the last two volumes than in the first two. It doesn't require a critic overly sensitive to the history of my home, of my city, New York, to note that the shift toward the lumpen in the series documents the rise in the homeless population over the decade in which the Nevèrÿon tales were written. (The young smuggler, Arly, Joey, and Udrog all involved specific distortions of specific models. And characters more generally fictional, such as Noyeed and Clodon, have, for various of their aspects, all too *many* models!) A critic with a more biographical bent could, throughout the series, doubtless tabulate the general movement of social classes under the writerly eye against the general shift in my income over the same period. (The vacillations of the freelance writer's wages are notorious!) But a more specifically biographical elucidation would not yield much to surprise, say, a reader of *The Motion of Light in Water,* among all these other market data.

Desire and the Law, S/M

Much of your work seems to be about imagining radical changes in bodies, desires, and sexualities, imagining new mappings of sexuality onto the body. While your work presents displacements of the limit of sexual possibility, as well as of power and authority structures, it is nevertheless also always about the Law. Your most recent Nevèrÿon texts, *Flight from Nevèrÿon* and *Return to Nevèrÿon,* both explore a highly coded, explicit, and visible intersection/coincidence between power and sexuality: sadomasochism. These narratives seem to be processing the contemporary debates around sexuality and pornography, debates which concern the relationship between fantasy and reality. The treatment of S/M in your texts contests a belief that fantasy is continuous with agency, that sexual scenes are literal enactments of social power relations. How might literary representations work to transform the meaning of particular kinds of signs in the range of human behavior that tend to be frozen and fixed in the collective imaginary?

SRD: In a discussion even veering near such topics, for some time now my rubric has been one from a lecture Foucault gave at Stanford University a few years before his death. He said:

> We must get rid of the Freudian schema. You know, the schema of the interiorization of the Law through the medium of sex (Michel Foucault, "Pastoral Power and Political Power").

Let me see if I can find some way among these darker stalls we have—by accident? by design—wandered in among.

I have been writing about S/M in the Nevèrÿon tales now since, really, the third story of the series, "The Tale of Small Sarg." But it would be wrong to take Nevèrÿon as some sort of cutting edge, some radical limit work, an enterprise lucid with insight and ultimately authoritative, about S/M practices, in any of their forms, gay or straight. In the course of writing these stories, I've had some very heated criticism from people in the S/M community. There are those who consider these stories of S/M activities to be the worst sort of pandering, pussy-footing, and liberal backsliding.

The libidinal calculus underlying Nevèrÿon's sexual economy is a conservative one, for example, and one I believe operates throughout humankind: What is forbidden is eroticized.

I don't suggest this is the only mechanism of sexualization. Nor do I say that what is forbidden is *necessarily* sexualized. But childhood proscription is certainly *one* common factor in sexualization—that is, it marks out a field where sexualization is more likely than not to take place. The accoutrements of S/M—the swastika, the leather gear, the whips and chains—are sexualized, I'm sure, in fundamentally the same way that the visible apparel, the underclothes, or makeup and colognes of the opposite sex are sexualized: through an intricate combination of availability/social proscription in childhood.

The argument that the sexual acting out of S/M fantasies is a literal "enactment of social power relations" suffers from the same flaw I find in the general Platonic argument against art, i.e., the reproduction of the evils-of-the-world in art must, themselves, be evil. This is mere sympathetic magic.

To assume a session of "sexual torture" between two consenting adults requires only minimal reorganization of what goes on in an actual session of political torture—and in any way manifests the same "power relations"–signs only gross ignorance of the context *and* the substance of *both* situations!

But we are speaking of the Law . . .

That Law is imposed, of course, on all sexual situations. And the social censure S/M has received is an example of that imposition. But the reduction of that imposition to a circular argument where S/M is censured by the Law precisely because it carries, reveals, manifests, and reproduces the Law's own hidden and embarrassing truth—that it functions at once as the Law's explanation, origin, and ever present evil—is a contradiction that calls for some firm demystifying analysis. We simply must challenge this view that various sexual acts carry the Law innately within them, momentarily to write out their truth for the historically sensitive reader.

The nineteenth century believed that power could suppress sex. Albrech's denial of love that empowers him to seize the Rhinegold and Freud's elaboration of sexual guilt and its subsequent repression both figure that belief. Both tell the same story. And the twentieth century is only the orphaned child—and orphans can be direct descendants too, as that century never tired of reminding us in its novels—of the nineteenth.

I don't think the question is one of fantasy and agency, with the slippery and finally a-locable line of intention, of praxis, constantly called on to divide the two at some pragmatic point that puts the ethical, the moral, and the good all on the side of behavior—of those who don't actually Do Bad Things, however much they think about them.

"Fantasies can all be purchased at the Old Market. But agents only work at the New." The tale is much too simple.

The reduction of the problem to agency/fantasy terms does more to stabilize the situation than to resolve it. The fantasy/agency "world" is a world where all men, where all serious men, where all (legally) important men, where all authentic men, walk around all day desirous of raping every woman they see—but by Great Moral Strength hold themselves within the bounds of civil behavior. This Moral Strength alone prevents them from becoming agents *of* their persistent fantasies. (Anyone not living within this fantasy world is no longer, by that Law, a real, a notable Man.) It is a world where every real, notable, or legal woman must—it is the Law—consider every man she sees a potential rapist. Only by an act of intention, of moral will (it is called compassion, it is called generosity, it is called virtue—though sometimes it comes through innocence, which is one with ignorance, whose feminine good can only be revealed by the victimizing behavior of the knowing male), can she speak or acknowledge any man with less than total terror. Some women, souls destroyed by that terror, break down and, deranged, run about, like maenads, seeking rape (according to the Law there is no sex, only rape—date rape, marital rape, rape rape, S/M). These women are ill, mad, and evil because they have broken the Law.

I think this fiction is a vestige of the Law. I think this story is what the Law presupposes. It is not—nor do I believe it ever was—the origin of the Law (though again and again people try to tell us that it was). But it is what the Law has always aspired *to*. And it is what the Law always repairs itself *toward*, every time it recovers from anyone's attempt to revise it.

The problem is that "fantasy" and "agency" are two terms, each metaphysically adequate to the other; the two are mediated solely by the transparent and immaterial faculty of intention—acting out, as the psychotherapists are so fond of saying.

Their relationship is one of complete metaphysical adequacy—which occurs only in that world where language is adequate to the real, and the real pays off in totally fulfilled desire. Myself, I don't know many people who live there these days, though it is the source of most of our rhetoric.

The AIDS novel that is the ninth tale in the Nevèrÿon series, "The Tale of Plagues and Carnivals," lost me, or at least considerably cooled, one friendship with someone working at the AIDS Foundation in San Francisco. It's very easy for writers—indeed, it's almost expected of us—to defend ourselves against such ideological attacks by saying, "Well, everybody *else* just doesn't understand that it's a novel—not a political tract." But, one, the Nevèrÿon series has a fundamentally different relationship to criticism from that of the single, unified work. Its serial form was a direct attempt to allow for the intervention of a changing and developing critical sensitivity, my own—or others, to the extent I could hear what they said and make it my own. Two, I have made too many ideological criticisms of other writers not to recognize the symptoms of a criticism that clearly has weight to it, even if I still remain blind to some of its elaborations (which, in both the case of the criticism of the series's dealings with S/M and its dealing with AIDS, I do). Still, the dozen-odd Nevèrÿon tales represent a dozen cross sections through a continuing, progressing dialogue with the world, not a complex synchronous position.

I remember when I first became aware of the political dimension of sadomasochism. Years ago, when I lived in San Francisco (the year Ronald Reagan first ran for Governor of California), some young men and women were sitting around my living room, discussing the way women were portrayed in film. A number of us had just gone to see Hitchcock's recently released *Frenzy,* and you might easily reconstruct the comments made about the constant and continuous portrayal of woman as victim in such movies.

One of the young men, indeed one of my best friends and a valued member of the circle, happened to be a heterosexual sadist. Over the previous years it had come out in the way such things, with time, do: rumors among us . . . a few passing, marginal conversations . . . a confirmation—when one young woman in the group, months before, had become anxious about what we were hearing—that his diminutive and quiet girlfriend (herself very much, by choice, *not* a part of our circle's center) was nevertheless "a consenting adult" who, indeed, gained considerable pleasure from their relationship. You probably know the machinery. There were moments in that machinery's workings that I'm sure were quite painful to him. There were others that were certainly ugly to me. But finally, he had been "accepted," which is to say by now his sexual preferences were only mentioned in the communicational margins in which such a group, as it considers itself normalized, *ever* mentions what it takes to be "abnormal" about one of its members.

At any rate, as we sat discussing this new, late-Hitchcock work, with its astonishing and attenuated tracking shot that retreats from the murdered woman's corpse, down the stairs, out the building, and across the street (blinking only once, when a bus passes before it), gazing fixedly back as though the camera painfully, longingly, obsessively wishes to remain, to return, to stare at the body, and the comic/horror sequence that answers it—the truck we follow up the night highway, as it bounces and spills its produce from the tailgate, and we wait for the nude female body we know is secreted among the potato sacks once more and finally to tumble out into view (certainly *this* is a film that demands a "market" analysis!)—, one young woman commented: "I mean, where is a woman supposed to find a role model? Half the time I see myself on the screen, I'm either being murdered because I've dared to step over some social or sexual line—or I'm a spineless wimp with no life, no interests, and not even sure I'm there."

And my friend chuckled. "What kind of role model am *I* supposed to have. The only time I ever see myself on the screen, I'm a raving psychotic maniac and murderer."

Some of the people in the discussion became quite angry here, anxious and confused—with most of the anger directed toward the young man. (Remember, this was 1969.) It wasn't the same thing at all . . . *His* situation was different. He was a man, and besides he was a man who . . . well, that's just not the same . . . well, it was different. People like him were . . . well, not people like *him,* but . . .

Today my reading of the anger is this:

We had gone to such trouble to "accept" him, to place his "perversion" in a specially guarded margin of discourse! (I know that margin well. I am black; I am gay.) Suddenly, he was daring to speak, for himself, wholly outside that margin, on the same grounding of equality with the rest of us: people who had organizations behind them, who had articles written about their situations, who had already amassed quite a discursive weight. What a flagrant usurpation of power—our power, which we had so generously, till now, "protected" him from!

Indeed, I had two revelations at that moment.

First was simply the realization that there was a sadist subject which might want the same range of rights, political guarantees, and considerations as any other desiring subject. And it was precisely the sense of apparent contradiction in that sentence that indexes the extent of the political outrage of their withholding.

Second was the realization that the problem with the popular representation of marginalized groups had nothing to do with role models. Rather, it had everything to do with public language. The rest of us in the group—we *had* no language to make distinctions between Hitchcock's homicidal murderers and our friend. And as we sat there, struggling with our anger because of it, largely silent while he was there, mumbling after he'd gone—*we* were the ones who had been brutalized, not by a lack of an artfully or even sympathetically presented "role model," but by the lack of social discourse. *Whatever* we wanted to say, *whatever* point we wished to make, *we* were reduced to inventing our own language about it, then and there—not a situation that encourages articulation! Indeed, it is a brutal task. To the extent our friend was a reader of films and a buyer in the market of popular culture, he'd certainly been as brutalized as we. But he *had* spoken. And his speech had left us all but mute. The crime (not his; nor ours) was a brutalization of what can be said. What can be lived—though it is equally susceptible to brutality—takes place on another level.

I'd gone through my own version of this, you may remember, when I was in the mental hospital—it's recounted in *The Motion of Light in Water*—and I first told my therapy group about being gay. Certainly that experience helped me recognize it when I saw someone else going through it.

Indeed, it more or less completed a social exchange process which the incident in the hospital, four years before, had begun.

Now, you've concluded your question with an interrogation of literary representations. But as long as we stroll so closely beneath the eye of the Law (that keeps this market under strictest surveillance), I hesitate to speak of literary representation—or of fantasy, or of science fiction. Let me rather write of writing.

I will only say—here—that what you will find in the Nevèrÿon tales, such as "The Tale of Fog and Granite," "The Game of Time and Pain," "The Tale of Rumor and Desire," or, perhaps more centrally, certain chapters in *Neveryóna, or: The Tale of Signs and Cities,* is that which I've always considered to be my very idiosyncratic and personal view—which is to say, such a view *must* be blind to the social markers in circulation through and around it, to the social forces that wholly constrain it. The fact that I might perceive such a view *as* "idiosyncratic," *as* "personal," is the superscription on a coin whose exchange rate I already know as it circulates in the cultural market of ideation and ideological provender that has so dazzled us. It buys only critique, review, demystification, and analysis.

Writing/History/Fantasy

At the end of "The Tale of Plagues and Carnivals" (1985), you describe that narrative as "a document," while reminding the reader it documents both "fictions" and "misinformation." In a sense, this text seems both to present a dystopian fantasy and to document a response to the contemporary AIDS crisis. Your recent autobiography, *The Motion of Light in Water* (1987), is another kind of document, one that critiques the memoir as a genre. As well it recalls a sexual landscape that, in 1988, seems a kind of utopia, of a sort it would be very easy for men—and women—who have pursued a certain sort of life style up till now to grow nostalgic about. In any case, taken together, these texts demonstrate certain possible relations between writing and history. Could you address that relationship and some of the questions it entails? How might fantasy structures constitute a form of response to the crisis?

SRD: Here, among the Aisles of History, one stall toward the edge catches my attention. Of all the possible quotations displayed, how surprising that we should find this one from a critic such as Hayden White, writing in 1973:

> I begin by distinguishing among the following levels of conceptualization in the historical work: (1) chronicle; (2) story; (3) mode of emplotment; (4) mode of argument; and (5) mode of ideological implication. I take "chronicle" and "story" to refer to "primitive elements" in the historical account, but both represent processes of selection and arrangement of data from *the unprocessed historical record* in the interest of rendering that record more comprehensive to an audience of a particular kind (Hayden White, *Metahistory*).

The italics are, incidentally, White's.

If we momentarily bracket those philosophical problems specific to language and representation, it's fascinating, paradoxical, and a bit disarming how quickly and completely what remains of the problem of the relation of writing to history becomes wholly covered by, absorbed in, and one with the relation of historiography to marginality. Let's reread the motto above—remember, it comes not from a history but from a "metahistory"—that we have (re)placed in that convenient margin: What a happy, innocent, and untroubled historian it is who believes that an "*. . . unprocessed historical record . . .*" somewhere *exists!* For that is, of course, the metaphysical grounding, the impossible and nostalgic object, the hopeless and heartless lie that stands as the barrier against the history anyone concerned with writing the margins must analyze, must struggle against, must all but kill themselves to overcome.

But must we go through an entirely new market analysis to reveal that, in whatever market, in whatever aisles, we finally set up the antique stall of the historian, *that* is the historian we all—from time to time—are and must be?

Somehow, somewhere, we all assume, at least in bits and pieces, that that which is written down (the Byzantine concept of history-as-document) will somehow dissolve this problem once and for all. (*Nevèryóna*'s chapters eleven, twelve, and thirteen dramatize, however, some of what I feel are the most important, because most overlooked, relationships between writing and history at that basic level.) Still, when we can appeal so unproblematically to (even momentarily), when we can cite in so untroubled a tone of voice, "the unprocessed historical record," it means (for a moment?) we have forgotten the outrage of having someone walk up to us, take the historical record from our hand, and with a glare of rage strike out a word, a sentence, a page, an entire text, substitute another, and hand it back with a silent dare or an articulate threat—often of death—never to expose or even mention the substitution; it means we have once again lost sight of the even more troubling fact that such a process of mitigation, of distortion, of outright lies segues seamlessly into and is indisseverable from (at least in its results) that process by which time and the shift of allegiances alone rewrite and rewrite by minuscule amounts the collective memory of a generation, until those who in 19— acted and spoke and proclaimed repeatedly that X was wholly different and distinct from Y, now shout as a slogan, in the frenzy of total belief, "In 19— X equalled Y," claiming that they never thought or even suspected otherwise, begging to be buried with that as their epitaph, as if that alone would allow them entrance into a paradisiacal afterlife. Those moves our motto relegates to rhetoric by the prioritizing of this "unprocessed historical" grounding *are* the efforts of other historians to undo what they already perceive as mediation, in search of a truth that is only and finally fixed in the fiction of their own account, once created.

In *The Motion of Light in Water* I give in some detail my experience of the U.S. media coverage of the Cuban Missile Crisis. But the book is exemplary, not exhaustive.

I was not yet sixteen, for example, the first time I went to a demonstration at the U.N. at which a minimum of five thousand people—and quite possibly ten—packed U.N. Plaza like Times Square on New Year's Eve, crowding the streets around it to two or three blocks away, so that movement in them was all but impossible. Home by subway that same evening, I watched the eight o'clock news show only a group of eight or nine picketers, near the building, while the announcer reported, "This afternoon, some protestors at the U.N. showed up to . . ." The sixties—and, as far as I am concerned, my youth—ended on the morning of April 1968, when I had spent the long night listening to the live accounts (unprocessed? No, they were oral, they were shouted, often in terror, often in amazement, complete with the sound of horses' hooves, the screams of young men and women being beaten, and the thuds of clubs on bodies, coming through the on-site walkie-talkies, the sound of broken glass as another police horse crashed its hooves into a phone booth from which a youngster was calling in his report of what was going on outside it), of the police brutalities in the neighborhood of Columbia University that ended the weeks of sit-ins there, as they were broadcast (live) over WBAI-FM the whole night long. Half an hour later, on the seven o'clock news on WOR-AM, I heard a newscaster declare, "Last night there were minor disturbances at Columbia University, where students had been holding sit-ins. But the police had the situation under control by 9:30."

Is *this*, then, the unprocessed record of that night and morning? Of course not. The painful fact is that all accounts are processed—for the taking of account *is* a process, indeed is many processes, many of them different and most of them having nothing to do with "truth." The theoretical insight I have tried to draw from this (in *The Motion of Light in Water*) is that without a conflict in processes, there *is* no history. History begins only when we do *not* know what happened—when there is disagreement over what happened. When everyone "knows" what happened (and I know you can detect the irony in that epistemological dictum), there is only mythology.

And nothing is forgotten faster.

If the experience of the concentration camp—the Jews in Germany, the dissidents in Russia, the Japanese Americans in the United States—is *the* experience of the first half of the twentieth century, surely major media lies and distortion (from the paltry examples I have given to the media black-outs of South Africa and the like) is *the* experience of the second half.

Yet between the two extremes of external and internal revision there are certain historical economies, which constantly emplot history, which perhaps *are* history. We can find them in our market if we only let ourselves wander a little a-field.

Here are three marginal areas I've experienced. They will all be useful for their marginal points:

1) The tapestry of individual perception.

2) The development of science fiction.

3) The reality of AIDS.

All three are topics few of us would have any difficulty locating, by and large, "outside of History", with its usual suggestion of a capital H for Clio's centered art. What happens, then, when they are brought *within* history—not as a margin to be crossed, but as a process always already begun that is now taken over, displaced, revised, and operationalized?

It is precisely the first area, the tapestry of individual perception, and its lack of centrality to the historic that marginalizes the lived experience of any man or woman—even the most biographized political potentate or popular personality. The actual flow of sights and sounds and temperatures and feelings and associated thoughts and thought fragments of which history is always, on some level, a reduction (yet seldom an account) is what keeps all of us as individuals at history's edge. *The Motion of Light in Water* was—as I suspect every such memoir and account is—my vague and illformed attempt to write my own, brief, limited, and inadequate chronicle, story, emplotment of that rippling and evanescent tapestry. But let me tell you here an alternate marginal tale—dealing not with representation but with psychology.

When I was a child, I had a nightlamp.

I received it as a Christmas present, age four or thereabouts. The woman who had roomed at the back of our house moved out, and my sister and I moved into the room that had been hers. And the lamp—a nautical affair, about nine inches tall, with brass base and brass shade, a reticulated green glass barrel between—was hung from a bracket at the right edge of the double doors, nearer the wall with the windows, too high for my four-year-old hand. It had specifically been given to me for Christmas, and I recall my childish uncertainty as to why, then, it had to be used for both me *and* my younger sister. At any rate, when my sister and I lay down in our separate beds, it burned, green and luminous like a starboard ship's beacon, till we went to sleep, and our parents, retiring in the next room, turned it out. I would wake in the morning to see it, hanging in dawn light, its brass brilliant under the rose and gold coming around the shade, the drapes, and through the fibreglass before the Seventh Avenue windows, its barrel a dead black-green when not lit.

But lest you think this is mere nostalgia for a gleam of light on metal, for the ribbed green glass, I mention that, in our house, there was almost always a catalogue of children's toys from FAO Schwarz, a large and well-known toystore down on Fifth Avenue. The catalogue's cover was colorful. Within, however, during the 1940s, only black and white pictures figured the objects for sale. One day, when I found it in with some old magazines and sat down near the living-room chair on the rug to page through the gray shadows of trains and trucks and doll houses and puppets and chemistry sets and tinkertoys, I came across a picture that, after a frown and a blink, I realized was of my nightlamp.

With the recognition came a memory.

Months before, on the other side of some temporal abyss including both a Christmas tree and a birthday party, my mother had sat down with me, in the chair before which I sat now, with the same catalogue, and, paging through it, paused to ask me whether I'd like this or that toy. She had stopped at this very page, pointed her polished nail at that collection of gray and amorphous shadows, and asked me whether I'd like *that* for Christmas ("It's certainly something you could use," had been her comment, half to herself, half to me). Doubtless I'd nodded and said, "Yes," because there were certain questions that if parents asked you, you just said yes to, even if you didn't understand them at all, only to avoid the upset that accrued if you said no. But what came with the memory was the realization that at the time when she'd first asked me, I'd had no concept at all of what the object in the picture was, or, as far as I could tell, what it was supposed to do! I have characterized the lamp as nautical: there were little spokes coming out around the base. And on one side there was a representation, again in brass, of a ship's wheel. During that pre-Christmas perusal with my mother, I'd had no notion of what this ornament had been supposed to be. But in the intervening months, no doubt from some boys' book illustration of sailors and pirates, the ornament had become legible to me—along with the purpose and the use of the object, from simply having it hang beside the door.

That night when I went to bed and the lamp was turned on, I lay looking over the edge of the covers at it; and the knowledge of the picture in the catalogue—its sudden legibility—lent a second level of meaning to the lamp. As the second image gives the stereoptical picture its depth, now the lamp seemed wholly a different object. Two transformations had occurred:

For the first time I felt that the lamp was actually mine. At the same time I could sense in the nautical suggestions those resonances with precisely the boys' adventures that had allowed me to read the object—but only through the mediation of the catalogue photograph. Only the discovery of the photograph of it and—even more importantly—the memory of the photo from a field of previous illegibility had opened up about the object the resonant aura of subjectivity (ownership, romance, property, adventure), which it had been clearly constructed to commodify: which is precisely where the sensuality of the object alight in the dark, agleam in the dawn, joins with history—of the sea, of boats, of trade and shipping lanes.

Certainly I could not indulge this sort of analysis, wholly entailed with a future history of language acquisition, at four! But as certainly, I never looked at the lamp again without remembering and—as children will—pondering the transformation. How had it happened? Why? And when other objects called for that same transformation and did not achieve it, I thought of my lamp. When still others called and succeeded, I thought of it.

Again, so that we do not assume the path from this stall to the whole wondrous and romantic field of the market-and-history that we began with is a simple one, let's pursue the process over the following account:

After four or five years, the lamp broke. Some tug on the electric cord, too rough, and the little switch, a foot down the doubled rubber line, no longer made the bulb inside go on, even when it was changed. Then the lamp was gone, perhaps taken to a repair shop from which it never returned. Perhaps in the attempt to see if it was or wasn't the bulb, my father broke the glass. ("Both of you, really you're much too old for nightlights now. You don't really need it.") The bracket, however, with its double wire hook from which the lamp had hung, remained by the side of the door, under growing layers of paint—beige, green, taupe, through the several paintings of the house—now, every day, for the next half a dozen years, a new image to confront. The room was no longer mine and my sister's; we each had separate bedrooms on the third floor. But down in what was now the living room, with the couch on the back wall and, standing between the windows, the large, Zenith console television (purchased in 1951, a year in the general "televisionization" of the country, when the relation of the American people to the image underwent a fundamental and historical change, of which such rhetoric as this is only a marker), the paint-thick bracket, over by the sliding door, was still there. And when looking at Korda's *Thief of Baghdad* or Laurel and Hardy in *Babes in Toyland* on the television screen (even in these first years, what former generation had seen so many hours or repeated narrative images so frequently, so fragmentedly? would any other generation experience the transition between the two modes? could that transition be historified by anything else *except* a meticulous account of the changes in the flicker and play of light on the retina?), or any of the other fantasy films that were my favorites, I might glance over at the position of that so much more minor mark of romance, memorialized now only by the bracket from which it had once hung, to feel, if not to wonder at, the relation of the two orders of absence, the flickering on the glass screen, and the place on the wall, only lit by that flicker and shifting gray, their mediations and articulations dimmer than the photo in the vanished and many times replaced catalogue from which, like the wonder it had been, it had once been chosen.

As a presence then, as an absence then, we are dealing with an incident, an object, of significance—a significance replicated, modified, developed with each look, daily and throughout years. But it is precisely this chronicle, this tale, this emplotment that holds these looks, these gazes, and their luminous contents to the historical. (Where is the unprocessed historical record here? Though I have many times thought about it, this is the first time I have ever told the tale.) It lifts them from the wholly engulfing pool of nostalgia that flows through Lethe into the surrounding ocean of nothingness and non-being. At the same time, by preserving their origins in the sensory flow, the same account assures that they can never be wholly free of nostalgia. (Can *any* history be free of nostalgia? What is *more* nostalgic than war memories?) Now I have written an autobiography, *The Motion of Light in Water,* which you've read. And you will find no mention in it of that nightlamp, its catalogue photograph, or its painted-over bracket. But the reason the tapestry of individual perception remains external to history is that, whatever that book may be to the reader, for me it is—today—only the absence of any mention of that lamp. That is what invalidates it. That is what makes it merely a mention of some happenstance occurrences in a life only a fool might seriously think more than marginally congruent with my own, certainly not central, certainly not with like historical import. And if (and certainly you already know this), somehow, in some ideal future edition, I added this account to complete it, to correct it, to revise and rewrite it, to bring it in line with history, the process of inadequation would only repeat itself, as I fixed on some other, absent object, and the tale I might tell about the complex of its sensory reductions.

Thus the tapestry remains almost always folded up on the historical edge.

The barrier that keeps it there, despite such occasional breaches as this (for these barriers survive not as absolutes, but as inescapable statistical tendencies over the play of historical enterprises), is the economy of exhaustion.

But I have cited two other examples, for the economy of *their* exclusions: the development of science fiction and the reality of AIDS, both, in their separate ways, demonstrate orders of "marginality," both of which can be analyzed in such a way as to highlight a transformative economy stabilizing the interplay of exclusionary forces that separate happenings and historiography.

Let me proffer you, briefly and succinctly then, two "histories of science fiction." The first I claim unabashedly, with all the crankiness of the self-styled scholar, is the True History of my chosen genre. The second I call, with the just-suppressed ire and irony I'm sure you can read in it, the Academic History of science fiction.

First, the True History:

From 1911, when Hugo Gernsback first wrote his vignettes of the technological accomplishments of his hero, Ralph 124C41+ ("Ralph one-to-foresee-for-one plus"), till 1925, when he republished them in *Amazing* and they began to serve as a model for writers of what Gernsback wanted as SF editor, we are in the precritical period of SF in which all the difficulties of the world are presented as amenable to scientific solution.

In 1913, Proust published the first of a series of novels, *Du Côté de chez Swann,* at his own expense in Paris. In that same year, Edgar Rice Burroughs published the first of a series of novels, *Under the Moons of Mars,* at *his* own expense in Chicago. Practically everything in excess of the similarities of these two remarkably similar publishing events characterizes the difference between SF and literature. At the same period, English Literature was being constituted as an academic discipline in the universities of England and America.

In 1926, Gernsback named his genre "scientifiction" and, in his magazine, called on writers to write stories "like those of Poe, Verne, and Wells." At this point, we enter the flowering of this precritical period in SF when scientism dominates the field.

In 1929, the readers of Gernsback's magazines renamed the genre "science fiction" in the magazines' letter columns.

In May 1930, Ray Palmer published the first fanzine, *The Comet.* Today, over 800 fanzines are published in the U.S.

Both the appearance of readers in the pages of the professional pulp magazines and the appearance of professional writers in the pages of the amateur fanzines describe a closeness between readers and writers still characteristic of science fiction and not found in the contemporary literary genres.

In 1937 John W. Campbell took over the editorship of *Astounding Stories,* which shortly changed its name to *Analog.* The tradition of technological and scientific innovation founded in the Gernsback era was continued; but with Campbell's higher writing standards, as well as a generation of writers who had grown up reading the genre to draw on,

Campbell—in the stories that he encouraged—inaugurated a critique of the philosophy of science, carried on under a program of theoretical plurality.

With the end of World War II and the explosion of the Atomic Bomb at Hiroshima and Nagasaki, the focus of SF changed to that of history. At the same time, the series story, popular for years, took on a new substance and relevance. Many such series were continued in such a way as to force a rereading of them: e.g., E. E. Smith's *Lensmen,* Asimov's *Foundation,* Heinlein's *Future History,* Simack's *City,* and George O. Smith's *Venus Equilateral.* Now the genre's range presented a view of plural theories of history that spanned from images of historical guidance by unknowable, mystical forces, through historical materialism, through notions of individual charisma as well as historical necessity. This constant dialogue kept the field healthy and lively. Embroiled in such eristic wrangles, these stories responded with varied sensitivity to everything from the war itself to psychoanalysis and ideas of technological determinism. During this decade, via the fan group The Futurians, many SF writers and editors with definite and committed leftist leanings entered the field (including Asimov, Wollheim, Pohl, and Merril, who were largely responsible for the growing sociological sensitivity of the field).

Also in 1937 the first science fiction convention was held in Leeds, England. In 1938, the first U.S. science fiction convention was held in New York (both attended by under fifty writers, editors, and readers). Thus began a tradition of SF conventions. Today over two hundred are put on in the U.S. every year, many with more than a thousand attendees—more than two every weekend. Along with the rise in fanzines, the SF convention established lines of movement between fan and professional that gave a texture and flexibility to the SF genre unknown in the literary precincts. Ray Palmer (of *The Comet*), traveling the communication lines he helped to lay down, eventually became a writer and an even more important editor. The road from "fan" editor to professional writer and/or editor has been traveled by many writers since, including Bradbury, Ellison, and Zelazny.

Responding to a demand from both readers and writers for an even greater social awareness of more local problems, in 1949 *The Magazine of Fantasy* (which two issues later became *The Magazine of Fantasy and Science Fiction*) was established under the editorship of Boucher and McComas. And in 1950 H. L. Gold established *Galaxy.* While *Analog* continued the tradition of technological speculation, the other two magazines mentioned committed themselves to higher stylistic standards and far greater sociological density—as well as sociological sensitivity. The fifties in science fiction represent a decade of increased literary sophistication:

the finest works of Sturgeon, Bester, Bradbury, Walter Miller, and the more sensitive stories of Judith Merril and Fritz Leiber, as well as the collaborations of Pohl and Kornbluth are characteristic products of this decade. By its end, Pohl was the editor of *Galaxy* as well as of the two other magazines published by the "Galaxy Combine," *Worlds of IF* and *Worlds of Tomorrow.* And Merril, between her annual *Best SF of the Year* anthologies, with their extensive commentary, and her monthly F&SF book review column, had become the field's most important critic—in a constant, productive wrangle with SF writer and critic A. J. Budrys, whose book reviews appeared regularly in *Galaxy.* At the same time, under the impetus of the new technologies in typesetting, the paperback revolution was doubling, tripling, quadrupling the number of inexpensive books that could be published. From the end of this decade through the first half dozen years of the sixties, science fiction would appear extremely hospitable to young (or just new) writers of talent and serious intent. Writers to enter the field in this period include Roger Zelazny, Joanna Russ, Thomas M. Disch, Ursula K. Le Guin, R. A. Lafferty, Larry Nevin, and myself. As well, during this decade, major SF writers such as Charles H. Harness, Cordwainer Smith, and Alfred Bester, away from the field for various periods of time, now returned.

In April 1964, in London, Michael Moorcock took over the editorship of the English SF magazine *New Worlds* from Ted Carnell. English writers such as J. G. Ballard and Brian Aldiss continued to publish there. But a number of new writers, many of them American, were attracted to the magazine—or, in some cases, actively sought by Moorcock, including Zelazny, Disch, Zoline (who functioned primarily as an illustrator), and Priest. As well, poets D. M. Thomas and George McBeth appeared there. Moorcock's sympathy with the range of experimental writing encouraged these and other writers to go even further in their search for new writing techniques and to focus their fiction on new problems. This island of production in the growing sea of SF production was characterized as the New Wave.

Other important islands of SF production at more or less the same time were the twenty volumes of Damon Knight's *Orbit* anthologies (that ran from 1966 to 1978) and Harlan Ellison's *Dangerous Visions* anthologies (1967, *Again Dangerous Visions,* 1972—the island with which I had the good fortune to be associated). Both of these islands were often spoken of by readers later in the seventies as "new wave"—though for critics interested in the distinctions between these highly individual islands, in terms of aesthetic programs, stylistic approaches, and thematic focuses, this is a rather obfuscating usage.

In April 1970 Moorcock stepped down from the editorship of *New*

Worlds and the New Wave proper—that particular island of production associated with *New Worlds*—more or less dispersed.

The end of the 1960s saw, most importantly, an explosion of feminist science fiction, In 1968 Joanna Russ's novel *Picnic on Paradise* continued her Alyx series from *Orbit.* Ursula Le Guin's *Left Hand of Darkness* appeared in 1969. Later Russ' story "When it Changed" (from *Again Dangerous Visions*) won the Nebula Award in 1973. And her novel *The Female Man* appeared in 1975. That decade was also characterized by the growth of academic interest in science fiction. The English journal *Foundation* was established in 1972, joining *Extrapolation* (1959); and *Science Fiction Studies* was established in 1973.

I will cease my history here, and only note that with this new academic interest we also get a new history of SF. That history is much simpler—and much briefer—to write; these aspects alone militate in large part, I suspect, for this Academic History's eventual triumph over the history above:

This new history posits an uncritical period that extends almost as far back as you want to go, through Kepler's *Somnium* (1656) and Cyrano's *Voyage to the Moon* (1657)—even to Dante or before. This precritical period runs, without articulation, up through the work of Verne (*20,000 Leagues Under the Sea,* 1870), Bellamy (*Looking Backwards, 2000–1887,* 1888), and Wells (*The Time Machine,* 1895) on into the twentieth century, sweeping up Zamiatin's *We* (1927) Huxley's *Brave New World* (1932) and Stapledon's *Last and First Men* (1932), *Odd John* (1935), and *Starmaker* (1937) as it goes.

The first important event of this history in what we *usually* think of as science fiction is 1937, when Campbell takes over *Astounding.* This begins a period which runs to Hiroshima, in which science fiction (claims this history) presents the world's difficulties as accessible to scientific solution.

From 1945 (Hiroshima) to 1950 (the establishment of *Galaxy*), this attitude slowly changes.

From 1950 (Gold's *Galaxy*) on, SF condemns the false and dangerous claims of science.

From 1960 through 1975, SF is characterized by a search for new literary techniques and the discovery of ecology . . .

And—*voilà!*—this history is done.

Besides the simplicity of this second "history," I would bring to your attention at least three overall patterns as you go back and compare them. One: most of the characteristics cited in the second history (belief in science, literary sophistication) happen ten to fifteen years *later* than they do in the first. Two: there is no mention of any specific incident or aspect that distinguishes science fiction, as produced in marginal pulp magazines and at the cultural boundary of America's reading practices, from literary production. Three: there is no sense in the second of science fiction as a concerted response of its writers, editors, and readers either to events among themselves or to events in the larger world—such as the Second World War. This "science fiction" simply grows, changes, reflects the world about it—but never responds critically in any way *to* it.

Besides the displacement of characteristics from one history to the other, the second may strike us as familiar in other ways. What this second post 1937 history mirrors almost perfectly is the history of the general middle-class attitudes toward technology and science in the United States.

The academic literary critics who, slowly, have made this the history of my genre are largely people who come out of a critical tradition where the "value of literature" is often assumed to be that it "expresses the spirit of the times." These critics work in an intellectual landscape where science fiction is a devalued form and considered a debased writing. Their overwhelming urge is to legitimate it; the overwhelmingly available method of legitimation is to create a history for it that "expresses the times." Since the technological concerns are still there in the *Analog* stories of the early forties, these critics highlight them—there—for the purpose of that legitimating history—even though those technological concerns express little or none of what is specifically interesting, new, overwhelmingly evident, or, most importantly, at odds with the establishment literary concerns (i.e., before the war, the critique of the philosophy of science and after it the exciting range of historical plurality) in the SF of that period.

As far as the fifties' "condemnation of the false claims of science," all one can say is that from the self-styled "Golden Age of SF" of the late thirties and forties to last year's cyberpunks, the range of science fiction has never been antitechnological—though certain writers have gained a modest crossover popularity (and practically lost their generic following as a result, e.g. Ray Bradbury, Vonnegut), by espousing such a position. But because a good deal of America went through an antitechnological phase from the end of the sixties through much of the seventies, a similar "phase" (in which these lost writers are privileged) is cited for SF.

But more important than all of this, what gets lost in this second history is that the writers of SF of this period were themselves, overwhelmingly, marginal—always marginal economically, often marginal politically (frequently to the left but sometimes, as with Heinlein, to the right). And they were writing in a tradition that was, first, wholly and openly expelled by the literary establishment of the United States. Second, they were writing within a tradition that has always seen itself opposed to the social and cultural mainstream. That, indeed, this tradition has a history of its own, different from that of either "literature" or "the times," concerned with different values—concerned with values different from those that the mainstream of our culture would occasionally attribute to it—should be expected. (Does one go to Christians for the history of Judaism?) But it is precisely the oppositional nature of this history that is abolished before an economy of legitimation/delegitimation. For what the Academic History of science fiction tells us is that the two economies are one—you cannot legitimate one thing without delegitimating another. And our initial stroll through the market has already shown, you'll recall, that this is the economy of valorization—the increased valuation of one object through the devaluation of another.

Isn't it a strange route that has brought us here to our third marginal topic, the reality of AIDS? But then, it is precisely the profusion of this market that requires this cheek-a-jowl packing of its products.

The reality of AIDS . . .

The writing of history . . .

Reality . . .

History . . .

Aren't we terribly close, in this juxtaposition, to something fundamental in our initial problematization? What is "history" the history of, if not of reality? That, of course, is the nostalgic cry that echoes in the motto we have by no means left behind—we have only wandered around to the other side of it.

Only, here, we must ask: what happens if, as in the case of AIDS, that reality is constantly and catastrophically—with the death of thousands as both result and cause—changing?

To historify—much less to chronicle, to story, to emplot—a changing reality (a reality that has changed so catastrophically in the seven years since the syndrome acquired a name [1982] or the five years since Gallo isolated a viral agent [1984]), suggests we are no longer engaged in history at all. We search for revisionary concepts to fix the task. Foucault's archaeologies? *Les histoires des mentalités?* Docudramas? They are scattered about in our market—and all are inadequate.

In my own emplotment of one period in that changing reality, "The Tale of Plagues and Carnivals"—when AIDS transformed from a disease without a medical cause to one with a presumed virus—my use of the term "document" should probably be read as a gesture to that inadequacy (a document wholly and heavily processed, if not a document such as, in *Neveryóna,* Pryn leaves ghosted in the wax on which she and Yrink inscribe and dispute the production accounts of the brewery where she works in the second half of the book, a document protecting this person, exploiting that one). I say this, because to read my use of "document" as a gesture toward some baseline reality or unprocessed history is to misread it—and, I suspect, to misread the whole Nevèrÿon series.

Yet, at the same time I know that from time to time, as in White's passage, it *must* be read in the other way, as much as it irks me.

If the historification of science fiction has revealed, through the economy of valorization, how one history replaces another, the changing reality of AIDS has made embarrassingly clear to me the way in which, through the economy of the mutual tripartite inadequation of desire/language/experience realities *must* always shift. And it is through this tripartite economy of inadequation that the economies of exhaustion and valorization both function.

The discrepancy between what we desire (want, wish for, expect) and what happens contours the space in which language repeatedly and repeatedly occurs. The discrepancy between what we say and what happens is the endlessly repeated locus of desire. And the discrepancy between what we desire and what we say revises and revises the space *of* what happens *to* what happens (our experience *of* our experience, if you will). Yet by the same tense tripartition, none of the three will ever be adequate to the other; and their inadequacies are a field for play, slippage, endless revision and changes on and in all three. For some time now I have believed that the various attempts to omit "what happens" (that most beleaguered category, lived experience) from theoretical primacy, to reduce it to desire and language alone, is, itself, the metaphysical move that (mis)establishes language as wholly capable of expressing, as wholly adequate for, and as completely transparent to, desire. It is a similarly structured move that, obliterating language, sets desire and action (another aspect of what happens) immediately flush. It is a similarly structured move that, obliterating desire, sees language as wholly adequate to experience. But this is why I stress the three and the economy of their mutual inaccessibilities.

Now AIDS has marked an area in the social market where language, desire, and lived experience have all functioned at great intensities—and often functioned in opposition. In the market of AIDS, whether it be the gay man trying to negotiate his pleasures, or the government official trying to negotiate a grant, what we say we do—or say we should do—is often hugely at odds with what we do do. Likewise, what we wish and what we are compelled to do have often been in equal tension.

Indeed, in many respects AIDS has acted as a microscope in which the ordinarily ignorable tensions between the three—language, desire, and experience—have been magnified to frightening size.

But let me refer only to a few lines from my 1984 novel, "The Tale of Plagues and Carnivals", that you have questioned: in July 1983, Peter, the volunteer AIDS worker at the GMHC, says at brunch: "But we still don't have any reliable statistical prototype for sexual behavior. In my own experience, I see a leaning toward IV-needles and passive anal. But that's what they're calling anecdotal evidence these days. Everyone's got some, and it's all different" (p. 206). And further on, the narrator muses: "CMV, ASFV, HTLV, Hepatitis-B model, retroviruses, LAV, the multiple agent theory, the popper theory, the double virus theory, the genetic disposition theory (the eternal Government Plot theory!), the two-population theory . . . no one will understand this period who does not gain some insight into these acronyms and retrieve some understanding of how they *must* obsess us today, as possible keys to life, the possibility of living humanely, and death" (pp. 217–218).

I think of both as two of the more "documentary" passages from the novel—though I will never be able to tell you precisely how far a taped transcription of that July morning's conversation would differ from my written account a day or two later in notes, or from my still fuller written version six months later from memory—in short, I could tell you nothing precisely of the "process" that produced this particular (let me call it historical) historical emplotting.

But now let us trace the status of these enunciations across the various "reality shifts" that have intervened between their utterance and now. Notice that as late as October 1984, when the book was in galleys and I was writing my concluding necessary and nonfiction postscript, the mention of anal passive intercourse and IV-needles was *still* considered merely "anecdotal." In my official postscript, I no more felt I could responsibly mention these than I could suggest magic potions or blessed talismans as cures. Indeed, *what* I felt obliged to write in that note, though everything inside me strained to modify it, was, "Given the situation, total abstinence is a reasonable choice"—though I am obliged to add now that total abstinence was never my *own* choice; though the "anecdotal evidence" I based my own behavior on was, as I look back on it, pretty shaky—if lucky.

By 1986 (two years after the book was written, a year after it was published) "anal passive" was now constantly referred to as "high risk" behavior, with its suggestion that there were other behaviors that were of lower risk, and with the equal suggestion that all sexual behaviors lay on a graduated scale involving *some* risk or other.

Since the February 14, 1987, edition of *The Lancet* published the Kingsley, Kaslow, Rinaldo et al. study, the reality of AIDS has undergone another equally catastrophic change. The result of this and like studies has been among the *least* disseminated information about the disease, so I will summarize it here. But let me start by saying that what this information may well mean is that we will come to look on the rhetoric of "high risk" (and "low risk") behavior—along with the rhetoric of "repeated sexual contact" that for several years now has accompanied it—not as responsible caution but rather as a discourse as murderous, pernicious, and irresponsible as the various antisemitic and racist pronouncements from Germany before and during World War II.

In the Kingsley, Kaslow, Rinaldo et al. study, 2,507 gay men, all of whom tested seronegative for HIV (that is, with no antibodies to the virus, and so who had presumably not come in contact with it) were monitored for six months. All were asked to fill out detailed sexual questionnaires. At the end of that six month period, 95 individuals had seroconverted.

Of those 95 individuals, from the questionnaires they kept, *all* but three had engaged in anal receptive intercourse *at least once.* Those three had all engaged in anal insertive intercourse. Also from the diaries of the rest, of 147 men who had engaged in oral intercourse but who had *not* engaged in anal intercourse, there was *not one seroconversion.*

Is such a study "conclusive"? Of course not. But so far I have not seen any study that contravenes its results. And what it strongly suggests is that—in terms of the sexual transmission of AIDS among gay men—we must throw out the whole notion of "high risk/low risk" behavior as well as of "repeated sexual contact." Eight percent of those who seroconverted had only a single encounter of anal passive intercourse: clearly, then, one encounter is enough, if it is with an infected partner. We can now say, in all reasonableness, that AIDS *is spread sexually by gay men through anal intercourse.* If it is spread sexually in any other fashion, that fashion represents a small or minuscule percentage of those who have contracted it.

The ramifications of this are monumental and tragic. It means that from 1982 people were told "total abstinence is a reasonable choice" who should have been told "do what you want but don't get fucked in the ass; and if you must, use a condom." That last is "realistic"—in all senses of the word—advice; that is, it's advice which is followable. The exhortation to "total abstinence" is not.

History has already told us that.

But it is arguable that with the proper advice, of the 70 percent of the

80,000 or more who have contracted AIDS sexually, 95 percent or more of them might still be alive! That is a staggering thought.

Yes, it seems there *are* two populations among gay men. There are those who get fucked—those who get fucked without condoms; and there are those who don't. And that is the difference between those who are at risk from AIDS and those who aren't.

Today, almost two years after Kingsley, Kaslow, Rinaldo et al., I can no more officially "advise" gay men to abandon all sexual precautions save those involved with getting fucked than I could advise those magic amulets. Such advice would be as socially irresponsible as it would have been to mention in my official postscript of October 1984 "anal passive" and "IV-needles" as "particularly" dangerous in the spread of AIDS. But the fact that—two years after the study—I can *not* say anything more specific in an official voice is one of the reasons the "anecdotal" has become *the* important language in the AIDS situation; its tales are what must be the focus of any history of the epidemic. (More accurately, what is required is a history of the abysmal split *between* the anecdotal and the official.) And that is because of the flagrant inability of all "official" language (be it mine, or Susan Sontag's purusal of the metaphors of AIDS) to deal with the situation in anything approaching a responsible manner.

The other terrifying fact in all this is that *there is no scenario available for the transmission of* AIDS *to women.* Similar studies, which must involve women keeping similar sexual diaries, have just not been done. Common sense suggests that a good number of those women who have contracted AIDS sexually have also contracted it anally. But the fact that no one has done a similar study to explore the possibilities of vaginal transmission in women is the single greatest piece of sexual oppression women have suffered in our day. The lack of any such study—and the endless excuses for it that I have heard, largely from men ("Women don't want to know such things." "Women won't give you such information." "You can't fairly ask women to write about such things.")—is criminal. But the absence of this information, either as monitored document or anecdotal document, makes the current criticism of "women's bodies" seem strangely misplaced; and until such a scenario is established, we live in an age that can only be characterized as monstrously heterosexually repressive—with that oppression as usual tendered almost wholly toward women.

From what we do know of the situation of gay men, there is a good possibility AIDS is a disease men can pass to women but that, save in highly unusual circumstances involving sores on the penis, women cannot pass to men. And while all my sense of symmetry rebels against the notion, it *must* eventually be documented one way or the other. Until it is, heterosexual women can no longer have sexual lives, but must live in the same anxiety ridden state of shadowy sexuality that characterized half a dozen years of the sex lives of gay men.

Such scenarios must become facts of history. But they have yet to be documented, written, and entered into our cultural market. The only way they can do so is through a careful and accurate articulation of language, desire, and experience. I can only conclude this meditation on history and writing with this observation—as an exhortation to vigilance, a *caveat emptor:* "let the buyer beware."

Once again, history begins as a field of active ignorance—only another term for what Husserl called "the passion to know." All research can do, as we use one document to untangle the processing of another, is inscribe that field with probabilities. For no document can ever be *known* to be a hundred percent correct. And the economies of distortion highlighted by our discussion of marginality are at work, of course, throughout. I say this as a gay man who lives his life against such probabilities day by day.

So there is to be no reading here, then, that this instability or these changing realities or the shift in these probabilities make them any less serious. They are just as much a matter of life and death as they always were.

At the end of your question you have made a gesture toward fantasy; and here, at the end of my answer, I'll gesture in return. To the extent that fantasy—the sort of fantasy I write, that appears in the margins of the SF shelves of bookstores, and at whose margins my novel about AIDS lingered for a few months in 1985—is a legible form, a lisible practice of writing, a formal fiction, it is no more exempt from these economies than any other writing practice, including history. And I would only warn the buyer (another *caveat*) that anyone who expects fantasy to escape them in any way, simply through its particular order of mimesis, will be bitterly disappointed.

What have we found, then, in this forage through our markets' margins?

That the economy of exhaustion is always at work between the tapestry of perception and its reprocessing into any sort of historical account.

That the economy of valorization is always at work when history is revised into being: for that economy is also the one that tells us history is never originally written, but *only* revised.

Finally, that the economy of the inadequation of language, desire, and experience forever creates the field on which the above economies (as well as the more blatant processes of external corruption, internal distortion, and media manipulation with which we began) can wreak their political violences.

The job the fantasy—or science fiction—writer shares with the historian is to work against all these economies, by pitting the goods of one market constantly against the goods of the other, by constantly comparing goods from one part with goods from another, before any price is fixed, before anything is bought.

5.

Some *Real* Mothers . . . : The *SF Eye* Interview

This text began as an interview conducted and recorded by Takayuki Tatsumi at Lunacon, in Croton, New York, in April 1987. I rewrote the transcription over the next month. It was published in a 1987 issue of Science Fiction Eye *(Volume 1, Number 3), edited by Stephen P. Brown out of Washington, D.C.*

The interview is dedicated to the memory of Alfred Bester (1913–1987)

Takayuki Tatsumi: Let me begin with a brief introduction. Last autumn [1986] it was very exciting to watch you teach science fiction—especially the cyberpunk writers—at Cornell University, where you were a senior fellow at Cornell's Society for the Humanities, and I had a chance to sit in on your seminar. Chiefly, you focused on a comparison of John Varley and William Gibson, along with a psychoanalytic reading of their works, giving us an insight into what's going on in the current history of science fiction. Today I'd like to discuss with you your thoughts on cyberpunk, and SF after cyberpunk, based on your experiences at Cornell. To begin with, let me ask you, how did you like Cornell?

Samuel R. Delany: Well, it was a wonderful experience. It gave me a chance to talk about some ideas that had been percolating down for a year or more. Also, it was just a chance to think.

Paradoxically, the one thing that professional writers—writers who earn their living from their work—are not encouraged to do is think.

I don't mean thinking about your work—how to make it better; how a sentence might be interpreted; how a story might be read; what you can use in everything from your afternoon walk by the grocery to the TV movie you catch at three in the morning. That's the way a hunter thinks about hunting, or a dry cleaner thinks about cleaning fluids. It has too much the mark of necessity and survival.

I mean thinking as an abstract process, where, in a social situation, problems—or even situations—are put before you, and, in discussion or alone, you're encouraged just to think about them. Since I've come back [from Cornell], I've finished one long story (or short novel), "The Tale of Rumor and Desire," that is part of a new Nevèrÿon book, *Return to Nevèrÿon.* I couldn't tell you directly how much of the Cornell experience went into it.

The landscape did.

There's one scene in a gorge, which is primarily one of the Ithaca gorges (at Treeman Park) transformed a bit.

TT: The influence of landscape upon literature is very intriguing. However, J. G. Ballard's "inner space" seems quite different from Gibson's "cyberspace"; Ballard's springs from his own experience in China; cyberspace functions both as the product of a high-tech imagination and as the playground for a certain stylistic experimentation. In this sense you were right when, in class, you compared Gibson's cyberspace to Alfred Bester's typographic experiments that configured Gully Foyle's synesthesia while he space-time jaunted in *The Stars My Destination.* Could you tell me a little bit more about the relationship between scientific idea and science fictional style?

SRD: My first thought, when you bring this up, is not so much a stylistic one as a formal one. Science fiction has often taken new areas of conceptual space, then inflated them with language. The very first turning to outer space as a real place to write about, by Leinster, Heinlein, Williamson, and Van Vogt, was very much the same verbal strategy.

Suddenly there was a new space to deal with.

Then you inject a great deal of lyrical language into this particular area and see what happens to it, happens in it. And that's what Gibson is doing with cyberspace . . . it's a similar strategic move. A thought on form, but it has its stylistic aspect—it makes a stylistic distinction.

TT: Did that have anything to do with your selection of the Robert Heinlein and Roger Zelazny stories for your seminar?

SRD: No, this is actually a pretty new idea to me. It's not one I've spent a lot of time thinking about. The selection of the Zelazny and Heinlein stories had to do with their approach to psychoanalysis—the use of psychoanalysis in Heinlein's "The Roads Must Roll" and in Zelazny's "He Who Shapes" . . . although the dream space in "He Who Shapes" is very similar to cyberspace: both are conceptual spaces that, with the help of technology, we can enter. You can die in either one. The language with which Zelazny talks about the dreams that Render can control is very different from the general narrative voice of his tale in the same way that the language that Gibson uses to discuss moving through cyberspace is different; in the same way that Bester's synesthetic language in *The Stars My Destination* is different. The original title for "He Who Shapes" was "The Ides of Octember"—which is to say, a figure of rhetorically distorted language. The ides of Octember, you'll recall from the story, is a time whose possibility or impossibility we can only even talk about when we are in the dream space created by the Ro-womb.

That beautiful, poetic, and ultimately noncommercial title was taken off the story by its initial editor, Cele Goldsmith, because it did not name the subject (in either sense) of the story. It was rather a verbal tag for a pertinent subspace—the space that the story was about. It was a sign of a space in which language could be distorted in a certain way, giving us access to certain purely verbal constructs.

TT: It reminds me of one of your own verbal constructs, your title *Starboard Wine.* Even the title *Dhalgren* is a tag for a particular process, created of expectation and verbal highlighting, rather than a name for a person or a place that the book will then observe, explore, or circle in on.

SRD: Outer space itself began as a kind of subspace that sat next to . . . well, planetary-surface-space.

TT: Roger Zelazny is one of the authors Gibson doesn't mention often. But surely his second novel, *Count Zero,* reminds us greatly of Zelazny. Does that also have something to do with it?

SRD: Maybe Gibson is blind to any mention of Zelazny because they're too much alike. There's a certain stylistic thrust Zelazny and Gibson share. Both of them indulge a kind of Jacobean gorgeousness, coupled with a love of the "hard-boiled." Also the initial excitement both generated in the SF readership at the very beginning of their careers—Zelazny from '62 to '67, Gibson between '81 and '86—is similar. The initial image of both is that of considered stylists.

TT: What about your seminar selection of another story, "Baby is

Three," by Theodore Sturgeon? That has something to do with intersubjectivity, as you've mentioned . . . perhaps?

SRD: Again, the reason I selected it, at the time (for one of the three introductory stories we dealt with before launching into Varley and Gibson per se) was because the frame of the story was a psychoanalytic session; and, at that particular point, I was dealing with science fiction's view of psychoanalysis.

The proposed structure of the seminar was first, you'll recall, to pull out of, or even to construct from, a reading of Heinlein, Sturgeon, and Zelazny a kind of composite science fictional view of psychoanalysis. I wanted to read this science fictional construct closely against Lacan, the two of them mutually critiquing one another. You'll recall from the seminar that, by and large in SF, the initial point of transference is not the father but the state. It's there in a patently politically conservative work, such as in Heinlein's "roads Must Roll," it's there in an insistently liberal work, such as in Zelazny's "He Who Shapes." It's put most clearly in Sturgeon's "Baby is Three," during Gerry's bit of free association, where he thinks: "I ate from the plate of the state and I hate."

Ten years ago Luise White (in the "Women in Science Fiction Symposium," *Khatru,* 1976) noted that, for a male-dominated field, SF had an astonishing range of active, vigorous women characters—far more than many of us suspected—authored indiscriminately by men and women. But she also went on to point out an overriding pattern: These women invariably worked either directly for the state, or for some male-run institution that controlled so much power and revenue, it might as well be a state in itself.

These are not patterns common to naturalistic fiction. But they are inescapable as soon as you turn to science fiction. From Susan Calvin (the psychiatrist in Isaac Asimov's Robot series) to Molly Million (the mercenary adventurer of Gibson's world), science fiction has an astonishing gallery of good "phallic mothers." But their bosses either are the state, or are financially powerful enough to challenge, threaten, and topple states. This fact is intricately related, somewhere in the political unconscious of science fiction, to the transference phenomenon we've already noted.

It was only after teasing out—or putting together—this theoretical superstructure that I wanted to use it to read a pre-cyberpunk writer such as Varley and a cyberpunk proper (if one can speak of such) such as Gibson, and see the movement from one to the other, as the SF field had made them centers of excitement and attention, in terms of it.

We were only partly successful.

But it's hard not to note that the psychoanalytic session turns memory itself into a kind of subspace: a space of narration, of nostalgia, of ideological intricacies (i.e., a space of blame and resignation), and of lyricism.

Paraspace would really be a better term than subspace.

If we're going to explore this idea further, we have to note that our paraspaces are not in a hierarchical relation—at least not in a simple and easy hierarchical relation—to the narrative's "real," or ordinary, space. What goes on in one subverts the other; what goes on in the other subverts the one. They change their weights all the time, throughout their stories. So calling it a subspace—with the prefix's strong suggestion of subordination—is wrong. A paraspace, or even an alternative space, with its much weaker—and more problematic—question of position and troubling supplementarity, is more to the point.

TT: In terms of cyberspace, it all does seem to have started with Bester's synesthetic effect. As we read through *Neuromancer,* we hear punk music throughout the visual images from the high-tech world. How do you describe that kind of syn-esthetics?

SRD: You can only draw it out from an actual examination of the rhetorical figures used to write about these paraspaces. I'd have to have the texts in front of me, and point out the actual verbal plays that constitute the text of cyberspace, that constitute the text of synesthesia, that constitute the text of the "Ro-Womb" in "He Who Shapes." It's the same kind of thing that happens in Algis Budrys' 1960 novella, "Rogue Moon." Inside that strange alien artifact—a hundred meters across, twenty meters high, and, significantly, on the dark side of the moon—things of great import happen . . . they result in death for Al Barker—again, and again, and again. Yet, these spaces are very different from standard FTL "hyperspace," that instrumental space we pass through in order to bridge great distances, where, in most stories, we spend only a second or two, a sentence or two. That's a functional and useful—and at the same time highly subordinated—space. In its functionality, in its usefulness, it's subordinated to the plot, to getting from here to there.

This alternative space is a place where we actually endure, observe, learn, and change—and sometimes die. With these paraspaces the plot is shaped, as it were, to them. And inside them, the language itself undergoes changes—the language the writer uses to describe what happens in it is always shifted, is always rotated, is always aspiring toward the lyric.

In the case of Budrys, the passage through this space splits the subject: into an M (or moon form) and into an L (or laboratory form, back on earth), while the space itself, merely a complex of "rules, and crazy logic; Alice in Wonderland with teeth," remains impassive, unresponsive, yet murderous.

Finally the synesthetic passages in Bester accomplish something very close to this same splitting, or doubling, of the subject: the Burning Man, that demonic version of Gully, which keeps appearing at moments of tension throughout the story, and whose origin, we finally learn, is that mystical conflagration in the cathedral, towards the book's climax.

It would be interesting to look at a number of these various paraspaces in terms of the way the language is used within them.

TT: You presuppose, very naturally then, a consistency between the scientific idea and your own style of working—or language: the technologically constituted paraspace becomes the locus of a more lyrical language. In your own work, *Babel-17,* say, the paraspace would be the discorporate sector—first in the port city, then in the great shadow ship. As in "Rogue Moon," this paraspace is also associated with death. It's the space where a whole necessary aspect of rhetoric, involving the shifters "I" and "you," is learned. In *The Einstein Intersection,* the paraspace would probably be the source cave—which is associated with history (and is also where Lobey first sees, in the old television, Kid Death directly): In these paraspaces death and history seem somehow to bear a relation at once antagonistic and complicit. In *Nova,* we only spend one brief, bright moment in it, when the Roc passes inside the hollow of the nova itself; and we encounter the words "deaths," "death," and "dead" at least five times.

SRD: You know, the one writer I never figured this applied to was me . . .

TT: It's interesting that in a later work, like *Triton,* your paraspace is completely social: the unlicensed sector in the Tethys complex, where the laws for the rest of the city don't hold. While in *Dhalgren,* except for the first chapter (and even there . . .) it's nothing *but* a paraspace.

SRD: Yes, what's that marvelous line from that appalling SF picture? I think it's *Slave Girls from Beyond Infinity.* Once they enter the temple, one slave girl turns to the other and says, "I have the strangest feeling the normal laws of time and space no longer apply."

TT: The distinction between ordinary narrative space and a technological lyrical paraspace is allegorized by the distinction between "narrative" language and "lyrical" language, then?

SRD: I suppose that holds as long as you remember that both ordinary language and lyrical language are equally rhetorical. There's a wonderful spot in "Rogue Moon," before Barker has entered the paraspace, where Hawks, who at the beginning knows more about the inside of the paraspace than anyone else in the story, is telling Barker what he knows: He describes the death of one of the previous explorers (the man's body looked as if it had fallen from a height of several thousand meters under terrestrial gravity), and Barker asks him a question: "Could that have happened?"

Hawks replies: "No."

And Barker responds, phatically, "I see."

To which Hawks returns, "I can't see, Barker. And neither can anyone else."

In short, the play of ordinary rhetoric—the "transparent" language that we all assume is, willy nilly, somehow apart from rhetoric—is there suddenly called into question. Its rhetorical quality is suddenly foregrounded. The ideas and ignorances it allows us to slide over and slip across are brought sharply to the fore.

But it's important that this happens, *not* when—somewhat anticlimactically—Hawks and Barker travel through the paraspace itself, with its "shafts of crystal transparency open[ing] through the folds of green and white, with flickering red light dimly visible at their far ends and blue, green, yellow heaving up from underfoot," its "crystalline transparent projections jutting out from the red wall," or its "enormous featureless plain of panchromatic greys and blacks." There, a more traditional notion of rhetoric is being foregrounded and, indeed, being allegorized by a set of colorful rhetorical figurations.

Nor does the allegory end there. In a science fiction text, ordinary space is just as technologically contoured as any of these technologically constituted paraspaces—from cyberspace to outer space itself. But ordinary space (like ordinary language) is the place where the characters are likely to forget that technological contouring, just as characters, enmeshed in ordinary language, are likely to lose the sense of its rhetoricity.

At least half of Theodore Sturgeon's verbal poetry was expended on lush, vivid, and precise descriptions of the emotions of his characters; but the other half was lavished on luminous evocations of astonishing machines that often performed impossibly complex technical tasks.

We've broached a very interesting, even exciting point: In science fiction, rhetoricity often allegorizes technology—and the awareness of technology; especially technology that's perceived as being beyond ours.

TT: Cyberpunk is often characterized by mirrorshades. We can see it first in John Shirley's *City Come A-Walkin'*. But the metaphor of mirrorshades is important not only because mirrorshades sound punkish, but because mirrorshades are described as the effect of a prosthesis—and frequently as prostheses that give us our own sense of reality.

I wonder if cyberpunk doesn't make the most of mirrorshades, at least partly inspired by your *Dhalgren,* in which Kid wears the optic chain, looped upon his body, a chain made up of prisms, lenses, and mirrors. As such, your chapter title "Prism, Mirror, Lens" is very interesting. Do you think the obsession with mirrorshades has something to do with what you've called "the distortion of the present?"

SRD: I've written that science fiction does not try to predict the future. Rather it offers us a significant distortion of the present. But to try and see the distortion that takes place on the reflective surface of a pair of mirrorshades as an allegory of science fictional distortion in general may be to stretch allegory to the tearing point—where the glare blinds us to its logic, to its psychology; where the sound of the music drowns out just the dialogue with the contemporary that distortion's significance encompasses.

Mirrorshades would seem, rather, to have something to do with the science fictional gaze. What are mirrorshades, after all? They're a thin film of reflective mylar. They cut off your gaze—at any rate, darken what you see. At the same time, they mask the gaze's source. Someone looking at you cannot tell whether you're looking at them or looking away. Thus they both mask the gaze and distort the gaze. They protect us against a painful light. At the same time, they displace the gaze of the reader, who must always look at himself or herself any time she or he seeks to find the origin of the gaze. All you can find is yourself—which I think is a nice allegory of what is happening in this particular kind of science fiction.

TT: Do you think of that in terms of psychoanalysis?

SRD: I think it suggests a psychoanalytic reading.

SRD: Mirrorshades constitute a state of mind?

SRD: Well, they constitute the structure of a particular displacement of the notion of vision—and since the whole notion of the gaze comes from Lacan, and from Lacan's emphasis on the mirror stage, the text becomes someplace where you look to see what's going on, only what you see is yourself looking at the text to see what's going on—while at the same time, the text presents a gaze that is somehow darkened, distorted, and reflected.

TT: You mean reading the literary text is just like looking at the text through mirrorshades?

SRD: It's not quite clear whether you're the one wearing the mirrorshades or whether the text is wearing them. I think in cyberpunk the text is wearing them—the mirrorshades.

TT: I'd like to take up the idea of prosthesis; because, in Gibson's and Sterling's cases, we can find a kind of ambiguous boundary between the human and the mechanical. In this sense we must say that cyberpunk's question is the very notion of boundary—as, for example, in the name of the hero of *Neuromancer,* Case. Gibson suggests that the human body is simply a case, a frame. Could this be the reason why your *Nova* is sometimes called the first cyberpunk novel?

SRD: Is it?

But how could I possibly comment on that?

One interesting thing about cyberpunk, however, is that, while usually we consider the prosthetic relation where the prosthesis is helping us to deal with some kind of loss that we've sustained, in cyberpunk some prosthetic relationships are deadly—like the sacks of poison that are going to melt and kill Case. Or the "prosthesis" in Tom Maddox's story "Snake Eyes." In Gibson's case/Case, the prostheses are deep inside the body and work to sabotage it.

Thus, in *Count Zero,* there's that extraordinary scene, after the holovid star gets blown up, where we see the man walking through the airport, carrying the case that looks like it was made for two billiard balls, and we just know that it contains her salvaged prosthetic eyes.

Not all of them are baleful, of course. The skeleton the performer wears in "Winter Market," and with Molly Million in *Neuromancer* and "Johnny Mnemonic," you don't know quite where the prosthesis ends and the body begins. There's always a kind of ambiguity—like Molly's mirrorshades that are actually replacement eyes.

TT: As for Molly, Gibson's characterization of her reminded me of Rydra Wong in *Babel-17* in some sense.

SRD: Ah, but the person she reminded me of most was Jael in Joanna Russ's *Female Man.* Both of them have retractable claws in their fingers. Both of them wear black. Both enjoy their sex with men. And there's a similar harshness in their attitudes.

I'm sure Gibson would admit that his particular kind of female character would have been impossible to write without the feminist science fiction from the seventies—that is, the feminist SF whose obliteration created such a furor when Bruce Sterling (inadvertently of course . . . ?) elided it from his introduction to *Burning Chrome.*

Sometimes it seems as though these male writers were trying to sublate the whole feminist movement unto themselves—which can only be done at the expense of history. But simply because the influence of the feminist writers is so strong on male writers like Gibson, I don't think we will ever be able to lose it historically.

It's always seemed to me that Varley, a writer whose feminist sympathies are pretty much there on the surface, was really trying again and again—now in "The Phantom of Kansas," now in "Overdrawn at the Memory Bank," now in *The Ophiuchi Hotline*—to wrestle with, to argue vehemently with, to somehow rewrite in a new and acceptable form, Budrys' "Rogue Moon." In "Rogue Moon," you'll recall, Al Barker, the man in love with death, dies again and again—and it doesn't really matter. Well, Varley keeps telling us, it's got to matter—somehow, at least to the person who dies. And yet the coherence of the story is always fighting that notion that he's putting forward—the notion of the reality of death—so that this oedipal struggle I see between him and Father A.J. is taken up and dramatized in his stories, in text after text.

Varley is, of course, *the* SF writer who has taken over the prosthetic as his own personal field. Heinlein's "Waldo" and the range of Varley's stories *are* the necessary texts in any examination of SF and the prosthetic.

Gibson, however, is constantly rerewriting Russ and Le Guin. We've already talked about what Gibson's Molly owes to Russ' Jael. (It's only the world of Russ's novel that makes Gibson's Molly signify in his: In Gibson's world, there are neither Jeanines nor Janets—only various Jael incarnations.)

But take a look at Le Guin's societies: They're all loose webs of courts, kibbutzim, and academies. As such, all their institutions are highly structured and very protected places.

Now hold up against this Gibson's Urban Sprawl, and you can suddenly hear the shrill—one yearns to say "hysterical"—protest against that ordered social template around which Le Guin organizes her world.

The bricolage of Gibson's style, now colloquial, now highly formal, now hardboiled, makes him as a writer a *gomi no sensei*—a master of junk. Applied to Gibson, it's a laudatory title. But it would be absurd to apply such a term to Le Guin. And it's precisely on that rhetorical level that he argues with, cannibalizes, and rewrites her.

But in science fiction, the intertextual dialogue has always been all.

TT: In a lecture you gave at Cornell on the work of biologist and cultural critic Donna Haraway and her article, "A Manifesto for Cyborgs," you referred to a kind of surplus of metaphor in terms of logic that is supposed to be produced by a kind of . . . deconstruction of gender?

SRD: The surplus I discussed was something that comes with any metaphor. A metaphor (or simile) always produces a logical structure—a structure that, in itself, is almost always wholly semantic. ("Why is a raven like a writing desk?" "Because Poe wrote on both.") But there's always a psychological surplus, poetic and organized far more at the level of the letter ("Feathers, leather, wings, wood, stone, bone, beak, brass, eyes, handles, claws, drawers . . ."); and the tension between the logical, semantic structure and the psychological, poetic surplus is, I think, what produces the energy and vividness of metaphor. The logic and the psychology in tension make for the cyborg view of the metaphor. The logic is the technological aspect. The psychology is the organic aspect. The two feed back on each other—in the same gesture with which they open each other up.

TT: What, in that view of metaphor, could necessarily change the orthodox view of the cyborg?

SRD: I don't think it changes the orthodox view. I think it grows out of the orthodox view. I think it recomplicates on the orthodox. It's the same kind of metaphoric distribution over itself that Derrida makes of the whole notion of writing, which goes out and subsumes voice and pulls it up against itself, until the boundary between becomes unlocatable, and recasts the whole notion of voice, so that you can have things that are purely oral, yet still partake of the notion of writing. It's a way of upsetting another set of hierarchies; but that upset is always an interim strategy. It's never absolute, complete, total, or finished.

TT: Insofar as the cyborg is the product of the prosthetic—or, in Derridean terms, that writing itself must be the product of a prosthetic process—there's still controversy going on over whether cyberpunk is a movement or a subgenre. But, for the time being, we can at least say cyberpunks have clarified their consciousness of the history of science fiction, as it's seen in Gibson's story "The Gernsback Continuum," and Sterling's essay "Midnight on the Rue Jules Verne" [*SF EYE* a1].

Gibson decomposes Gernsback by mocking his aethetics of the streamlined, whereas Sterling decomposes Verne by reconstructing his image from a punkish viewpoint. How do you place them in the history of science fiction, actually in view of the age of the New Wave? Perhaps the image of "cyberspace" might be another version of "inner space."

SRD: Inner space . . . ?

Certainly that's a tempting reading.

But looking back on it at this point, "inner space" seems to me to have begun as a very conservative notion whose main strategic function was to legitimate science fiction for the New Wave—to make SF look more like literature by overtly importing into it the literary priority of the subject. To say that all the technological paraphernalia and images in SF were really keys to the socially, biologically, and cybernetically internalized world of the post-Romantic, post-Freudian "subject" was to throw out (or at least to repress) precisely what was important, significant, and truly alive in science fiction. It was a way to give up all articulate readerly (and writerly) response to just what, in science fiction, could critique that social, biological, cybernetic construction of the subjective: the playful presentation of a socially and scientifically analyzable, linguistically and poetically malleable object.

Writers who espoused inner space had to be, almost by definition—no?—anti-technology.

Cyberpunk is pro-tech. Thus it *can't* be pro-inner space, QED . . . ?

Excepting the rather silly film that, this past year, gave a biological literalness to the term, "inner space" was wholly psychological in its constitution, its function, in its deployment—at least during the period of its use as a critical term by the New Wave. First off, no one ever went there. It was an insistently aspacial term (what was spacious about it was also wholly ironic). It was a space of interpretation. It was occasionally indicated in the text; but it was never pictured and dramatized.

Cyberspace is, on the contrary, apsychological. It is the place we go to learn about information. Within it, we can gaze out (not in) on General Motors and see just how much bigger it is, in terms of what it knows, than the database on the PC in the apartment next door. In it, we can destroy each other (Chrome can be burned down to its informational grounding) or we can die. Cyberspace exists entirely as a technological consensus. Without that technology it could not exist, be entered, or function. It's much closer to Popper's notion of "World-3" (the world of texts and data that interweaves and stabilizes the world of human beings) or Chardin's "Noösphere" (the sphere of abstract knowledges presumed to be generated by, and encircling, the biosphere) than it is to anything internal and psychological. Indeed, successive technological realizations of those and like images have organized the nostalgia, or the ravenous hunger, for the informational totality the bourgeoisie has experienced since the middle of the 19th century—a nostalgia, a hunger implicit in everything from the Love of Wise Old Men (like Gandalf) to the ascendancy of computers themselves as middle class toys, a nostalgia which catapulted writers like Verne and, later, Wells (they were known, first of all, both of them, as writers who *knew* so much; Wells, indeed, was probably the first intellectual—as opposed to artist—celebrity; after all, his best creative work was *merely* science fiction; and as soon as he reached that celebrated position, he was invited to write a history of the world—which invitation he accepted and did pretty well at, everything considered) to an astonishing public popularity. Wells, for a while, was simply the most famous man in the world. That same hunger doubtless propels, now and again, the current extrageneric bourgeois interest in some aspect of science fiction, once it's been labeled with a catchy enough term.

How does one place the cyberpunks, then, against the New Wave? I don't know whether one can. There was the New Wave. Then there was the entire explosion of feminist science fiction—in many ways a political and stylistic counterwave. The cyberpunks come after that—again, in many ways a reaction.

Jeanne Gomoll has brought it specifically to our notice in her open letter to Joanna Russ, in the last issue of *Janus*. It's interesting that the feminist explosion—which obviously infiltrates the cyberpunk writers so much—is the one they seem to be the least comfortable with, even though it's one that, much more than the New Wave, has influenced them most strongly, both in progressive and in reactionary ways—progressive in its political cynicism, reactionary to the extent that cynicism can only be expressed through a return to a certain kind of macho rhetoric that was dated by 1960, and that really belongs to Britain's "Angry Young Men," Philip Wyllie, and a whole lot of other—let's face it—second-rate writers. Yet, in characters like Molly . . . you know, the great irony of the cyberpunk movement is that the most quintessentially cyberpunk story is Connie Willis' "All My Darling Daughters." And Willis is very seldom—or never—thought of as a cyberpunk. Yet, if you wanted to choose one story that is more cyberpunk than any other one written, that would probably be it—and it's written outside the movement, and probably six or seven years before it even got going!

TT: One thing that pleased me most in your class was your discussion of Alfred Bester, then John Varley, then William Gibson. If we are taking the viewpoint of cyberpunk, I think it is possible to reconstruct the American history of science fiction, beginning with Bester, Chip Delany, John Varley, and William Gibson.

SRD: Well, again, you're indulging that same cyberpunk patriarchal nervousness. You're omitting the Russ/Le Guin/McIntyre/Vinge axis, without which there wouldn't *be* any cyberpunk. Is it this macho uncertainty that keeps on trying to make us black out the explosion that lights the whole cyberpunk movement? without which we wouldn't be able to read it? without which there would not be either the returning macho or the female cyberpunk characters who stand up to it?

When you look at the criticism cyberpunk has generated, you notice among the male critics this endless, anxious search for fathers—that finally just indicates the general male discomfort with the whole notion of paternity. Which, in cyberpunk, is as it should be. Cyberpunk is, at basis, a bastard form of writing. It doesn't have a father. Or, rather, it has so many that enumerating them just doesn't mean anything.

What it's got are mothers. A whole set of them—who, in literary terms, were so promiscuous that their cyberpunk offspring will simply never be able to settle down, sure of a certain daddy.

I'm a favorite faggot "uncle," who's always looked out for mom and who, when they were young, showed the kids some magic tricks. But I have no more claim to a position on the direct line of descent than any other male writer. Sometimes they like to fantasize I do. But that's just because they used to like me before they knew anything about real sex.

To the extent that they can accept mom and their bastard status—which I think Gibson does—these writers produce some profoundly interesting and elegant work.

To the extent they rebel against them—and the one point Gomoll couldn't seem to make was that this search for fathers is part of the *same* legitimating move that ignores mothers—the work becomes at its best conservative and at its worst rhubarbative—if not downright tedious.

But movements are always controlled by such ironies. They never quite contain themselves. They're never wholly at one, at rest, at any kind of balance point with their own, always imposed from the outside identities: the Name-of-the-Father that never quite fits. That's what bastardy in such a context means. As long as we keep those ironies in mind, we have a strategy to keep the term cyberpunk from settling down, from congealing, from totalizing into something rigid and restrictive—we can keep it "under erasure," if you like.

TT: A cyberpunk writer like John Shirley is not so feminist.

SRD: He represents, I think, a more macho aspect of the movement—and perhaps, at least in his fiction (his criticism is something else), one of the less interesting aspects, only partially because of it. But I admit: I haven't read any of the *Eclipse* trilogy yet. That might change my mind entirely. And his ideas on the place of politics in art are some of the most interesting—and intelligent—I've heard in years.

Intriguingly, the writer whose work has been pulled forward and placed at the head of it all—Gibson—is the one who most responds to the recent (and by no means completed) feminist history of our genre, and in an extraordinarily creative way—in a way similar to the way that Varley (who is the most non-cyberpunk writer you could have) responds to it, too. Shirley and Sterling might take a lesson. The simple truth has been that the test of the novel is always in the crafting of its female characters, from *Daniel Deronda* and *Great Expectations* to *Anna Karenina* and *Madame Bovary,* from *Women in Love* to *The Waves* and *Nightwood.* For better or worse, science fiction novels are—yes—novels. *Ulysses* would be as impoverished without Joyce's Molly as *Neuromancer* would be without Gibson's.

And because we all learn to write fiction first and foremost from other fiction, neither men writers nor women are granted an a priori easier time. The problem of creating believable—much less good or great—women characters is not a jot easier for women writers than for men.

That's why, finally, it's a fair test, too.

TT: I suppose a kind of male—or macho—tradition seems to be, for better or worse, what "historical consciousness" actually is.

SRD: If that's true, it's very sad. Bruce Sterling is a dazzlingly astute—and joyfully inventive—critic. Truly, I envy him the insights he can pull out from the most cursory survey of current social textures. Still, the one place he too much resembles the literary critics from whom his own rhetoric again and again tries to dissociate him is in his fear of the political.

It goes along with the cynicism. It begins as an attempt to keep the cynical stance pure; to keep its ironies exerting equal pressure in all directions. But quickly any critic worth his salt (and I use "his" here advisedly, though conservative women critics—Helen Vendler, for example—suffer from it just as much) sees that, without some political leavening, that cynicism is already at work for some very ugly (and ideologically determined) ends; ends that are just as political as *The New York Times* editorial page and probably much nastier.

Sometimes the critic senses it, but hopes no one else will. That's just bad faith. We cease to take such critics at all seriously as soon as we notice. At other times, the critic begins to fight against his own blindness, against his own all too easy assertations, his areas of slovenly thought, his own conceptual bad habits.

Then we get some exciting work.

The conscious critico/political fear is that if you let the political—or the social—into your literary purview just the least little bit, it will get out of hand, take over everything, and render the enterprise trivial and hopelessly vulgar in a truly pernicious way.

What critics who have this fear (and it's a particularly American one, by the bye) don't—or won't—realize is that only by inviting the social—the political—into critical studies gracefully and graciously right at the beginning is there any hope of making it behave itself once it's inside, making it keep its feet off the coffee table or giving everybody a chance to talk without boorishly hogging the conversation. And, no, it will never learn which fork to use nor be sure when and when not to use its napkin. But, as hosts, we must make allowances—which is not to let the reins of the party go, but to keep a clear vision of our own priorities, while not forgetting that running *this* soirée is work!

Critics who think they are abolishing the social—or the political—completely from their criticism are simply revealing their vast and overwhelming nostalgia for an era when criticism was seen (it never really was) as a much easier job than it is. We either articulate our politics; or we cleave to a very conservative politics.

The conservative streak in the range of sympathetic cyberpunk criticism is disturbing. That streak is most likely the one through which the movement will be co-opted to support the most stationary of status quos.

TT: Bruce Sterling's and Lewis Shiner's "Mozart in Mirrorshades" not only decomposes Mozart but develops a concept of cybertime. How do you find the topic of temporality useful in science fiction?

Maybe we've been focusing on the topic of space, and we didn't have any concept of inner time. We had only inner space.

SRD: The involutions of time in science fiction are in general very primitive. Even in stories like "By His Bootstraps" and "All You Zombies," the thrust is constantly toward linearizing time—toward taking something that initially seems like a knot and declaring that somehow it's linearly negotiable. With the time knots—the temporal complexities that science fiction presents—there's always a sense that they're being untied by the plot. I think it's interesting that for the longest time in science fiction, during the fifties and even the early sixties, when somebody said you were writing an experimental story, they meant you'd written a story with a flashback in it! This was the height of literary experimentation! (This simple-mindedness was what the New Wave was originally rebelling against.) I think this was indicative of a general attitude toward time. How else to specify it, I'm not exactly sure. In *Parsifal,* Wagner has Gurnemanz (I think) say the line: "Here we are turning time into space."

And that may just be what science fiction, because of its commitment to narrative—and to a fairly simple concept of narrative at that—is condemned to: to take temporal complexities and dramatize them in simple spacial, and often inadequate, terms. At its best, such as the Burning Man we've already mentioned in Bester, it can be stunningly effective.

But cyberpunk (if not science fiction itself) has got the same problem that so many of us postmoderns are stuck with. It isn't sure whether it's a sexy bastard like Oedipus who knows all the answers—or an innocent bastard like Parsifal who can't come up with the questions.

As we live day to day, we pass through a very complex set of temporal intersections, yet somehow science fiction is always simplifying these, giving up on them, and there doesn't seem to be any way to fight it. I think it has something to do with the time-bound context that narrative takes place in. Somehow, there's a feeling in SF that if the temporality is really lost, even for a moment, then we don't *have* a narrative anymore. We have something else. We have a verbal construct.

And as we've said: verbal constructs in SF are usually at the service of those paraspaces. They avoid all entanglements in the temporal complexes that literature has used them to represent since the beginning of High Modernism.

Science fiction—and that's the current cutting edge of science fiction—seems to be committed to narrative in a very simplistic way. Gibson even glories in that simplicity. But it still sounds reactionary to me. I'm afraid there's nothing in cyberpunk I've seen to date that's spoken to the problem of temporal complexity in a way that strikes me as different from anything else in science fiction. If there had been, it might not be so popular.

TT: Do you like any other cyberpunk stories, say, among the ones included in the *Mirrorshades* anthology?

SRD: I like most of them very much. I think "The 400 Boys," the Marc Laidlaw story, is very good. I like the Pat Cadigan story, "Rock On." I think it's a very good anthology, all the way through. There're stories that make me kind of wonder what they're doing here, like Greg Bear's. At the same time, it opens the thing up in an interesting way. I absolutely understand why Sterling didn't include, say, "Johnny Mnemonic" among the Gibson offerings. But I still wish it was there—and, in ten years, I think people will miss it. As I said, I just wonder why "All My Darling Daughters" isn't the book's lead story.

You know, I was doing freelance work for Arbor House last summer, and I pretty much wrote all the copy on the jacket and collected the quotes. If you want, you can call me a recent cyberpunk packager.

TT: Greg Bear refuses to be called a cyberpunk.

SRD: The problem with that is simply that you can't "refuse to be called" anything. You can only refuse to respond to the call. What you're called never has anything to do with you. It does, however, have a great deal to do with how you're talked about—which has a great deal to do with how you're treated. And how you're treated has everything to do with you.

That's one reason why you better not refuse to respond, but fight for better treatment—for you and all the other bastards.

TT: In a recent issue of the rock magazine *Spin,* Dr. Timothy Leary writes an essay called "Cyberpunk."

SRD: Oh, did he? I haven't seen that.

TT: In that essay, he says that Gibson not only fuses high tech with low life, but high tech with high art. Certainly his second novel, *Count Zero,* borrows that aesthetic image of "the box" from Joseph Cornell. Here's another prosthetic. And it records the fact that some people try to reconstruct science fiction in the context of modernism, I mean their sense of science fiction.

In general, what do you make of such prosthetic possibilities in terms of your critical position that science fiction cannot be defined?

SRD: Just because it can't be defined doesn't mean it can't be described.

It can be described. It can be located. You just can't specify its necessary and sufficient conditions, which is what a definition—by definition—must do.

TT: And it can be grafted—can be combined with something else.

SRD: Of course.

TT: That's very interesting. Though it can't be defined, it can—always—be combined.

SRD: You might argue that it is always-already combined with something else. Genres never arrive pure. They are always-already impure by their nature. And science fiction is one of the most impure. That indeed is half its glory. Science fiction has always looked around and absorbed images from art and science, and it's done both constantly—Ballard taking all the images from Yves Tanguy and Dali with one hand and images from the space program with the other. It's a process that happens again and again in the field. In that sense, I think, *Count Zero* is a very traditional science fiction novel—and beautifully so.

TT: Gibson's sense of language itself seems prosthetic, as is typically manifested in his coinage "Neuromancer"—a combination of neurotic and necromancer and (and a pun on) new romance. But it is you who have been best known for grafting various terms.

I find it quite impressive that at several universities, including Cornell, you've been using the language of science fiction, which often rejects generic distinctions, and the language of teaching, which always starts with generic distinctions. Don't you find the combination of science fiction and teaching very . . . prosthetic?

SRD: One of the delights of teaching science fiction is that not a great deal of it has been done, so you're really in a new field. Thus I think it behooves one when teaching science fiction to move slowly. The difficulty is having to bring the vocabulary of literary criticism to science fiction with great care; to remember that you're taking a vocabulary vouchsafed by literary studies and moving it outside the literary precinct. You have to proceed very, very carefully. It involves critiquing literary studies themselves, as you appropriate one term after another—or as you decide that you can appropriate this term but that you can't appropriate that one. It's been my experience, for example, that when you deconstruct (to use a common, current term) a science fiction text, you indulge a very different operation from the one you indulge when you deconstruct a literary text—a text of naturalistic fiction, poetry, or philosophy.

In science fiction the undecidable (or the deconstructable) is always organized around this question: Is the particular phrase you're trying to read closely a piece of information telling you about the fictive subject, or is it a phrase telling you about the object structure of the fictive world? Most competent SF readers carry an innate sense that a term, phrase, or sentence can't do both—or at least not both at the same time. So this is what becomes radically undecidable in the science fiction text.

An example I've used frequently: In Thomas Disch's story "Angouleme," there's a character named "Miss Kraus." This is a story that takes place in June and July of 2024. Miss Kraus in the story walks around in Battery Park with a crackpot placard protesting the destruction of seagulls. Now when Disch wrote the story in April of 1970, there was a real woman in New York City whose name was Miss Kraus. She went around the streets with various placards—just as does the character in the story taking place in 2024. At least once the real Miss Kraus was the subject of a small *Village Voice* article.

One recalls Tolstoy getting the idea for *Anna Karenina* from the article on the railroad suicide of an unknown Russian woman. But notice what different problems of interpretation this leads to with the SF text.

Do you extrapolate from Disch's narrative that his fictive "Miss Kraus" in 2024 knew about the real Miss Kraus in 1970; that, somewhere, she'd read the old *Village Voice* piece and taken her name consciously from her avatar? Disch tells us clearly in the text that, because of her wedding ring (a sign that she's really a Mrs.), "Miss Kraus" can't be her real name. Does this society offer its ordinary citizens this sort of access to the details of its own past . . . and the writer's present?

But perhaps it's simply a poetic borrowing from the real world of 1970, grafted onto the text, to stand as another sort of sign—a sign outside the world of the story, a sign that merely floats, as it were, on the textual surface, without intruding into the implied structure of the narrative world—to alert (to gesture or merely to indicate for) the allusionarily and historically informed reader what sort of crackpot the story's Miss Kraus, in fact, is.

Where inbetween are we supposed to read? To what degree is the sign merely textual, and to what degree is it submerged within the narrative, recomplicating it to suggest objective social conditions and occurring social incidents, choices and decisions belonging to the story's characters and world?

As a textual sign, is it merely an indicator of subject, or, within the story's narrated world, does it have an objective weight?

And why can't it be both?

Well, if you read it one way, it says that Miss Kraus is historically aware, has a sense of irony and historical mission, however distorted. It says she is a creature of considered consciousness and conscientious resonance, who knows—and who has even constructed—where she comes from. And, above all, it says that the world of the story, however oppressive, offers her the possibility of this historical access.

If you read it the other way, however, it says exactly the opposite: it says that Miss Kraus is naive, simple, a textual configuration of poetic indications, taken from history, but that she is wholly unaware of it nor able to control it. It says that the possibility of historical access is elided from the fictive world by the same rhetorical gesture of poesis that names and constitutes her.

But you can't really decide between the two readings.

There's nothing in the text that lets me know how I'm supposed to read this name "Miss Kraus" against the historical-*cum*-contemporary fact of the name's origin. Since there is a historical source for the name, does the character have access to this history or does only the writer? It's undecidable from the text.

To complete the deconstruction, of course, we would have to undo the ideological distinction; and that would require perusing the text for the other dozen places within the story where names are rendered inappropriate or ambiguous. But that is not our purpose here. We only want to indicate a beginning.

This is how we almost always have to begin the deconstruction of the SF text. This is the kind of thing that becomes undecidable in science fiction, which is very different—is a question you simply don't have—in naturalistic narratives. Now, in *Anna Karenina,* I believe Anna reads an article about a suicide. But no one reasonably asks whether Anna did or did not read the article that inspired her own creation—even if the words of the two articles were identical. Which is to say, the implied irony would always float on the surface of the text, a commentary upon it, but without ever becoming an element of the novel's objective world. If we took the sign as absorbed by (and contouring) the fictive world of the novel, it would render Tolstoy's text a kind of metafiction simply inconceivable among the realistic Russian novels of the 19th Century.

The temporal dimension of SF, however, makes it a very reasonable question to ask of "Miss Kraus." And that's where deconstructing the science fiction text takes us into entirely different historical (and ideological) questions from the deconstruction of literature.

TT: Does that difference control your sense of teaching science fiction?

SRD: Yes. As we use words that are borrowed, very carefully, from literary studies in teaching science fiction, we end up going in radically different directions—directions that almost invariably take more cognizance of history . . . which is why I like to teach science fiction.

6.

Science Fiction and Criticism: The *Diacritics* Interview

This text began as an interview conducted and recorded by Takayuki Tatsumi at Novacon III, in York, Pennsylvania, on November 2, 1985. Over the next year I rewrote the transcription. It was published in the Fall 1986 issue of* Diacritics.

Takayuki Tatsumi: Let me begin by expressing my congratulations on your receiving this year's Pilgrim Award at the last SFRA (Science Fiction Research Association) conference. In 1984, you seem to have been quite prolific. You finished a novel, *Stars in My Pocket Like Grains of Sand,* and a critical book, *Starboard Wine.* Although Walter Meyers, in presenting the award, did not mention the latter title, clearly SFRA appreciates your consistent critical activities.

In the introduction to *Starboard Wine,* you try to identify science fiction criticism as a counterpart of science fiction, based on an analogy between the port side and the starboard side of a boat. Could you give me a deeper sense of the relation between science fiction and science fiction criticism in terms of this most recent book?

Samuel R. Delany: First, thank you very much for your congratulations. The image of prolificacy my 1984 publications leave is, alas, an illusion of publishing schedules. *Starboard Wine* contains essays written before 1980. And I'm ashamed to say how many years I pecked and picked over *Stars in My Pocket,* once it was, for all practical purposes, finished. Though now and again I have my energetic bursts, I'm really a very slow writer.

But to your question about science fiction criticism.

* The interviewer would like to thank Richard Ryan for help with a long and difficult transcription.

The analogy in the *Starboard Wine* introductory essay doesn't situate science fiction criticism against science fiction itself (though that's an intriguing reading). Rather it tries to situate, however ambiguously, that old opposition, *parole* against *langue*—or, if you will, utterance against grammar, the imaginary against the symbolic. "Port wine," in my analogy, along with "left," "the heart," "red," and "the portside ship's beacon," form a web of signifiers whose nodes all have immediate referents, while the webbing itself is only associational—that is, it merely serves to guide us among the references. The associations are merely meanings: signs, if you will, of the most immaterial order—unuttered mnemonics whose only reading is, "This way to a reference." "Starboard wine," on the other hand, while it certainly has meaning, has no referent: nevertheless that a-referential node can help orient us in the greater web of meanings and references when we lose our way. The narrator of my introductory critical fable learns this when he's out on the nearly featureless Atlantic Ocean.

At least one purpose of criticism is to give utterance to (or fix names to, or even to create anew) the a-referential patterns that order references. The relation between orders of reference, orders of meaning, orders of fiction, which is the relation we deal with when we talk about the relation between "science fiction" and "science fiction criticism," has always been slippery. One writer writes a text about an imagined experience. Another comes along and writes a text about an experience he or she imagined—what else is insight and understanding?—about reading the first text. The second writer is called a critic.

One problem with science fiction criticism is that those formal critics who've been recently writing texts about reading science fiction are not used to telling stories about science fiction texts. Often these formal critics have been trained only to tell stories about texts in other genres entirely—about texts clearly situated within the literary precincts. Frequently you find them telling the same old literary stories. This is a little sad.

In the '40s and '50s, in the informal criticism of SF that appeared in fanzines—amateur mimeographed periodicals put out by enthusiastic readers—and among the book review columns of the professional SF magazines, there was a call for increased sociological density in the SF then being written. The best SF writers responded to that call with works such as *The Space Merchants* by Pohl and Kornbluth and *The Stars My Destination* by Bester. Judith Merril moved from the stark but simple images of "Only a Mother" to rich, social tales like "Dead Center." (She, of course, was also one of the critics who was most articulately voicing the demand.) And Theodore Sturgeon was able to respond with a fictive texture far denser, far richer, far more vivid than that of the SF he had written in the past—a good example of writers responding to critical pressure in a positive way.

Formal criticism of SF in the last ten years—between the middle '70s and the middle '80s—seems much less clear about what it's calling for. I think this is because formal—or academic—criticism is done largely by literarily oriented critics. They just aren't used to making active demands on literature. When you're writing about Dickens, Defoe, or another dead author, there's not much point in declaring: "I would like to have seen it done *this* way." But SF is a very live and lively practice of writing. If the demands are thoughtful and sensible, there's always some SF writer somewhere who will find the suggestion interesting enough to give it a try. And if—as happens on occasion—the readership responds? Well, then, you've changed the genre.

But science fiction has always been immeasurably more intimate with its readers, with its critics, than has literature—at least than literature has been since World War One (when some critics, like Terry Eagleton, would say "literature" as we know it began). The criticism that arrived in the SF magazines and in the fanzines, in that it made specific demands, had a kind of energy, if not sophistication, that current academic SF criticism lacks. I don't think current academic SF criticism is sure what kind of criticism it is. Academic SF criticism, as generally practiced, is very unclear whether it's thematic criticism or whether it's a more theoretical enterprise. While the larger world of literary criticism moves on into deconstruction in one direction and into sociohistorical research in the other (the two of them from time to time coming together to lend each other real support), academic SF criticism seems unsure of its theoretical presuppositions, both as to its object and its methods. There's still too much vulgar Marxism and unsophisticated thematic reductionism in the criticism I see in *Science Fiction Studies, Extrapolation,* and the various other places where formal criticism appears.

In the fanzines (and there are more than 700 of these amateur publications printed yearly in the U.S.A., Europe, Central America, Australia, and Japan) the best articles, the richest ones, the ones that have the most energy and insight are the most traditional—that is, the ones that pose their criticism in the form: "This works. This doesn't work. This could have been far more effectively done this way. This part is a disaster because . . . ." In the academic journals, of which there are two-and-a-half (*Science Fiction Studies, Extrapolation* and, out of the North East London Polytechnic, *Foundation*—I won't say which one of us is the half: any of us could claim that status), the richest and most energetic pieces seem to be the theoretical ones, the ones that ask, "What enables this text to make sense?" But, sadly, these articles are rare.

TT: Donald Hassler, President of SFRA, told me after the conference that from now on we should pay more attention to critical elements already present in your stories as well as to your criticism itself. In fact, particularly since *The Ballad of Beta-2* (1965), your SF has made itself a form of SF criticism. As a result, we are unable to apply the traditional binary opposition between fiction and criticism to your writings. It is here that we can locate your metafictional and/or meta-science fictional tendency, which leads us to call you "the purveyor of crisis." To what extent have you been conscious of criticism within SF—as well as SF within criticism?

SRD: I have to start by saying that it's always struck me as amusing that academics so often favor *The Ballad of Beta-2* among my SF novels. It is, after all, the story of a graduate student involved in a research project in galactic anthropology—my only novel that centers on an academic.

Now *that* was a very easy story to tell, the one I just implied: Academics pick out *The Ballad of Beta-2* for special favor because it's about an academic. I have many referents for it. But it's still such an easy tale I suspect it's not a very interesting one. For that reason, I think the best way to approach that particular text critically, if one *is* an academic, might be to take that rather dull story I just told and try to tell a more interesting story about *it*. What is *really* going on in that story—not my texts alone, either *The Ballad of Beta-2* or the insipid story about it that has so many referents, but what is going on in the larger story that *combines* my SF novel with the obvious tale these referents have just prompted me to tell?

One of the best critical plots I know is this: "Most people who just glance at the situation see X, Y, and Z. But if you look more closely, you'll notice P, Q, and R. . . ." With the emphasis only slightly shifted here and there, it's the plot of Auerbach's *Mimesis,* Burke's *Philosophy of Literary Form,* and Barthes' *Sur Racine.* Right now, it's a particularly useful plot for SF criticism, because there are so many dull, obvious stories in circulation about science fiction. "Science fiction is about the future." "Science fiction is about science." "Science fiction is the mythology of the industrial age." You have to remind people (even people who've never read any science fiction), sometimes, just how well they know these old stories (rather the way English speakers who've never seen or read Shakespeare's plays still know all too much about them). Unfortunately, too many SF critics never get beyond the first half of the tale. Then they sit back and think they've done it.

Now about the story you just relayed that Donald Hassler has passed on to you: There exist all sorts of critical elements in the work of SRD, from his first story about an academic on. Well, yes, it would look that way, if you just glanced at the situation. But if you look more closely, you'll notice the plots of all my first eight SF novels, which take us back well before *The Ballad of Beta-2,* hinge in some way or other on the interpretation of a text. In the very first, *The Jewels of Aptor,* it's a matter of which of two versions of a hymn is authentic. In the *Fall of the Towers* trilogy, the whole problem is to locate the writers of three texts and to salvage their writings. And in *The Ballad of Beta-2,* of course. . . . But, really, it's impolite for the writer to go on at too great a length telling stories about his stories.

The fact is, my critical concerns with science fiction were pretty informal through most of my first seven or eight novels. Any interest you can read into my work about any critical problems of SF per se in anything I wrote before 1975 is largely an accident of allegorical *richesse.* Oh, I was interested in problems of writing, problems of language, problems of life, and problems of art. But a slightly more interesting story, I suspect, for whatever you want to make of it, is that as soon as I became critically and articulately interested in problems of the SF genre per se around 1973, '74, and '75, that's when the overt signs of SF as a genre began to vanish from the surface of my texts.

I suppose what I'm saying is that I can see an energetic, creative interrogation of those early SF novels in terms of the status of the text, the progress of the text, the conceptual range of what is considered textual in them; such an interrogation might produce a critique that was, first, interesting and that, second, might even discover or create some associations that would allow readers to move around in those early novels more easily. As a critic, I'd be rather interested in reading it. But "Critical Ideas as Expressed in the Science Fiction Novels of Samuel R. Delany"—Lord, that strikes me as jejune! But it's just the sort of piece the current uncertainties of academic SF criticism militate for.

Certainly science fiction from the late '60s on was most exciting at precisely the place where the traditional generic boundaries were most heavily under attack: I mean the SF of what was then called "The New Wave," which was centered around the British magazine *New Worlds.* What gave us a sense of SF as a genre was the dissemination of science fiction elements outside the traditional SF boundaries and, indeed, the infiltration of elements traditionally outside those boundaries into the SF precinct. That's what made our generic status a question. Until that time everyone knew what SF was—it took place in the future, and/or it had rocketships and ray guns in it, and/or it was sold from a particular bookshelf in the store. The graduations of its generic aspects ranged from the semantic conventions of the SF sentence to the economic distribution mechanism of the SF text. Within the field we all knew none of these aspects could serve as definitions—as necessary and sufficient conditions. (*All* formal genres resist definition: Intersubjective objects can not be defined; and genres are nothing if not the socially shared codes—however partial that sharing—by which readers read them.) Still, it was uncanny just how well they did as functional descriptions under the real demands of readers and writers and editors and magazine distributors and book publishers and bookstores. This is what informed Damon Knight's "meta-ostensive" definition of the late '50s with its considerable wit: "Science fiction is what I point at when I say 'science fiction.'" Unless we remember those simpler times—or are *they* just another too easy story?—we're likely to say of Knight's quip today, "What's so funny?" or at least see the humor as lying in another area from where it did then. But it was only when the functional limitation on these generic aspects began to break down that the critical question—in all senses of the phrase—became "What *is* the SF genre?"

TT: In order to push this topic further, let's turn to *The Einstein Intersection* (1967), one of your most fascinating SF novels, which might be read as treating with the definition of SF itself, contrasting Einstein with Gödel. We might regard this as the intellectual crisis that, moreover, reflects the human crisis in terms of nuclear war. I can't help thinking of some of what T. S. Eliot described in *The Waste Land* (James Gardiner pointed out some of the similarities in "Images of *The Waste Land* in *The Einstein Intersection*," *Extrapolation*, No. 18, May 1977). As a postmodern writer, how do you accept the modernist thematics and stylistics?

SRD: Before I tackle your terminal question, I must take on some of your ticklish presuppositions. I think it's on page 4 of *The Metamorphosis of Science Fiction* that Darko Suvin first uses the term you used in the midst of your question, "definition," in terms of SF. And on page 7, he writes, "SF is, then, a literary genre whose necessary and sufficient conditions are the presence and interaction of estrangement and cognition. . . ." It is, of course, those words "necessary" and "sufficient" that make this a proposed definition. Well, the fact is that the presence and interaction of estrangement and cognition in a literary work are simply and blatantly insufficient to produce SF. If they interact in one way, they produce fantasy. If they interact in another, they produce surrealism. If they interact in still another, they produce criticism. And it can be argued that as well as insufficient, they are not really necessary either. There are too many space-operas, as familiar to readers as the last fifty of them read, in which there is no cognitive thrust at all. And if these are excluded—by definition—from the genre, then we have no definition at all. Nor is that even taking on the rather considerable problem of describing, in a necessary and sufficient manner, just what "estrangement" and "cognition" mean in an SF context anyway. But this notion that SF *is* somehow definable is an idea that haunts the academic discussion of SF as much as it haunts the informal discussion that has filled the fanzines since '39. If SF were definable, then it would be the only genre that was! No one has found the necessary and sufficient conditions for poetry. No one has found the necessary and sufficient conditions for tragedy, for the novel, for fiction. If SF is, as Suvin calls it, "a full fledged literary genre," why should it be the single one to *have* necessary and sufficient conditions?

The answer is, of course, because it's "scientific." The dream of scientificity that haunted early structuralist criticism also haunts science fiction. Indeed, it is the same dream. Even the ideological filiations follow awfully similar lines: The connection between SF writers of the 30s and 40s and the leftist politics of the period is now mentioned, now repressed, now romanticized; but it's seldom researched or analyzed. Of course, in both cases one must realize that this scientificity is a dream, a phantasm, a ghost. The best way to deal with ghosts is to research and analyze their historical formation (even with such a self-evident ghost as the scientificity of science fiction). But you don't hold seances and table-tapping sessions in hope of giving it more solidity than it already has—not if you want criticism worth the name.

In terms of science fiction, we're also dealing here with an underlying uncertainty about what constitutes a genre, about SF's aspirations to generic status, and about those borderline cases—borders that writers like Vonnegut and Malzberg and Piercy and Ballard and Lessing and Ellison and Atwood, from the '50s on, have been claiming to cross, now in this direction, now in that one—that both problematize and constitute the SF genre-effect we have today. But we'd do better to turn to something like Derrida's "*La Loi de genre,*" which is nothing *but* an interrogation of generic *un*certainties, as a model for where to locate, at the theoretical level, our generic problems. Though that essay only tantalizes with the most tenuous suggestions, I find it a better model than Suvin's theoretically shaky positivities, however well meant.

Now let's look at your question about SF and modernist themes and styles.

Science fiction and even more so science fiction's despised younger cousin, sword-and-sorcery, are today's major heirs to the Wagnerian legacy that so inundated modernism, that was the total surround of modernism, that, indeed, up until the post-Edwardian invention of "literature," was modernism. All we have to do is step outside this hotel room where we're conversing and look into the halls of this SF convention to see people wandering up and down in capes and armour; we have only to look into the art show at the end of the corridor to see the dragons and the views of the Eternal Cosmic Spirit that are the contemporary Wagnerian spawn. (I believe last night I even saw someone come in with a bear!) Modernism grows wholly out of the concept of art—the creation of Serious Art—that Wagner fostered throughout his life and disseminated through the institution of Bayreuth, that spread throughout Europe and the United States in the 1870s, '80s, and '90s up until the Great War—by which point it had settled, pretty firmly in place, and where it remained up until World War Two. The First World War made Wagner's influence uncomfortable. The second dropped a curtain over it entirely, almost wholly repressing his name as the most pervasive artistic influence on modernism. Stephen Dedalus, who, throughout *Ulysses,* carries an ashplant (like Wotan, in *The Ring*), when he raises it to strike the chandelier in Nightown, cries out, "Nothung!"—Sigfreid's forging cry. (*Nothung* means, of course, crisis; Sigfreid was your original "purveyor of crisis"—not I.) At the end of *Portrait of the Artist as a Young Man,* Stephen wrote in his journal: "Welcome, O Life! I go to encounter for the millionth time the reality of experience and to forge in the smithy of my soul the uncreated conscience of my race." Well, the sentiment and the metaphor were Wagner's. All the major modernists, from T. S. Eliot to D. H. Lawrence, to Proust and Thomas Mann, were Wagner's children—at least the ones most popular in America. It's just not fashionable these days to point it out. (Ezra Pound's exhortation to the artists of his generation, "Make it new!" is only his restatement of Wagner's exhortation in a letter from the early 1850s to Liszt: "*Kinder! Macht Neues! Neues! und abermal Neues!*"—Guys! Make it new! New! and then again new!)

As soon as you have something suppressed, something that it's intellectually unfashionable to talk about, it becomes pervasive at the level of the repressed. So, in a sense, precisely as we forget the Wagnerian influences in modernism as a gallery of specific Wagnerian images, Wagnerianism as a set of values, of attitudes, and as a presumed framework for art rushes in to swamp almost all considerations of modern art. Our theater today *is* the theater of Wagner—Wagner was the first person to turn down the lights in the auditorium and have illumination only on the stage. The commercial Hollywood movie is, let's face it, the *Gesamtkunstwerk.* Wagner was the first person officially to forbid talking in the theater. He was the one who instituted the custom of not clapping between movements at a concert. When you went to Wagner's *Festpielhaus* at Bayreuth, you went to Pay Attention to a Work of Art; and, today, when you Pay Attention to Art, you are in the midst of Wagnerism. The respectful, silent, attentive, pseudo-religious attitude we bring to serious art *is* Wagner's legacy—as, today, it is the controlling aspect, attitude, and framework of modernism, whether theatrical or literary.

Because SF developed largely outside, and often in opposition to, literature, and largely outside literature's ideological constraints, it kept—in the subgenre of sword-and-sorcery—those Wagnerian images, where they could be recognized, intact, by anyone. (As I said, all you have to do is look out the door into the hallway.) At the same time, and for the same reason, it was also able to critique the Wagnerian aesthetic attitude and the associated ideological constraints, which literature fell victim to by repressing the images that had, till then, carried them. It's no accident (as Adorno was so fond of saying) that the first woman to win a Hugo award in the professional SF writing categories, with her stories of dragons and dragon riders, was trained as an opera singer, after she left Radcliffe.

The SF critique of modernism, if you want to call it that, was practical and hard-headed: The artwork shall not be venerated in the mode of a religious object—ever! The SF writer is *not* an author—that is, an authority figure: a source of interpretive constraints. The SF audience is probably the most intelligently enthusiastic audience I know of—certainly for any current practice of writing. But it is not the silent, pseudo-religious enthusiasm modernism has taught us to bring to art.

In that sense, SF has just anticipated postmodernism by a little.

In the same way that Joyce's stream of consciousness was an early, but direct, outgrowth of the Wagnerian monologue and its theory (through the influence of *Les Lauriers sont coupés,* by Edouard Dujardin, editor of *La Revue wagnerienne* in Paris), the ubiquitous present tense, used by novelists from Pynchon to Alison Lurie—and that as well I see today in three-quarters of the poetry submissions to *The Little Magazine,* on which I've been a poetry editor for two years (that wholly artificial and unspeakable tense which has become the omnipresent and uncritical sign of the literary)—is only the most recent outgrowth of that monologic aesthetic in which art itself denies all dialogue, contest, agonism, and history to become an individual subject's representation *of* an individual subject (or series of individual subjects) *for* an individual subject, with the exciting, material, impinging social object relegated to a wholly secondary position—when its existence is not outright denied. But because most literary readers—not to say writers—can't historify much of this, they too become its victims. We have managed to escape a *bit* of that in SF, while still maintaining enthusiasm, intelligence, and analysis, for which I am quietly, smally, but happily grateful.

TT: I never imagined that Wagner was an influential figure on your works.

SRD: He's not.

I don't think I sat down and heard my first Wagner opera all the way through till 1977. My point is, he's a nonconscious influence on almost all current western art. At least if you are using terms—as you did—such as modernism. By the First World War the three human beings on whom more books, monographs, and articles had been written than any others were Jesus Christ, Napoleon Bonaparte, and Richard Wagner. Since than, Marx has probably joined their company.

TT: Is it the interest in late romanticism that encouraged you to keep writing heroic fantasies, such as the Nevèrÿon series?

SRD: Yes—if you'll allow that interest to be an antagonistic one. Wagner and Baudelaire were the late romantics from whom modernism arose. But, though we are willing to acknowledge Baudelaire, we are not quite so willing to acknowledge Wagner—although they share many things. Baudelaire was a great champion of Wagner, especially "Tannhäuser," when it was performed in Paris. Both could be viciously antisemitic. (Somewhere in his diary, Baudelaire cries out for the extermination of the Jews.) And they both maintained intriguingly ambiguous attitudes to the notion of *l'art pour l'art.* One minute they wanted it. The next they were demanding social relevance. Which is to say, all these notions and stances were givens of the nineteenth century. In these aspects, Baudelaire and Wagner were *too much* alike, even if these are the shared presuppositions that allowed them to talk to one another, as it were.

TT: The critical approach toward the relation between modernism and postmodernism has been traditionally binary. We have been forced to decide our viewpoint between continuous and discontinuous perspectives.

SRD: Literature has an established critical tradition and condition. Its continuities have been so inculcated, so sedimented, so ossified that they have become the skeleton allowing us any and all articulation about them, around them, no matter how muscular, how nervous, how excited those articulations happen to be. To disrupt that ossification we *have* to stress discontinuities—or we are furthering that ossification. (As they used to say in the '60s, if you're not part of the solution, you're part of the problem.) SF's informal critical tradition, in terms of the millions of fanzine pages written and published since 20-year-old Raymond Palmer produced the first issue of *The Comet* in 1939, has been an almost entirely proscriptive enterprise. That is to say, the vast majority of it, written by men and women under twenty-five (and a staggering proportion of that written by boys under twenty), has not paid any serious attention to either continuities *or* discontinuities. Rather, it repeatedly held each text up against an ideal model of its own form, an enterprise that helped hasten the internalization of a formal set of codes, today widely shared by a considerable readership, that allowed SF to reach generic—or, if you prefer, critical—mass in the astonishingly short period of sixty-five years. Academic SF criticism, which has only really existed with any solidity since 1958, rather than concentrating on intrageneric continuities, has by and large manufactured only a spurious and much debated set of intergeneric similarities that, without clear-cut task or theory, tend to self-destruct almost as fast as they are posited.

This means that the *serious* SF critic today has both to construe and to deconstruct. That is to say, the very serviceable critical plot I was talking of before, "Most people who just glance . . . ," is one for which literary critics can frequently omit that opening part, because, with any canonical text, that part is so well known. But SF does not have a canon, nor does it have the critical tradition that supports a canon and holds it to shape. So, for a while at least, SF critics are struck with having to tell the complete story every time. But that is why I can make noise about the strategic opposition between continuities and discontinuities in terms of science fiction—noises I would be the first to find unacceptable in the present literary situation.

TT: Returning to *The Einstein Intersection,* I would like to focus on its protagonist, Lo Lobey, who is characterized as a black mutant Orpheus and appears to reflect your own background as a black. Lorq Von Ray in *Nova* is also significant: He is an interstellar mulatto. According to the biographical data available, your elementary education at Dalton immersed you in the linguistic differences between black children in Harlem, where you grew up, and white children around Park Avenue, where you went to school. Can you explain in more detail how experience developed your keen awareness of language?

SRD: Well, you've set up a context in which you are stressing the continuity between my characters and me. Therefore, strategically, I'll try to talk about discontinuities, not because you are wrong, but only to open the question a bit further.

I've always liked to write about characters who, on the one hand, have done the same kinds of things, or had the same experiences, that I've done or had. On the other hand, I've also been trying—very carefully, even from the very first SF novels I wrote in my early twenties—to write about people whom I've *seen* in the world doing those same things. When you're writing about a character in a given situation, it's important to know what that situation *feels* like, from the inside. But it's also important to know what someone in that situation *looks* like, from the outside. You want both sides, especially in the kinds of experiences that make you aware of the differences between social classes.

Certainly, in terms of my being black in the United States, the experiences go on from the time I walk out of my door to the time I come back home. And I bring them home with me. Asking me to specify one or another as representative is like asking a farmer with a haystack to pick out the most representative straw. You just can't do it. Any straw picked out is going to be provisionally representative at best.

My experience of language? Well, here it was my mother and aunts, talking over coffee around this or that kitchen table, now in Harlem, now in Bedford-Stuyvesant, now in Montclair. There, it was the urgent stories my school-friends whispered to one another as we played on the school roof or sat together in the lunchroom, across from the library on the school's third floor. Now, it was the obscene, easy, chuckling tales of the men who loitered by Louis' corner shoeshine parlor, where every Sunday I had to stop to get my shoes polished on my way to church. Another time, it was a professional Irish storyteller who came to our school to enchant us with his richly bebrogued adventures of Jack—always youngest of three brothers—and various fairy folk. Now it was the small, brittle black woman who tutored me in remedial English in her top-floor Edgecombe Avenue apartment. Later it was the bilingual jokes of a bunch of Hispanic boys I taught remedial English to, when I was seventeen, under the auspices of my neighborhood community center. And there was, of course, the language that flowed under eye, here in a novel by Jane Austen, there in one by Dickens, now in ones by Himes, Yarby, Killens, now in my father's readings of Dunbar and Twain, now in an aunt's recitation of James Weldon Johnson, here in the caption of an E. C. horror comic, there in the thought balloon of some *Mad* or *Panic* parody; and of course in science fiction. And of course there was more. What I speak of is the range of idiolects anyone growing up in a great American city hears and reads, in any number of situations, from a night at an imported production of *Midsummer Night's Dream* by the Old Vic at the Met to the instruction on the back of the box. Their shared, banal lesson, I suppose, was simply that narrative was constant among them.

My experiences as a black in the United States, if I am a black writer, must go into my work: There's no way I can keep them out. But I'm more aware of the way they go in in terms of macro-structure than in terms of micro-texture. Certainly the choice of a character like Lorq (*Nova,* 1968) relates to my own experiences as a black. Even in *Babel-17* (1966) to deal with an Oriental woman in a basically extrapolated American context comes from my being a racially marginal man. In *Dhalgren* (1974) my half-American Indian hero only distorts my own situation. *Triton*'s (1976) protagonist is white and male—the one book of mine in which the thrust toward the main character is almost wholly critical: What's wrong with him? Why doesn't he function properly? Why can't he be honest with himself? Or with others? That critical view reflects the situation of somebody who looks at whites in this society, from the margin, and must ask: What's wrong with them? Why do they act that way?

But I hope you can see: It's not my characters, who, at the level of the subject, are somehow congruent with some fancied Real Life of the writer. It's rather situations, irreducibly social, among many elements in my books, which are analogous to social situations I have seen from the edge, been centrally trapped in, or gone careening through.

Characters as such simply don't exist. There are only characters in situations—in history, if you will. But that's not "History" with any sort of capital H, which becomes mired in the Imaginary confusions that are idealism through the same theoretical strategies and gestures by which we seek for it the totality of the Real. This history is rather a progression of sensation-saturated fragments of the day and night, any one of them lax and banal in this direction, luminous and tense in that one, always accessible to some analysis when it is related to other fragments (sometimes a very great deal of analysis, too), but still too fleeting to be wholly open to more: fragments in which impressions and inattentions sit side by side with the known and the unknown, with the observed and the mistaken, with the accurate and the erroneous, with the clear and the cloudy, with right facts and wrong judgments, with knowledge and ignorance—all of them only the always already past play of sediment and structuration, yet never without that excess we call the future; fragments whose constitutive aspects always include other objects, other subjects, other sediments (in all of which the notion of the "other" splits under the very pressure of analysis the split "self" applies to locate it), as well as psychology and sentience; fragments that are at once too numerous and too ill-bounded to leave more than the most reductive data on the theoretical level, but that are nevertheless the material seat of all pain, joy, humiliation, birth, satisfaction, hunger, frustration, vitality, exhaustion, lust, community, contest, chaos, love, torpor, work, rage, and death.

This notion of the self-inseparable-from-the-material-universe-and-all-we-don't-know-about-it that is one with the notion of the-self-in-history-that-is-all-we-do-know-about-our-universe (history: that which we can narrate, however, awkwardly, however figuratively, however incompletely) is what stands against the notion of the modernist subject—that subject so easy to represent (in some eternally infinitive mood) by a voice endlessly and lyrically singing its isolated monologue, accompanied by an exquisitely articulated and intricately colored orchestral psychology that is grounded only in a dream outside of historical time (whether the dream is called the "collective unconscious" or the "mythological") that is presumed to explain (whether the explanation process is taken as "imaginative" or "scientific"), through a series of allegorical translations of that dream, the greater historical mechanisms the subject seeks to understand by standing outside of history and dreaming.

But it doesn't really matter if that monologue is Wagner's or Baudelaire's or T. S. Eliot's or James Joyce's or Ezra Pound's. I think we can locate a common view of the subject at play among them all, a view now affirmed, now contravened, but that still shows enough of an outline to warrant our speaking of it, however interimly, as we have.

The alternate view of the subject I tried to sketch out I don't know whether I'd dare dignify with the term postmodern (or antimodernist) subject. Still, it's a view of the subject some of whose lineaments now and again I can descry in a number of our postmodern marginal enterprises: some black fiction, certain feminist fiction, various approaches to criticism, much science fiction, some gay fiction. . . .

A piece of practical advice once moved through the SF world. Murray Leinster (1896–1975) told it to Theodore Sturgeon (1918–1985), who passed it on to Judith Merril (1923–), our consummate critic, who wrote it down in an article in F&SF in 1962, where I read it: "It was the basic device for generating a plot. Start with a character, someone with certain strong, even compulsive personality traits. Put him in a situation which in some way negates a vital trait. Watch the character solve the problem . . ." ["Theodore Sturgeon," 1962]. Some people might wonder why such a formulation is so central to *science* fiction. Yet look around you at the mundane fiction, of the most naturalistic sort, published today: That's just not how most people would characterize the fiction of Ann Beattie, Raymond Carver, Jayne Ann Phillips, Ethan Canin, or Breece D'J Pancake. Oh, I know some will leap on the notion of solving the problem. But even if the problem is *not* solved, the important SF presupposition is still there.

Plot, story, diegesis, history, the solving of problems *or* the failure to solve problems—the whole generation of fiction only begins when character *and* universe, subject and object, are conceived, seen, and set in a *local* tension. I choose to see in this device a manifestation of that particular antimodernist, paraliterarily narrated subject-that-doesn't-even-exist-without-objects SF has taught me look for, to find, to propagandize for, even as I consign much in the device that strikes me today as too executive, as too proscriptive, to the realm of the metaphorical or to the historical givens among a tradition of writers who considered themselves craftsmen first and artists secondarily, if at all.

It's a wonderful device with which to read or reread a whole range of fictions—especially SF. As advice? Well, what writer could follow it slavishly, tale after tale? But what SF writer could fail to recognize in it a vividly figured aspect of the world she or he writes in dialogue with; and thus what SF writer could fail to recognize in it a presupposition that makes his or her side of the dialogue make sense?

Now would you like to consider black fiction for a moment? Some white critics expect the black experience to be reflected by black writers in comparatively stereotyped terms. Unless a writer, white or black, is writing about blacks these critics can recognize as black in a particular way, the critic grows afraid that the writer—the black writer—is just not black enough. When I meet with this in white critics, today I just laugh. The answer, for me, seems obvious: "I *am* black. I and my work *are* the evidence for and of blackness. It's *your* job to rearrange the criteria in terms of the evidence I present you with—not mine to fit my work into your white scheme of what 'black enough' means to you."

I said it before: If you're a critic, tell me an *interesting* story. That goes for white critics criticizing black writers. For what it's worth, that's not a criticism I've gotten from black critics. Because we're on the inside of the problem, we—as blacks—realize it's a bit more complicated. We're not so fast to stop with only the story's first half, sure that, if the writer's not wearing his blackness pinned to the most traditional part of his sleeve, the emperor's naked.

TT: I'd like to take *your* fiction for a moment, if I might. Isn't *Dhalgren* a dream outside of historical time—and a huge one at that—of an extraordinarily formal and near Wagnerian, if not Joycean, complexity?

SRD: It's very much a dream. But the one thing it *isn't* is an Explanation of History. It's an analysis of much that's American. But I haven't seen any critic yet who was even tempted, in the midst of all that allegorical play, to read some total historical schema into it. And I'm rather proud of that.

No, let me take that back. Stanislaw Lem dismissed the book as "just more 'twilight of the West.' " I suppose you *couldn't* frame a dismissal in more Wagnerian terms than that. Still, I suspect that's because Lem read as wholly allegorical descriptions that American readers—at least most urban American readers—recognize, through the allegorical skrim, as all too realistic portraits of vast areas of our great American cities: burned-out, underpopulated, all but abandoned. The specificity of those descriptions weights the reading away from the universal and toward the local. At least I hope it does.

Cozy, folksy, reassuring, Tolkein was writing a three-volume explanation of history. (Who was it who called *The Lord of the Rings* "Wagner without the music"?) Not I.

TT: The extrapolation of the American situation in your sense seems a fiction technique closely related to the traditional way of writing SF.

SRD: You assume there *is* a traditional way of writing science fiction. . . . You may be confusing a way of reading with a way of writing. But I see what you mean.

Well, if you're a science fiction writer, those are the generic conventions you have to work with and within. You're stuck with them, for better or worse. The thing to do is see what you can make them into. What you want to do is take those conventions—and break their necks!

TT: What about Butcher in *Babel-17*? Although at first he looks like a slave, later the linguistic explosion makes him free. Is the linguistic system a kind of slavery for you?

SRD: Again I detect an embryo allegory between me and one of my characters in mitosis within your question. Let me stall its formation just a little. The Butcher was, for me, primarily an object of desire. He was someone I wanted to possess; not someone I wanted to be—or, indeed, thought I already was. I wanted to rub up against him—like a large, dangerous teddy bear. Here and there I'd seen aspects of him in the streets, or now and again glimpsed him in the pages of other books. So I polished him up and put him in a novel, where he would be safe. Or where I would be safe from him—at least for a while.

Now to your question.

Glibly speaking, *all* speaking subjects are trapped in Nietzsche's "prison-house of language." But who are these glibly speaking speaking subjects who so speak? (Isn't "glib" the perfect modified with which to characterize that particular linguistic figuration for the materiality of language?) What do they risk (what can they win? what can they loose? and what *must* they remain blind to?) by reminding us of that slavery?

(Perhaps I remain blind to one or another three volume explanation of history I accidentally wrote in this decade or that, while I wasn't looking. . . .) A writer is usually someone who gets a masochistic enjoyment out of being enslaved to that particular house. I used to say very frequently—and have written occasionally—that you only gain some control over language when you become clearly aware of all the things language can*not* do. I love language. I love the specificity of English. I love to play with it. And I love the way it plays with me.

TT: So there exists a kind of "love-hate relationship" between you and language?

SRD: With more emphasis on the fact of love. Oh, certainly the hateful side is there. There's always the frustration that comes with the problems I try to solve. But if you don't enjoy trying to solve the problems (that's probably where the masochism lies), you wouldn't have become a writer.

TT: Can you be sadistic rather than masochist about language?

SRD: I don't think it's possible. It's all variations of masochism. With both sex and language, I think the sadists who take themselves *too* seriously are fooling themselves just a little. Sadism is a matter of desiring the desire of the masochist so strongly that, eventually, that desire becomes sexualized. Sadists almost always go through a masochistic period first, even if it's in early childhood. But it's surprising—and reassuring, at least in sex—how rarely you run into that sort of self-deceived sadist. The vast majority of the ones I've known personally have a pretty clear memory of the earlier stage and a pretty clear understanding of the process of transformation. One of the great crimes of the Frankfurt school, in *The Authoritarian Personality*, was the writers' uncritical association of real sadism—the social sexual practice—with social blindness, personal cruelty, and political oppression. They thought that sadism—which is, of course, the material social strategies of real people split by a particular formation of desire, some of which practices are responsible and some of which are irresponsible, and, as with any other social group, some of whom follow those practices and some of whom balk at them—was a safe metaphor, something so anomalous, so beyond the cultural pale, that they could pretty well use it anyway they wanted. It was an attempt to make their topic glitter.

But what they did was blind a generation of thinkers to what was actually going on in a whole range of social and sexual life with a whole range of men and women, children and adults, white and black, Jewish and gentile, gay and straight, rulers and ruled, oppressors and oppressed. They momentarily forgot that sadism is traditionally known as "the perversion of philosophers"–philosophers as they were. And why.

TT: In relation to this "glitter," I've always been struck by your obsessive use of the image of the jewel, as in *The Jewels of Aptor* (1977). What's more, in *Empire Star* (1966) you even gave the role of narrator to a jewel itself. How did you get concerned with this image? Do you simply owe this to Sturgeon's *The Dreaming Jewels?*

SRD: Oddly, not to Sturgeon but to an old science fiction TV program, *Tom Corbet: Space Cadet.* It was a fifteen-minute TV show (back in the '50s when there were such things), on when I was nine or ten. At one point Tom and his cronies encountered some mystical jewels; and, watching them on television, I thought the glittering objects the program used to represent them were the most beautiful things I'd ever seen. Later, I discovered they were little geegaws, about the size of walnuts, with dozens of spikes radiating from the center, a glass gem set on each. There was a whole pile of them on keychains at Woolworth's! Eventually I bought one of my own. Obviously the prop designers had gone to Woolworth's and thought they were beautiful too. That's the banal origin of the image.

The thing about jewels is that they have many bright and sharp-edged faces. They're signs of wealth, adventure, and power. Their variety comprises a sentimental code: diamonds for constancy, rubies for passion, emeralds for jealousy. . . . They reflect and refract the light that passes through them. In so doing, they shatter unitary images. Look through them and things become at once fragmented and multiple. The refractive quality of cut gems is a metaphor for analysis, brilliance, and pluralism. And, in excess, banality.

TT: Let's take the theme of technology in SF, which has often been contrasted with the theme of science. Do you make some such distinction?

SRD: For purposes of informal conversation I must. Since other people make it, if I wish to talk to them—even about obliterating it—provisionally I have to go along with it. On a more theoretical level, however, I don't know whether it's such a useful distinction after all. I'm not so sure I'm ready to say that science and technology are two different things.

TT: Is there any way in which, for you, science and technology disclose a contradictory relationship?

SRD: I think the problem with the terms—and, indeed, the concepts—is somewhat similar to the problem recently articulated over the distinction between anthropology and history. A good number of historians, of a more marxian bent, have claimed that anthropology, as it is usually studied, has no real and valid object: that a study of culture that is not also a study of the material history of that culture is no study at all. To study the abstract system—the culture—by which a given society functions without talking about the economics, food patterns, weather and housing, population pressures, transhumance and husbandry, and the political and social adjustments to them all, and what's more, not only how these factors impinge on the lives of the people today, but also how they impinged on them a generation ago, five generations ago, or five hundred years ago, is not to study anything real, these historians claim. It is to give object status to something that is ontologically only an aspect of an object. They go on to historify their argument, pointing out that "anthropology" began as that subject one had to read in the British university system if, indeed, one was destined to go off and work in a colonial country for the British foreign service. Anthropology—the study of the "pure," "uncontaminated" "culture" of an "anhistorical" people—was, they point out, the study of all those aspects of the society one needed to communicate with it, to manipulate it, and to control it, along with the systematic suppression of all the elements that might lead one to respect it, to grant that people an equal political status, to comprehend and respond to their sovereign rights and desires—a suppression of what might lead your ordinary Englishman to a view of an autonomous people struggling with the same problems as the rest of the world and deserving of political integrity.

From the notion of oneself as a subject *outside* of history it's a very easy step to that of a people—a collection of subjects—*without* a history.

Nevertheless, history was what confirmed the humanity of Europe. That's why no other society was allowed, by Europe, to have one. Non-European countries, unless like Japan they went to war with Europe, were only allowed a more or less anhistorical anthropology. (What's important, I suppose, about the "postmodern" subject-in-history I tried—and, doubtless, failed—to evoke in that lyric blurt above is that it's a notion of history-and-the-subject that can be denied to *no* one. As soon as you do, you're misreading it.)

A very similar analysis can be made, intraculturally, about the relation of science and technology. Science tends to be seen as a discipline which has as its object a set of purely mental functions apart from any materialistic mooring. Rather the materialist world, from time to time, embodies it as technology. But science exists as the revelations of incontravertible truths by pure acts of mind—even when those acts are called "observations"; even when what is observed is organized by "experimentation."

In no way, understand, do I suggest that intellectual activity cannot proceed apart from its pragmatic applications. That would be to deny that the cultural aspects of a society—religious, aesthetic, philosophical, or scientific—existed. But an aspect is not an object. And in the same way that the notion of a pure culture (the presumed object of anthropology) becomes one with an imperialistic ideology that justifies abuses toward a society because that society "has no history," the notion of pure science as a materialistically uncontaminated mental activity, which, as it constitutes a presumed object apart from technology, can then be infused into technology's artifacts that proceed to manifest this mentation, is quite possibly the major conceptual disaster by which technological abuse proceeds: Because technology partakes of this spiritual quality that is "the scientific," it is beyond criticism. Conversely, those who would condemn the uses of technology marshal their evidence only to confirm that it is the spirit—science—that is evil. This essentialist bickering gets us nowhere.

TT: This again brings me back to *The Einstein Intersection,* in which you seem to have meant science by the Einsteinian convex curve and technology by the Gödelian concave curve.

SRD: You are still caught in a certain dualism that leaves both concepts—science and technology—too impoverished for my tastes. That dualistic reduction (into one object wholly mental, and one object completely material, one seen as wholly abstract and thus beyond criticism, the other seen as wholly and pragmatically determined—thus amounting to the same thing) is, I suspect, the locus of the abuse.

Myself, I would start by positing an area, that is also a disciplinary object, richer than either (and which I would favor, yes, with the name technology—not at all an innocent term or choice, it certainly displays my materialist biases), while relegating the aspect of it which usually goes under the rubric of science to "theory," or some such move. And I would make it clear that "theory," even among those who work with it exclusively, such as cosmologists or abstract mathematicians, is not an object; it is rather and always an aspect of an object and, therefore, dependent on and responsive to other object aspects, however we maneuver it.

The Einstein Intersection you must remember was begun when I was twenty-three. I'm now forty-three. At the time I was fascinated by the

Gödel theorem from the famous paper of 1936. It seemed to mark out the rational limit of rationality. But in that paper, Gödel specifically warns against using his theorem metaphorically: Obviously he was aware of its metaphorical urgency. But the theorem as he posited it was only a logical aspect of arithmetic systems.

Now in my SF novel, absolutely ignoring Gödel, I do precisely what that wise man warned us not to. In that book, Gödel's theorem becomes *nothing* but a metaphor. There was a great risk there—and unless one is willing to face that risk as a critic, and talk clearly about what is at stake in such a risk (i.e., what was lost), I don't think there is much you can say about the "Gödelian" aspect of the book. Indeed, it's arguable that for just that reason the book *has* no Gödelian aspect—though Gödel's name is bandied about in it.

By the way, something that might interest your readers. *The Einstein Intersection* was originally titled *A Fabulous, Formless Darkness.* The first publisher changed the name for commercial considerations. But after two decades the book will be reprinted next year, as part of an omnibus edition (*The Complete Nebula Award Winning Fiction,* Bantam Books, 1986) with its proper title restored. That makes me very happy.

TT: Resistance to the existing system is, I believe, what characterizes both the SF of the '60s New Wave, with which you were, however inaccurately, associated and the current cyberpunk movement in SF, with which you have been quite vocally sympathetic. But for a moment let me pay special attention to Philip K. Dick. Although his works have sometimes been regarded as part of New Wave SF, *Do Androids Dream of Electric Sheep?* triggered the movement we now call cyberpunk when the text found its visual possibility in Ridley Scott's *Bladerunner.* It seems to me that the key to the cyberpunk movement lies in this difference between written Dick and visual Dick.

SRD: Alas, I can't let you have your moment quite so easily—at least not without betraying my SF critical enterprise for the last ten years. I've written other places that I think the academic tendency to import a resistance—or what I usually call an oppositional—model to explain various SF phenomena, such as the New Wave SF of the '60s and now the cyberpunk movement of the '80s, is inappropriate and distorting. Since I've discussed it before, perhaps I shouldn't take you to task for it here. I'd just like to point out, however, that when the first novel from a new, cyberpunk writer like Gibson takes both the Nebula Award (which is voted on by all the six hundred odd SF writers and editors who make up the SFWA) and the Hugo Award (which is voted on by the approximately fifteen hundred readers who register in advance for the World

SF Convention), how much resistance to the cyberpunk movement can there in fact be between this new movement and the field? My own perception is rather that, once editor Gardner Dozois gave the cyberpunks their name in the pages of *Isaac Asimov's SF Magazine,* the entire SF field, readers and writers, took them to its bosom as some of the most interesting and energetic SF production going on right now—as indeed they are.

But you were asking about Dick.

I've always felt the thing that makes Dick popular—with, indeed, the people he's popular with—is his stories' insistent endorsement of what, from time to time, has been called "the liberal-Jewish worldview." This is a worldview I certainly grew up with and, short of an outright radical social reorganization, is the worldview I subscribe to: If it's not the best of all possible *Weltanschauungen,* it's immeasurably preferable to all sorts of others lying about. And it's certainly the one in this country most likely to sustain a radical dialogue from which its humanist reductions may be critiqued.

The problem with Dick is simply that he wrote so much and, often, so badly. I mean sentence by sentence. What people claim to like in Dick is his constant interrogation of reality: What you thought was real is always turning out to be illusion. What was solid is always a dream. What was certain becomes uncertain. But what remains solid underneath it all is the liberal ideology beneath that material uncertainty: and that's very reassuring to a certain readership. On all the other points in your question, I agree—though I think Gibson's image of "cyberspace" has more to do with Disney's *Tron* than Scott's *Bladerunner.*

TT: What was and is the New Wave for you now? How do you like what J. G. Ballard has written recently?

SRD: "New Wave" is a historical term that refers, for me and for most working SF writers over thirty-five, to a group of writers who were publishing in *New Worlds* magazine from about 1965 to about 1970. Applied to too much else, the term becomes merely mystificational.

The most recent works of J. G. Ballard are quite fascinating. Ballard was, of course, both in the minds of readers at the time and in the minds of writers at the time, the most aesthetically energetic and the most representative writer of that particular island of SF production, dubbed "the New Wave" by Judith Merril in 1966 (in a kind of parodic gesture toward the French cinema's *nouvelle vague*). Ballard's most recent work is, of course, his fascinating autobiography, *Empire of the Sun.* But although it takes its title from a work of proto-science fiction, *The States and Empires of the Sun,* the fragmentary second volume in a proposed trilogy of utopian satires by Savinien Cyrano (the historical Cyrano de Bergerac), its science fictional element is nonextant.

TT: But in general you yourself are thought of as part of the American counterpart of the New Wave movement.

SRD: And so was every other SF writer who entered the field between 1960 and 1970 who was not a regular contributor to *Analog Magazine*—the spiritual antipode from *New Worlds.* (A tally of the writers who published in both would probably slay forever the oppositional model that distorts most academic assessments of the New Wave.) That is to say, once the term was cut loose from a very specific group of writers, with a specific aesthetic program and a particular publishing outlet, and was used to designate various and sundry essentialist oppositions at work without border, boundary, or citable locus throughout the sea of SF production in the late '60s and early '70s, as perceived by this academic or that, the term loses its object and becomes merely a way to propagate historical distortion.

I simply was not a part of the New Wave as it existed at its historical moment. I very much *wanted* to be a part of that exciting and vigorous island of production in the sea of '60s SF. Like the vast majority of SF writers at the time, I was sympathetic with it as a program, even if I wasn't wholly bowled over by all the stories. (Who was? Still, this sympathy, which was almost ubiquitous among the active writers at the time, is another reason why the oppositional model is inappropriate. There were probably no more than half a dozen critical voices who felt the New Wave was in principle a bad thing.) But the SF I was writing back then—*Babel-17* and *Nova*—was basically space-opera. The aesthetic program of the New Wave was oriented toward near future SF, like Moorcock's Jerry Cornellius stories, Disch's *Camp Concentration,* Pamela Zoline's "The Heat Death of the Universe," and, of course, Ballard's series of "condensed novels" that finally became in his collection *The Atrocity Exhibition.* Whatever their range of experimental writing techniques, whatever their science fictional thrust, these stories all tended to reflect the world of the here and now very directly. (Or the world of the there and then: This *was* 1967.) The New Wave just wasn't interested in space opera, no matter how well written. Nor should they have been.

The one story of mine that *New Worlds* printed, "Time Considered as a Helix of Semi-Precious Stones" (1969), was published over editor Moorcock's objections, through the good offices of his American assistant, Jim Sallis. Moorcock felt—and felt quite rightly—that there were other magazines that *would* accept this kind of tale. Therefore printing it in

New Worlds was at best a waste of pages that might be better given to a more unusual *type* of story that might have had difficulty finding a home in the standard SF magazines. Unfortunately my story went on to win me my fourth Nebula Award as well as a Hugo Award from the World Science Fiction Convention at Heidelberg. And so it managed to establish a spurious link between my name and the New Wave. If only because of that, the story has always been something of a sore point with Moorcock. Although he and I were (and are) friendly, he nevertheless makes a point of disclaiming it when he can. Nor do I blame him. I try to set matters straight too when I get a chance. But it violates one of those simple-minded stories everyone likes to tell.

A strong and terribly important characteristic of SF is its accepting quality. Almost immediately, various stories that *were* much in the spirit of the stories that were appearing in *New Worlds* began to appear, if not in *Analog*, then in *F&SF*, and the various magazines of the *Galaxy* combine. Damon Knight's hardcover *Orbit* series was established in the United States—which became an island of production of its own, with its own particular tone and texture. If I were going to use the phrase "American counterpart to the New Wave," the *Orbit* series' twenty-one volumes are what *I* would cite. (And I never published in *Orbit* either.) The publication of my story in *New Worlds* is a clear and positive example of the accepting quality common to the whole SF genre. But to make anything else of it is to remain stubbornly oblivious to historical fact in the name of a very simple-minded tale of oppositions that never existed and oppositions overcome by efforts never made. But, as I've said and written before, the oppositional model you affirm with your statement about "Resistance to the existing system . . ." no more provides valid organization for the historical evidence remaining from the New Wave than it does for the popular and exciting cyberpunk movement right now. Critique is not resistance—even vigorous, polemical critique. It is how that critique is received that determines resistance. And that's what people who talk in terms of opposition fail to historify.

TT: The last time I met Thai SF writer Somtow Sucharitkul, he told me that he had just had a very emotional talk with you on the phone.

SRD: That was shortly after Theodore Sturgeon died. Sturgeon's death was very moving—and very upsetting. Sturgeon was a very important writer to me. When I was an adolescent and then a young man, Sturgeon's stories gave me days, months, years of soaring joy; he made writing seem both wonderful and possible. If words could do what he made them do—not that I had a jot of his talent to do it—then writing was a justifiable thing at which to spend my life. Then, when I was in my early thirties, I first met the man—and discovered that this extraordinary artist was also a real and human being, who was proud of his children and grateful for praise and would put his arm around you and hug you, or make jokes about salads, or discourse on Japanese beer, or laugh with you or listen to you while drawing on his pipe.

Then, a dozen years later, he died.

When Somtow's appreciation of Sturgeon appeared in *Fantasy Review,* I was deeply touched. And I phoned Somtow to tell him how much it affected me.

Yes, it was a very emotional conversation. I cried.

TT: Now let me move on to your most recent novel, *Stars in My Pocket Like Grains of Sand.* It is widely accepted that one of the New Wave's achievements lies, according to Colin Greenland's *The Entropy Exhibition,* in the violation of taboos—specifically in dealing with the problem of sexuality among others. Even in your earlier works, for example *The Einstein Intersection,* you problematize traditional views of sex by inventing three biological sexes. And in *Stars* you appear to push this problematization further, by dealing with the homosexual relationship between your characters Rat Korga and Marq Dyeth. I would like to ask: How did you set about to make the exploration of gayness effective in SF discourse?

SRD: Again, you must allow me to back up just a bit. You say that one of the New Wave's achievements lies in its breaking taboos in order to deal with sexuality. I don't think you can really locate any particularly energetic exploration of sexuality in the historical New Wave: Ballard, Disch, Zoline, and Aldiss are, if anything, rather asexual writers as far as their SF goes. At least in terms of affect.

Another island of production—another American counterpart, if you prefer—was comprised of writers who were drawn into Harlan Ellison's monumental anthology project, *Dangerous Visions* (1967). Indeed, if you want to locate me on a particular island, that is doubtless the one on which I belong. But it also must be stated this island was of a different density and a different stability from, say, the island represented in England by *New Worlds* or the island represented in the U.S. by *Orbit. New Worlds* was a magazine; and *Orbit,* a hardcover series of anthologies, went through some twenty-one volumes. In both there was real feedback. The same writers published in them again and again. *Dangerous Vision* was also a series of anthologies. But there were only three of them—the last of which has still not been published. And each writer only appeared (more or less) once. Ellison's aim, even if he did not achieve it, was to get *something* from everyone in the field. But it was a strongly edited series. (My first submission was rejected.) Thus it was a very affecting experience for many of the writers—especially the younger ones; but some of the older ones as well.

Now on *this* particular island, sexuality was, indeed, an articulate concern. In much the same way that Moorcock wanted stories for *New Worlds* that could not be published other places, Ellison wanted stories for *Dangerous Visions* that could not appear in other places. Yet I think anyone will agree that *Dangerous Visions* had a very different tone and texture from *New Worlds*—not to mention *Orbit* on the one hand, *F&SF* on another hand—and *Analog*.

The *development* of the concern with sexuality, what made "sexuality in SF" something more than a masculine yawp demanding to be let blurt a few more dirty words, what made it a topic for exploration and for science fictional manipulation, what took it beyond the initial explorations of Farmer's "The Lovers" (1952) or Sturgeon's "The World Well Lost" (1953) and *Venus Plus X* (1960) were the works by those writers most concerned with feminist questions as they emerged in the middle and late sixties. Certainly the strongest of them were the women writers who came to prominent attention at the time: Russ, Charnas, Le Guin, and later Tiptree, McIntyre, Varley (male), Lynn, and Sargent: a very, very strong current in the recent sea of SF production. Even if that current has not precipitated an island, it's only because it has not associated itself with a specific publishing outlet.

Now that we have that straightened out, we can go on to *Stars in My Pocket*—if it still interests you.

TT: What interested me most in this book was your deconstruction of maleness itself rather than your championing of gayness. This is important, because while the concept of femininity is powerfully deconstructed by the current feminism, that of maleness is not questioned yet to the full.

SRD: I take your comment about the deconstruction of maleness as a fulsome compliment. Thank you.

Myself, though, I wonder if a phrase such as "the deconstruction of maleness" might not, in the long run, be more applicable to another novel of mine, *Triton*. There, a certain masculine psychology, treated as a social object, is analyzed down into its conflicting elements until it can no longer be radically distinguished from a certain "femininity" that men begin by defining and distinguishing as wholly apart from and supplementary to the masculine. In *Stars in My Pocket* I don't really do more than subvert the notion of masculinity. In the rather darker second volume, I hope to show that subversion is more apparent than actual—precisely because it is *not* analyzed, because it is *not* deconstructed.

TT: The reason I focus on this problem is that with this new framework of gay literature you seem to have added another Chinese box of minor literature, to use a term from Delueze and Guatari, to the existing Chinese boxes in your writing—for example, black literature, pornography, science fiction, speculative fiction, SF criticism and heroic fantasy. As to the possibility of black literature as minor literature, Henry Louis Gates, Jr., maintains, in his work, that black literature is not simply a complex formal reaction to the western literary canon, but tends to revise and reflect western rhetorical strategies even more than it echoes black vernacular literary forms. What role has the structure of minor literatures played for you?

SRD: "Minor literature"—women's fiction, feminist fiction (another area), black fiction, gay fiction, experimental fiction, as well as all the commercial genres (not to mention their ubiquitous overlaps)—has become, I suspect, the model for the literary itself. Literature is a marginal, strategic, and subversive activity at play in the social margins of politics, industry, advertising, and the media, and the minor literatures are, of course, on the margin of the margin. "The margin of the margin" recalls Derrida's "the signifier of the signifier" as the model for all signification.

Minor literatures become privileged in that their situations refract, explain, and finally control the larger literary condition, which they analyze literature down into. Literature with a capital "L," to the extent it still exits after the recent theoretical onslaught, still sees itself as reflecting life in some direct and unbiased way—largely, I suspect, through the offices of psychology. As soon as we admit, by whatever figural means, our bias as real and living writers, we *become* minor, of course. I think if any white, vanilla-heterosexual male were honest enough to write from the position that he and his class had some of the *real* problems they do through a set of historical constraints locally manifested, *that* would probably be dismissed out of hand as the *most* minor of minor literatures—precisely because it would blow open the whole literary game, the game in which the white-male-heterosexual *position* is assumed to be the particular dream-outside-of-history in which, today, everyone could, of course, live comfortably and, there, be Masters of

History—if only we'd all leap ever so lightly into it . . . as if (1) they would let more than a token number of us in, assuming we all wanted to go, and (2) they could possibly exist in the particular dream they do without their material, social, oppressive relations to the rest of us.

The unbiased, apolitical literary text presents directly a major truth of life (putting aside all that contestatory, minor, politically oriented writing). . . .

The pure unmediated voice presents directly a true and authentic meaning (putting aside writing itself). . . .

We know the form of the argument.

Minor literature (and/or paraliterature, if you will) refracts, contests, and agonizes with this other "unbiased" literature, calls it to task, puts it in question, and, with violence, appropriates, desecrates, ignores, falls victim to, and brilliantly recuts the multiple facets of its conventions. Certainly that seems to be the thrust of Professor Gates' contention, as you have just related it to me—a contention I can concur with. That Gates wants to take this to the rhetorical level gives me a huge, critical sense of relief. The evidence, in terms of black literature, is there from *Our Nig* through *Black No More* and *Their Eyes Were Watching God* to *Mumbo Jumbo* and *The Color Purple.* So I wouldn't be surprised if people began to pay more attention to paraliterature, if only because of its modular priority in terms of the larger, illusory, literary schema.

But we'd best not forget that literature, at least since the rise of the novel, has *always* existed in the same predatory, appropriative, violent relation to folk literatures, minor literatures, paraliteratures. It is these bright, violent, multiple infractions (are they really so much "misprisions"? Can't we read into them more individual anger in one direction, personal smugness in another, and—across the board—social necessity and ideological motivation than is covered by the suggestion of mere mistake?) that allow the text to mean.

The metafictive argument, which we've just ambled into by a back metaphor, is one I only balk at when it becomes reductionist and proscriptive: Instead of "Literature refracts other literature, and that refractive process is what constitutes the literary," too often we get "Literature reflects other literature and that's *all* it does or can do or should do or try to do; therefore that is all we should ever talk about when we talk about literature," which is just terrorism and *not* the same thing at all.

Literature—whether a particular piece right through here is being judged minor or major—will reflect just about anything you want to read into it. . . . *if* you read intensely and intelligently enough. So will paraliterature. That's why texts are unmasterable. I'm tempted to say that's *how* they're unmasterable, too. But we mustn't sabotage our *bons mots* with too much precision. That just insults the reader.

TT: At this point, what I really want to ask is if you've ever felt that it is your biographical life that has persistently allegorized the fates and possibilities of minor literature within you—black literature, gay literature, science fiction, and so forth.

SRD: At least once I've used my life directly in my work. In one of the (so far) nine Nevèrÿon stories there's a section, in the seventh tale, "The Tale of Fog and Granite," in which the main character goes to the end of a bridge, very early in the morning, the terminal side of which, at the old marketplace, functions as a kind of prehistoric public transportation depot.

Well, in the ninth tale, "The Tale of Plagues and Carnivals"—a tale with a more experimental surface than some of the other stories—I include the actual journal entry, recounting an actual early morning visit to the Port Authority Bus Terminal, on which that part in the earlier tale was based: The reader can see, if she or he is disposed to, what was reflected, altered, reversed, revised, or distorted from the journal text in order to form the fictive one. But rarely is the rewriting so direct. Basically that was an experiment in method.

TT: Haven't you felt that it is you yourself who have been allegorized by minor literary genres?

SRD: Do you mean that, in critical terms, I have received a certain sort of packaging? I suppose I have. But it's as I said to your first or second question: the relation between orders of fiction is always problematic. This is true of the relation between autobiography, which is only another kind of fiction, and more traditionally so-considered fictive forms.

But if you will allow me to point it out, I detect a certain allegorical closure throughout the range of your questions this morning. Earlier, you asked if certain characters in my novels were allegories of the writer. Then you suggested that the text itself might be an allegory of my life. Now you ask whether the writer's life is allegorized in the minority genres themselves. I suspect this particular allegorical circle is another literary importation: The life mirrors the text mirrors the genre mirrors the life. But I question whether this is an interesting story for a critic to tell, at least here in the precincts of SF. Against the tug of that closure, I'd rather hold your final question open.

Currently, literature has at least three critical allegories that it finds energetic and intriguing: There is the old "New Critical" allegory where the text is read as an allegory of its own aesthetic engendering. The second is the one so brilliantly carried out by Paul de Man in one direction and Barbara Johnson in another, where the text is read as an allegory of its own interpretive problems and aporias. The third is Shoshana Felman's brilliant variation on this in "Turning the Screw of Interpretation," where the text is read as an allegorical anticipation of the critical dialogue grown up about it. But there is some difficulty, if not danger, in importing these allegories of reading into SF criticism. The first smacks a bit too much of idealism and the sublime. And the latter two presuppose canonical texts which have garnered a set of critical interpretations, a range of critical problems. This has not yet happened to the truly interesting SF texts.

But there are other allegories of reading one can pursue with profit through the paraliterary domain. For example, an interesting allegory for an SF critic to tease out might be the way in which the power relations depicted in the SF text allegorize the power relations between the literary genres and the paraliterary genre of SF. Another example: Since the SF text that takes place in the future invariably poses some critique of the lacunaic structure of history, the SF critic might want to read minutely and carefully over the way in which the relation between the SF writer's life and the writer's SF text allegorizes the historical critique dramatized by the text itself. And still another: To the extent that it extrapolates on science, the SF text always poses a critique of one or another aspects of the current philosophy of science. The critic might then try to read in detail the way in which the relation between the specific SF text and the greater SF genre allegorizes the critique of the philosophy of science dramatized in the specific SF text. . . .

But to specify these allegories is to see them proliferate about us. They are complex allegories. They are allegories that would demand a sophisticated, articulate, and knowledgeable critic, at home with theory, philosophy, history, science, and science fiction.

But wouldn't these allegories produce more interesting critical fictions, more informative and interesting stories—here where we pause at the beginning of serious SF criticism—than would a simple and circular closure that does not even retain the sharpness of focus to produce an exciting *mise-en-abîme*, a closure before which the silent and attentive—dare we say religious?—contemplation of correspondences between "author," "work," and "genre" only marks a thrice reiterated confirmation of the monologic subject, heavy with late-romantic significance, stalled among the sundered and essentialist concepts of Individual, Culture, and Society, each, in its interminable reifications, alienated from the others?

7.

Sex, Race, and Science Fiction: The *Callaloo* Interview

Robert F. Reid-Pharr sent me the following half-dozen questions for an interview to be part of a section on Black Science Fiction, proposed by editor Charles Rowell for his extraordinarily wide-ranging journal of black literature, Callaloo, *in 1989. I responded in writing. The interview was published in the Spring 1990 issue.*

Robert F. Reed-Pharr: Sex and sexuality are recurring themes in all of your later works. I wonder what meaning, what insights, you believe it's possible to glean from an examination of sexuality, particularly that of the sexual "minorities," the homosexual, the sadomasochist, the participant in cross-generational or "anonymous" sex. Here I am specifically referring to your characters Gorgik and his sexualized slave collar, Kid and his sexual trespassing of gender and age boundaries, Marq Dyeth and his use of "the runs."

Samuel R. Delany: I suppose the first thing your question brings to mind is Yeats' comment that sex and death alone are the topics complex enough fully to engage a mature mind—not that I agree with Yeats. History is another topic I'd add, with the rider that the mind which is only concerned with sex and death, and not concerned with history, probably is quite wanting in what most of us would recognize as the mature.

But we're perhaps privileged today in our knowledge that sex and death are, themselves, historical. They play different parts in our world today from the parts they've played at other historical moments, not to mention the parts they play today at other geosocial sites.

My father was an undertaker in Harlem, and I grew up, for all practical purposes, surrounded by corpses—the dead of our community who were being prepared for burial, according to community rituals. That experience helped to create what I've come to consider a fairly healthy view of death—but a very different one from, say, the view that a child raised in a war-ravaged or famine-ridden land might have . . . though such views might very well be equally realistic, and are clearly important.

It's also a very different view from the one that grew out of my own father's childhood encounter with death, that I've talked about at the end of another interview, published as "The Semiology of Silence," in the journal *Science-Fiction Studies* (see Part I, Chapter 1).

But *your* question was about sex.

From World War II to the present, I can't imagine a period of *greater* historical change in attitudes toward sex—not to mention toward death. (Can one of these change *without* the other's changing?)

In the decade in which I was born, the prevailing attitude was that, for those who could confine their sexual behavior to an extraordinarily limited range, sexuality, if approached properly, could become the grounding for total and transcendent happiness—especially for women. But for anyone whose behavior strayed outside that range, even for a moment, sexuality would become the dark, terrifying, and inexorable ground for doom, defeat, degradation, death, and misery. Moreover, this was as it should be.

The civil rights movement asked some fundamentally historical questions and in the course of that interrogation questioned—ever so slightly, as we can judge today, though that questioning appeared radical enough at the time—the sexual stereotypes entailed in racial ones. Besides fanning the flame of civil rights, World War II had already produced a general loosening of moral strictures that was to widen the split established as far back as the twenties, and exacerbated by the thirties, between a bohemian, or underground, culture aspiring to free love, wild music, and a range of enhanced experiences on the one hand, and, on the other, a mainstream culture that felt that it was its own particular duty to compensate for the excesses of the war by an overly rigid, *echt*-American, and ever-smiling domestic perfection.

In the sixties, the women's liberation movement, followed by the gay liberation movement (both of them using the civil rights movement as fundamental model), now began to push for an even more radical and self-consciously analytical questioning of sexual expectations all through our society than the "underground culture" had informally initiated. The underground, the overground, the left and the right each became, in turn (especially for feminist critics), objects of scrutiny.

Let me say that as the women's movement and the gay rights movement have gotten away from the civil rights movement as model, both have found themselves backsliding into far more reactionary positions than, at former times, they once dared to occupy. But the reason for this is, I suspect, that the questioning both began with was *so* fundamentally radical that, since material changes didn't arrive to stabilize some of the answers, those answers simply couldn't be held onto; and we've watched some of those answers metamorphose back into more reactionary forms, for want of a materially realized society to support them. What the civil rights model privileges is, of course, a constant review of power, money, violence, education, freedom, shelter, health, and food.

You have to know the state of all of those—and have some sense of the history of them all—practically day by day, if you're going to stabilize any sort of theoretical progress, in any radical liberation program—racial, genderal, class, or sexual.

There is a very naive—but probably necessary—question that is practically impossible to escape, given where we seem to be in this historical process:

"Given the fact that I sit where I do on the sexual map, can sexuality become the basis for *my* total and transcendent happiness?"

Now personally, I think that's a very historically constrained—even distorted—question. It's a question that, despite the most understandable pathos, could not even be asked if the astonishingly retrograde presumptions of that (overground) 1950s view of sexuality hadn't been internalized and uncritically accepted. And anyone who answers that question either "Yes" *or* "No" is essentially working to establish a very retrograde view of sexuality itself.

Yet some form or another of this question is what a good number of readers come to my work with. Naive as it is, I have great sympathy with it. The fact is, I'm always having to teach myself, then reteach myself, then reteach myself again, why and how it's invalid.

Now to call the question invalid is not the same as answering it with a "no"—and thus dooming oneself to a life of ascetic chastity. That's never been my answer. It's not today in the age of AIDS. Nor was it ever, yesterday. It means, rather, again and again asking yourself how sexuality is constituted into the life you happen to be living, now, today—whatever period your life is in: whether it be the thirteen years or three months or eight years you live with a mate or a lover; whether it be the three years or ten years or three months your sexual activity is more or less limited to what is available in the various promiscuous lanes of our society—heterosexual or homosexual; or whether it be the three weeks, or three months, or three years when, through whatever combination of decision and circumstance, your sexual behavior is confined to the masturbatory. In fact, even to ask the question—how is sexuality constituted in my life, now—is to realize that the categories suggested by those three clauses (sex with a mate; promiscuous sex; masturbation) are, in themselves, of the same reactionary order as the internalized presumptions that underlie that most naive question we began with—that, indeed, such analytic categories, and the assumption of their logical autonomy and experiential adequacy for the understanding of sex, may *be* the internalized presuppositions that support the conservative view of sexuality in the first place.

Sex is a process to be integrated into one's life over an astonishing range of specific and bodily ways. And the frightening, troubling, deeply unsettling insight we all now have to live with is that that range of possibilities *far* surpasses the ones suggested by the oppositions faithful/promiscuous or masturbatory/abstinent that lurk under and finally all but constrain the tripartite division we began with: lover/promiscuous/masturbatory.

Questions such as these, I've tried to dramatize in my fiction from various sides, starting with *Dhalgren* or some of the stories—like "Aye, and Gomorrah . . ." and "Time Considered as a Helix of Semi-Precious Stones"—written just before it.

I suppose I do agree with Yeats in that sex is often an older man's or women's preoccupation, if only because of the pressing problems it brings to the fore through aphanasis. Sex plays a much larger role in the personality than the simple dispersal of physical pleasure, so that when, with age, it starts to go, some very real reconfigurations of the personality have to take place once again—reconfigurations as violent, and as difficult, if not as outright painful, as those which occur around the dramatic increase of sexuality during the changeover from childhood to adolescence.

As a gay man pushing fifty, I'm aware that the older person knows most of what she or he does about sex through the holes and absences in the personality its increasing failure begins to highlight.

Those absences are the site of *pure* desire—sometimes the most painful of states, which the young, by and large, simply do *not* have to contend with.

To return to your question, however: I write about homosexuality because it's been the site of most of my own sexual experience.

As for sadomasochism, I began writing about it because, at one time, for many people it represented some sort of sexual limit case—although in just fifteen years that has changed enough to mark, I feel, notable headway. At least I'd hope that was the case among my own readers. If some of my stories provided "laboratory conditions" for the *gedanken* experiments with which they've reached some new understanding, then—no matter how the stories are judged—I'm pleased.

RFR-P: It's immediately apparent in much of your work that you are concerned with "the problems of representation." You constantly reiterate the fact that the written text—like one of Venn's mirrors in "The Tale of Old Venn"—is reflecting reality rather than simply providing a transparent window through which the reader experiences some unmediated "nonrepresentation." Yet though it is often impossible for the reader to forget that s/he is indeed experiencing a representation and not reality, the reading experience is still quite enjoyable on a visceral level. The work is always "sexy, compelling, exciting." I wonder if you could talk about how you are able both to force the reader to maintain some critical distance from the text while pushing him/her to an emotional identification with the characters that makes the reading of a Delany novel or short story more than just an intellectual exercise.

SRD: I'm fascinated by the way your question exhibits such an ambiguous attitude to the "representation" problem about which it turns. You say that "the written text . . . is reflecting [i.e., reversing the values of] reality" and thus is functioning as a mediation (although "reflection" is usually a metaphor for textual transparency, as in the text that "holds the mirror up to nature"); yet only a handful of predicates later, you can talk of the text as "pushing [the reader] to an emotional identification with the characters" that suggests that, when the text is being enjoyed (when the experience of the text is both "visceral" and "intellectual"), somehow mediation is no longer as important.

At one point, "critical distance" functions; at another, no "critical distance" is in effect: rather, the text *is* an experience.

In your question that causal opposition seems to be based on the fact that when the text registers as "sexy, compelling, exciting," then somehow we have escaped into some sort of encounter with the world in which textual mediation diminishes.

Well, while I think all the implied terms ("critical distance," "lack of critical distance," "lack of awareness of mediation," "awareness of mediation," "the text is an experience," "the text is not as enjoyable an experience when it is only intellectual," "the text is more enjoyable when it is both intellectual and visceral") in your argument are valid, I think the oppositional relations you manage, willy-nilly, to set up between them all ("critical distance" is to "lack of critical distance" as "text as intellectual" is to "text as visceral *and* intellectual" as "lack of enjoyment" is to "enjoyment" as "awareness of mediation" is to "lack of awareness of mediation") are simply wrong.

There are primarily intellectual texts (from newspaper articles to scientific reports) that we accept as unmediated just as there are texts both visceral and intellectual that foreground their mediation. There are some highly intellectual texts that I have enjoyed far more than some very sleazy texts that were both intellectual and visceral. And no matter how visceral and intellectual a text may be, the farther away in time its origin, the more generally aware of its mediation we are. Paradoxically, the further away in time its origin, the less aware we tend to be of its specific foregroundings of its mediation. And, at different times, we might be critical—or noncritical—of any one of them.

This interview might be considered, for example, as the interplay of two primarily intellectual texts, one of which is trying to foreground the rhetorical assumptions that mediate—indeed, that constitute—the other; which necessitates the one's remaining blind to much of its own rhetoricity.

The poststructuralist lesson we are conveniently forgetting here is, however, no happier a lesson than the one we just arrived at in our consideration of sexuality. Indeed, it is much the same lesson:

It is precisely at the point when we are most caught up in the text, when we are most aware of the story *or* the information that it purports to convey (and most unaware of the text as such, that is: of the text's rhetoricity) that we are *most* ensnared, trapped, and victimized by mediation, by rhetoric itself.

The point is, we never *escape* it.

The choice we have, rather, is to be critical of the power of mediation over us—or to be victimized by mediation because, for a few pages or a few paragraphs, we have become blind to it.

Textuality *is* mediation per se. To experience textuality for moments as *invisible* is to *confirm* mediation's strength—not to deny it.

But even when mediation is—momentarily—invisible, it doesn't "vanish." Some readers—the late James Blish (that fine science fiction writer and exemplary Joycean), was, oddly, one of them—simply refuse to go along with any text they read as *intentionally* reminding them of its mediation. But they tend to be readers committed to a very rigid antimodernist aesthetic—an aesthetic that, fortunately, is not all *that* common. And if they were consistent with themselves, they could enjoy neither Shakespeare (with his endless plays within plays and his constant cross-genderal puns on the sex of the actors playing women disguised as men) nor the range of romantic poetry, which, with every rhyme and trope, constantly declares that the poet is writing a poem.

I happened to escape reading that way (or trying to write that way) because of two factors: One was logical, the other historical.

It's easier to give the logical reason first, then continue as though the historical one was an outgrowth of it, when in truth it's the other way around.

But—logically—by the time I was in my early twenties, I'd figured out the following contradiction. On the one hand, the commercial writers around me, whenever they got hold of a critical platform, were forever calling for writing "that did not attract attention to itself"; they championed a writing that was "wholly transparent." On the other hand, they were also calling for writing that was "concise, vivid, inventive, and insightful."

Well, it finally cleared for me:

One: Writing that does not attract attention to itself is always writing that is most like most other writing. That is the *only* writing that can even approach the illusion of "transparency."

Two: Writing that's concise, vivid, inventive, and insightful is fairly rare—especially in commercial writing.

Three: Therefore, commercial writing that *is* concise, vivid, inventive, and insightful *will* attract attention to itself *because* it's rare and is *not* like most other commercial writing.

Thus the whole commercial writing enterprise is based on a contradiction and—thus—its program is impossible to follow. Like the rest of our critical apparatus, it presupposes a golden age when all writing was good (i.e., when high quality was ubiquitous), which we have now fallen away from. The split and fallen state it assumes we have reached is not very different from the one that literary studies, with their assumption of an anterior period of classical unity, are basically founded on. . . .

The historical aspect of all this was one I seldom see spoken of today—but much of the "entertainment" literature of my childhood and adolescence consisted of the plays of Giradoux, Anouilh, and Cocteau: as well as the Gide of *Oedipe* and *Thesée,* the Camus of *Caligula,* and the Sartre of *Les Mouches.* I remember my seventh grade English teacher reading us *Amphytrion-38* and the whole class responding with delighted laughter. And I was ten or eleven when I was taken to Broadway to see Michael Redgrave in *La Guerre de Troi n'aura pas lieu* (aka *Tiger at the Gates*); I was still quoting lines from it in stories I wrote when I was twenty-four. Cocteau's account of the Oedipus legend, *The Infernal Machine,* was the first play I read all the way through, in the fifth or sixth grade (just before I read Lillian Hellman's *Watch on the Rhine*). The point is, these were all plays of the Resistance; many of their writers were highly political; or, like Cocteau, they verged on the surreal. But all had turned to mythology—and turned to it in wholly self-conscious ways. The characters in their mythical plays were *founded* on anachronism: They were constantly stepping out of their roles to remind the audience, with the same line by which they confirmed their wholly modern stance, that they were entirely textual—rather than transparently historical—creations.

When Katharine Hepburn, playing Eleanor of Aquitaine, declared to

Peter O'Toole, playing Henry II, in the movie *The Lion in Winter,* "Oh, for God's sake, Henry—it's the middle of the eleventh century!" not only did I laugh with the rest of the audience, but I felt, not that the reality of that insistently "realistic" movie had been shattered, but rather that it had been heightened: I can't conceive of a time when people *didn't* project the progress of a lifetime or a decade onto the whole of eternity—and while I'm sure that, in the eleventh century, there were other ways of expressing it, that's still what the anachronism figured for the audience; that was the base of its satirical thrust at the present—and, thus, of its humor.

In one sense, I just kept on doing more or less the same thing that the writers I'd enjoyed up till then had been doing all along.

In works like *The Einstein Intersection* or *Nova,* to remind the reader that mediation/representation was the name of the game was, in itself, nothing new. I'd enjoyed it in writers from Shakespeare and Shaw to André Gide and Alexander Trocchi. If anything, I was brought up a bit short by the occasional science fiction voice claiming, in one review or another, that such moments broke the bubble and destroyed all possible enjoyment.

RFR-P: I am certain that you would agree that while science fiction is one of the more popular of the literary genres it is also one of the least respected critically. What does it mean to you as a writer, particularly one so concerned with critical theory and linguistics, that you write in this undervalued medium? Have you been afforded some artistic or professional "freedom" because of your choice of science fiction as your primary vehicle? What difference does publishing with houses like Ace versus more mainstream houses make on the artistic and professional life of a writer with your particular sensibilities?

SRD: Certainty is, of course, a dangerous position for a critic to assume about anything. And what my critical theory and linguistic concerns immediately force me to do is to state that, while popular, science fiction is *not* a literary genre. Historically it develops primarily outside the literary precincts and—moreover—you cannot understand what it does and how it does it unless you have a clear vision of its historical development in fundamental opposition to what SF has always seen (however clearly, however cloudily) literature to be.

For us to assume, here, that SF is a "literary" genre would be to mire us in the same sorts of contradictions that a white interviewer, interviewing someone black, would ensnare the whole discussion in by beginning a question:

"I am certain that you would agree that while blacks constitute one of the great races of the West, they are also treated by whites as one of the most inferior. . . ."

The fact is: The crime is not a matter of a "great race" treated as an "inferior race." It is rather that a complex of lies, contradictions, and obfuscations is fundamental to the very notion of race and has been used to oppress and exploit a group of people who occupy a certain historical position, who have arrived at the present along a certain historical trajectory.

If such a discussion is to be anything but bombast on both sides, the black in question had better halt the white interviewer at the start and make that clear from the beginning.

Again, the fact is: Literature as we know it today is a local illusion. The notion of a self-evidently superior group of texts, which eventually defines an interdependent group of literary genres (genres in which, at any given moment, the vast majority of specific examples are appallingly written and not worth consideration, but all of which are nevertheless a part of literature while somehow, still, falling outside it), genres which, in their idealized form, nevertheless constitute "literature" per se, is not very far from the notion of a self-evidently superior group of individuals, which eventually define an interdependent array of civilized social categories (social categories in which, at any given moment, the vast majority of specific individuals behave barbarically and follow only the path of ethical least resistance, but who are nevertheless at once a part of civilization while they constantly act outside it), social categories which, in their idealized form, nevertheless constitute "civilization" per se. Well, "the civilized," when it is presented without irony, is the fascist concept that grounds its inverse, "the primitive"; and it is the opposition between the two which grounds the idea of "race."

Now to say that literature is an illusion is in no way to deny that there are beautiful, rich, and rewarding texts—any more than it suggests that there are no courageous, ethical, and socially aware people. We enter the realm of illusion only when we take these very real things and hypostatize from them a transcendental (rather than an ironic) category, such as the "civilized" or the "literary," that at once causes them and that they cause.

I hope it's beginning to come clear that, basically, I am answering all your questions with a single reply.

You ask have I been afforded any particular freedom by choosing to write SF—or, perhaps, by publishing with nonmainstream paperback houses such as Ace?

Well, I might mention that, since 1978, I *haven't* published with Ace—once the Science Fiction Writers of America audited the company and found that it had stolen some $19,000 in royalties from me . . . and hundreds of thousands of dollars from a number of other SF writers. No, I don't think there was any particular freedom involved.

Let me hasten to point out that the current Ace Books has no managerial continuity with the company of which I just spoke. From editorial to accounting, it is an entirely different and—today—quite respectable institution. But I mention that sad moment in the history of SF publishing simply to remind you that a ghetto is a ghetto. Life there is usually harsher and harder than life in those precincts that drain money, goods, and energy out of that ghetto, and whose own vitality, if not survival, would be seriously compromised without the ghetto—as "mainstream" culture would be compromised without its constant invigorating thefts and more covert appropriations from the precincts of popular culture, be they that of popular music or of mysteries or of science fiction or of what-have-you. Ghetto culture is something to be analyzed, respected, and understood with compassion—even awe. But there is little to romanticize about it, in terms of such overarching notions as "freedom"—or, for that matter, power, money, violence, health, food, shelter, or education.

The lessons one learns in the ghetto about all such topics are not usually pleasant ones.

RFR-P: Following the previous question, I wonder if you could discuss the ways in which you have challenged the traditional—and often repeated—narratives found in much science fiction. It seems that you are self-consciously pressing against the barriers of both "traditional" hardware narratives (*Nova, Triton, Stars in My Pocket Like Grains of Sand*) as well as the sword-and-sorcery narratives (the Nevèrÿon series).

SRD: Here, of course, is the place where I must turn around and defend "ghetto culture"—that is, the science fiction ghetto: and defend it with the language, the metaphors, the rhetoric that accrue to me as a black writer who grew up, till age fifteen or so, in New York's black ghetto, Harlem.

In thematic science fiction terms, I have been an extremely conservative SF writer. The New Wave of the 1960s, for example, which various academics are always trying to place me "at the head of," was actually a group of far-looking writers from whom I was all but excluded precisely *because* of my SF conservatism: I was interested in space operas and hardware at precisely the point when they, with great vigor and energy, were turning away from such writerly pursuits as puerile.

The Nevèrÿon enterprise, for example, is to articulate for adults the hidden and subterranean currents that are forever at play in the largely infantile genre of sword-and-sorcery: to make explicit—and use the tale as a stage radically to explore—the sadomasochistic and homoerotic elements without which Howard's *Conan the Conqueror* would never have survived, nor proliferated into a subgenre of its own.

Yet the argument can be—and has been—made that, since the genre *is* infantile, why not simply leave it behind and go do something else? My essentially redemptive crusade, which seeks to reread Howard and Moore and Leiber and Russ and Moorcock and Saunders, may at worst be doomed *by* that fundamental infantilism and at best can only create a highly specialized verbal inflation—four volumes and seventeen hundred pages worth, so far—of the most limited interest.

That, at any rate, is the most elegant form of the argument against my work, as I see it.

Now there are many SF and fantasy writers who honestly feel that my work for the last fifteen or more years has been wholly misguided, if not deranged. Paradoxically, I feel that such a judgment is finally *more* informed—without being in any way more correct—than the extrageneric view that sees my enterprise as revolutionary *in terms of the genre.* The only view less informed is the one that sees my enterprise as, somehow, fundamentally literary and having *nothing to do* with the genre.

My answer to that most elegant form of the argument, as I tried to present it above, is that, finally, it strikes me as just a refined restatement of the commercial argument I outlined for you with your second question. The commercial contradictions in the reception history of these texts as they have been published—*Dhalgren, Triton,* the Nevèrÿon series—suggests strongly to me that something else is really going on behind that argument as applied to those books. Too many people seem to have already found something in them of value. What I am doing in almost all my books is the genre equivalent of "gender bending." That's how all genres expand, progress, survive. It's a paradox that when the results look *most* revolutionary, that's when the writer is *most* attending to the tradition.

I would be very happy for someone—other than me—to ferret out what, really, *is* going on behind that argument, in terms of my last twenty years' work. But to attempt such an analysis under the categories available within a model that sees me as somehow fighting *against* the genre from which I draw all my sustenance, inspiration, and strength is doomed to the same sorts of mystification that we are all too familiar with: the argument that sees every successful black as one who has successfully fought—or fought down—the socially detrimental factors that make *all* blacks into muggers, thieves, drug addicts, prostitutes, and sociopaths.

Even such distressing—and I believe, fundamentally distorted—statistics as the widely bruited "fact" that one out of ten black males in New York City will spend some time in jail *still* means that *most* black males (nine out of ten) will not. Black society is still constituted by *most* of the people—male and female—in it. All that unhappy statistic ultimately suggests is that a far higher percentage of blacks in New York City will have first-hand knowledge of the unhappy and oppressive lessons to be learned from the machinery of penal enforcement in our culture than will most whites.

If you want to look at radical writers in SF terms, look at Bear and Laidlaw and Willis and Kessel and Robinson and Sterling and Cadigan and Waldrup and Vonarburg and Bisson and Kress. These are a handful of the SF writers who are currently working to enlarge the boundaries of the genre. These names are nowhere nearly as well known as mine. And there are positive and political reasons for that. Let *them* speak to you about the problems of life in a writerly ghetto.

RFR-P: I believe that your work, your aesthetic, is evolving from one in which your life and voice are "hidden" in the text to one in which they are indeed the subject of the text. First, I wonder if you agree with this point. Second, I wonder if you could describe the process by which you have come to self-consciously use your self, your "character," as the material with which you create. To put it bluntly: How did Samuel Delany move from writing works about "other worldly" characters residing on other worlds to writing about the early years of Samuel Delany, a talented black gay science fiction writer in New York City with his wife, the equally talented Marilyn Hacker?

SRD: Do I agree with your first point? Yes. But I've always funneled the macro-structures and micro-structures of my life into my work. What's happened, I suppose, is just that, as I've garnered more and more attention in the last fifteen or twenty years, more and more of my experiences are of the sort that accrue to someone our society is observing for its various reasons—experiences of the sort that you only have when those observation processes are turned on you. At this point there are six books on my bookshelf—not by me—with my name in the title or subtitle: I've started to pay attention to how other people have been paying attention to me and have taken some of the more general aspects of the things I've noticed for my material.

I suppose I wanted to bring some awareness of historical process to bear on such notions—with whatever sense of tact I could. But that enterprise is what, say, *The Motion of Light in Water,* my autobiography of a couple of years ago, shares with §9.82 of "The Tale of Plagues and Carnivals."

RFR-P: I know that earlier in your life you seriously considered giving up writing to become a rock singer. I also know that you have directed at least one film, that you have written half a dozen books of criticism and/or social comment (*Heavenly Breakfast, The Jewel-Hinged Jaw, The American Shore, Starboard Wine, Wagner/Artaud,* and *The Straits of Messina*), and that you published four issues of a quarterly, *Quark,* with Marilyn Hacker. How then did you come to the point of fully accepting fiction as your primary means of communication? Also, in what ways have your experiences as a singer, director, critic, and editor shaped the skills—and the vision—which you bring to writing?

SRD: Well, the fact is, I don't know whether I *have* fully accepted it. In 1987 after I finished the Nevèrÿon series, I went on to accept a position as Professor of Comparative Literature at the University of Massachusetts. Since then, I've written no fiction. I didn't expect to; nor have I tried to. My primary energy has gone into teaching—which I've found rewarding.

The projects I see ahead, to the extent they involve writing, are mostly nonfiction.

None of this is, of course, engraved in stone. I've also directed a couple of plays; I've acted in some others. I was an editor on the board of a poetry magazine for three years. One summer, not so long ago, I worked as an editorial assistant in a commercial publishing house. I've also raised a daughter and, as well, worked on the continuity of a couple of other peoples' films.

Would you think I was being wholly eccentric if I raised the same sort of objection to the notion inherent in your question of a "self" that accepts *or* rejects such metaphysical states as "being a writer of fiction" (or of being a musician, or a parent) as I have to some of the other rhetorical presuppositions in some of your other questions?

To be effective, to produce any practical results, any such "acceptance" has to have an intensely local quality to it. "What must I do to write this passage *now?*" "What does this music require at *this* moment, in *this* situation?" "What parenting does this child need *here?*" The emotions rumbling under and around such questions (rather than any such articulations themselves) produce anything and everything, valuable or disastrous, that falls out of our lives.

I've given up writing fiction a number of times. Coming back to it often has the quality—as you say—of "fully accepting fiction as [my] primary means of communication." But then, giving it up in the first place had the quality of fully accepting something *else* in place of it—very possibly something that didn't involve communicating at all. But I've given fiction up enough times to know there's no real reason to worry about it. It's not even something to dignify with a term like "writer's block"—I don't feel in any way that my writing is out of my control, which seems to be what "writer's block" is about. I want to go on teaching a while—and writing, when I do, about the things that come up in conjunction with it or in opposition to it.

Part II

1.

The Kenneth James Interview

In Spring of 1986, I spent a productive and pleasant term as a Senior Fellow at Cornell University's Society for the Humanities. Then an undergraduate at Cornell's Risley College, Kenneth James first interviewed me while I was in residence. A few months after I left Cornell, Mr. James sent me a set of follow-up questions. That second set of questions and the answers I wrote to him constitute "The Kenneth James Interview." This is its first publication.

Kenneth James: The relation of the artist to his society is a recurring theme in nearly all of your novels. The central characters of your stories are, almost without exception, artists of some kind. In SF the protagonists are often scientists: logical, analytical types. What interests you in the artist's creative and emotional responses to the world?

Samuel R. Delany: Well, back when I was writing my first SF novels, I was married to a very fine artist, the poet Marilyn Hacker—so that the relation of the artist to *her* world was something I had a chance to observe day to day. It went along with walking down to the 2nd Street supermarket to do the shopping or going around the corner to the storefront office on Avenue B to bring Mr. Greenberg his rent.

Marilyn *was* the logical, analytical type. She had (and has) a wonderful sense of humor and a wide and raucous silly streak. Sometimes she could be emotionally very guarded, or, sometimes, emotionally all over the place—probably one compensated for the other. But logic and analysis dominated, much in the way they do in the traditional mathematician. (So much for the clichés about poets.) There used to be a radio program, which eventually moved to television, called the *The Quiz Kids,* in which a panel of precocious youngsters sat around in caps and gowns and answered bizarre questions sent in by adults. For a season just beyond her toddling stage, Marilyn had been the youngest Quiz Kid. She was also an avid SF reader—as was I—by the time we met at the Bronx

High School of Science. Having been a certified child prodigy—she went on to college at fifteen and had all but graduated by eighteen, when we married—she was very wary about exposing herself to new areas of information. Since she'd always been able to turn in a pretty spectacular intellectual performance in just about any area she tried, the prospect of being a beginner again, even for a while, was not one, as a youngster, she cherished—though, Lord knows, there were enough areas about which she was already awesomely informed. (New life experiences, on the contrary, she sought out with astonishing gusto, given that she was so physically frail.) But when, for example, some years later, I became interested in poststructuralism and literary theory, she couldn't have found it duller. Ten years after our separation and divorce, though we're still friends, she, I'm afraid, still regards my interest in such things the way you might the interest of an otherwise reasonable acquaintance in acupuncture or astrology.

At any rate, in the years just before and after our marriage, watching this thin young woman in thick glasses (with, at the time, a two-foot length of dark bronze hair down her back) write her early poems, being around her while the detritus of daily life, from a paint flake cracking from the ceiling while we were having some intense discussion to an anecdote a friend told her about a nearly supernatural incident that occurred while he was at a Vermont boys' school in World War II, transmuted into lines of dizzying musicality, not to mention being the poems' first reader, was hugely exciting.

It made my whole adolescence and early manhood an adventure.

The actual poetic process is not something I've ever written about directly—at least not in my SF novels. I don't remember ever writing about what it looked like, or how heart-catching it could be to be around. To convey that, you'd have to transmit something directly of the impact of the poems themselves, of this half-line undergoing its more and more luminous revisions, of that tercet suddenly aglow from the heat of its final cadence, or of the whole poem, all its pieces mortared wonderfully in place—an impact that, yes, may be greater for someone who's seen the engine working with the case off.

But we'd inherited—probably from the uncritical part of a leftist leaning to our adolescent politics—the notion that, however personally committed you were to it (and we were about as committed to writing as two adolescents pell-melling into adulthood could be), art was—no matter how thrilling its creation—a secondary social activity in the greater social scheme.

To write a fine sonnet was a wondrous feat; but to build an apartment house was to change the world . . . we were caught up in some silliness like that! But that was the other reason why I felt it necessary to keep the creative act out of the *center* of my novels.

About four months after our marriage, when she was just nineteen, while on scholarship to the Art Students' League in New York, one darkening November afternoon as she was leaving the 57th Street building, Marilyn was accosted by an interviewer and some cameramen, doing a section for that night's ten-o'clock TV news. "Why, in this age of science," he asked her, along with a dozen others making their way home, "do you want to be an artist?"

"I don't really see that much difference between them," Marilyn answered, into their lenses through hers. "Both are based on fine observation of the real world."

And if you can avoid the vulgar leap that joins fine observation of the world contingently to direct representation of the world, and if you don't mind the fact that "real world" has neither a capital R nor a capital W but is rather a social construct given by a consensus that your own observations may well contravene, contradict, or revise, then you have a big plank in our aesthetic platform back then—and, I suppose, now. Because, like Marilyn, I saw the best of them as fine observers, I thought artists were good people to *tell* the story. Look over their shoulder, I felt, and you might see something interesting. But for that other, basically ideological reason (the secondary status of art in general), I felt that the *making* of art shouldn't be the primary topic of the story told.

Although, today, I'm much more inclined to grant artistic effort the same status I would to ditch digging or dry cleaning, I still don't believe I've ever based a whole story, much less a novel, on what an artist at work really looks like, or goes through when she's working, or what the situations are that disrupt that work, deflect it, or slow it down.

To the extent that some of those early SF novels are social microcosms, the artist had to be there—the poet, say, in *The Fall of the Towers*. Which is to say, your question begins most astutely: The relation between the artist and the world was, however obliquely, what from time to time I turned to. Oh, there are artists aplenty in my books and stories; but in those same books the creative process is, with only a few exceptions, a given—not an object of dramatic analysis. When I write about artists, I'm fond enough of them. But the psychology of the artists as artist is something that—save, perhaps for bits and pieces of *Dhalgren*—I never found a fictive topic of consuming interest.

The real reason was, as I said, ideological bias; today, I suppose, it's just habit.

KJ: While you maintain that the act of artistic creation per se does not interest you as core subject matter for a story, "The Tale of Plagues and Carnivals" from *Flight from Nevèrÿon* seems to write itself before our eyes. The "author" periodically interrupts the narrative to address the reader directly and makes it very clear that the story, as well as the entire Nevèrÿon series, is an evolving work of art and of criticism. This kind of self-documenting commentary suggests to me that one of the primary concerns of *Flight* is, after all, the creative process. In light of your own previous comments, what could be more deeply concerned with the creative process than a self-critiquing novel?

SRD: Well, you can make too much of a statement such as "I don't find the creative process *per se* interesting." Not contradicting anything I've already said, that's still a relative interest. With "The Tale of Plagues and Carnivals," I'd only note that one main concern of the whole Nevèrÿon series, along with sex and power, is narrativity itself. The commentary's thrust is, I suspect, more toward the workings of narrativity than toward the workings of creativity.

There are some meditations on the creative process wedged here and there into *The American Shore.* (If you're criticizing a work of art at a certain rigorous level, you have to have some stated or implied model of what "creating" it consisted of.) My view of what artistic creation actually is hasn't changed much since I wrote about "fictive creation" in that 1978 book.

The one place where creativity is visibly foregrounded in the Nevèrÿon series actually lies *between* two stories.

Section 9.7 of "The Tale of Plagues and Carnivals" is a journal account of a trip I took down to the Port Authority Bus station at five o'clock in the morning to catch a bus to Philadelphia for an academic conference, "Post Barthes/Post Bakhtin," at Temple University in 1982. Most readers will recognize it as the basic material for Chapters 4 and 6 of "The Tale of Fog and Granite," where the young smuggler comes down to the Bridge of Lost Desire and, after his encounter with the one-eyed man, takes off with the student he picks up as he starts his journey south. If you like, you can go through the two sections sentence by sentence to see how the journal entry was transformed, expanded, reversed, enriched, or cut to create the fictive account. Does one become an allegory of the other? Does one critique the other? Do they say different things? Do they make different statements about epistemology, society, or writing?

These, I guess, would be the "creative" questions one might ask about the two texts and how they relate.

The commentary in "The Tale of Plagues and Carnivals" seems to me—though I am just the writer, and therefore not a privileged interpreter—more in the line of commentary on narrative problems, political problems, problems of enunciation and enunciational juxtapositions. If you want to say, though, that there's a necessary overlap between the two—creativity and narration—I wouldn't object.

KJ: While rereading *Neveryóna,* I recalled a statement made by a student after your reading at Risley Residential College at Cornell University. The student commented that, in recent years, your writing style seemed to have become less experimental and more straightforward. I remembered your rather surprised reply that in recent years your writing had caught critical flak for doing just the opposite. Now when I compare the surface style of *Neveryóna* and the rest of the Nevèrÿon stories to that of *Stars in My Pocket Like Grains of Sand,* which was apparently written concurrently with the series, *Stars* appears to be written in a more exotic and dense style than the series, which seems comparatively "straightforward." And yet you mentioned to me that you considered the Nevèrÿon stories the more important work to you. Perhaps I'm confusing surface difficulty with literary worth, as English students often do, but I'm wondering if you might elaborate on your own evaluation.

SRD: The final evaluation of any work must be left to the reader. What do I mean when I say the Nevèrÿon tales are more important to me? Well, they've occupied me, almost obsessively, for more than ten years. Hour for hour, more work has gone into the Nevèrÿon texts than anything else I've ever written—certainly more than went into *Stars.* And the series taken as a whole comprises more words than *Dhalgren* by twenty percent.

This is probably too glib for an overarching answer, but it may be something to keep in mind. Most of the work on a text goes into simplifying it, clarifying it, expunging unnecessary clumsinesses, redundancies, and hitches in style and flow. While you retain its complexity, you work the text to present that complexity as simply as possible. The "straightforward" effect you cite may just be a *product* of the work that's gone into it—if not a product of the conception's initial intensity.

Had I put in the same sort of work on *Stars,* it may have seemed *less* "exotic" and "dense"!

On a whim, I saved all the drafts of the most recent Nevèrÿon story, "The Tale of Rumor and Desire." In a notebook, it began with a couple of weeks of notes, back in January '87. Then, from the first eight-page typed draft, to the final hundred-plus page text, there are approximately twenty-five versions, before one went to the publisher, Arbor House. You just won't find that much *labor* over the text of *Stars.* And that's characteristic of the Nevèrÿon stories. In general, once the first draft of a Nevèrÿon scene is finished, in subsequent versions, sentence by sentence, the text becomes simpler and simpler.

The novel, *Neveryóna,* has three places where you can look through, into the undertext (as it were). One is Gorgik's "market monologue." Another is Madame Keyne's monologue on sexual beauty. The third is the Earl's monologue on writing. It would be too much to say these passages resemble my first drafts in some way—a draft which, at other places, was refined to an easier and more accessible narrative. But they certainly represent the kind of *thinking* that underlies the entire book—indeed, the entire series.

I'm very pleased that, in your initial letter requesting this interview, you singled out the market monologue for praise. People who dislike the series usually point their criticisms precisely there—and at the two others, Madame Keyne's and the Earl's. I certainly hope narrational pleasures are there through all the stories. But I suspect the greatest joy to be gotten from the tales is formal—formal ways in which a reader's various critical perceptions of one incident (and the language narrating it) mirrors his or her critical perceptions of another. The journal entry about the Port Authority and the fictive account of the Bridge of Lost Desire are only among the more blatantly refractable.

On the other hand, I have to be prepared, for the series may be my *Romola*—*Romola,* you remember, was the historical novel George Eliot put years of work and research into—and wrote in a special style she invented to convey its historicism and its humanity. (I looked at some of the market scenes in *Romola* as well as in [Robert E.] Howard in preparation for the market sections in my own book.) "I began it a young woman," she said, "and finished it an old one." It was very much the novel she felt closest to—and was the one that most drained her.

But today, like Flaubert's *Temptation of St. Anthony,* we find it all but unreadable.

KJ: Something I've been meaning to bring up is the influence of poststructuralism and semiotics on your work. I'm only peripherally familiar with that whole school of thought, but it's difficult not to notice that poststructuralist texts tend to be incredibly abstruse. Now I understand that ideas can be complex and difficult to express, but the notion that some ideas are so complex that you practically have to reinvent the language in order to express them seems pretty suspicious to me. No idea is *that* complex; it just can't be. I understand that some of my problems with these texts stem from poor translations, and that these critics may, in terms of their linguistic philosophy, be trying to "practice what they preach"—but I'd like to be sure that writers like Derrida and Lacan aren't pulling the wool over my eyes—and their own. What do you think?

SRD: What you've brought up is the whole problem of "difficult discourse"—I've often wondered if it shouldn't be called the problem of "complex rhetoric." Certainly it relates to the Nevèrÿon stories: The readers who dislike the series find what you call "straightforward" hopelessly ornamental, baroque, "literary," and—even more so—too unyielding of any narrative progression to be worth the struggle. (Paradoxically, a few readers among this group make an exception for "The Tale of Plagues and Carnivals"; but I couldn't tell you if it's tone, topicality, or form that makes this one tale more readable to them.) The place you have to start any discussion of difficult discourse in America is with the whole notion of "complex" language and "simple" language, as we Americans traditionally respond to it.

Our country values "common" sense and "simple" language. It's part of our whole democratic notion—part of a necessary vision of democratic workings. What this means, however, is that to speak or write a complex rhetoric is to speak *against* the American grain, as it were—to speak outside the American tradition. This is one reason difficult discourse initially raises our suspicions and distrust.

I first read Orwell's "Politics and English Language" back when I was fifteen, and I still swear by the essay. Take a look at it. For a writer, there isn't a better work to mold a basic approach to language.

But, given Orwell's historically sensitive and moving argument for clear and common language, you still have to ask: What are the *reasons* to speak against the grain—to speak outside the tradition? There are a number of philosophical reasons that take a fair amount of complexity to explain. But there's at least one reason that can be put in the "simplest" language you want:

Thousands of lies, reams of nonsense, and barrels of bullshit are put out each day in unadorned, straightforward language. And they're swallowed right down—because no one is initially uncomfortable *with* the "simple" rhetoric. People assume sentences such as "Thousands of lies, reams of nonsense, and barrels of bullshit are put out each day in unadorned, straightforward languages," are somehow *less* rhetorical, and more transparent to truth, than, say, this sentence which both criticizes the assumptions about it and quotes it—when, indeed, both sentences are equally rhetorical, only coming from different rhetorical traditions, the inner one only more familiar than the outer (or marginal) one.

Because "simple" language is the language we have come to trust, it's easier to utter falsehoods and nonsense in it. Because "difficult discourse" is the language that, by tradition, we *dis*trust, we've always got someone ready within it to poke holes in the newest offering, ready to call that offering into question, ready to show that the currently aspiring emperor really is buck naked. To the extent a writer has a choice whether to present his or her ideas as difficult or simple discourse, to choose the difficult is to choose the road along which people are waiting to ambush your ideas, attack and hack them into dead pieces, where people are ready to dismiss you out of hand or simply to bury you by ignoring you, where the cruelest criticisms lie in wait for every statement. And a whole circle of people wait outside the critics of difficult discourse to declare: "No idea is that complex: it just can't be"—so that difficult rhetoric may be the braver choice *because* it invites distrust and criticism from the outset.

There are other social arguments for difficult discourse: One claim is that difficult discourse is less co-optable than simple discourse.

Also, in difficult discourse understanding spreads more slowly. There's a greater gap between those who *do* understand the ideas and those with no idea at all what those ideas are about. Simple language, on the other hand, tends to produce a circle of people who understand and another circle around them who misunderstand, with no very clear distinction between. The very speed at which understanding and misunderstanding alike spread and intermingle in situations of simple discourse tends to blend understanding and misunderstanding into a hopeless mass and mess, so that, over a given period, ideas put in simple language lose their strength and precision relatively quickly, even when they are important ideas.

A case in point is the history of science fiction, which has traditionally been presented in the simplest language—with the results that half that history doesn't exist any more. The mangling of the history of the New Wave is a good example. That's something I lived through and observed and know from first-hand experience. But even an account as well researched as Colin Greenland's *The Entropy Exhibition* is strangely distorted—*because* it fails to analyze theoretical assumptions and presuppositions. That analysis could only be done in a far more complex rhetoric than Greenland is comfortable with. I just wish Greenland could have dealt with the paradox—what that paradox meant—that the New Wave itself was, if not anti-intellectual, at least anti-theory and against complex rhetoric, for all its literary experimentation. (I keep wanting to wave historian Fernand Braudel's statement in the face of so many SF historians: "Without theory, there *is* no history.") In many ways the New Wave was a highly conservative movement. But you can't say, in simple language, "The New Wave was conservative," and have people do anything but blink their eyes in confusion, under the impression you've just presented them a contradiction in terms.

Another argument in favor of difficult discourse: In a social field where simple language is the privileged rhetoric of the everyday, complex rhetoric will attract people who (one) by temperament tend to think against the grain and who (two) are smart enough to deal with the rhetorical difficulties.

Difficult discourse delays popularization of truly important ideas until nonpopular thinkers can become deeply familiar with the work, and can form a slowly growing group that, when popularizations *do* begin their inevitable distortions, is there to critique those distortions and alert people to the problems inherent in them.

In short, you can reasonably argue that, in a social field *that privileges simple language,* to choose difficult discourse inaugurates a critical process, a stabilizing process, and a preservative process that works to criticize and stabilize important ideas for the good of the ideas themselves.

But here we must move on to the philosophical level and leave aside practical and institutional problems.

What we call "difficult discourse" is not, of course, simple and innocent complexity for complexity's sake. Most of what, today, you and I recognize as "difficult discourse" stems historically from the German academic tradition. (When Goebbels made his famous and frightening statement, "When I hear the word 'culture,' I reach for my gun," what he meant was specifically German academic culture, i.e., "difficult discourse"—one of the few places where people *were* trying to criticize Hitler and German National Socialism.) As that tradition moved to France and, finally, produced structuralism and poststructuralism, yes, this tradition picked up a particularly French accent. (The French allowed in the fragment sentence to balance out all those three-hundred-plus-word anacoluthons.) But, like any rhetorical tradition, there are those who write it well and those who write it badly.

At this point, I've read most of the Derrida that's been translated; some of it I've reread many times. I certainly have no sense that he is—as you verge on suggesting—an intellectual charlatan.

But I'd point out that on occasion he has called himself an "intellectual clown. . . ."

And now and again you'll encounter the phrase "the laughter of Foucault. . . ."

There's a comic aspect to difficult discourse that people daunted by the rhetoric fail to see. The comedy is not the sort that produces belly laughs (though it does sometimes). Someone once said that any truly intelligent argument is always a comic performance. This is the level where you begin to appreciate some of this writing.

Lacan? I've read the translations available and many of his commentators; I've led reading groups and seminars in his work. My early encounters with "The Seminar on 'The Purloined Letter,'" "The Insistence of the Letter in the Unconscious," and "Speech and Language in the Field and Function of Psychoanalysis" were rich and exciting. But while a number of his ideas—and, even more so, idea-galaxies—are important for our concept of the subject, of transference, and for psychoanalysis in general, I find it harder and harder to keep up my own interest in him.

But that's no reason why you shouldn't explore him.

There are still a few books promised by writers I greatly enjoy (Jane Gallup, Shoshana Felman) about Lacan that I'll devour with great interest when they appear—but that's more because I'm interested in Gallup and Felman than in Lacan himself any more. Still, having some familiarity with him will mean I've got an entrance into what *these* very exciting writers are writing about.

As for Derrida, some "entrance points" into his work have been more or less established, that is, essays that an ordinarily astute American reader can start reading and get a good intellectual purchase on what is going on.

I wouldn't advise *any* one to start with *Of Grammatology* or *Margins of Philosophy* or *Writing and Difference.* The long essay on Plato's concept of writing, however, in *Dissemination,* called "Plato's Pharmacy," is a wonderful work, which repays careful reading and does not require excessive prior knowledge. The essay "Differance," contained in *Speech and Phenomenon,* while not at all easy going, is still comparatively generous with its rewards to someone who comes to it cold. The same can be said for "Structure, Sign, and Play" (in *The Structuralist Controversy,* edited by Macksey and Donato) and the three interviews in *Positions.* In the course of these, if you also read some of the writers in dialogue with Derrida, you'll be better prepared to go on to some of his other works.

If you've read *some* Nietzsche, some few essays *about* Nietzsche, at least one Nietzsche biography, and have been curious, from a feminist viewpoint, about Nietzsche's all too rampant misogyny, you'll enjoy immensely Derrida's essay published in a small pamphlet by itself, *Spurs.*

If you haven't, however, you won't.

One problem with Derrida is that he's a brilliant and well-trained academic philosopher. His "deconstructions" of western philosophy proceed as a set of commentaries on the texts of previous philosophers.

These essays not only undertake close readings of (often) marginal pieces of other philosophers' works, but they presuppose a professional philosopher's familiarity with the study text as well as a professional philosopher's familiarity with the traditions of criticism that have accrued to the philosophers in question. Given that these are the readerly expectations of his essays, it doesn't make things easier that many of his points are made with ironies, plays on worlds, puns, and the like. But this is what the "complexity" of Derrida generally analyzes down into.

Certainly the essays in which comic aspects are most in evidence are the ones in the debate between Derrida and John Searles over the "speech-act theory" put forward by the late English philosopher John L. Austen in his 1955 William James Lectures, *How to Do Things with Words* (Harvard University Press, Cambridge Mass., 1962). The debate includes Derrida's "Signature, Event, Context," Searles' "Reply to Derrida," and Derrida's exhaustive and witty reading of Searles' reply, "Limited Inc" (contained in *Glyph* numbers 1 and 2). But you really *do* have to follow the *whole* thing—from Austen on—to know what's happening. Or, to use a Derridian phrase, to know what's at stake. Still, for a delightful read, it's worth the couple of slow days at the beginning to get through Austen's little book, in order to enjoy the rest of the exchange. Followed closely *from* the beginning, there are a good *number* of belly laughs before you reach the end!

When you say, "No idea is that complex," the preceding is really the only argument one can oppose to it: a series of specific texts, that you read, that you enjoy—or that you don't enjoy. The "idea" that Derrida is so often trying to get across—if you can call it an idea—*is* complex: The reason it's complex is because it's not so much an idea as it is a repeated demonstration of a process, in situation after situation, where meanings that at first glance seem clear, total, and masterable are shown to be undecidable, incomplete, and full of slippage and play. The sign that we are near one of these faults—these verbal optical illusions of masterability which must be analyzed (or, to use the term most associated with Derrida, "deconstructed")—seems to be any time we are in the presence of some metaphysically valorized opposition that purports to be a tension between equalities but is really a socially fixed hierarchy: for example, white / black, good / bad, speech / writing, inside / outside, male / female, culture / nature, etc.

Among these "equal and opposite" terms, the first term is always socially more desirable.

I've mentioned Shoshana Felman once. Let me recommend to you her essay "Turning the Screw of Interpretation," most recently republished in her collection *Writing and Madness*. Let me also recommend

Barbara Johnson's fine book *The Critical Difference.* (She also translated Derrida's *Dissemination.* I commend them because they are wonderful writerly performances—the same way I would commend Jane Gallup's *Reading Lacan.*) As I'm shortly going to say to you all over again, when I get to your next question, "profound ideas" are a happy adjuct of this business. But pleasure in reading is primary; and a careful encounter with these writers, these texts, is an inroad to some wonderful reading pleasure.

KJ: The next question would be, how did you first become interested in literary theory, semiotics, and the like? What idea did these texts present that appealed to you, and how does it relate to SF?

SRD: Well, it was certainly an interesting process. Back in 1967, I spent some two or three months adapting, producing, and acting in a two-hour radio play for WBAI-FM in New York City, based on a short novel of mine called "The Star-Pit," which had appeared a year before in an SF magazine called *Worlds of Tomorrow.* I got a call at the back room of the little apartment on 123rd Street, where Marilyn and I were staying with our friends Joe Soley and Paul Caruso, from a man named Baird Searles, whom I'd never met before but who eventually became a good friend. He was the head of WBAI's Drama and Literature Department. And the first time I went down to the old offices and studios, then in the third floor of an old private house on East 38th Street (they've moved several times since), I stepped into his office to find myself staring over his secretary-cum-assistant's desk at a young woman I hadn't seen for several years, but who had been a good friend of mine from the time I was fifteen or sixteen to a year or so after I'd gotten married, at which point she'd drifted out of my life.

Her name was Judy Ratner, and she'd been in Marilyn's French class at NYU, where the two of them had become great friends—and I'd somehow become part of the circle.

At any rate, it was warming to take up the friendship again. A few months later the radio play was finished. Working with Sue Schweers ("Lee," in *Heavenly Breakfast*), I'd finished hundreds of hours of post-production work on the editing, music, and special effects for the play, gone up and visited Jack Gaughan (where I wrote "We, In Some Strange Power's Employ, Move on a Rigorous Line"), come back to the city, sent Marilyn off to San Francisco to be with Link, joined the Heavenly Breakfast Commune, and, when that broke up, gotten my own ground-floor-back apartment in a tenement on 7th Street between Avenue C and Avenue D. One day I stopped in to see Judy up at the WBAI studio, and while we were having lunch together, she took out a Mentor paperback and asked me whether I knew it. It was called *Madness, Sanity, and Civilization,* and it was by Michel Foucault.

I'd seen it up on the psychology bookshelves at the old Eighth Street Book Store or down near the floor in the psychology departments of Marlboro's and Brentano's—bookstore chains in the city at the time, all since driven out by Dalton's and Walden's. "It's really very interesting," she said. "Why don't you take it with you and read it."

So I did.

A day or two later, I'd finished the first fifty pages.

I confess, I drew a perfect blank.

I had no idea *what* I was reading. Was it a history? And, if so, a history of what? Madness? Poverty? Crime? But it was all mixed with meditations on the notions of "hot and dry" and "cold and wet." And it had been dredged in the most obscure and complex rhetoric. I put it down, convinced it was beyond me. About the only thing I took from the book was that it had been translated by Richard Howard, whose name I'd seen on a number of English versions of other French books, some of which, like his translation of Gide's *The Immoralist,* I'd greatly enjoyed.

Not long after that, I walked into the Eighth Street Bookstore to see, on the front desk, a pile of the new Foucault hardcover, *The Order of Things,* from Pantheon. Somehow, I got to read the opening meditation on *Las Meninas.* It made a *little* more sense. But not much. And that New Year's Eve (1968), a few days after delivering the Ur-version of "About 5,750 Words" at the MLA (and, I believe a couple of days before, getting drunker than I'd ever been in my life with Michael Perkins at the end of a criticism session on *Equinox,* that produced a four-day hangover), I flew off to San Francisco.

We skip a year or so until I was living in the Albert Hotel, back in New York City, when, sometime late in 1972, I settled down on the orange, threadbare bedspread, to read Lévi-Strauss's *Tristes Tropiques.* By that time I'd read one or two desultory pieces by Barthes. I'd still never heard the names Derrida or Lacan. I'd read a handful of essays by Lévi-Strauss (such as the often reprinted study of the Oedipus myth), but though I'd heard of "Structuralism," I had no sense of it as a school or movement. I couldn't have told you two other names besides Lévi-Strauss's associated with it. To me, it was all vaguely connected with the essays by Noam Chomsky (*Syntactic Structures, Aspects of the Theory of Syntax*) I'd been reading at the same time.

As I began to read over Lévi-Strauss's thoughts on tourism and the primitive, I did connect the density and pacing of his sentences with those pages of Foucault I'd read a few years before. I also connected it with various essays by Charles Olson. About Olson's prose, I'd already realized: Those massive, tortured sentences, so proud and protective of their own awkwardnesses, were much like those in the fiction and poetry (but *not* in the nonfiction!) of Paul Goodman; they were the detritus of a mind truly attempting to think new things in a new manner, and struggling not to lose the newness—and, for the sake of that struggle, giving up a certain grace and polish for the raw excitement of insight. What Gertrude Stein had tried to do for the process of ordinary thought, Olsen had been trying to do for the process of extraordinary thinking. I recognized some of this pacing in Lévi-Strauss. But I also realized, even from a translation, that this was writing under the control of history and tradition to a much greater extent than Olson's—even if I didn't know what tradition (it's German academic, as I said earlier) it was.

About fifty pages into *Tristes Tropiques,* there's a chapter titled "Sunset." In February '34, young Lévi-Strauss was on a tanker, plowing about the southern French and Iberian coasts. In the course of the journey, he found himself, day after day, watching the sun rise and set. He writes:

> I watched enthralled from the empty deck as, every day, for the space of a few minutes, in all quarters of a horizon vaster than any I had ever seen before, the rising and the setting of the sun presented the beginning, development and conclusion of supernatural cataclysms. If I could find a language in which to perpetuate those appearances, at once so unstable and so resistent to description, if it were granted to me to be able to communicate with others the phases and sequence of a unique event which would never recur in the same terms, then—so it seemed to me—I should in one go have discovered the deepest secret of my profession. . . .

Following this declaration, Lévi-Strauss places a passage he composed, in observation of a sunset, on shipboard back in '34.

It ran on for eight pages.

I'm not even going to *begin* to quote it!

Go look it up and read it yourself. It starts on page 55 of the Pocket Books mass market paperback.

But it was one of the phenomenal reading experiences of my life. It is—and all it is, is—a description of what happens during a sunset, as observed from a boat deck. Half a page into it, most readers will recall, with amusement, Goethe's quip: "Even the most glorious sunset grows boring in less than half an hour."

Well, these eight pages are quite dense enough to take a good half-hour, if not an hour, to read. They describe an event that occupies no more than ten minutes in its unfolding. But it would require a fool to find them less than fascinating. To the extent Lévi-Strauss challenges Goethe's off-handed witticism and wins, it's an intensely comic victory. I laughed out loud half a dozen times at the sheer, dazzling ambition of the piece. And when I was through reading it, I had an understanding of a style of thinking *and* a style or writing that I had not had when I began it. That afternoon's reading was my first gut insight into the intricate rhetorical surface that, more than anything else, seems to characterize structuralist/poststructuralist writing.

If I had to synopsize the insight that passage gave me in a sentence, I'd say: "In this writing, ordinary processes are slowed down and fixed with a comparatively heavy, if not ponderous, diction, to allow us to see what is really going on—things that, often, we've only watched rush past."

But if you don't catch, first, the *pacing* of the thought propelling such sentences, as a reader used to the conversational speeds of thought in most writing you'll just be lost. That was why I'd gotten lost during my first encounter with Foucault. I'd had no idea where we were starting out from, or where Foucault was taking me—nor, above all, any concept of the careful and considered pace at which I was to be taken there.

But that, more than any of the institutional reasons I've cited, or the philosophical reasons that are so frequently drawn from them, is where the real excitement of "difficult discourse" lies. To read the best of these studies is a fascinating *reading* experience. But, yes, it helps to have some preparation as to just what kind of experience to expect. Otherwise, it can all become verbal mush.

Shortly after that a new edition of Foucault's *Madness and Civilization* came out (the word "Sanity" now dropped from the title); I reread it; and it made a *lot* more sense to me this time. Indeed, the culminative effect was as great, if not greater, than Lévi-Strauss's passage had been. I read *The Order of Things* and, in England a little later (when I flew to England at Christmas 1972 I took the Doubleday-Anchor reprint of Jacques Ehrmann's issue of *Yale French Studies,* from 1966, which was simply called *Structuralism;* and that is still, along with Macksey and Donato's *The Structuralist Controversy,* the best introductory anthology I know of), Barthes' *Writing Degree Zero* and *The Elements of Semiology,* as well as Lucian Goldmann's wonderful and clarifying little book, *Philosophy and the Human Sciences.* But now my reading spread out in the field far too much to bother specifying.

But that afternoon, on the 10th floor of the Albert Hotel in 1972, is where I date my serious reading in structuralism, semiotics, and theory from.

Anyone familiar with my own writings will, of course, recognize that such an epiphany as I had that afternoon was by no means accidental or random. In the middle sixties, I'd had my own mornings and evenings on boat decks in the Mediterranean. And in essays such as "About 5,750 Words" (1968) and "Thickening the Plot" (written early in 1972, only months before I read the Lévi-Strauss passage) I'd made my own attempts at slowing down the reading and writing processes to examine their details. Perhaps a week before, in a paroxysm of enthusiasm, I'd read aloud Auden's "Caliban to the Audience" to my young friends Mark Gawron and Lee Amack, when they'd come to visit. And I'd also been reading in John Ashbery's *Three Poems.* So I was rather like a supercooled liquid waiting for the crystal to drop.

But the real revelation was, to borrow Lévi-Strauss's words, "to find a language in which to perpetuate" those fleeting processes.

My book *The American Shore* (1978)—a close, slow, and detailed reading of Thomas Disch's SF short story *Angouleme*—has much more to do with Lévi-Strauss's microscopic examination of that winter sunset in 1934 than it does with, say, Barthes' *S/Z*—which, though I'd certainly heard of it before I began my own study, I only got hold of and read when I was three-quarters of the way through my own first draft.

You'd also asked if there was any particular idea that attracted me in all this reading—over and above the simple excitement of stylistic energy and phenomenal retardation. Writing the introduction to *The American Shore,* I thought I'd found such an idea that, if it wasn't common to everything called structuralism, was common to those examples of it *I'd* found most interesting. It was

> the general concept that meaning is not contained in the sign but is extrinsic to it, i.e., that the ontological location of meaning, more or less acknowledged with Sausure's appropriation of the Stoic division of sign (Greek *semeion*) into a signifier and a signified ("the perceptible *signans* and the intelligible *signatum*" writes Jakobson in *Main Trends in the Science of Language* . . .), lies in the signifier's relation to other signifiers, and that the signified is therefore always a web of signifiers, malleable in four and possibly five dimensions, the gathering into signification of any part of which invariably further excites that malleability (and that the relational field in which all this finally registers *as* meaning is the neural web of the sentient body). It is what we can say of the gross organization, synchronic and diachronic, of that web that we see as the reward to be gained from the study of any given sign, any set of signs, or any signifying figures. . . . (*The American Shore,* p. ii)

Today I wouldn't have the gall to write such a sweeping totalization of the field of intellectual endeavor I'd been dipping my toes into for only half a dozen years when I wrote it. I now know what I was balking at was essentialism. And I know the provenance of the arguments against *and* for essentialism is far longer—and more complex—than I had any notion of when I was writing the *Shore*. Yet there still isn't anything in the statement that profoundly bothers me today—which is only to reveal my own ideological blindnesses, for anyone who wants to trace them out.

Nor is it an accident you can find so many of the terms in the quoted paragraph popping up again as names of organizations in *Stars in My Pocket*, "sign," "web," and so forth.

How did this idea relate to SF? Well, for an answer there, you must struggle through (or to) the *Shore* itself. It's among my favorite of my books. (If the Nevèrÿon series is my *Ramola*, then *The American Shore* may be my *Eureka*.) But it was not the idea (of the endless displaceability of meaning) that was so important. Rather, it was what, with that idea as a given assumption about the way the world worked, you could go on to show: the things that Foucault, Barthes, and Derrida were showing.

What's so hard to explain today to young people on the verge of structuralism/poststructuralism, coming to it through graduate school courses, is that the stuff made its first impact in the sixties and seventies as incredibly exciting *reading*—even on someone like me, wholly outside the university. As has happened to many people, I've found my interest in Lévi-Strauss falling off over the years. (It parallels my growing disinterest in Lacan.) The very things that made him initially so exciting and, among some of the other writers connected with the dialogue, comparatively accessible seem, over the long run, associated with several attitudes and ideological blindnesses I find it hard to go on pursuing. But I will always be in his debt for that initial moment of insight and excitement.

But we have to remember Foucault, Derrida, and Barthes claim our attention because (like Carlyle, Ruskin, and Pater; like Walter Benjamin and Simone Weil) they are astonishing *writers*. And if you are responding to them intensely, it is as writers that they are exciting you. This doesn't mean they aren't thinkers—aren't historians, philosophers, social and literary critics. But a thinker thinks in words. And the thoughts and the words can't be separated. (It seems I've been saying this for some time now. . . .) For readers really turned on by these writers, while intellectual contexts can be given (or even created) around them, their texts can't be synopsized and re-presented in consumable paraphrases any more than can the texts of Pound and Stein, Joyce and Yeats. And that's the best answer I can give to your question about how my interest began.

2.

The Susan Grossman Interview

In 1988 Susan Grossman wrote me to request an interview, and in late April of that year in New York we had a long recorded session, followed by a very pleasant lunch. Some weeks later Ms. Grossman's transcription arrived in the mail. I reworked it. This is its first publication.

Susan Grossman: What made you decide to write your autobiography, *The Motion of Light in Water: Sex and Science Fiction Writing in the East Village: 1957–1965?*

Samuel R. Delany: For years now various people have said that, in my various critical articles, I've tended toward promiscuous autobiographizing. In criticism, I've always been generous with personal anecdotes about the incidents that led me to what some critics are comfortable presenting as mere abstract ideas. Well, I decided to give in to that tendency and run with it—or let it run with me, at least for this book. That extraordinary American novelist Willa Cather once said in an interview she gave in 1921 that the "years from eight to fifteen are the formative period in a writer's life, when he unconsciously gathers basic material. He may acquire a great many interesting impressions in his mature years but his thematic material he acquires under fifteen years of age." I suspect Ms. Cather drove her stakes in a bit too early, however—or, more accurately, she staked the field very precisely for those writers whose theme is—as hers was—the movement away from the family and into the great world. For the eight-year-old, the family, whether a loving and supportive one or a strict and repressive one, is a given at the same time as it marks out a space separate from the World. The family is a seamless fact, powerfully real, that controls all of life and living. That goes for chaotic, shattered families just as much as for stable ones.

For the fifteen-year-old, however, that same family is becoming analyzable. The fifteen-year-old writer begins to see her family as a series of interests, prejudices, habits, responding *to* things in the world, reacting *against* them. Some of those interests are even in conflict with each other. The fifteen-year-old must struggle with the realization that the family only exists in its particular form because, within it, X dominates Y for a particular end. And that's in the nicest and most loving families—as well as in the most hateful ones.

Somewhere in the course of that realization, such themes as Cather's are formed.

For the science fiction writer, though, things are different. The SF writer's overarching theme is likely to be the discovery that the world itself is negotiable. SF's grand concern is that the Great World—physical and social—that always commences as a set of appearances, be it the appearance of a sumptuous and tuneful party where the rich and lucky glitter, or of a garbage-clotted alley where the homeless amble and scavenge, or of the wheeling stars above both that change through the night, are, all of them, despite their appearance, explainable. Observe any of them long enough (and never shun technology as an aid to observation), and explanations will come forth.

The period where this major revelation strikes is both longer than, and differently placed from, the discovery of the family's limits: say, from, twelve to twenty-three. (That, incidentally, despite the dates, is the real age range covered by *The Motion of Light in Water.*) Those are the science fiction writer's formative years. You might even say that SF is the writing of adolescence—if you'll allow Literature with a capital L to be the writing of childhood. As postmodern fiction appropriates more and more of science fiction's attitudes, rhetoric, and themes, the important dates in the writer's life, when she "unconsciously gathers basic material," move further from the ones Cather set out (which, after all, do very nicely for writers from Charles Dickens through Virginia Woolf) to lean toward the ones I've located.

I've always thought I had an interesting life between the ages of thirteen and twenty-seven or thereabouts. After that, I hope, the work becomes interesting.

SG: Your life after that point settled into something more or less conventional?

SRD: I wouldn't call it more "conventional." But writing now took up a lot more time and thought. Correspondingly, the life was less . . . anecdotal.

SG: I'd wondered why you chose to focus on that period.

SRD: Well, for one thing, in social terms it marks the transition between the fifties and sixties. Things really did change about that time. Changes occurred in everything—sex, politics, art. I wanted to chronicle a bit of that change as I'd seen it.

SG: Because you were inside a lot of it? I particularly enjoyed the opening of the book when you explained that you had a certain perception of events; but when you sat down to chronicle them, or when somebody else sat down to research your chronicle, you found the reality—

SRD: Some of the reality—

SG: —objective reality, at least—

SRD: —didn't follow the way I remembered.

SG: But that the subjective reality was just as important in shaping who you were. That made me smile and sit back and think about it a while, because it's exactly the same experience everybody has—if they have someone outside to corroborate it for them. In writing a memoir or an autobiography, what do you find out about yourself? Do things surprise you as you set them down?

SRD: Well, what happens is that—as you set things down, as you write things out—incidents take on the order in which they come to you while writing. But that may not be the order they occurred in.

Often this new order obscures the old one.

At one point I gave the manuscript of *The Motion of Light* to my former wife, Marilyn Hacker. Her comments were fascinating. She remembered many things as happening in a very different progression from the progression I remembered. Often her order made more sense than mine did—even to me! Overall, Marilyn was very supportive of the project. She made lots of suggestions, almost all of which I took or responded to. I don't know whether writing such a memoir is critiquing yourself or inventing yourself. Perhaps the process is somewhere between the two. A lot of people talk about writing memories down as "getting rid" of the events. I don't think that's what happens. But you can make a case for the benefits of putting events into a kind of order so that you can see their significance more easily.

SG: But it doesn't get rid of them any more than psychoanalysis "gets rid of" them.

SRD: Right.

SG: Thirteen years after your separation and eight years after your divorce, are you still friendly with Marilyn on a current basis?

SRD: Well, we have a fourteen-year-old child in common. We both admire each other's work. The respect is still there—very much so.

SG: Her current work seems very different from what I've read of hers from when you two were teenagers. Some of the images from when she was younger were so violent.

SRD: Well, certainly vivid. She's one of the most vivid poets writing. Her particular voice is very specific, very sensory, very rich. The classical poetic task of painting a location and an epoch over the range of the work is one she accomplishes insistently well. Certainly in twenty-five years her poetry has matured and deepened and broadened—all those good things. But there's a great deal of continuity in that voice. The sensibility is a lot more sophisticated at forty-five than it was at twenty. But I can recognize an equally intricate poetic craft at work in both periods.

SG: I imagine it's exciting to be able to witness that continuity in an artist.

SRD: Yes, it is—very exciting.

SG: You've mentioned a few times—in *The Motion of Light in Water,* and in other things you've written—that you were worried about the transition from being a prodigy to being an adult artist. You talked about—the piece is in your first essay collection, *The Jewel-Hinged Jaw*—about the fact that there are few SF writers producing over the age of 35. They're trotting around to various science fiction conventions, but they're not writing much—or much of interest.

SRD: Well, there *were* a number who were trotting around at the time—and not producing.

SG: Today, are you satisfied with the transition as you've made it?

SRD: That particular essay I wrote when I was thirty or thirty-one. Now, at a ripe forty-six, things don't look so grim. Which is to say, I still seem to be working. I'm comparatively happy with what I'm doing—I don't know if anybody else is, but I keep myself entertained.

SG: That's probably what's most important. It's nice to have a certain level of financial security and a certain amount of approbation.

SRD: Yes, that helps.

SG: What of your own work do you like most—what did you enjoy writing the most? Really, that's two different questions.

SRD: And both are hard to answer. I think the Nevèrÿon series is my favorite, though, on both counts. Minutes ago, of course, I left the galleys to the second volume of the British edition of the series back on my dining room table, where I was working on them till I had to come downstairs and meet you here. I must say, galley correcting is going rather slowly. But that's partly because the weather is nice and I'd rather be outside than in.

Generally I feel most comfortable with my most recent things. I really have had more fun with them. The more organized and ordered a piece of writing is, the more fun I have with it—I'm sure you picked that up from *The Motion of Light in Water.* And the Nevèrÿon series (the overall name of the four volumes is Return to Nevèrÿon, by the bye) is certainly the most ordered and organized work I've tried.

SG: There have always been repeating elements among your books—things that circled back around from one story to the next. Is that something you find in the real world? Is it something you look for—or is it something you impose on the various tales you write?

SRD: I think it lies halfway between—between something you find and something you impose. We see repeating patterns. We see patterns that reflect one another. This constant reflection of one pattern by another is the central conceit running through the tales in Return to Nevèrÿon's four books—with the added factor that a reflection reverses the structure of the elements it reflects. And a reflection of a reflection does even more complicated things—a notion I picked up in the late '60s/early '70s, a couple of years before I started the series, from G. Spencer-Brown's little book on the calculus of indication, *The Laws of Form* (1968).

But the reflections one indulges in memoir making give you, for better or for worse, your sense of civilization as ordered and negotiable. Also, because the reflections are never exact, because no one pattern is ever wholly explained by previous patterns, because those reflections always involve one or another form of distortion—and because what makes you sensitive to images from one direction makes you blind to those from another—it also assures that civilization remains unmasterable, new, and alive.

An examination, not of the content of the reflections, but of the distortions between them, the unclear spaces, the moments of fogging, the scratches, the places that let you know a reflection, rather than "reality," is involved in the first place, teaches us about the reflective process itself. It's rarefied stuff—but that's what I'm playing with in the eleven Nevèrÿon tales. It's a very formal game—certainly not to everyone's taste. But it's kept me amused.

SG: Which of your works did you have the most trouble with?

SRD: The hardest book I ever wrote was *The Towers of Toron,* the second volume of The Fall of the Towers—the early SF trilogy I did between '62 and '65. That's chronicled in the memoir—I was just twenty when I began it. The sheer size of the project, the perseverance it required—well, it just demanded more thought, more simple physical energy, than I'd been prepared to put out.

I'd written one novel—and I suppose I'd thought writing a trilogy was simply a matter of writing three novels in the same way, one after the other.

That's often what trilogies are.

But because I'd planned the work as a trilogy from the beginning, it meant writing three novels each of which could stand alone; but at the same time, each had to deepen the experience of the one before it. Taken together, all three had to form a coherent whole. In such a case, the work and organization isn't simply additive. It goes up exponentially, volume by volume.

By the third volume, I'd realized the work I would have to do. Once I knew it, I kind of jumped in and—as best I could—tried to do it. But the second volume was the one where I was *learning* that—and I just kept balking. I kept fighting the work—and ended up having to do a lot more!

It seemed to take forever.

Dmitri Merezhkovsky's fine and wondrous novel *The Romance of Leonardo da Vinci* is the second volume of a trilogy, Christ and Antichrist; *Leonardo* is arguably the best of the three. The first volume, *Julian the Apostate* (published here as *The Death of the Gods*), seems too thin to modern readers, and the third volume, *Peter and Alexis,* is—for most

American readers, in its extant translation at any rate—too metaphysical, too contrived.

But the second volume, *Leonardo,* is rich, magical, endlessly inventive, and very human—certainly it was one of Marilyn's and my adolescent favorites.

Lawrence's *Women in Love*—certainly *his* best novel—can be looked at as the central volume in a tryptych that includes *The Rainbow* on one end and *Aaron's Rod* on the other.

But the Merezhkovskies and the Lawrences are the exceptions.

Too often middle volumes of trilogies just sag. One thinks of Robertson Davies' Deptford trilogy. Or Tolkien's *Lord of the Rings.* I think it has to do with getting hit by this underestimation of the work the whole project will take.

At any rate my trilogy rather droops in its center panel.

SG: I guess *The Fall of the Towers* is one of my all-time favorite books. I was perhaps twelve when I first picked it up. It gave me permission to break out of strictures I was taught in grammar school—because here was a real book, by a real writer, doing all these amazing things! At the same time the images struck me as just stunning and brilliant and beautiful.

SRD: Thank you very much!

SG: We had to do a reading—I was in seventh grade, I think—from some book. I decided to choose the scene where Vol Nonick's wife is being tortured to death. So here is love and sex and death all laid out for my seventh-grade class. My teacher just sat there with her hand over her mouth. She didn't say anything. Then she said: "Well, that was very . . . interesting."

SRD: That's rather astonishing. At twenty or twenty-one when I wrote it, certainly the last thing I would have imagined was a seventh grader reading it out loud to her class—though had I known about it, I'd have been thrilled at the prospect.

Perhaps the single anthologization I've been happiest over—I mean deeply happy with—was when a page-long section from *Dhalgren* was included as a student model for prose in an elementary composition textbook. Much of the classical poetry that survives from Greece and Rome is lines or sections of poems, you know, that ancient grammarians included in their texts as fine samples of various grammatical usages. Certainly up through *Dhalgren* one ambition I had for my writing—

however wide of the mark it fell—was for it to be a classic prose for its era.

SG: I also had to audition for a play that year, and since I couldn't find a monologue I liked, I put one together from the Fall's scene, in the first volume, where Prince Let is in the forest and the forest guard Quorl is explaining to him about Tloto being a sentient being. I think my teacher found that rather perplexing without a context!

SRD: As the writer, of course, what I remember is the working time. That particular section was written several years before the trilogy's first volume. It started as part of a novella I wrote when I was eighteen. I'd just come back from the Bread Loaf Writers' Conference, where I'd had a working scholarship. With a number of other young writers, I'd waited table in the conference dining room that summer. The novella was about a young waiter at a summer resort, who finally runs away from his job, lives in the woods, and meets a kind of hermit—the model for the forest guard Quorl. The young man has stopped speaking. But slowly, over a time, the hermit brings the young man back to speech—in the book, the hermit became Quorl, teaching Prince Let to speak again in chapter eight of volume one. When I wrote that first volume, I simply lifted the section from the earlier story, changed the names—and tightened a few sentences of discription.

You say you were fond of it in the seventh grade.

I was fond of it, too.

I'm very touched that it meant something to you.

Difficulty in speaking, difficulty in articulating has always been a problem that greatly moved me. Correspondingly, for me, those who help others express their own ideas, their own feelings, who empower others to seize back authentic and effective language have always been my heros. It's very warming to hear you responded to that, too, even this many years after the writing.

SG: What are your pet peeves with publishing these days?

SRD: Well, today's peeves aren't terribly different from yesterday's—or the peeves I had when I first began to publish in 1962.

But they're certainly more intense.

Ideally publishing should be an editor, at a publishing company, reading a manuscript and saying, "I like this book. I want to publish it." Ideally, the book is then printed, distributed, people buy it, like it, or don't like it, tell their friends—who buy it, like it, or don't like it. And the process goes on. Eventually, the sales more or less index the audience's like or dislike of the book.

Publishing today, however, involves anything and everything *but* that process.

Today the editor must select a book entirely in terms of the pre-extant "slot" it fits in. Then the book is sold to bookstores on a synopsis (usually no more than three sentences long) and a cover—as well as on the hype the salesmen give it as they go from store to store, distributor to distributor . . . salesmen who, in most cases, will never read the book. Again and again you hear editors say, "It was an interesting novel. But it's just not something we can do." Again and again you find editors publishing books that don't interest them as much as things they've had to reject. Today, in order to sell a book not only do you have to advertise it, but you have to advertise the advertising! "Will receive a hundred thousand dollars of national advertising!" the ads for the "Lead Best Sellers"—a prearranged slot—declare in *Publishers' Weekly*, which is what you must say to get the bookstores to start ordering large amounts of copies!

Purely in terms of the "slot" the book goes into, an advertising budget is arrived at. Purely on the strength of the advance orders (from people who haven't read it) a print run is established. This becomes the "target" sale the company aims for.

Generally speaking, only hardcover books that have a "target" above twenty-five thousand have a chance of becoming genuinely popular: Those are the only books set up to go back to press quickly enough should the orders and reorders come in heavily. With paperbacks, only those books that are targeted at over a hundred thousand have a chance at becoming bestsellers—for the same reason.

But the ordinary—or "midlist book" as it's called (whose initial printing is three thousand, five thousand, even fifteen thousand copies in hardcover)—simply *can't* become a bestseller, even if it sells out in a month. The stores aren't geared for reordering such titles. And the paperback book that sells fifty thousand, seventy thousand, eighty-five thousand is in much the same situation.

Now that's seventy, eighty-five thousand copies of a book that sells for $3.95 or $4.95. We're talking about items over which, during a run of time, some 375 *thousand* dollars will change hands—yet the ordinary laws of supply and demand have no chance of coming into play, as a determinant of success or failure!

It's the difference, of course, between "ideal capitalism," which, whatever legal restraints have to be imposed on it, our country was founded on; and consumerism, which is what we actually have. The problem with consumerism is that the consumer him- or herself is the one person in the equation with *no* power to change the system. And consumerism in any area of the arts is deadly. It wholly muffles the dialogue between artist and audience—when it doesn't simply silence it.

And the situation has gotten worse over the years. Fifteen years ago I wrote a novel that went on finally to sell a million-odd copies in paperback and at the same time produced some excellent critical reviews.

My editor has told me in no uncertain terms that if I submitted the same novel today, they would not even be able to publish it—not because the audience isn't there, but because the "slot" isn't. And without the "slot," there's no way to start the machinery working that distributes and disseminates books to a buying public.

SG: It seems that, no matter what the demand is, there aren't enough copies on the shelves. How do you know what the demand is anyway? They don't seem to release many copies to bookstores. Even though there are science fiction bookstores—specialty stores, where science fiction is accepted as "real" writing (sometimes)—I still find that you've got a certain amount of new releases and then . . . it's out of print!

SRD: That's because, as I said, supply and demand don't come into play. For the middlemen to stall the process at a point where they can stabilize a steady, predictable, and unchanging profit, where everything is sold and nothing is left over, they have to stop it well below what the demand might be. If the system were allowed to run wild, you'd have—here and there, at surprising and unpredictable local points—much larger profits. As well, overall, you'd also have much larger profits.

But there'd be more unpredictable failures, too. And the logic that consumerists use is that the instability and unpredictability of the system in the long run—the wear and tear on it, as it were—would be more costly than those overall profits would compensate for. The side effects of stabilizing the system in the way it has been range from built-in obsolescence when the system produces tools, cars, and appliances, to fostering illiteracy in the audience and a total lack of quality in the product when the system is trying to promote art.

Consumerism survives by locating—or by artificially creating—such cutoff plateaus. Right now science fiction has more or less found itself at one. Today science fiction makes up roughly 16% of all new fiction published in the United States, in terms of copies sold. But it's only 14% in terms of titles sold. Well, for the last eight years, publishers have found that whenever they try to push up the number of titles beyond what it already is, they start losing sales on other titles. At this point, the number of titles times the number of overall copies is a constant. You raise the number of titles, and the number of copies per title sold goes down. You start printing more copies, and the number of titles that sell goes down. That's because you have a fairly fixed readership.

SG: A few years ago I encountered my first example of cyberpunk. I wonder if it's becoming a problem that you can't get published unless you're picking up on this new genre.

SRD: No. Certainly cyberpunk is not threatening the run of more conventional science fiction—at all. In fact, we'd have a more interesting field if there *was* some real economic threat from the cyberpunks.

Right now they include, yes, some of the more exciting young writers we have. But the cyberpunk phenomenon is only meaningful when you remember it marks a polemical boundary. There are writers equally exciting on both sides of the line. Bill Gibson, Bruce Sterling, Tom Maddox, John Shirley, Pat Cadigan, Marc Laidlaw, Rudy Rucker, Greg Bear, Lew Shiner—these are some of the more interesting writers whose names have been linked, more or less appropriately, to the cyberpunk movement. But on the other side of the border, you *must* read, among writers of the same age, Connie Willis, Kim Stanley Robinson, Karen Joy Fowler, Octavia Butler, Paul Parks, John Kessel, Lucius Shepard, Nancy Kress, Howard Waldrop, and Susan Palwick. If you don't, the cyberpunk movement simply makes no sense. And I don't think you would be particularly surprised that, while there's only one woman—Cadigan—associated with the cyberpunks proper (who, yes, are getting the lion's share of the publicity), there are a good many woman on the far side, just as exciting as the boys' club across the way.

But to the extent that cyberpunk represents one of several aesthetic peaks over the range of current science fiction, it's rare that an aesthetic peak ever poses any real, commercial threat to the valleys running through the field.

SG: I was thinking more in terms of new writers.

SRD: Well, I've been working part-time at a hardcover publisher's—the recent financial security hasn't been all *that* great, actually. The company has a strong SF line, which includes a number of the most exciting cyberpunks.

But in the office, the new novel that the SF department is all excited over—by a new young writer—keeps getting described from desk to desk as: "It's like the best Heinlein or Asimov novel you've ever read."

Or, "It's a great SF military adventure—only it's got something really different about it."

Now I haven't read the manuscript in question. I have no way to know if these descriptions are accurate or just the enthusiasm-of-the-week you have to generate on such a job to keep it bearable.

But notice they don't describe the exciting new book by the new young writer: "It's like William Gibson, only with a certain military overlay." They don't describe it: "It's got all the technical insight and invention of Bruce Stirling, but with a more adventurous thrust." In short, the hot new novel, even in this most progressive of SF departments, is still described as "Heinlein-plus," as "Asimov-plus." Not as "cyberpunk-plus." And that's because there're still no cyberpunk "slots." Nor will there be for a while.

In commercial terms, cyberpunk is a subset of the SF adventure, with only a critical existence—but no real commercial presence.

SG: Do you have any other thoughts on new writers?

SRD: In terms of new writers, you know, we've had an interesting switch since the sixties. When I first began publishing science fiction in 1962, I was twenty. True, I was a bit young, but at that point, new writers coming into SF averaged about twenty-two, twenty-three, twenty-four years old.

Recently a woman named Kathryn Cramer did a study and discovered that the new writers today come into the field at thirty-three, thirty-four, thirty-five. It intrigues me that, in terms of the cyberpunks, the "new young writer," William Gibson, who's been publishing for five years, is only six years younger than aging, old, establishment me—who's been publishing for twenty-six years. I'm a grand old man at forty-six and Gibson is a hot young whippersnapper at forty.

I wonder if that rise in age among the entering writers doesn't mark something a bit unhealthy for the field.

Myself, I'd like to see writers coming in younger. Certainly young people out there have talent. But what it suggests is that an economic filtering system is discouraging new writers—is rejecting them outright in a way it wasn't when I was nineteen or twenty.

I wasn't unique, either. My contemporary, John Brunner, sold his first SF novel at seventeen. Grandpa Asimov was eighteen or nineteen when he entered the field, back in the late '30s. And within the SF world a whole gallery of writers are remembered for starting particularly young: Vance Aandahl, Mark Geston, James Sallis, Marc Gawron . . . all were in print before their twentieth birthdays. But those are names of the fifties, the sixties, the early seventies. Not the eighties—when a new writer is more likely to be thirty-five than twenty.

SG: It might have something to do with the whole age curve of the United States moving up.

SRD: Perhaps.

SG: Also the fact that people tend to stay in school longer. These people are getting out into the work force later. Maybe it takes them a certain amount of time to acquire familiarity with technology. That's a thing you pick up in school.

SRD: But if you're going to be a technophile, you're a technophile by sixteen or seventeen. I can't think of anybody who wasn't interested in technology by twenty-one, who became interested in it by thirty—though I know of a number of people, interested in science in their teens and twenties, who swung 'round to the humanities a few years later: Both the culture critic Donna Haraway and the literary critic Carol Jacobs began as biologists. Think of the number of writers who started out to be engineers: the French poet Paul Valéry, the German novelist Robert Musil, the English poet W. H. Auden. . . .

But examples of people moving from the arts to the sciences don't come to mind so quickly.

Perhaps there are some. But I haven't encountered them.

SG: That's not true in my circle of friends. I started out an art major; but I got my degree in biopsychology.

SRD: Well, it's rare in my experience. But I'll certainly take note of it. It's interesting that things like literary criticism, for example, are getting such a hard edge to them. The intricacy and difficulty associated with critical theory, poststructuralism—that sort of thing—have produced a niche in the softer disciplines for people with a more scientific bent. I wonder if that's compensation for the situation we're talking about.

SG: Do you think that the boundaries between the races, between genders, perhaps between classes are getting fuzzier?

SRD: Perhaps it's more accurate to say that such boundaries are always socially constituted. And what is socially constituted can be socially displaced, socially dissolved, made more malleable by certain social changes or made—indeed—more rigid by other changes.

SG: Obviously people's physical characteristics are fairly stable.

SRD: But physical characteristics are only one element of "race." People with red hair are just as physically distinguishable as people with brown skin or as people who are overweight. But the races are not constituted by physical characteristics alone. Heredity is the key factor in race. Though now and again people have been mistaking me for white all my life, I'm still black. And my daughter, who is quite blond, is also black. Still, people with darker skin generally suffer, as a group in this society, a whole set of distinguishing treatments and prejudices that people with, say, red hair, blue eyes, and fair skin—as a group—don't suffer. And, of course, in this society, people who are overweight suffer a whole set of prejudices and—let's call it by its rightful name—oppressions that are entirely different from the ones people with red hair or people with dark skins suffer (unless they happen to be overweight and black too). The point is, the constitution of physical characteristics into social groups, around notions of heredity, which then receive certain sorts of social treatment (or who then escape certain other sorts of social treatment), *is* the social constitution of such boundaries.

The malleability goes for gender distinctions just as strongly. Believe me, in Greek and Roman times gender distinctions were very different from what they are today.

Today, when you hit thirty or forty, and you've watched such boundaries fibrillate through a decade or so, you tend to think: "Gosh, the distinctions are blurring." But, really, they've been fibrillating over thousands of years. And some of the changes have been much greater than anything we've watched in the last twenty.

But as you age from twelve to twenty-three—there, you see, again those privileged years for the maturing of the science fictional imagination—you first become aware of that fibrillation and finally have a perspective from which to comment on it.

There's a wonderful quote from some Egyptian priest around fifteen hundred BC, who wrote in some treatise on papyrus—or perhaps a letter to a friend. I don't remember the exact translation. But it boils down to: "The young people nowadays. I just don't think they have the moral stamina or the values that will let them survive into the next generation."

SG: And there's nothing new under the sun.

SRD: Or, possibly, this Egyptian priest was too aware that everything he saw under the sun *was* new. And he didn't think that the old staid values were going to persist too much longer. But the truth is that the old values are always under attack. Clearly there are moments when the attack is stronger than others.

SG: There was a passage in *The Motion of Light in Water* where you stepped out and said you hoped that after the AIDS crisis was solved, it would do something permanent to people's—

SRD: It's interesting how everybody goes to that paragraph, which is on page 175, incidentally, as the center of the book. Just recently I did a reading at (of all places) a dance club called Tracks. The people who set up the reading asked me to include that paragraph.

SG: It's important.

SRD: Yes, I think so too. It makes me suspect that perhaps the changes from the fifties to the sixties were not *just* because I happened to go from being a teenager to being an adult.

All during the forties and fifties, you would hear again and again: "There's been more changes in the last fifty years than there have in the last thousand." That fifty years saw the advent of the internal combustion engine and the electric light, radio and TV, movies and central heating, air travel and air conditioners, iceboxes and gas stoves, baby food and baby bottles, buildings over four and five stories high, dishwashers and disposable diapers—hundreds of developments that radically altered the structure and texture of everyday life.

But it wasn't until the late fifties and early sixties that the explosion of information produced some real changes in people's worldviews—changes that actually registered not in a few intellectuals but over the range of middle-class and working-class society in this country.

Again and again all during the early sixties I used to find myself in this conversation with various white people who had come from various places away from the large urban centers of the country: "How could I be prejudiced?" they would ask me. "Up till two years ago I never even *saw* a black person. I didn't know there were any? Every six months or so, I heard that there were black people somewhere in the world, in my little home in Mohucket, Idaho." Then, in the next breath, they would tell you how they were frightened of black people, they felt uncomfortable being around us, they didn't know how to talk to us, but from what they could tell, we certainly seemed to have a natural sense of rhythm and were able to sing and dance well, and wasn't that wonderful. But this, of course, wasn't prejudice, was it . . . ? Today, however, even if there aren't many blacks in Mohocket, Idaho, television and movies at least allow people there to see that blacks exist. And now AIDS has let people know that open homosexuality exists—that people approach their lives in sexually different ways. And that represents a real change.

SG: I guess if it's totally out of your context, you can't be "ist"—racist, sexist, whatever—if you've never had to deal with it. I guess any sort of "ism" requires a frame of attitudes to be inside of.

SRD: Absolutely not. It can just as easily be a frame of attitudes to be *outside,* as well. Because we gain it over a historical period, we lose track of what a hard-won state civilization is; and when civilization goes, the first thing to go with it is the freedom, the egalitarianism, the notion of equality and equal treatment between individual and individual, reflected in the notion of equality before the law. The two instincts always there to battle the notion of civilization are first, "Might makes right," and, second, "The strange and unknown is dangerous, evil, and must be destroyed." The sad truth is that when civilization breaks down, it doesn't take a generation for these notions to reassert themselves—it can take as little as seconds!

The point is, people who are racist, sexist, or homophobic are just uncivilized—Freud's unhappiest discovery was that civilization is not a matter of aspiring to some sort of ideal primitivism. It demands repression. What must be repressed is fear. What must be repressed is the desire—often in response to fear—to display our might where we're sure we'll win; where, to put it in civilized terms, we're sure we can get away with it.

I don't mean such people have any less culture, in, for example, an anthropological sense than some others.

But ethically, it's not that they are *within* a frame of racist, sexist, or homophobic ideas. Rather, they are largely *outside* a frame of egalitarian ideals. What brings you inside such a frame of ideals is having to deal with social difference on a daily basis. But the people who do not have the necessary problems to solve by egalitarian means—which are, in the city, the most efficient means—tend to be simply and brutally controlled by fear of what's strange, and that fear seems to them rationally justifiable because they feel sure right is inherent in any exercise of their own power against that fear—whether it be the power of jokes and humor to allay anxiety, or the power of personal censure and individual self-righteousness in argument, the power of vigilantes to bring about what the government has said may not be done, or simply the power of the vote. And they are angered when anyone suggests that they overcome their fear or that their own powers and privileges to fight what they fear are not self-justifying.

In this light, an interesting point might be made, that nineteenth-century anthropology has conveniently muddied for us: The periodic sacrifice of virgins, that was indeed discovered in a number of primitive tribes in those years, was actually a sacrifice of women who had reached a certain age without bearing children. In terms of tribal behavior, whether or not the woman had had actual sex was usually not in question—though whether or not she had a male protector, that is, was married, might very well have been. Still, it was easy for nineteenth century England, with no concept of birth control, to rewrite that primitive situation as the "sacrifice of virgins." Am I arguing that the childless woman was strange and scary to a primitive tribe? Certainly she was rare, so that quite probably she was. But what is more interesting from the point of view of the "civilized" men who were putting together these narratives, which still control our vision of "primitive" cultures, was that what they were actually inscribing in these stories was their own immense resentment of the women in their own Victorian culture—all of whom, the best of them, or in their best years, were "virgins," of course—who were withholding sex from them, in deference to the scarcity system a male authored legal and economic matrix had engendered.

But that's a much better model of how sexism and racism works for today than turning to the Ku Klux Klan.

SG: Well, people are always going to utilize information in different ways.

SRD: Oh, absolutely, but I think—

SG: Just the availability of information.

SRD: Yes, and I think that things that make people hungry for information are far more subtle than simply what people are told they should want to know about. Fortunately.

SG: I've read papers where you've been discussed as a black writer. I've heard you discussed as a gay writer—do you see yourself as a proponent of anything in particular? If I think of you as anything, it's probably as a feminist writer. Do you see yourself as an educator or anything?

SRD: Well, I see myself as writing from a particular position. That position is black; it's gay; it's male; and it's far more contoured by the marginal workings of science fiction than what I take to be the central concerns of literature, that is, those concerns organized around "the priority of the subject."

I have a great deal of sympathy with a lot of feminist thinking. I couldn't call myself a feminist, however, because I don't think a male *can* be a feminist, no matter how sympathetic he is to women's cause. It's not my fight—it's yours. And I am of the group you will have to take power from, if you're to win that fight—if only the power to oppress you.

How sympathetic then, other than intellectually, can I be?

It's like a white person calling himself a black militant. It just doesn't quite . . . you know . . . wash. I can be a feminist "fellow traveler," if you will. But that's it. That was part of my political education. And, indeed, when a man started calling himself a feminist, that was the definitive sign he didn't understand what feminism was really about, anyway.

Recently, I've been barraged by a set of books, coming out of academia, all pointing out "male feminists," in which (some) women use the term and men use it also. I grew up in a particular ideological location where not using such a term was simply the custom. These people obviously grew up in another context. Now I must say, as I read these books, I see all the co-optations that I was warned against, that I was taught the custom was instilled to guard against, and that the idea of "male feminist" was claimed to represent. Among the male and female scholars who use the term, that co-optation seems rampant throughout their studies, their essays. And a good number of the other scholars who contribute seem to be spending much of their time pointing this out. But it's all too easy just to dismiss such work by the symptom, rather than to analyze what's in excess of that symptom—the failure of most political thinking.

But I may have to review one of these books, and I'm trying to figure out how to say all this politely.

SG: As though it were something you should be able to say to the author, were he standing in front of you or reading over your shoulder.

SRD: Something like that.

SG: That's a quote from one of your essays, "Shadows."

SRD: Yes. I recognize it. And it's something I still believe. Though occasionally, when you're reviewing something essentially political, it strains that critical precept near to breakage.

SG: Not all people worry about being politic. Some people make their reputations by being just the opposite.

SRD: Well, it has little or nothing to it do with being politic—which has a connotation of self-promotion about it. It's just better for your inner peace—also it's the most efficient critical stance. I certainly don't mean you should never get angry, or that you should never say bad or meritricious work is bad or meritricious. Certainly get angry when anger's called for—and anger is frequently called for. But anger can be expressed politely. Politeness may even be the wrong word—unless we take it to a kind of root meaning: "the proper way to act in a city." (That "polite" and "politic" come from the same root warns us how easily one can turn into the other—and we must stay on guard against precisely that.) It's something that goes along with the notion of disinterest, that very nonobjective state people occasionally call "objectivity"—which has nothing at all to do with being objective, but has everything to do, rather, with keeping the analysis at a certain level of precision. Well, you just can't maintain that level when you're jumping up and down, screaming, and calling names.

But that's why I call for a sophisticated critical tact.

3.

The K. Leslie Steiner Interview

This interview was first proposed in 1992 and carried out entirely in writing in 1993, for an issue of The Review of Contemporary Fiction*—where a much shorter and much different version indeed will appear. This is its first full publication.*

K. Leslie Steiner: Your book *Silent Interviews,* due out shortly from Wesleyan University Press, collects a shy dozen, major, meaty interviews, that have appeared in publications as diverse as *Diacritics* and the *Comics Journal.* But, looking through my Delany files, I find a dozen more: still other interviews from both Virginia's *Callaloo* and Montreal's *Science Fiction Studies,* as well as Massachusetts's *Contact,* Washington's *Lambda Book Report,* and local newspapers from Lawrence, Kansas, to Orono, Maine: vis-à-vis most of us, even most writers, you're a widely interviewed man.

Recently, however, you've discouraged personal interviews. You've urged those who would interview you to write their questions and send them to you; and you respond in writing—often very generously. *Silent Interviews* is restricted to such written interviews. And our own interview here is another through the mails—so far, five letters from me to you, twelve from you to me, and two brief phone calls—but no face-to-face contact.

What's the reason for this? Is it to maintain privacy, control of what goes into print—or what?

SAMUEL R. DELANY: The answer requires a counterquestion: What's the purpose of an interview in the first place?

If the interviewee is some sort of criminal and the idea is to spring the embarrassing and unsuspected question—"What *was* in that maroon attaché case you were seen passing to the security guard outside the building the night of July 16th?"—so that you can report the stutter, the confusion, the embarrassment that signals guilt, complicity, and malfeasance, perhaps then the live interview has a place.

But if the interview is investigative in a deeper sense, and the purpose is to find out what the interviewee actually *thinks* about matters, the written interview is more concise and efficient.

In the live interview, to questions of any complexity my answer will be lots of hemming, hawing, and sentences less than half completed while I think again—unless the topic is one I've written about within the last months; or one I've been asked about many times already; or one that's formed the subject of a class or lecture I've given recently. I can only answer a question with any ease or eloquence—or even articulateness—if I've had a chance to rehearse. Thus, precisely as the question is new and interesting, the live answer will be a botch.

KLS: What kinds of questions do you like, then, in an interview?

SRD: I've done a *fair* amount of thinking in the past fifty years about the problem of representation, the relationship between art and politics, or the place of theory in writerly explorations. All are areas I'm comfortable, if not happy, to explore with an interviewer.

Of course some questions are more likely (more likely than questions of representation, politics, and theory) to come to an interviewer's mind when she or he is addressing me, as a writer of science fiction stories and sword-and-sorcery tales—questions I abandoned long ago, because their terms were invalid and the problems they were meant to solve could be handled far better by devoting thought to wholly different matters—often a complex of different matters.

Such questions include:

"What makes a good plot?"

"What's your definition of SF?"

"Where do you get your ideas?"

Well, when an interviewer asks me such questions, I have to reconstruct why I don't believe there *is* such a thing as plot for the writer in the usual sense; or why SF belongs to a category of object, as do all written genres, for which it is impossible to find necessary and sufficient conditions (that is, it belongs to a category of object that resists definition in the rigorous sense of the word); or that ideas are *not* things but—even the simplest of them—complex processes, and as such don't "come from" any "place," but are rather process-responses to any number of complex situations.

With such questions, many of the ideas I'm dealing with are counterintuitive. And counterintuitive ideas can't be explained quickly to someone who doesn't have a firm handle on them already. Nor can you deluge someone with six or seven new counterintuitive ideas at a shot—

not if you expect the person to understand what you're talking about. Nor can you expect that person to give back a reasonable account of those ideas after just one hearing.

A temperamental reason why I prefer the written interview may be even more important. That's simply: I'm a writer. My thoughts are *formed* by writing. When I want to think with any seriousness about a topic, I write about it. Writing slows the thought processes down to where one can follow them—and elaborate on them more efficiently. Writing *is* how I do my thinking. Thus, if you want to understand what I think, ask me to write—not to speak.

KLS: Is there any formal aspect to the written interview that characterizes it—identifies if for the reader?

SRD: Yes. The interviewer's elaboration around the questions tends to be meaningful, rather than random. The questions themselves are more to the point. And the answers make sense.

KLS: On my Delany shelf are five books devoted to your work—books with your name in either title or subtitle. There are three others with substantial sections (a whole chapter or more) about you—a lot of attention for a writer just fifty. What's your response to this attention?

SRD: When it's for the work, I'm pleased. Before she died, Jean Rhys characterized literature as a great, clear lake of felt and careful writing, to which each writer tries to contribute his or her tiny trickle. The bad writing inevitably sinks into the ground to be forgotten. The good winds its way along till it joins the lake.

The fact that a few people run over to your particular streamlet—before it's absorbed one way or the other—and cry, "Look! The waters here have a particular clarity, sparkle, and freshness! As well, beyond its apparent transparency and purity, the most intricate complex of tastes and colors makes it what it is!" and they do so, moreover, in a way that attracts a few more readers—well, what writer would *not* be grateful? That's why you work on it as hard as you do.

On the other hand, something about that attention troubles. Good writing seems to project a personality. That's part of what makes it good. But the attention often becomes some judgment *on* the personality. While the writer is alive, this can be painful. So much criticism of living writers is critical discontent over the gap between what the critic perceives as the "real" personality and the personality projected by the writing. This is particularly the case if one is, as I am, a black writer, a gay writer, a writer who works largely in the paraliterary genres rather than in the traditional literary ones—that is, the writer belongs to a group which, itself, is a text projecting personality constraints. But what I'm speaking of is a problem for the most canonical of literature:

T. S. Eliot—whose personal asceticism led to a bare and intellectual poetry of infinite complexity.

Virginia Woolf—whose crystal vision grew so intense it finally encompassed madness and—ultimately—suicide.

Samuel Beckett—whose isolation generated a more and more minimalist work as a reflection of his own greater and greater despair.

Well, believe me, that's not how Eliot or Woolf or Beckett experienced it.

But there's hardly a remembered modernist—from Hart Crane and Jean Toomer, from H. D. and William Carlos Williams, from Djuna Barnes and Zora Neal Hurston, from Pound to Wyndham Lewis, to Hemingway and Gertrude Stein—for whom we don't have an instant life . . . a life that only obscures the relation between the actual complexities of any artist's working life and the work.

That "projected personality" is perhaps the greatest illusion contributing to what Baudrillard has called "the ecstasy of communication." Another counterintuitive notion: The writer does *not* project his or her personality. Rather, she or he creates a verbal machine which allows the *reader* to see aspects of his own or her own personality reflected back, but—analytical ability, precision of perception, emotional depth or perspicacity—lensed to a greater intensity, an intensity which suggests a personality we all very likely, writer and reader as well, aspire to, a personality we feel we have contact with while reading. Quite possibly, the writer—as a reader of his or her own text—has contact with it while writing, and feels it a part of him- or herself. But if the writer yearns to be that personality too blindly—too convinced that it is, indeed, his or her own—the results can be tragic.

KLS: When critics give accounts of your work, do you recognize them—or agree with them? Do you think they do you justice?

SRD: Justice is a more complicated phenomenon than critique. (It's most civilized quality is mercy.) Therefore I won't broach it here.

But Rilke said that fame was the sum of the misunderstandings current about you. And he was right. One reason for this is the many fundamental misconceptions of the sort I've been talking about.

As a limit case: In a posthumous collection, you read a cheery letter the writer wrote a friend on November 4, 1923. And you assume, reasonably, that on November 4, 1923, the writer was in a more or less cheery mood. But I've written letters in which, between one word and the next, a lover or a spouse has engaged me in an argument that has lead to tears and rage, book throwing and what all, at the end of which—two hours, or two days later—I've gone back, finished the sentence, finished the letter (just as cheerily as I began it), the whole text sealing out and over the argument, with no mention of it—though the argument was, both in content and intensity, far more important than the presumed cheerfulness for which the letter might later be taken as biographical evidence. I wish I could say such limit cases were rare. But, from time to time in my life, they've been nearer the rule than the exception. How, then, does one use the letters of Keats, of Woolf, of Crane to construct a vision of the specificity of an objectively lived life?

In the criticism of fiction we are, of course, fairly used to "exotic," if not off-the-wall, interpretations. I harken back, however, to one of those books you mentioned with my name in the title, which proposed that a woman character in a novel of mine was really a man. When I read the assertion, I took it as having a certain metaphorical margin. But at least three readers, who apparently cared about such things, wrote me to ask whether *they* had missed something, or if the *critic* had misread—a not untoward assumption with that particular book, as it was a science fiction novel in which a number of characters ended up a different sex from the one they started out.

But the point should be, I suspect, that misunderstanding is a matter of how critical assertions are taken.

Now I'm a critic too; I write a fair amount of nonfiction. But because a number of my ideas—to repeat myself—are counterintuitive, some are hard to grasp and often even harder to *précis.* Writing about them is particularly problematic for the critic who doesn't share them, or who actively disagrees with them. Speaking about them to someone not already easy with their apparent paradoxes is even harder.

KLS: Could you give an example?

SRD: Take the fundamental notion governing most of my SF criticism for the last fifteen years: that science fiction is—as are *all* practices of writing, as are *all* genres, literary and paraliterary—a way of reading. This is *not* a definition of science fiction because it applies as much to poetry, history, pornography, and philosophy as it does to SF. But it takes a while to settle oneself with the notion that science fiction is nothing *more* than a way of reading; it is nothing *less;* it is nothing *other.*

A critical notion that goes along with this: The only meaningful things we can say about SF *as* a genre tend to be about the way in which the way of reading that *is* SF differs from the way of reading that is poetry, say, or the way of reading that is naturalistic fiction, or the way of reading that is philosophy; or we can point out similarities shared between the way of readings that is SF and other ways of reading. Both are pursuable lines of study because what affects these ways of reading is specific and material: publishing policies, printing conventions, economic situations, sociological and historical events, readerly and writerly responses, educational contexts—as well as, of course, semantic conventions. Alerting people to the ways material forces contour the way of reading that is SF is a good deal of what my critical project—as far as it entails SF—has been about.

Intuitively, however, most of us feel that there is something out there in the world called science fiction—novels, stories, films, and TV shows. Even SF poems. Even SF paintings. Whatever it is out there, this science fiction, it has certain aspects—certain rhetorical features—that distinguish it from other writing or from other narrative forms that are not SF. Thus it would seem—intuitively—we are free to respond to this thing in the world in various ways: We can interpret it in various ways, and not lose sight of the fact that it *is* science fiction.

If this were the case, however, then science fiction would belong to the category of objects, like Chippendale chairs and Ford motorcars, that can, indeed, be defined: It would have its necessary and sufficient conditions.

Survey the criticism of science fiction that's been written since the genre was named in 1929, however, and you'll find that no one—absolutely no one—has been able to come up with these necessary and sufficient conditions. Moreover, thousands on thousand of pages have been devoted to the task. What one does find, instead, is that—as is the case with all written genres—there are an infinite-seeming number of sufficient conditions for science fiction: Those are the conditions about which we can say: "If it exhibits these features, it's always *possible* that it's science fiction." But there are no necessary conditions at all—not one! Those are the conditions about which we can say: "If something exhibits these features, it always *must* be science fiction."

Now, you need both for a formal definition.

At the point you realize there *are* no necessary conditions, however, you can do one of two things. You can give up the intuitive model; you can speculate that maybe SF is not a thing out there in the world, characterized by its aspects (its rhetoric), in the same way that Chippendale chairs or Ford motor cars are. And you can look for a better model—or you can do what has generally been done within the science fiction field: you can change the meaning of "definition" itself to something less rigorous, more informal, and go on playing the same intuitive game, hoping the inadequacies won't get you into too serious trouble.

But, just as intuitively, you might realize that what characterizes written genres is simply different from what characterizes Wedgewood china or Aubusson carpets—easily definable objects. Genres exist as vast and complex sets of codes, shared by thousands, if not millions, of people. It is not necessary that everybody shares all of the codes (indeed, *nobody* does), or shares them in exactly the same way. It's sufficient merely that any two or more people share an unspecified "enough" of them, for those people to be able to talk together in a way they find more or less satisfactory about texts their codes tell them belong to the genre. Thus, these codic complexes are discourses—soft-edged and changeable but—thus, again—*not* definable.

Thinking about the problems people first have accepting counterintuitive ideas, I'm thrown back to a charming anecdote about the philosopher Wittgenstein. Walking across the Cambridge grounds one day, deep in a knotty cogitative problem, Wittgenstein suddenly stopped a colleague walking toward him and demanded: "Why do people always say that it was self-evident to primitive man, looking at the sun, that the earth stood still and the sun moved through the sky around it?"

"Well," suggested his colleague, who, sensible to the philosopher's excitement, wanted to be helpful, "it just . . . *looks* like the earth stands still and the sun moves around it."

"Then what would it have looked like," replied the excited Wittgenstein, "if the *sun* stood still and the *earth* were moving?"

There is, of course, an answer to Wittgenstein and his colleague that counters both their intuitive approaches to the problem: It is not a matter of what it *looks* like at all. It's a matter of what it *feels* like. Because we can't feel the earth's turning, we might assume it stands still. We feel the same lack of motion standing six feet from the pole, where we are circling at less than a third of an inch each minute as we do standing at the equator, where we are rushing along at slightly over a thousand miles an hour. But that's why, in both places, and at all in between, people trusted their bodily feeling and assumed the sun was moving and the earth was still.

Intuitively in our culture, the self-*evident* leads us to *look* for a *visual* answer—rather than a kinesthetic one. But that's where the paradox and humor of the anecdote come from.

Now the anecdote's heuristic thrust reminds us that the counterintuitive model produces the same appearance as the intuitive one—only it explains with greater economy and elegance a number of less obvious subtleties such as the regular turn and tilt of the stars and the otherwise erratic courses of the planets across them.

What my new model of literary genres, including SF, helps explain is not only the differences, but the overlaps—and the mechanism for the endless appropriations back and forth—between SF and other genres, literary and paraliterary, as well as the changes all undergo.

In discussions of science fiction, when people who have changed the meaning of definition encounter the work of someone who has proposed a new model, often they find it difficult, or sometimes even dangerous, to give up their intuitive model. Often at first they assume the new model *is* a new, informal definition. And their accounts of it often take on the syntax, if not the vocabulary, of their old model. When I talk about SF as a way of reading—the way of reading that *is* science fiction—for example, this becomes for them the way of reading *associated with* science fiction.

The material conditions that I see as actually forming the way we read that is SF—that contour, constitute, and create science fiction; that constitute the discourse of science fiction—such critics try to understand in terms of material conditions that change *the way we read this recognizable thing in the world* that, for them, is SF. For them, an essence has been left *un*changed. For me, once those material conditions have affected the way we read, science fiction *has* changed.

For them, SF *has* a way of reading.

For me, SF *is* a way of reading.

But they tend to see the rhetoric I use to make this fine but wholly pervasive and functional distinction as crabby, cramped, and—often, at just the places where it challenges their model—impenetrable.

But you might say to me: "Well, surely you believe that there are things called SF texts in the world—*apart* from our way of reading them." To that I would answer, no, I don't.

Simply consider what would happen if all the codes that constituted the way of reading that is SF were removed from everyone's mind at once. First, no one would be able to read the *language* the stories were written in. And that way of reading, for me, even extends to the way we recognize the fact that pages with undecipherable marks on them *are* texts—that certain objects are themselves readable. Or, indeed, that something—the paper which is now covered with strange marks—is a textually meaningful object in itself, or was once a textually meaningful object, back when a vast number of other codes were known. In short, if you struck all the codes that constitute reading science fiction from all the minds around, you would strike the ability to read any thing else as well.

And if they were struck, no, there would literally *be* no science fiction in the culture.

KLS: Myself, I wouldn't say that to you: I've been reading you far too long. I would comment, however, that in much the same way as "writing," for someone like Derrida, has come to mean something more complicated and broader than sitting down to scrawl a *pro forma* note to the landlord accompanying the rent check, so "reading" for you has become a more complicated and broader process than running an eye over the list of contents on the back of the cereal box, while waiting for the morning coffee to drip through.

SRD: Yes—or rather: for me, reading has expanded to include all we do in such a situation, from taking in the fact that it's a cereal box at all and not a novel by Coover or Perec; that it's breakfast time; that we pay a certain kind of attention to what's written on that cereal box, and not another kind; the ways we might put that information to use, in terms of diet or medical situations; how we remember those contents for so long and not longer—indeed, the set of material forces that constitutes, finally, "the contents listed on the back of the box" as we read them.

KLS: So critics of science fiction have either the option of changing the notion of definition or changing the notion of reading . . . ?

SRD: Yes. Though I'd be more specific; they have the option of *reducing* the notion of definition to that of functional description; or of *broadening* the notion of reading considerably. But yes.

KLS: That's an interesting idea. . . .

SRD: You've hit on the fact, of course, the most sophisticated theorists have stressed again and again. Both the new-fangled theoretical critics, like me, and the old-fashioned thematic critics (as they are often called) are really making remarkably similar moves. The fundamental difference in what is going on is largely rhetorical—with the new-fangled critics using a lot of complex rhetoric to hold stable a very slight presuppositional, modular shift in the notion of the object of study. Still, in terms of science fiction: If you move from the literary genres to a paraliterary genre like science fiction, some concepts are going to have to change.

The question is simply which ones.

My reasons for wanting to leave the meaning of definition alone and for wanting to broaden the meaning of reading (rather than "to liberate the word," about which, despite what my friend Professor Samuelson has written elsewhere, I care nothing; like most writers, I'd rather see words used more carefully than more freely) are finally political. By reducing the meaning of definition, the science fiction critic cuts off a lot of people with whom he or she might have a productive dialogue—philosophers, say. If you change the meaning of logical terms, how are you going to benefit from what logic might have to say about what you're doing? Broadening the meaning of reading strikes me, however, as a critic, a reader, and a writer, *as* liberating. Honestly, it feels good! And by the same token, it vouchsafes the possibility of dialogue with those other critics, in other areas, who have broadened the meaning of writing and reading in other critical fields.

Fifteen years ago, my stress on the differences between science fiction and literature was seen as quite threatening—both by writers who had devoted their lives to writing fine science fiction and by critics who had devoted much of their lives to promulgating science fiction's literary value. That was because the only difference usually spoken of back then was the qualitative difference: Literature was good; most science fiction was ghastly. The oppositional stance to that position had always been some form of—no, they're the same . . . at least the best science fiction is.

But to me they obviously *weren't* the same; and once I began to write about the differences, at first people assumed the differences I was writing about, especially as some of them were fairly rarefied and hard to follow, must mask some form of the old literary argument: Literature is good and SF is bad.

But to cite the title of a book by Barbara Johnson published only a little later, we live in "*A World of Difference.*" Difference is information.

The differences between SF and literature I was discussing excited me; and I tried to write about them as if they were exciting. Five or six years later, the same critics began to read me as saying: "No, because SF has all these exciting differences from literature, SF as a genre must be *better* than literature!" Well, that's patently absurd.

Today, now that my critical interests have moved about a bit and I'm paying more attention to literary texts per se, the SF critics are saying: "Oh, look! *Now* he seems to think that literature is okay after all! Certainly has changed *his* tune, hasn't he!"

Well, though my ideas *have* changed, developed, and been refined over the years, *that* path doesn't outline the change. And the critics who think it does (not a mistake Professor Samuelson makes, by the bye) just aren't addressing what I'm doing—or have been doing.

In my SF criticism, the appreciation of literature—no, the love of literature—supports it all, just as my love of science fiction supports it . . . unto the ideological critiques of literature that, from time to time, I've offered.

At one point or another all the intuitive notions have been mine. But giving them up—even the intuitive idea of literature as a hypostatized category in itself—has made me love the wonders of words and sentences and what they can do and have done in literature and paraliterature not a jot less. If anything, jettisoning those notions has allowed me to love those wonders even more.

KLS: In the midst of all this, what is the place of the aesthetic? Do you have an aesthetic theory?

SRD: In the interplay of all these counterintuitive ideas, a specifically aesthetic theory might seem a risky business at first. With Nietzsche, we learned that God was dead. With Barthes, we learned that the author was dead. With Foucault we learned that man was dead. (It's interesting that people who have no problem negotiating these other demises again and again balk at this one—to me the most important.) With Derrida we learned that the world is constituted of language and that language is undecidable. With de Man language reached new levels of undecidability, where it became undecidable whether or not something *was* undecidable. Then, with Rorty and Davidson, we learned that language doesn't exist—and Atlantis would seem to have toppled wholly into the sea!

In the midst of such commonsense catastrophes, to speak about aesthetics might appear, at least for the moment, willfully perverse. But I am nothing if not perverse, and I *have* an aesthetic theory: It is simple and not counterintuitive at all, though at present it's not a very popular one. My theory is simply that human beings *have* an aesthetic register. Like the registers of hunger and sex, the aesthetic register is fundamentally appetitive. It manifests itself as a desire to recognize patterns, both spatial and temporal; its particular appetite ranges over spatial and temporal fields of continuity and contrast, of similarities and differences, of presences and absences—the field of texts, of fictions.

Classical aesthetic theories assumed that an appetite for the beautiful and the good lay at the center of the aesthetic register: and while lots of translations can take place between classical theories and my theory, because mine does *not* center on beauty and goodness but on order, my theory is *not* a classical theory.

This theory that the aesthetic is a human register, as autonomous as hunger or sex, explains the vexing situation that Republicans and Democrats both can enjoy Mozart, that midwives and state executioners both can love Artemisia Gentileschi, and that the guard who turned on the gas at Buchenwald and the resistance worker who gave her life to smuggle Jews out of Germany both might have delighted in Dickens.

Most people can follow the above argument as far as music and painting are concerned. But the narrative arts in this context strike them as more problematic.

Let us look at that problem, then: When representations of events are arranged in certain patterns, often they suggest moral arguments. But I hold that it is the pattern that satisfies—that appeases—the aesthetic appetite, even when we staunchly disagree with the moral arrived at.

Who today can agree with the "Great Man" theory of history toward which the vast complexity of incidents and characters weaves through Tolstoy's *War and Peace*—though it does not lose its place as one of the world's finest novels for that! Though there is no novelist more aesthetically pleasing in her or his organization of events than Jane Austen, it's the rare reader today who can really approve Austen's moral message in *Emma,* in *Persuasion,* or in *Mansfield Park.* In *Pride and Prejudice* the Bennett sisters come home in the late afternoon from watching a soldier flogged, as happy and as bubbly as a teenage party returning from an afternoon at the tetraplex, watching the latest Disney Studio animation: We bracket a certain monstrousness in Regency Society for the sake of Austen's incredibly satisfying pattern making, as it weaves her always astute observations on desire and social aspiration among her women and men into the tapestry of her novel—as the Nazi who enjoyed Dickens presumably had to bracket a certain "naive liberalism" for the sake of Dicken's macro- and micro-patterning.

But in narrative art the aesthetic is almost always confounded—it began with Plato and continues to this day—with the moral (i.e., the vision of the good) which the patterns necessarily manifest; thus, even when the patterns are isolated, they would seem to comment on whatever was referred to by the work of art: topic, milieu, moral stance, or the emotions or sensations that are allied to the work.

We only broach the counterintuitive with the realization that a pattern made with oranges is *not* the same as the "same" pattern made with apples—much less with exploded cartridge cases: The aesthetic elements form their pattern not only with the other elements "inside" the aesthetic object, but also with elements "outside" it. (Those quotation marks are needed because the complexity of the patterns is such that the inside/outside distinction vanishes fairly quickly: which is to say, actually art works *have* no insides.) The problem of individuating aesthetic patterns is identical with the problem of individuating meanings in philosophy. Still, it is the apprehension of pattern, not of emotion, that satisfied the aesthetic—though one often learns to enjoy the emotions and material allied to them as well.

My theory also explains the counterintuitive paradox that, while the aesthetic register has no particular political content itself (other than to suggest the political right to have available, at least in the Good Society, a free range of possible satisfactions, as there might be rights to a range of sexual, medical, and material freedoms), any *particular* aesthetic object *must* be political. And that is because the political, important as it is (after all, it defines the real), is *not* a register unto itself. It exists only as a range of questions that can be asked (and possibly answered) of any object (aesthetic or otherwise), and not as a presence or an essence *in* an object.

The aesthetic appetite can be refined or brutalized, can be developed or stultified; it is as socially malleable as the appetite for food and sex are socially malleable and can manifest itself in as many ways. In the same way that saints and villains both possess it, it can be allied both to pleasing and to abhorrent material—or material that different people find abhorrent or pleasing for different reasons. And people can perceive the aesthetic element in objects or materials of both sorts.

The theory suggests an explanation to that other paradox—why there are people with wonderful imaginations and great self-discipline who are nevertheless dreadful artists (since neither imagination nor self-discipline necessarily presumes a desire for patterns strong enough to create them); it also suggests an answer as to why the ability to play music well is not the ability to compose it (since a talent for underlining and highlighting patterns already there is not necessarily the same as a talent for creating them). Here I think Harold Bloom's observation that artists rebel against the fear of death more strongly than other people is more to the point than questions of imagination. So is Richard Rorty's reading of Bloom's observation: Artists are people who rebel against the failure to create.

What the aesthetic is intimately allied to is the ability to recognize genres—that is, to read and recognize patterns at a higher level of complexity.

That the contrasts and continuities that constitute aesthetic patterns are recognized as falling *within* genres *and/or* across genre boundaries seems to me—very likely—entailed with the aesthetic itself. Many years ago I wrote, about Walter Pater's observation, "All art aspires to the condition of music": Yes, and so does everything else. But people are just getting to the point of realizing (with the work of Rorty and Davidson, as

I noted earlier) that language and its meanings are a kind of complex musical behavior—in the sense that Rorty calls "nonreductive behaviorism."

KLS: Although I've written several times about your work, and although you've written—at great length—about mine (I mean your four books about Nevèrÿon), we've still never met. But in writing back and forth during the exchange of questions and answers for this interview, at two places you suggested I phrase a question differently. To both suggestions I happily complied. At least three places, I've suggested you elaborate on an answer that you gave that I wasn't quite clear on—

SRD: What you suggested was that I *rewrite* three answers. And let me hasten to add I was equally happy to cross out and write again, more fully, more clearly—

KLS: All right. And at least once I rewrote a question of mine to bring it in line with an answer you'd written, an answer which I thought was more interesting than the question I'd asked—to make me (and, I suppose, you) look better, as it were. Also, a couple of times we've both suggested cutting up longer sections, yours and mine, with comments from the other, to make the whole more conversational.

SRD: True. At this point, without checking the whole correspondence, I couldn't tell you which of us was actually responsible for which lines, phrases, or words—in the last three, this, or the next, entry.

KLS: Oh, yes: and at one point, early in the exchange, you asked me how I felt about dropping two sections of questions and answers (the section on Lacan and the section on George Eliot) that together totaled more than fifteen pages; and I wrote you back, yes, I thought they were better left out—for clarity and concision's sake.

But this means that, to someone privy to all the notes, drafts, and side-correspondence supporting this text, the clear demarcation of what in this interview is strictly "you," Chip Delany, and what in it is strictly "me," Karen Steiner, would be, to put it mildly, problematic.

In terms of the production of these questions and answers, at least in their final form, our separate identities are really a rhetorical fiction.

SRD: That's right. The problem of the "interviewing subjects" and their supposed identity, we might call it.

KLS: In both cases that identity is quite split, if not shattered.

Similarly, there's the problem of when and where this interview is taking place. In your study in New York City? Or at the paper-scattered, blonde wood worktable by the morning window at my kitchen in Ann Arbor, where I'm writing—

SRD: Actually, I've been drafting my response for the last couple of pages in my notebook, in bed in my bedroom, a bit after midnight, while, under the blanket beside me, with the shoulder of his red T-shirt poking out, Dennis snoozes and snores. (We've been unpacking book boxes all day from the previous weekend's move from Amherst back to New York City. It took me two years finally to believe Dennis's often-repeated exhortation he had no problem sleeping with the light on, and that I should feel free to turn it on, to read or to write, whenever I liked. Me, I couldn't do that at all. But he actually means it.) But yes, the point is: Does it take place over some metaphorical postal-phone line?

KLS: Or perhaps in some ideal living room—

SRD: Or radio or television studio—

KLS: —of the mind, that's finally *neither* your bedroom at midnight nor my kitchen at dawn? At any rate, would you perhaps close out our discussion with some more comments on the written interview and the scene of (its) writing?

SRD: It's certainly a fascinating topic—if only because it's the first where you've asked me directly about what we've been wrestling with indirectly till now: the problem of fiction itself.

By that I mean the problem of character and setting—and their relationship to actuality, to what happens, to experience, if not to language and desire.

KLS: Certainly you believe (counterintuitively, no doubt) that none of the three—character, setting, and reality—exists . . . ?

SRD: I don't believe that the first two exist in any hypostatized form that allows them to come apart from the text. As to the third, in no way contradicting what I've said already, I believe the real is synonymous with the political. That is, it's what you *have* to deal with, one way or the other. But, no, I don't believe in any transcendent and metaphysically grounded real that is somehow present, either perceptually or mystically.

(If you can substitute "political" or "politically" in any of your sentences for "real" or "really," then I suspect you're probably okay. If not, you're using it transcendentally, and should probably be using "actual," "actually," "intense," or "intensely"—if that's what you actually mean.)

Were I writing a scene in a novel, say, in which two invented characters were talking to one another—or, indeed, if I were writing a nonfiction account of an overheard conversation between two actual people I was sitting in on—fundamentally I'd have the same problems you and I are having as collaborators, making this interview read "realistically."

Whole narrative industries function, however, on the intuitively more accessible model of drama—where the terms character and setting originated, before they were appropriated by prose fiction—a model in which, yes, characters and setting can be considered separately and apart.

Only a couple of days ago I went in to proof my Introduction to the new volume collection of Neal Gaiman's *Sandman* comics at the offices of D.C. While there, I was told two people in the Development Department wanted to speak with me and I was ushered upstairs and into an office where a man of forty-five in a tie and pinstriped shirt told me: "I've been a fan of your science fiction since I was in high school. For me, the worlds you created in your stories were the most vivid I encountered in all my SF reading. Here at D.C., we're trying to work on some new science fiction projects. We're wondering if you would do some work for us, in which you'd create some worlds for us to set some science fiction stories in?"

You can see, certainly, he was working from the theatrical model. It's hard to explain to someone in such a situation that what they're asking for is virtually impossible—that the vividness of the world or setting in a science fiction novel or story is as much a matter of *where,* for example, in the course of the scene, you mention the details of its description, as it is *what* those details are; or, indeed, to explain that the fact those details are written with a minimum number of words—especially adjectives—is a direct factor in how vividly the reader perceives the scene.

I might come up with settings for them—but they will be just as dull as anyone else's.

For a moment in the history of western narrative, writers actually tried to create setting separately, inserting them before the scenes began. But the results were not vivid scenes, but leaden descriptions—sometimes of ten or twenty pages—while the scenes following them read as if they were located no particular place at all.

Chekhov signals the end of that whole approach to narrative, with his explanation of the "telling detail." He explains, somewhere, that you can spend paragraphs describing an old mill under the cloud-streaked moon, how the water rushes over the wheel, how heavy and dank its stones are, and nobody will actually see it; but merely mention how the moonlight catches on a bit of broken glass lying on a mossy flag atop the millrace . . . and the whole structure rises, vivid and visible, before the moon-slashed night mists of the reader's mind!

There—at least one structure in the Atlantis is returned to us!

But in terms of what the modernist writers and beyond are after, Chekhov's is cheating a bit—which is to say, his telling detail works *because* it follows the leaden, un-telling description.

The great American science fiction writer Theodore Sturgeon is the first writer I know who knowingly took the Chekhov technique the step further to articulate what he, and the modernists from Joyce and Woolf through Updike and Barth, were after—at least on the stylistic level. In a letter he wrote to Judith Merril in the early fifties, he explained: The way to write a vivid scene is for the writer first to visualize every aspect of it, from the paint drops on the new brass doorknob plate, to the bare wood window frame and the putty-smudged panes with their labels not yet scraped from the corners, to the trowel swipes on the ceiling's unpainted plaster. Then do *not* describe it. Rather, the writer should move his or her character—the harried new home buyer, the tired construction worker with his can of beer—through the scene, in whatever emotional state he or she is in, mentioning only those details that impinge on the character's consciousness.

Those details will *become* the telling details that make the scene shimmer intensely into life. What's more, Sturgeon pointed out with great insight, the scene the reader imagines will *not* be the same as the scene the writer imagines; but the scene the reader envisions will be as immediate, as vivid, and as emotionally charged for the reader as the writer's scene was for the writer. What Sturgeon is doing of course is mapping out the emotional connection between character and setting that is the precise reason that, in textual fictions, character and setting will *not* come apart from each other the way the Development Department at D.C. Comics might wish.

But any reader of novels must at least intuit the grosser terms of that relation. Alan Breck Stewart—certainly Robert Louis Stevenson's most appealing character—exists only on the sea and in the heather. When he enters the streets of a city (and in *Catriona,* sequel to Alan's initial presentation in *Kidnapped,* Stevenson goes through incredible machinations to keep him outside), he loses all immediacy. But most readers can put together a list of characters—Heathcliff, Mrs. Haversham, Captain Ahab, Dr. Matthew Mighty-Grain-of-Salt-Dante-O'Connor—who live intensely only against specific fictive 'scapes.

The implied advice in Sturgeon is to tune out the conscious mind and open oneself up as completely as possible to the imagined character and the imagined scene. But that's probably code for opening yourself as wide as possible to your intuitive sense of the narrative conventions that let you know when and where to place those spare, nonexhaustive details—a reasonable strategy, since we learn such conventions intuitively by exposure.

As a critic I want to be free to talk about Stevenson and Sturgeon in the same argument—if not Neal Gaiman and Allen Moore. I want to discuss Coleridge and Crane (Stephen, Hart, *and* Nathalia), Joanna Russ and George Eliot, Chekhov and Lacan, together and without apology. But I think that requires having a strong and pointed notion of their differences so that the dialogue they can create has its greatest actual, most intense, and political—*not* transcendental—meaning.

So, finally, where do such interviews—between two voices, two writers, two fictive characters both of which are creations of hand and neither of which has necessarily ever sounded on the air—occur? They occur where all fiction does: where the unconscious, that decides the undecidable by reading the language of the Other into the silences of the other, is flush with the preconscious, that provides us with the range of the recognizable: a juncture for which all lisable surfaces—the page under eye and beneath the thumb, the movie screen beyond the audience's darkened heads, and cathode ray tube's imaged glass within its plastic or metal nacelle—that is, the text, are today the visible sign.

KLS: Thank you.

Appendix

Anthony Davis—A Conversation

Weeks after the premier of the opera X: The Life and Times of Malcolm X *at the New York State Theater at Lincoln Center in New York City, Henry Lewis Gates, Jr., suggested I come to his house to interview composer Anthony Davis. The interview was conducted on November 9, 1986, in Ithaca, New York. When I submitted the transcript to Mr. Davis, I asked him to rewrite anything he wanted to. It came back with only the lightest editing—and that entirely for facts. I felt it only fair to edit my own comments in the same spirit. This is by far the most traditional interview in the book, then—not really a written interview at all.*

Samuel R. Delany: I'm talking here, Sunday morning, after a pleasant brunch at Henry and Sharon Gates' house, with Anthony Davis, composer of *X: The Life and Times of Malcolm X,* which premiered a few weeks ago at Lincoln Center in New York City.

Victor Hugo's son, Francois-Victor Hugo, did the translations of Shakespeare into French which Boito used to work on his libretto for Verdi's *Otello.* In the introduction to his translation there's a long passage in which Hugo explains that of course Othello isn't *really* black, that Desdemona couldn't possibly have fallen in love with him if he was: He's obviously an Arab or of some strange and romantic race that makes him not really black.

But in the margin of his own personal copy, Boito has jotted a succinct and pithy note:

Pertanto sta negro! "But he *is* black!"

And this is arguably the controlling thought behind Boito's libretto, if not Verdi's opera.

From *Aïda* and *Otello* to *Porgy and Bess* and *Lost in the Stars,* we as blacks have been opera-ed, have been operated upon, have been operationalized by white composers so that there seems to be a kind of massive charge running from white musicians to us as black subjects. How did you and your brother, Christopher, who devised the story, and your cousin, Thulani, who wrote the words, feel as blacks usurping this particular position in what's certainly perceived by most opera goers as an all-white field (with the possible exception of Scott Joplin's *Treemonisha*)—a field in which blacks have traditionally been the *objects* of white operas?

Anthony Davis: Well, we felt very good about it. We said: This is a opportunity to have our own voice—to deal with our own history, our own characters, and with our own people, in our own voice. Blacks *have* always been the object of operas: Today I was just looking at *Four Saints in Three Acts* by Gertrude Stein and Virgil Thomson. Black people have always been symbolic for white people, particularly in opera; in a sense it frees whites to deal in a mythological way with other subjects through us. In *X* I was trying to deal with our own myths. I always thought of Malcolm's as one of the great stories—and myths—of our day. I felt it was really ripe for operatic treatment.

SRD: Did it ever occur to you guys, even jokingly, to write an opera entirely about whites?

AD: Sure. My brother had this idea: he said the sequel to *X* should be *Brigham Young*.

SRD: Wonderful! Now, opera is often an intellectually beleaguered art. Because of its direct connections with the theater, people have a tendency not to take it seriously at the time it's being done: It's very theatrical, grandiose—deals with the passions. But as soon as the opera sits awhile, it becomes the object of a great deal of intellectual energy by critics. Was it Joseph Kerman in *Opera and Drama* who said that examining its opera is the way you test the health of a culture?

Were you at all weighted down by this contradiction between the frivolity of opera, on the one hand, and the terrible, terrible seriousness with which people can take it, on the other?

AD: No, I don't think that affected me. I was never convinced of opera's frivolity to begin with. There's a tradition of light, comic opera. And there's a tradition of poorly put together melodramas. But when I looked at my models for opera, at the operas I admire, I really felt that you could create something epic; you could create something tragic; that you could make a unique theatrical experience, heightened by music. And that's what we were trying for.

If anything, the criticism has been that we weren't frivolous *enough*. But I never thought frivolity was appropriate.

I felt I could have fun with Malcolm X and fun with the times and the characters. But I felt it should be serious fun. I would play with it, but I knew that underneath was something deadly serious.

SRD: Were there particular things you wanted to do in this opera that you'd seen done badly in other operas—things you didn't want to do in this opera that you knew didn't work in other contemporary operas?

AD: Oh, yeah!

SRD: What were some of them?

AD: I'd seen lots of operas that used basically theatrical dialogue. The librettos were plays, where you'd have one line, then another line, and another line—a lot of modern twentieth century operas are written this way. They're very talky.

Well, that's something I wanted to avoid.

I was interested in building melodic material, in a way that wasn't realistic. People don't talk in long phrases. When you have two or three characters, you weave them—rather than let them speak in the normal way a discussion goes, where you listen to someone and then respond. Our decision not to use normal language, to make it poetry, was because—I've always found this—if you write with everyday speech, it moves the musical setting toward plainsong, which didn't really interest me. That's something I'd heard in other operas and decided early on I wanted to avoid. Basically, we were dealing with certain kinds of arguments that reflected a whole way of understanding our historical and cultural situation. When you understand Malcolm and you understand, let's say, the street life around him—well, we had a whole rationale to express; and it couldn't be expressed in everyday speech.

First off, you don't have the time you have in a play. Look at a libretto. An opera libretto is fifty or sixty pages long. It's not structured like a play. So you really have to think of it in terms of—

SRD: This was the reason Thulani used that somewhat elevated diction?

AD: Yes. You have to use images and you have to use metaphors. Just the conceit of having the characters sing, rather than speak, takes it out of the realistic mode. If you plunge back into realism, either in language or in action, it can compromise the abstraction implicit in the music.

SRD: What made you turn to opera? Had your writing included symphonic forms?

AD: Yes. I'd written two symphonic works. I did a work for the Brooklyn Philharmonic (which was also done by the New York Philharmonic); and I did a work for the San Francisco Symphony, a piano concerto. After I had done my first orchestra pieces and was looking for the next thing to do, it occurred to me that opera would be a logical step. Also, I felt my music was uniquely dramatic. Most composers—my contemporaries—are very uncomfortable with drama. They're uncomfortable with the notion of music having dramatic tension. It's partially the legacy of John Cage that's brought that perception about. But I always felt that drama was present in my music; so I decided opera would be a natural form for me.

SRD: What were your first experiences of opera? How did they affect you?

AD: My first experience listening to anything like an opera was probably Kurt Weill. When I was a child, my father had the records of *The Threepenny Opera,* with Lotte Lenya—and I was terrified of it! I remember listening to it Sunday mornings: Every Sunday morning he'd play it. And I'd hide under the table.

SRD: So opera was very powerful?

AD: Yes, it was *very* powerful. My father had some Wagner records. But I wasn't really interested in them at that point. It took me a long time to get over the racism of Wagner to reach the music.

In school, at Yale, I did an intense study of nineteenth century opera, particularly Wagner and Strauss. I had to do a lot of analyses, particularly of Wagner. Later on when I began my own exploration of opera, the first ones I attended at the Met—my violinist plays in the Met orchestra and he gets me into the operas—were mostly Wagner. I learned a lot from them; from *Parsifal,* which is one of my favorite Wagner operas, and *Die Walküre,* which is another of my favorites. They provided interesting models.

SRD: You mentioned *Parsifal.* I was wondering—in fact I wrote it down among my notes to ask you—whether *Parsifal* might have been, in some ways, a model for *X.* If not *Parsifal,* possibly *Tannhäuser*—

AD: They were the first two operas I ever saw.

SRD: *Tannhäuser* and *Parsifal?* The reason I ask is because you have that wonderful, spiritual climax in *X*, where Malcolm, in Mecca, is with the chorus of praying men. And it's very hard to see it and *not* to think of *Parsifal.*

AD: Yes. Basically that's about the search for faith—it's about faith; and, in *Parsifal,* about Christianity.

If you want to make an argument for where minimalism began, you could say that *Parsifal* was the first minimalist opera. Probably the second act of *Parsifal*—I'd start with that.

Bringing back motifs, using thematic material in different sections of the opera to link it, insisting on recurring themes—that all comes from Wagner. I was building toward that moment in the third act—I always thought of that as the climax—the moment in Mecca, when Malcolm sees his name: El-Shabazz—naming is so much a part of black culture. Where he discovers his religion, he discovers *who* he is. That moment where he does it is the resolution of a kind of quest.

SRD: When we were talking last night, you mentioned Janacek as a favorite composer. Do Janacek's works have anything to do with, or any bearing on, *X?*

AD: Well, I came to Janacek a little later. I had already started writing *X.* My director, Rhoda Levine, had done the premiere of *House of the Dead,* which is one of Janacek's greatest operas. She'd also done a number of his other operas. She'd told me about him, and as a birthday present she gave me the records. So I began to study it. I was fascinated with it. But it will probably influence me more in the *next* opera I do.

SRD: Janacek, then, is a recent enthusiasm?

AD: Yes. I think what's interesting about him is his ability actually to deal with melodrama, to deal with family situations in a fresh way. And also his use of orchestration—he's a beautiful, a wonderful orchestrator. He really uses the orchestra to paint with—and the call and response between the orchestra and the voices. The voice says something and the orchestra responds. It's a very different form from what I do.

SRD: What were the circumstances around *X*'s beginning—how did you come to this particular opera that a month ago we all saw at the New York State Theater at Lincoln Center? How did it grow up?

AD: It was originally my brother's idea, about five years ago. He said,

"Why don't we do a musical about Malcolm X?" I said, "A musical?" I couldn't do that. I thought, well, maybe I could do it as an opera.

Then, three years ago, we brought in Thulani; and we started to write it.

We received some grants for it. Finally it was done at the Kitchen, in downtown New York City. We did a series of workshops—one at the American Music Theater Festival in Philadelphia. It was a whole learning process, because none of us had ever done an opera before—though our director, Rhoda Levine, had had lots of opera experience.

The libretto was written—mostly—first. I worked with it, edited it, then set it to music. Sometimes I would change lines around—I always brought in more ensemble material. That's my tendency.

We started from the beginning with a synopsis. My brother would submit a synopsis. We'd argue about it, the three of us. We'd tear it apart—then we'd go back to it. But after about a year or so we had the structure together. And we'd already written almost two acts.

SRD: In terms either of the writing or of the production, do any incidents or anecdotes stand out?

AD: Mostly I remember my director having problems with the fact that I liked having orchestral interludes in the opera. She didn't know what to do with them.

SRD: Interludes [laughter], just like a real opera!

AD: In a way she didn't understand what happened when the words stopped. And I just said, you know . . . it can stop. I mean there doesn't have to be talk all the time. It's not a play.

In Louise's aria, I used to have a long orchestral interlude, and I didn't have the recitative leading up to it—that was written later. I thought, well, maybe I could put recitative over this and it would help. It did. It really became a very nice moment in the opera.

For me there've been a lot of funny things; for example, in the production you saw, the characters Street and Elijah were played by the same singer. Originally Street was a bass-baritone part and Elijah was a tenor. When I auditioned Thomas Young, and we agreed that he would be Elijah, he told me he was singing in a club downstairs in my building, at Manhattan Plaza. He said why don't you come hear me.

I went; and I'd never heard a jazz singer as good as he was before. I'd already accepted him as an opera singer—to do Elijah Muhammed's part. Now I said, well, you have to do Street too.

SRD: It certainly adds a resonance to the opera to have Street and Elijah the same singer.

AD: I think it's great. It ties the work together. When we did the first workshop performance, one problem was that Street disappears after the first act—and Elijah Muhammed comes in. That means most of the characters Malcolm confronts in the first act disappear for the second; and that's a structural problem. Because you have no conflict; you have no sense of protagonist/antagonist. This gave us an idea how to effect that continuity and it also made a connection between Malcolm's two father figures . . . . That was lucky. When I heard him sing, I told him, "Well, you're going to do Street too."

I had to transpose the Street part up a fifth, because of his voice. It took a little extra work; but it was worth it.

The problem is, I don't know if anyone else in the world *could* do both parts.

SRD: At one point in the early scenes of the opera there's a long section where Malcolm is mute, where he doesn't sing at all. Now when a character in an opera stops singing, it makes a very powerful statement to an opera audience. What was the feeling that you wanted to project there?

AD: Well, we wanted to see the way he was being affected by things around him—the way he was taking things in. Silence is a very demanding thing for an actor, especially an opera singer. One of the demanding things about Malcolm's role is that the singer has to be able to listen. In the whole first act you're responding, you're changing, you're being affected by the people around you. You see Street, you see all these others—his mother, earlier on, and then Ella. The big payoff is the aria at the end of the act, when he finds his voice; and that voice comes out in rage. Finally he can express himself as a man—but only at the end of the act.

We always had fights about why can't you have him do or say something here, react to something there. But we decided to go with the notion of making Malcolm's first-act aria that much more powerful by not letting him sing as an adult until that point. There, song makes sense: he's a man in prison, and he's down, he's at the bottom of his life. Then you hear his response to the whole of what he's seen before.

He talks about his father. He talks about his mother. He talks about his whole situation. And that was what we were trying to set up.

One thing I was very concerned with was the relationship of the chorus to the soloist. I wanted to create a sense of Malcolm's community.

Because Malcolm is a public man—and a political man—it seemed rational to me always to show him in the context of other people.

SRD: The first time we hear Malcolm; it's as the child's voice—a very rarefied boy soprano singing just after his mother's mad song. This is followed by Malcolm's long silence—almost twenty minutes. After this terribly weighty quietness from just the one character—of course, music is going on all around that silence and certainly that's effective—the next music from Malcolm is a man's voice.

Yes, it's very strong.

Indeed, the opera struck me as very *richly* musical. In the generous *New York Times* coverage during the week before the premiere, there was some talk of it's being a jazz opera. But what I heard seemed to be a lot closer to the tonalities of German music in the beginning of this century—Berg, Schoenberg; even if it wasn't using their serial techniques. In that sense you could say the music was very conservative. How does this assertion strike you?

AD: Oh, I don't know what that means, because—

SRD: Not as a value judgment, but just simply as—

AD: No, I *would* accept that. It's funny, because music has been so divided. What's radical in music is a somewhat different thing today: the use of an improviser, I think; employing certain rhythms and repetition—those kinds of things. Academics have tried to define musical development only in terms of harmonic and melodic material. But basically the end of that kind of development was the twelve-tone school. You had responses to it, from the minimalists, to the Cage stuff, to the electronic stuff. I think *X* hearkens back to a more conservative mode. But then, I'm very interested in form—form in music.

Musically, I've never been able to accept the arbitrariness of chance operations. Really, music has been hiding behind certain intellectual concepts, or—better—hiding by not allowing itself to be expressive, by not allowing itself to be direct. And directness is important to me. It's also been hiding, I think, by being afraid to confront form: It's been afraid to create works with the same kind of formal development one hears earlier in twentieth century music. A lot of my contemporaries haven't developed their music formally in the ways earlier music does.

SRD: The thing that comes to mind when you say that is the way in which the various scenes in *Wozzeck* are each in a different musical form: Act One, Scene Four is a passacaglia—actually a chaconne—with twenty-one variations on a twelve-note theme; Act Two's five scenes form a five-movement symphony with the first scene the sonata movement and the fourth a double scherzo; Act Three, Scene Four, is an invention on the key of D-minor . . . and so forth. Were these the kinds of formal structures you were working into *X*? They're things that would be very hard for a general audience to pick up, without being told, even after several hearings.

AD: Well, I don't use a twelve-tone system. There's a sense of tonality, a sense of key structure. I was trying to be consistent within the dramatic structure by reinforcing it through the musical structure. I have recurring themes, recurring tonalities, also certain recurring intervalic relationships. Often I think of the key as a rhythm—not just a succession of tonal intervals. It can be a pattern.

Throughout the whole opera I use this B-flat/A-flat major second.

I put it in the opera so many ways, I was getting embarrassed about it. Every conceivable way. It became a game for me. You start playing these games. I mean, I'd never written anything of this length. It's almost required of a composer to justify the length by having everything connected. By the time you get to the third act, everything you do has to have some relation to something you've done before. There's no way you can introduce something completely new. From the opening of the overture you hear that opening interval.

That's the recurring motif: You hear it all over the opera.

I do it in different ways. At the same time I was consistent. One time I had these twenty-five B-flats paired with this pedal-point A-flat that I use. The first time you hear it is with the quartet of men after Malcolm's father has been killed. Then you hear it again when Malcolm first starts his ministry on 125th Street. He says: "When I was little, they called me nigger; they called me nigger so much I thought it was my name. . . ."

And everyone laughs.

But what's underneath it is the same rhythmic pattern, the same ostenato, that you heard underneath the report of his father's death: "They say that Earl was on the tracks; they say a streetcar ran. . . ."

So I had these little jokes. But the idea of using these recurring ostenatos, these patterns, bringing them back, bringing back the mother material—you know . . . [He hums]. I brought that back in the second act with, "Who shot the bomb and destroyed your home? . . ." I brought that back, because, even if the audience doesn't realize they've heard something before, it still affects them in a subliminal way. It gives depth to the scene: All of a sudden they say, "Oh, man!"—because of the emotional weight that comes from the way you used it before.

Also I had these rhythmic games. Once I had a conductor come up to me and say, "What's this with the number eleven in your music? The whole opera is in eleven." Eleven this and eleven that. . . . Eleven-eight. I had patterns of eleven. He showed it to me, and I mean it *was* there—everywhere. I remember when I was studying Machaut's or Dufay's motets, that kind of thing about using numbers, like in isorhythmic motets—where you're using certain lengths in different ways as the underlying structure of the music. That's really, really prevalent in my work. I would go back to a certain pattern, and I might turn it around, and do it a different way. For me what was fascinating was the whole notion of constantly borrowing from something you did before. In a sense, you're always building musically on something that happened in the past. So the opera has an overall development. It hearkens back to more dramatic forms—as opposed to the Italianate form of Verdi, which, while beautiful, is more a question of tunes. Verdi's operas, in a way, are structured not unlike a Broadway show. But because of the beauty of the music and what's within the infrastructure of it, it becomes something else.

But I was more interested in the form of Wagner and Strauss, which was more through-composed.

SRD: As you discuss the structure of your opera, clearly it's through-composed. Yet you seem comfortable with terms like recitative and aria, terms and concepts that "through-composers" of operas, like Wagner, tended to eschew. You apparently think of your opera in those terms. You didn't find any difficulty dividing the opera up in your own mind in patterns like that? Or did you? Or is it just for my benefit—because you're talking about it with me?

AD: It's very funny. I only had one *real* recitative in the whole opera. I mean, someone would say, oh, you know, that's a recitative. And I'd say, yeah, you know, you're right.

SRD: The premiere night for *X* had very much the sense of an Event. It was impressive to go into Lincoln Center and see three-quarters of the audience black. For me, that was a truly marvelous thing! But at one point in the opera Malcolm sings, "I don't hate white people." And suddenly—and it was the *only* point in the opera, where I did—I had the feeling: We've only *rented* this space . . . from *them.* It was almost as though that particular line was somehow being given *to* the white establishment structure that controls the art-world of this country. At no other time in the opera was I made aware of that larger—

AD: Right!

SRD: Did you at all feel this was some kind of placation that had to be included in the piece? Or was it just an attempt to show several sides of Malcolm—an attempt that I overread?

AD: No. Actually it says, "We don't hate the white man." But it's also meant to be funny. You have to consider Malcolm's humor in terms of the whole passage [Sings]: "It may sound bitter. It may sound like hate. But it's just, but it's just . . . the truth! We don't hate the white man: His world's about to fall. But it' just, but it's just. . . ." There again, I'm playing with the music. It's the same music that you have behind, "They called me nigger; they called me nigger so much I thought it was . . . my name!" It was a gas to try to capture Malcolm's humor. It's always in his speech. But also it's in how he would say serious stuff: He could do that with humor too. Also he uses repetition, which is great for me. You can use the classical comic motif three times—bam! pow!—hit you with a zinger! That was hard to do because a lot of opera singers aren't used to that. [Sings:] "When I was little, they called me nigger; they called me nigger, they called me. . . ."

When Avery Brooks did it—because he's more of an actor, who came up through the whole black tradition of improvisation—he would improvise by talking in between the music. It was unbelievable stuff. And every night it would be different. "When I was little . . . yeah!" Then he'd catch someone's eye and make them respond. By the end, he had the whole cast going. He'd sing "They called me. . . ." And someone would come back with, "Yeah, well *what* did they call you?" That whole thing created an atmosphere of Malcolm *with* the people around him on the street.

No, I didn't try to placate. The only time I had to placate, really, was with the *other* side.

HLG: Our side.

AD: We had to be very careful in dealing with the break-up between Elijah and Malcolm and the issues that represents. Also we were dealing with people who're still alive. Betty Shabazz, Malcolm's wife, was right there, watching the opera—where someone is singing *her* words!

SRD: Yes. That's a real situation that has to be dealt with. In the overture to the opera, in the production, the curtain starts out open; and during the overture, one after another, all the characters come out. Is that written into the opera? Or was that simply the director's notion of how to do it?

AD: It was the director's notion. But soon it became a part of the opera.

I remember the first rehearsal we had, she came in and said, "Well, where's the overture?"

What overture? You write the overture after you write the opera, right? I had no idea that . . . oh, you want an overture?

"Yeah, I'm staging the overture."

You're *staging* the overture? I guess I'll have to come up with an overture for this.

So that's how it happened.

I had this piece that was written for a Robert Hayden poem, called "Middle Passage"—a piano piece. Basically that's the piece that became the overture.

It was kind of interesting, because, we're all in the "Middle Passage," somewhere.

SRD: In a way the staging seemed—well . . . I said at one point that the music seemed conservative without a value judgment: It seemed to come out of the German tonalities, structures, you know, of Schoenberg, or Berg.

The staging seemed conservative in a different way. It struck me that the basic model for the staging was *Our Town*—Thornton Wilder's old show with no scenery. For me I found that detracted from the musicality of the opera. I wanted something more radical in the presentation to underlie the complexity of what I heard as real musical invention and richness.

AD: Her idea of having the actors create the scene often came because there was so little time. I move from scene to scene so fast musically that the transitions have to be made pretty fast . . . Thornton Wilder—I'm not sure what the relation is to that. I think it could be done other ways. I could see other ways of doing that opera. But I felt that we had committed ourselves early on to how she was doing it.

SRD: What are your thoughts for future operas? Is there anything there you'd be willing to share with us?

AD: Well, yes—a number of them. First I'm going to do an opera with Debbie, a science fiction opera. It'll give me the opportunity, for one thing, to use a smaller cast—about eight singers in it and, I guess, some supers—some actors in it, too. It'll give me a chance to do a more lyrical form of opera.

It'll also incorporate some of the experiments I've been doing with electronic music. I've been working on a project at MIT with a computer. What I've done is to take spoken language and manipulate it. For example, I can change the speed of speech without changing the pitch. I can isolate different parts of the sound. I can make really beautiful musical effects with just spoken words. You can find all this music *within* speech.

The opera is going to be about issues of telepathy and the responsibilities that come with it. I want to have people hearing words and thoughts all the time. What would that really be like. And how do you express that in musical terms. You'd hear these fragmented musical statements, that could come from the computer, interacting with voices, and with spoken language.

There are two twins in the opera . . . and a mother, a stepfather, and a real father, who's what's called the gashulya: someone who's been surgically altered to live underwater. I have a painter friend who does black-light paintings—he does all his painting in the dark [laughter], and he's dying to do this: In the set we could use ultraviolet light so that when you look at the backdrop, it would just look like it was going back for miles. So underwater landscapes are possible. It'll be completely different. It couldn't be *more* different!

SRD: The Swedish Nobel Prize-winning poet Harry Martinson wrote a poem, *Aniara,* that was the basis for a science fiction opera thirty or forty years ago. Did you ever come across it?

AD: No, I haven't. I'd like to. Who wrote the music?

SRD: I don't remember[1]—if the mumbled truth be known! But it took place on a generations-long interstellar journey. And there was a singing computer in it, called the "Mima."

Are there any things that you think an opera composer should *never* do?

AD: Should never do? No. [Laughter.]

SRD: I mean, something that will always make the results bad. So that you'll end up with a bad opera? Is there a mistake that you see contemporary opera composers making that you have decided that you will never make?

AD: Actually in terms of subject matter, no. I would say no.

SRD: Not necessarily subject—but musically.

AD: Oh, yes. I think . . . don't write a play. You can't sing a play. I would say that's the main thing.

For another opera I was thinking of doing something on the *Invisible Man,* by Ralph Ellison; I'd love to do that. And I had an idea for this opera called *Tania,* based on the Patricia Hearst kidnapping. I really wanted to do that. [Laughter.]

SRD: Broad political ideas.

AD: Yes. It would be like *Lulu,* you know? It's another identity story, but it's a tragedy in the sense that the woman never finds it. First she identifies with her boyfriend, then with her family and that life; then she identifies with her captors and Cinque, and that whole thing. But it has a comic element. You see this woman emerge with her battle fatigues and then you see her identification, later on again, with her prison guard, whom she eventually married. I'd probably be sued, but it would be fun.

SRD: It's certainly an interesting notion.

HLG: I sense a relationship with Afro-American literature, in terms of your wanting to develop a relationship *between* the music and the literary tradition. Where does this come from, or why?

AD: It's probably genes. [Laughter.] I mean, man—you couldn't be in my father's house and *not* do that. I think that's where it comes from. We first talked about Malcolm X, I remember, sitting at the dinner table. We talked about the possibility of doing something with that. And *The Invisible Man* too. I always heard it with music.

HLG: Really? And he plays it in music, as Louis Armstrong.

AD: Louis Armstrong—I would do that. I have a friend, Olu Dara, who's this trumpet player. I even know who would play the trumpet in this. And I'd have him do that. But the orchestration I would put underneath it—it would be so *out!* It would be like the strings and stuff that you hear. [Sings.] Like, "Struttin' with Some Barbecue," or something.

SRD: Is there any advice that you would give a composer who was thinking about writing an opera? At this point, having emerged from your first large-scale professional production, what would you tell a young composer aspiring to write opera?

AD: Find good people to work with, mainly. And find subject matter that grabs your emotions—that's important to you. It can't be done as an academic pursuit. There's too much involved. The subject matter has to be important.

SRD: I remember years and years ago, when I was, ever so briefly, at City College, Rudolf Bing came and talked to us when he was head of the Metropolitan Opera. There were some of us there who were interested in opera. I'd been involved in writing one myself, only a year before. But I recall that, basically, Bing told us: "Don't bother."

Your opera, he said, will never get produced.

He said it very nicely. But basically he was saying, "Don't waste your time writing an opera." Now of course this was twenty-five years ago—

AD: He was right.

SRD: The actual mechanics of getting an opera on the boards—from the point of view of someone sitting in the audience, it looks daunting! How does that happen?

AD: Well, we were told a number of times that we should scale down the piece, make it a music theater piece so that you could do it in repertory theaters—that kind of thing. But we decided early on that it was for an opera house. They're going to have to swallow this one whole. [Laughter.] It's been an interesting phenomenon just how we've been able to get into this position—how we've been able to get City Opera to accept us. Actually, I never really approached them. They came to look at the opera at BAM [the Brooklyn Academy of Music] and that's how we got there.

SRD: It was originally done at BAM?

AD: No, we were doing a workshop at BAM; and people from the City Opera came to see it. But I think basically what there is, is a void. No contemporary American opera has really taken in people's imagination. The reason *X* became the phenomenon it has, and has had the success it has, is basically because we stepped into a situation where there was nothing there. There wasn't that much of any quality. And so it was unique. It had very little to do with the black and white issues; there just weren't that many good operas around—period. The field was really open.

I think that as a black composer, I had a tremendous advantage, in that our tradition has never strayed that far from the voice. When we write music, when I improvise, I can *sing* what I improvise. For me music has *never* been that far from the vocal traditions. I was talking to one of my contemporaries, about the black composers I know, and I said, "You know, it's really open for us." For example, the whole academic school of modern classical music, from after the 1940s—people who have been inspired by Schoenberg and Berg and Webern and those people—basically haven't been able to create an opera that anyone wants to hear [Laughter.] And so, basically, there's a real opportunity for the Afro-American tradition to become the dominant force in opera in America.

I really feel it.

SRD: Is it that nobody wants to hear their operas—or that nobody wants to produce them? I know that when I hear of a new opera, a new contemporary opera, I *go*—if I possibly can. I remember in London, going to see *The Mines of Sulfur*—by Beverly what's-his-name.[2]

AD: Yes, I go too.

SRD: The idea of a *new* contemporary opera is something very exciting for me. On the other hand there's the barrier of the production costs, just the realities of production, that stand in the way of people hearing—

AD: You know basically there's a musical problem, in that people don't really go to new operas. Opera has always been on the border between what would be "high art" and "popular art." There has to be something immediate in an opera. When you write an opera, something has to create an immediate response, an immediate musical response.

But that means you have to communicate on a number of levels as a composer: The first level is the melodic interest and whether you can draw an audience into the music. The patronage system has resulted in the composer's isolation—the patronage system which *is* academia, which is basically the substitute for the Church, or the substitute for the Court, or for the other forms of patronage. The isolation it's created makes a situation where the works are not written for any real audience; or they're written for a very small audience. But opera has to be on a larger scale. At least it's supposed to be.

HLG: Don't we encounter racism when we start to juxtapose blackness and opera? Didn't you encounter some of it?

AD: Yes, of course. Definitely that's true. There's an attempt to dismiss what I've done. But that's something you have to—

SRD: How so?

AD: Well, the *New York Times* critic, for example, said that basically *X* was just a polemic, and that it was just about words, it wasn't about music—basically he wasn't able to deal with what's in the music at all. And then the next *Times* critic used an argument about vernacular art. This was Rockwell—it was really a funny thing. He was very condescending. He said, it's a very good effort for a first opera, etc., but he wished that we would become looser. He compared it with Duke Ellington's *Queenie Pie.* He said that *Queenie Pie* came from an era when black composers felt less self-conscious about letting their vernacular roots show and allowing their audience to have a good time. [Laughter.] Here we go again. I think that there was this kind of response. What was amazing to me was that to see the response of the audience. We were sold out for every performance!

SRD: You had an incredible amount of support from the community. Any opera that I go to *and* my mother goes to, three days later (without a word from me, either: when we talked to each other, a week later, we were both surprised that each other had seen it)—I mean, *that* opera has won over the community!

AD: We got standing ovations. But in the *Times* piece they were trying to dismiss it almost as if it hadn't happened. They were trying to dismiss what had happened. The work was a success. It managed to communicate to an audience. No one would have had that response if it were just "about words"—whatever that's supposed to mean.

HLG: The *Times* wanted it to be more like a musical.

SRD: Why isn't this *Porgy and Bess?*

AD: Also he said I had to make my ideas gray.

HLG: What an insult! As opposed to black or white?

AD: Yes. I think that people are wrestling with the whole notion of black art being serious art; white folks always have a problem dealing with the notion that this is a serious work of art. I would say that my opera is no more vernacular than *Lulu*. If you're going to say that's vernacular, fine. But to talk about "vernacular art"—those arguments are so confused. Shakespeare is vernacular, you know. But they're not talking about it in those terms, because when an American critic says that, it *can't* be said without racism. It's about class distinctions and it's about racial distinctions. It's about those kinds of things and not really about the art or the work.

SRD: I only saw the first *Times* review, and it was a clearly a very tentative review by somebody who was—equally clearly—neither comfortable with the Event nor comfortable with the music.

The *Times*, remember, is *not* a highbrow culture organ. It's furiously middle-brow; and nobody seriously interested in the development of art—especially anyone black—is going to read it as anything else. I assume that a good number of the black people who attended those sold-out performances knew how to read those very frightened, up-tight and oh-so-predictable reviews.

And I would imagine that most people who had heard *X*, then read those reviews, would have felt, at the very least: "Wouldn't it have been nice if this man had said *something* about what happened last night *in the theater*." On whatever level: either on the stage, in the orchestra, or with the audience.

AD: Well, the *Times* critics couldn't. Of course I believe *X* works on all these levels. But I think that they couldn't possibly, considering who they are, speak out: That just won't happen right away. It's very funny: Critics outside New York were able to do that. But New York is too political. It's too much about their stance on cultural politics, not about reviewing a work. And trying to see where the work falls in terms of what they're trying to advocate.

SRD: Whenever you conceive of yourself as an arbiter of culture, rather than as a creator of culture, you become purely a political mouthpiece—of the most vulgar sort. And, sadly, that's the problem with most New York critics who have a major outlet. And it doesn't matter what the political slant of the work under review.

But think how strange it must have been to *be* a white critic in that audience. They were in another world—a world they'd never been in before. *We* were in another world—let's face it—that most of us certainly haven't been in very often. But it was ours. It wasn't theirs. And that must have been very upsetting. The upsetting part I suspect was not that that world was hostile to them. That, they—some of them—could probably have dealt with. Rather it was ignoring them. And that, I'm sure, was far more disorienting.

After all: What do those reviews, largely, say? Please pay more attention to the traditional values we whites have imposed on operas about blacks that we've written and approved of in the past: looseness, entertainment, melody. And what excludes them is a major opera house full of black people, giving a standing ovation to a black-authored work that's musically rigorous, run through with wit, and steeped in passion.

AD: I found it funny that no one would say what the audience *was*—the fact that the audience who turned out for *X* was so overwhelmingly black, and that that's unique for an event of this kind. There's been no phenomenon like it. I felt a little disappointed with the reports, in those terms; but I guess I shouldn't have. That's the major sense in which I feel I haven't had the recognition for what was really achieved. But that happens all the time.

HLG: People don't know how to read it or hear it.

AD: I thought that was unfortunate. I think also because of the political—

SRD: It's as if all of the *reviewers* turned into Parsifal and were unable to ask the proper questions.

But I remember the same thing happening back in the middle sixties, with a very different sort of opera: in 1967, Al Carmines' and Helen Adam's *San Francisco's Burning* played over three weekends at the Judson Poets' Theater to packed houses with twenty-minute standing ovations each night. But the *Village Voice* reviewer—we're not even talking about the *Times* here—gave the most lukewarm of reviews, wondering if this was "what a musical evening really ought to be," hardly mentioning a performance or a performer, and *never* referring to the standing-room-only audiences and their thunderous approbation.

There was so much flack over that, I recall, that two weeks later, after a column full of letters, very grudgingly the *Voice* re-reviewed it at a slightly higher level of enthusiasm . . . once the run was over.

Which only means that what we're talking about here is the particularly, and specifically black *form* of the "new art work" problem. And, of course, it does have its own and very real black form. But that form shares congruences with other, very real problems.

AD: Also, it's so easy to write about the subject matter of this opera. The subject matter is one reason it got produced, too. It grabbed people. But it also enabled them not to deal with what was being done *with* that subject matter. And that's too bad. But I anticipated that; it will take a number of years before people really understand or really listen to the opera, to what it actually does. It's funny. The audience will do that before most critics will.

SRD: There's a kind of tradition in conducting opera in New York, for some reason—certainly all the operas that come out of Lincoln Center—to conduct them small. Do you know what I mean? I remember Levine conducting *Tristan* one evening as though it were Debussy. Did you feel that the conductor conducted it with the sonic richness you wanted? Were you happy with the sound of the opera, in the house?

AD: No. But there are reasons for that. The acoustic balance. The house is very difficult. The orchestra basically had to play very quietly throughout the whole thing to have the singers be heard. Ideally, you would want to be in a position where the orchestra could play out so that the richness of the music comes through more. It's kind of like hearing the music through cotton gauze: because they couldn't really play out. Some of that had to do with some of the performers having trouble projecting through the orchestra in that house. But if I do a record of it or something, that won't be a problem. You'll be able to hear everything.

SRD: I'm waiting for the small-score to be published, so that I can sit there and follow it.

HLG: How about the rhythm?

SRD: Again, that goes back to what we were saying before about jazz . . . . What was jazz doing in the opera for you and what is rhythm doing in the opera for you as a composer?

AD: Okay. In terms of the so-called "jazz parts," I think that basically I was using them to set up time and place—the early sections in Boston.

SRD: You were using jazz for musical scene-painting.

AD: Yes. I tried to get into the big-band period—Lionel Hampton and Duke—because we were talking about dance halls and dance hall stuff. I was trying to use the music to create the scene. Then I thought I would set up a healthy tension between that and the expectation, so that when you actually get *to* the dance hall, the music goes somewhere else. Finally you realize that the dance hall is really about a kind of alienation, and not really so much about the dance. In his aria at the end of the opera, Malcolm sings, "You can jitterbug and prance, but you'll never run the ball." I took that as a model for the dance hall scene. In terms of rhythmic use, I see something more complicated. In the opera, I'm trying to use the rhythms as the building blocks of the drama. As the rhythm becomes more complex, as there's more rhythmic density, you get a certain tension.

SRD: There's a great deal of cross rhythm.

AD: Yes. There's a clash of rhythm, of rhythmic structures, using repetition to create tension. I find that rhythm like that creates tension. And I use—I guess, the word would be—antiphony, antiphonal choirs, basically *pitting* them against one another, while you have one recurring line. For these moments, using the chorus in that way, I divide up the chorus in different parts and then have them go at the same time. So you have these warring choirs. I do that with the orchestra, too. I might use radically different material for different parts of the orchestra, and have them occur simultaneously, so that there's a sense of development out of conflict between opposing musical ideas. That was really something I tried to work on in the opera all the time.

Also the use of rhythm *as* tonality. In a way I think my study of South Indian music inspired me to that. I studied with a master drummer. Certain talas have a sort of—well, when you switch from one tala to another, from one pattern to another, the change is very significant. It's not only the raga—or scale—that determines the emotional impact, but also the rhythmic structure: how you subdivide the rhythms.

I tried to be pretty systematic about this. I was very careful about where I introduced new rhythmic material—usually at very significant points in the opera. In the opera, rhythm is always the metaphor for violence—for the underlying violence. Even though there might be a melody above it, and, if you isolate the melodic material, it might even sound gentle, what's going on underneath is tense—the inner workings of a demonic machine. That's what I wanted to create: a kind of machine going on and on. I felt aggressive with the whole idea of how Malcolm, in the opera, says, "I'm going to beat you down," and the *beat*—you beat it. I'm going to beat these things into you, you repeat and repeat. Beat it, beat it.

It's not some serene thing where you use repeating structures and sit back and get in this mesmerized, or hypnotic, state.

I was more interested in the way music can push people and shove them in a certain direction: call it manipulative. It's a strong word. But that's what it is.

SRD: The first act of so many operas—from *Don Giovanni* and *Tosca* to *West Side Story* and *Phantom of the Opera*—ends with a stretto, a great marshaling of all the voices on the stage. But *your* first act ends with a single voice, singing alone. It creates a great deal of tension with the form opera audiences usually expect. It is, I think, a very effective way of highlighting your main character's struggle. And, of course, he's in jail, wholly isolated, while he's singing.

To change the subject, somewhat: Have there been any concert productions of the opera that you have been particularly satisfied with in the course of its life?

AD: Yes. I did a concert production in Springfield, Massachusetts. I'm going to do some more this year, different excerpts from it.

SRD: Have there been tapes made of those and, if so, is there any way I could get hold of one? So that I could listen to it again.

AD: I have tapes from the Philadelphia production. I have a bootlegged tape from the City Opera production. There are some tapes—of varying quality because it's usually illegal to make them.

SRD: I was once a super at the Met in Samuel Barber's *Anthony and Cleopatra* that opened Lincoln Center back in 1966 or '67; I got to see it from the inside through its five or six performances. It struck me that, as an opera, it was just not very interesting. Nor do I particularly mean the music. There was a static quality to it *as drama* that did not make you want to surmount the very real and necessary complexities of the music in the way that a *Wozzeck*, a *Lulu*, or an *X* does.

I don't think that "the larger audience" you must appeal to is the Broadway audience. The audience you have to appeal to is that audience interested in new aesthetic experiences, the audience who is serious about its art—*these* are the people who somehow have to be talked to by the work. One reason I enjoyed *X* so much is that I felt the music constantly aimed at that part of me; and that's at least one of the reasons I liked it as much as I did.

The music was taking me as seriously as I was taking it.

So I hope we get a chance to see it in several different forms, with new productions. Is there any possibility of this happening? What has been the response to it in terms of its falling into some repertoire somewhere?

AD: Oh, it's been very good. There's a possibility of doing it in Atlanta—and in Houston, at Houston Grand Opera. We're going to do a completely different production in London, I think. With a different director. I'm not sure *what* that's going to be. I have a feeling that we'll probably star Avery Brooks in that production. He may end up directing too. I wouldn't be surprised—because he *is* a director. . . . Then we're also trying for a film version. We've had a lot of interest from video and film people, and we have to decide whether to film the production, you know, as a PBS kind of production; or BBC. Or whether to *make* a film, which would be something different altogether. Or maybe do a kind of combination of the two: a video production that would incorporate things on stage, or on a stage set. It's a delicate balance. We'll be working on for a while.

SRD: That might make a good finale for our conversation. I think we might declare our interview to be officially over now. Okay. This was fun. Thank you, Henry, for your questions and comments. Tony, it was wonderful getting a chance to talk with you.

NOTES

1. Swedish composer Karl-Birger Blomdahl (1916–1968) premiered his opera *Aniara* at the Stockholm Festival, in May 1959. The libretto was by Erik Lindergren, based on the book-length poem by the Swedish poet Harry Martinson.

2. *The Mines of Sulfur,* by Beverly Cross.

Index

Other Books by the Author

Fiction

The Jewels of Aptor
The Fall of the Towers:
  Out of the Dead City
  The Towers of Toron
  City of a Thousand Suns
The Ballad of Beta-2
Babel-17
The Einstein Intersection
Nova
Driftglass (stories)
Equinox (The Tides of Lust)
Dhalgren
Trouble on Triton
Distant Stars (stories)
Stars in My Pockets Like Grains of Sand
Return to Nevèrÿon:
  Tales of Nevèrÿon
  Neveryóna
  Flight from Nevèrÿon
  Return to Nevèrÿon (The Bridge of Lost Desire)
Driftglass / Starshards (collected stories)
They Fly at Çiron
The Mad Men
Hogg
Atlantis: Three Tales

Nonfiction

The Jewel-Hinged Jaw
The American Shore
Heavenly Breakfast
Starboard Wine
The Motion of Light in Water
Wagner / Artaud
The Straits of Messina
Longer Views

About the Author

Samuel Delany was born and grew up in New York City's Harlem. He is best known as the author of science fiction and fantasy novels; his books have won Hugo and Nebula awards. He has also published several books of nonfiction, including critical studies of literature and a volume of memoirs. Since 1988 Mr. Delany has been a professor of comparative literature at the University of Massachusetts at Amherst.

UNIVERSITY PRESS OF NEW ENGLAND publishes books under its own imprint and is the publisher for Brandeis University Press, Dartmouth College, Middlebury College Press, University of New Hampshire, Tufts University, and Wesleyan University Press.

LIBRARY OF CONGRESS CATALOGING-IN-PUBLICATION DATA

Delany, Samuel R.

Silent interviews : on language, race, sex, science fiction, and some comics : a collection of written interviews / by Samuel R. Delany.

p. cm.

Includes index.

ISBN 0-8195-5276-3 (cl).—ISBN 0-8195-6280-7 (pa)

1. Delany, Samuel R.—Interviews. 2. Authors, American—20th century—Interviews. 3. Science fiction—Authorship. I. Title.

PS3554.E437Z476 1994

813'.54—dc20 93-35913